Princes of Hollywood

C.S. Berry

Author Note

Dear Reader,

This is pretty standard, but if you're related to me, please stop reading right here. Seriously. I'm not ready to look across a table and have you ask me so have you ever. . . Because no. Now go read something less spicy and don't talk to me about it.

I'm so excited to give you The Princes of Hollywood. This is the first book in a series. The books are meant to be read in order and there will be cliffhangers.

Princes is new adult with a slight age gap. I wanted to build a heroine who has been missing that piece of herself that she'll find with her new "family."

I don't shy away from sex scenes. There is plenty of group spice, but beyond just sex, she develops personal relationships with each of her guys. That's just how I roll.

Princes is very much about consensual play.

While I tried to be as conscious of proper play within BDSM, please remember this is a fantasy. While everything might be possible, always go to a more trusted source for information than my book.

I truly love this story and hope you do too. If you want to connect with me, my Facebook group is C.S. Berry's Spicy Executive Suite. You can also follow me on Instagram, but I generally post about the stories that are ongoing (which may contain spoilers).

For a list of detailed content warnings, please visit my website csberry.com. Or check my P.S. because I want to give you the option to skip in case of spoilers.

XOXOXO,
C.S. Berry

P.S. Content warnings: Heroine has a past of sexual assault by people close to her. This will be explored as the series goes on, but it is alluded to in book one. The main premise of the book is she is taking a job as a sobriety buddy for an actor. The hero went to rehab and needs to remain drug-free/alcohol-free for the movie.

Chapter 1

Boulevard of Broken Dreams

Greer

"What's this about a job?" I hide in my bedroom with the phone up to my ear, huddled on the double bed which takes up most of the room as my ex is currently watching football on the TV. Loudly.

"This actor needs a live-in PA. He talked about it with his agent while I did his makeup today. I texted you the details." My best friend, really my only friend in L.A., Bristol Walker sighs. "You can't stay at that apartment, Greer. Not with the asshole who cheated on you. If Will wasn't already living on my couch, I'd have you here in a heartbeat."

My ex yells loudly at the TV as if it offended him. Honestly, I don't know what I saw in him. I would leave, but we're both on the lease and neither of us could take it over on our own. Well, I definitely couldn't.

"I've got a job already." I pick at a loose thread in the sheets. Waitressing at a small diner doesn't exactly bring in the big money plus they've cut my hours recently.

"One that's a dead end and will never pay you enough. Look, call for an interview. The worst thing that happens is they suck and you say no." Bristol covers the phone and her voice mumbles to someone in the background. She comes back to me. "One interview. It's room and board, plus salary."

"I don't know how to be a personal assistant." Something hits the door, startling me. I can't stay here.

Chad keeps trying to convince me we should get back together. He's not sorry; he's just hit a dry spell. I've been sleeping on the couch, but last night he tried to carry me back to the bed. Like I would forget what he did. I don't need a guy who cheats on me. Fortunately, I woke up when he tried to lift me and told him off. Given his grunts last night and his limp this morning, a few of my kicks must have landed hard enough to sting.

Hopefully that will stop him from trying that shit again.

I don't even like him anymore, and I haven't exactly been missing our lack luster sex life either.

"Fine. I'll call the number." It's not like I have family to call for help. I've been on my own since the day I turned eighteen. Before that really.

"You won't regret it." Bristol sounds confident, but I can't be sure. My life isn't exactly coming up roses these days. I'll be lucky to get an interview.

We end the call and I pull up the text she sent.

Needed personal assistant available immediately
Must be drug free and submit to random drug testing
Must be able to work day and night

It isn't much information. I pluck at my lower lip while I stare at it. The door swings open and Chad saunters in. Disgust wells within me. He's a good-looking guy in his board shorts with his button-up shirt open to show his fit physique. He looks like he stepped out of the nineties. His bleached blond hair only adds to the image.

When he flops onto the bed beside me, he gives me this look with his brown eyes that used to do it for me. Until it was also doing it for

Sandy and Melanie and who knows who else. Now I just roll my eyes.

"What do you want, Chad?" I wrap my arms around my legs, drawing them out of his reach so he can't touch me.

"I'm thinking you need to pay more for rent since I'm not getting any now." He reaches out and tugs on the leg of my jeans. I almost hiss at him, but I bite my tongue. I still need to live somewhere. This is marginally better than the streets and I pay for it, so I have a right to be here.

"I can't afford more," I say through gritted teeth. We agreed when we moved in that he would pay more than half because at the time I couldn't afford it, and he really wanted this place over the place I could afford. Now, I really can't pay half.

He smiles his cocky, arrogant, knowing smile. "You could put out then. I'll let you stay here rent-free."

"Fuck you, Chad." Fuck this. I scramble off the bed and slide my feet into a pair of flip flops.

"Come on, Greer. It's just fucking." He collapses back on the bed like the whiny bitch he is.

I grab my backpack and throw my laptop into it before grabbing some random clothes out of my drawer. I'm not sure where I'm going, but I'm not coming back here tonight. Even the floor at Bristol's would be better than this.

He rises on his elbows and makes a kissy face. "You always liked it when I went down on you."

I roll my eyes. It's not like he did that often. Only when he thought I'd reciprocate. Usually, I'd just pretend to come to get him to stop. I go into the closet and grab a few other things, just in case I get the interview.

When I come out, any words of indignation die on my tongue when I see he's stroking his cock with a pair of my panties. I wish I'd stayed in the closet. How did I ever fall for this asshole's bullshit? "You're such a waste of space."

"Where are you going, Greer? You've got nowhere to go. No

friends. I'll be your friend…if you suck me off." He grins as he strokes his cock.

I sneer at him before charging out of the apartment. Clicking on the number for the ad, I haul ass to the elevator, listening to the ring-tone. Almost a year of my life wasted on that asshole. Even though we always used condoms, I got checked because the last thing I wanted from him was a STI.

"What a fucking asshole," I mutter as I step in and press the first floor button.

"Bad day?" a deep, groggy voice asks on the line.

Fuck, shit. No need to make it worse. "Yes, but I'm hoping to apply for the job as the personal assistant."

Fake it 'til you make it is what my foster mother always said. She was talking about smiling and being happy, but it applies to a lot of things in life.

"You do drugs?" His voice is gruff like he just woke from sleep. It skitters pleasantly down my spine.

"No, but would you believe me on just my word?" I lean against the wall of the elevator as the car moves to the first floor.

"I have a drug test here with your name on it." The rough voice helps calm me down even as it keys me up. It's been a while since Chad and I—a disgusted shudder runs through me. Mistake number one thinking sex equals love. From now on sex is just sex.

"You don't even know my name." I glance at the one light bulb still working in the elevator. This whole place is a shithole. I just want to find somewhere nice to live. Maybe I'll find an apartment to share on the internet.

"Maybe I'll just call you poppet." He chuckles. "I'll text you the address and you can come by to pee in a cup. We'll talk about things."

The way he says *things* makes my pulse throb. "How will you know it's me though?"

"What's your name, poppet?"

"Greer Morrow." The elevator stops on the first floor, and I walk into the lobby.

"Sounds very old-school Hollywood. I like it, Greer Morrow." My name rolling off his tongue is like melting wax dripping on my skin. Hot, dangerous, tantalizing.

My phone buzzes with a text and I'm sure it's Chad. That helps cool any fantasies about the voice on the phone. "Who do I have the pleasure of speaking with?"

"Roarke Flynn."

My insides burst with nerves. Had I just been low-key flirting with *the* Roarke Flynn? Sexiest Man Alive two years running? Whose sex scene in *Lost in Vegas* gave me the best self-administered orgasm of my life?

My throat closes a little and my mouth gapes like I can't find air.

"C'mon, poppet, it's not that shocking, is it? It's not like you're seeing my cock for the first time." There's humor in his tone, but oof, yeah, not seeing that. In person. Only on the big screen.

I clear my throat. "Would I be working for you?"

"Somewhat," he hedges, his voice still gritty and low. "But we can discuss that when you get here. I'll send you a text. You on your way now like a good girl?"

Fuck. Sparks bolt through my whole body at those words. "Yes, I'm coming—"

His deep, rich chuckle cuts me off. "Not so fast, poppet. We should at least get to know each other a little first."

Heat floods my face. This is dangerous, but I have nothing to lose. "I'll be there."

"I'll be waiting."

I don't bother changing, but fling my bag into the trunk of my heap on wheels, Old Betsy. Better clothes might help a little, but showing up in the old Volkswagen Jetta that's seen much better days is going to clue them in to how desperate I am for a job. Besides, this is who I am. Take it or leave it.

Most people leave it, but at least I'm not putting on pretenses about being someone I'm not.

The GPS leads me to a set of gates. Beyond the gates, trees line a road that disappears into the sky. I press the call button on the box and wait. The ocean is just beyond the house. I can hear the waves and it helps ease some of my nerves.

One of my best memories was at the beach. I don't have many good memories to draw on.

As I wait, a white car drives slowly behind me. Could be paparazzi? When I start to turn, they drive off. Weird.

"Yes?" The static-crackled male voice doesn't sound like Roarke.

"Greer Morrow to see Roarke Flynn." Time to play professional.

"For fuck's sake, Roarke did you order a prostitute?" It sounds like he's yelling into the house. A second passes while he waits for a reply and I die a little inside. Not that kind of professional.

"Oh shit. Did you hear that?" he says after a moment.

Heat claws its way up to my hairline. What the hell am I walking into? "Um, yes."

"Fuck, sorry." The gate buzzes and opens slowly. "Come to the main door and I'll let you in."

I consider backing up and just driving away. Surely, I can find another job and a place to live. Maybe I could just drive down the coast until I run out of gas or Old Betsy dies. Suddenly, I'm regretting not changing out of my oversized T-shirt and jeans with flip flops. I could have done something with my long hair instead of leaving it in a messy bun.

When the gates fully open, I pull forward. Might as well make a complete fool of myself. At least they won't mistake me for a prostitute. As I crest the hill, the house fills my vision. White multiple stories with enormous windows. Gorgeous. It's massive and as I pull up the driveway, there are two four-car garages on either side of me.

Neither Old Betsy nor I fit in here, but at least I'll meet my Hollywood crush in the flesh. I can tell my grandkids someday that I met *the* Roarke Flynn and they'll say *who?* Because who knows actors from when their grandparents were younger.

I grab a tube of cherry ChapStick out of my purse and swipe it over my lips. And that's all the makeup I have with me, so it will have to do. I'm a mess. My insides churn with nerves. Why am I even here?

Pressing my head against the steering wheel, I take a deep breath. This is insane. Bristol works in the Hollywood machine. She wouldn't lead me astray. If she thinks I can do this, then hopefully I can do it.

Fake it 'til you make it.

When I step out of my car, I smell the ocean on the wind. I can't see it from here, but I can hear the crashing waves and feel the salty air on my skin. What would it be like to live here?

Our apartment in the city is as far away from nature as possible. But here, fruit trees and greenery surround the house. The lawn is lush green grass making me itch to slip my flip flops off and dig my toes into it.

Drawing in a breath, I climb the stairs leading to the door. As I approach, I see the shadow of a very tall man walking toward the glass door. He comes closer. His light brown hair is an unruly mess, almost covering his hazel eyes. He's only wearing a pair of gray sweats. His bare chest is defined and a black tattoo crawls over his shoulder against his tan skin.

He opens the door and gives me a self-deprecating smile. "Sorry about that. You never know with Roarke."

His voice rolls over me like warm molasses and a shiver of awareness rushes along my spine. He holds his hand out.

"Wyatt."

I take his hand to shake it and feel a pulse of attraction flow through me. His eyes roam over me. I'm short so it doesn't take him long to look me over, but his eyes are interested when they meet mine.

Shaking off the awareness, I smile. "Greer Morrow."

His hand slides from mine. I resist the urge to rub my hand to rid it of the tingles he left behind.

"Follow me." He backs into the house. As I follow him across the warm wood floors, I take in the white rugs and furniture with dark green throw pillows. The fireplace is black. The open room flows into a dining room with walls of accordion glass doors open to a shimmering blue pool. A wine room peeks out from behind the dining room table.

I'm used to the normal height ceilings of my apartment, but these ceilings are taller than two of me, standing on top of each other. It's beautiful and a little cold at the same time.

At least it distracts me from checking out Wyatt's ass. Which I send a silent thank you to whatever woman invented gray sweats. Wyatt's back is just as defined as his front and that ink trails over his shoulder to spill down his back.

"We don't get a lot of visitors up here." Wyatt leads me around the wine room into what I think is supposed to be casual rooms? There's a kitchen and another dining table and more accordion doors to the outside and another two sets of living room furniture.

"Poppet, you made it." His dark voice is even more dangerous in real life.

I swear my panties melt and I almost don't want to turn to see this man. But I also can't resist. Turning, my heart beat ratchets up. Roarke Flynn stands before me. Golden hair, stubble on his square jaw, blue eyes shining like he has a spotlight on him, and a grin that is contagious.

I almost don't even realize I'm smiling back. When he closes in on me, he smells as good as he looks, sandalwood and spices.

"Sorry about the whore talk. I don't normally pay for company." That voice. My God. He takes my hand and a live wire jolts through me. He doesn't seem to notice as he draws me to the couch. "Sit. We have much to talk about."

"We do?" I collapse on the couch as my knees finally give up. My blood thunders so loud through my veins I'm not sure I can even hear him. I shouldn't be here. This type of life isn't for me, I've already proved that once before.

"Of course. This is an interview, poppet." He sits across from me. And then he winks. At me. A giddiness rushes through me like I've had too much to drink. Or at least, what I think too much would feel like.

I always wondered if I'd be the type of girl to get star struck. My foster mom Mary had her share of famous friends, but not one of them made me feel like Roarke does. His focus on me is intense.

"Wyatt, bring Aiden and Mason. We should do this as a group. After all, if poppet gets the job, she'll be living with all of us and making sure our every desire is met."

I swallow so hard I cough. He gets up and sits next to me rubbing my back.

"Don't die now, poppet. The garden is new. I'd hate to dig you a spot in it." The heat of his body is like a drug I can't help but crave.

Lifting my gaze, I sigh at how close and how perfect he is. Seriously, it's no wonder he reigns at the box office. He's gorgeous and overwhelming in real life.

He tips my chin and studies my eyes. "You seem like a brandy girl."

"I don't drink," I murmur on autopilot because he's touching me and all my thought process has devolved to that single touch.

He tilts his head like he can't believe what he heard.

"For fuck's sake, Roarke release the poor girl before she has a heart attack."

My gaze jerks to the familiar voice. Aiden Clyborne, tall, slender, but built, with a voice that women would beg to read grocery lists. He's been in some of my favorite movies. His slightly curled, tousled brown hair looks windswept. His light blue eyes don't miss a thing as he moves in to take my hand.

I barely process the jolt from his touch. I'm awestruck.

"Aiden, but from the look on your face you know who I am."

Releasing my hand, he gives me a wary smile like he's afraid I'm going to fangirl all over him.

He's not wrong. It's on the tip of my tongue. How much I adore him in every film. But I keep my tongue from wagging.

Roarke laughs and moves across from me again. "She likes me best, Aiden. Mason Randall and Wyatt McBride." He nods to the other two men. "This is my poppet, Greer Morrow."

My face heats at him claiming me as I look to the last man to enter: Mason Randall. Mary used to talk about him. This up-and-coming director who her paramour was mentoring. Unlike the others who give off some warm vibes, Mason is all dark from his black hair to his piercing blue eyes. He looks at me as if he already knows who I am and what I'm about.

And he definitely doesn't like it.

I straighten my back and sit as tall as my five-foot frame allows.

"You answered the ad?" Mason takes a seat and sits back as if this is his meeting and he'll be the one in control of it. Power radiates off him and that energy makes me want to misbehave. Not that I'm going to, but I don't do well with authority figures.

I need this job.

"My friend sent it to me," I admit. "She thought it would be a good opportunity."

Mason's eyes flow over me, taking my measure. I don't cower, but fuck, do I want to. He'll be the decision maker in all this. I'm not good enough for whatever this job entails or even to sit on this beautiful cream couch in my outfit that probably cost me twenty bucks. Not compared to these gorgeous men in their expensive casual clothes.

I'm going to do my best to make them overlook my shortcomings, because I want this.

All of it. This house. This life. These men. To play pretend like my life isn't one long train wreck. Just for a little while live a dream until I have to wake up.

Chapter 2

I'm a Survivor

Greer

"Actress?" Mason doesn't waste any time, starting the interrogation. "Model?"

I stifle a chuckle and raise an eyebrow, even as my hands grow clammy. I'm five feet tall, not exactly model material. Glancing down at my current state, I give him a look that asks *really?* "Neither."

"Do you know how to cook?"

"Yes." It's one of the things I love to do. One of my foster mothers, Cindy, was a baker.

"Cleaning up will be part of your duties, but we do have a maid who comes by twice a week for deep cleaning. We'll have a list for you. Do you have a problem with that?" His dark eyebrow lifts, challenging me.

"Not at all." I've spent years picking up after other people.

When I glance Roarke's way, he winks, making my whole body flush with heat. This is worse than any test anxiety I used to have. I'm hyper aware of all of them. The other guys lounge nearby, studying me. I twist the bottom of my t-shirt around my finger to give my hands something to do.

"Your main purpose will be to keep Aiden sober." Mason glances at Aiden, who snorts and leans back like he doesn't have a care in the world. "He's fresh from rehab and we have a lot of money riding on this film. We can't have the fuck ups like his last film."

It'd been in all the tabloid news: his divorce and subsequent breakdown, followed by a stint in rehab. I don't look at him, knowing that's what he expects. I always hated the pitying looks from people like you meant to fuck up your life. Like you're flawed somehow for feeling things deeply.

"You obviously didn't show up intending to try to seduce any of us." Mason waves a hand at my outfit and smirks.

A breath rushes out of me and I meet his eyes with an honest gaze. "My ex was being a dick, so I left in a hurry. Roarke asked if I could interview now, so I came straight here. I'm looking for a job and somewhere to stay. Not a man to bone. Besides I'd hate for you to think I'm polished all the time. That would take hours to accomplish."

"See, told you you'd like her. No fuss no muss." Roarke chuckles and pushes Mason's shoulder. Like Roarke could get all that from our brief phone conversation.

Mason barely moves but glares at Roarke. Not moving his gaze from Roarke, Mason says, "We'll need a urine test now and a blood test later. Unfortunately, someone will need to go into the bathroom with you to make sure it's *your* urine."

Roarke opens his mouth, but Aiden stands. "I'll do it. People have been watching me pee for the last few months. It'd be a change to watch someone else."

I don't think my face can get any redder as he gestures for me to follow him. When I send a quick glance at everyone else, they all just watch us go. This is a normal thing apparently. All right, I'm just going to follow *the* Aiden Clyborne and pee in front of him.

Fuck. How humiliating. But then I think of Chad wanting a blow job and know I'd do anything to get out of that place. Fuck, I'd probably blow all of them to get out of that apartment. My cheeks heat more as that thought doesn't actually repulse me. It must be this place and being starstruck.

We walk down a set of stairs and pass a movie room. This is a one in a million chance to see how the other half lives. My mouth drops open as I take in the expensive fixtures and pretty decorations. Did they pick this stuff out or did a decorator come through?

With my attention distracted by all the pretty things, I crash into Aiden's back when he stops. His back is hard as I steady myself on him.

"Sorry," I mumble as I take a step back.

He smells like oranges and I want to lean into the scent. But when he turns, I hustle back trying to look like I wasn't just sniffing him. He raises an eyebrow with that face that makes the bad guys cry in his action films.

Intimidating as fuck. I clasp my hands tight behind my back.

"Don't run the water. When you're finished, let me know and I'll come in and get the sample so you can wash your hands." Aiden's voice is smooth like the best chocolate.

"Wait?" I point to the bathroom. "You aren't going with me?"

He steps closer and lowers his voice, suddenly his heat and that citrus scent surround me and it feels overwhelmingly intimate. He glances toward the upstairs before returning his gaze to me. "I've peed enough in front of strangers to know how dehumanizing it is. If you let me pat you down, I can make sure you aren't hiding any bags of urine on you."

"First, ew. Second, people do that?" I tilt my head as I meet Aiden's blue eyes.

"Yes, addicts do that. They do a lot to get their fix." He drops his gaze before meeting my eyes again. "So what's it going to be?"

I bite my lip and try not to stare at him, but fuck, who wouldn't. Even if he weren't a famous movie star, the guy is hot. The thought of his hands on my body makes my insides swirl with heat. But going pee in front of him would be humiliating.

Normally that's a relationship killer, and while I don't think I'll be in a relationship with him anytime soon, I will have to work with him day in and day out. So maybe some boundaries would be good.

I hold out my arms and spread my legs like I'm being arrested.

He shakes his head, but a hint of a smile quirks his lips. "This won't take long."

"Is that a short joke?" I give him a look like I'm offended. It's not like I haven't heard them all.

"You are quite small." He goes down on his knee and the top of his head is eye level with me. He looks over my baggie t-shirt and sighs. His light eyes lift to mine. It's so weird to look down at someone. "I swear this isn't a line, but this would be easier if you took off your t-shirt."

Uh, fuck, yeah, that would be fine, but...

"I'm not wearing a bra," I whisper loudly. I can't even hear the guys upstairs talking anymore. It feels like we're completely alone.

He arches an eyebrow. "I've seen tits before."

I cock my eyebrow back. "Not mine you haven't."

"I'm a professional actor." His face is completely emotionless. "I've been on set with some of the most beautiful women in the world without their tops on. I'm sure your breast are..."

That pause is uncalled for as he gestures toward my chest. I cross my arms over my breasts and glare at him.

"Quite adequate." He grins like I'm one of those women on set who needs convincing to take their tops off and be filmed. "However, if we don't do this quickly, I'm sure Roarke will be down here any minute. He loves to watch almost as much as he loves to be watched."

My mouth drops open. That implication sounds very sexual. I glance over my shoulder like he might bound down the steps intent on watching me pee. Yeah, that's not happening.

Before I can second guess myself, I grab the hem of my oversized shirt and take it off, dropping it to the side before crossing my arms over my breasts.

"Larger than I thought." Aiden's words lack any inflection, purely formal. His eyes lift to mine and there's a gentleness in them I wasn't expecting. "I'm going to pat down your hips and legs. Then you'll turn around for me to check your back. I'll check your t-shirt and then you can put it back on."

"Okay." In the world of humiliating stories from my life, this doesn't even crack the top five. It's not pleasant, but I can deal with Aiden Clyborne having seen my breasts. Hell, maybe I'll even tell my imaginary grandkids too.

Aiden nods and his gaze shifts down. His large hands encircle my waist, brushing my bare skin and an involuntary shiver works through me. He pauses.

"Sorry," I say.

He works his hands down the outside of my legs. "Not sure what you're sorry for. I'm the one feeling you up when we've just met."

Having this superstar of a man kneeling before me is already intoxicating, but with his hands on me... fuck me, he's gorgeous even this close up. His fingers trail up the bottom of my pant legs along my calves, touching my bare skin and sending dizzying sparks throughout me. I suck in a breath and look up at the ceiling.

Think of something gross, like Chad. It doesn't seem to help.

"I guess I'm used to apologizing." Words spill out of me as he checks my other calf. Warmth surges through me as he trails them gently up the inside of my legs. "It's easier to say sorry and have the other person dismiss you than to acknowledge what you feel sometimes."

"Turn around please."

I lower my eyes to his, but he's keeping his face devoid of emotion. Turning, I glance toward the stairs, wondering if someone really will come to check on us. Aiden's hands settle on my hips and I inhale sharply at the feel of him behind me.

"It's my turn to apologize, but I'll need to touch you between your legs."

"Like a TSA check." Done by one of the sexiest men alive. My blood boils. "Oh. Yeah, whatever you need to do."

Like it isn't a big deal that Aiden Clyborne is going to cup my pussy. I don't think I've ever been this wet and hopefully he won't be able to tell.

"Honestly, I'll be quick." His fingers tighten on my hips.

"I bet you say that to all the girls." It comes out before I can stop it.

"Maybe." He chuckles. "It's been a while."

My heart clenches thinking of his brutal divorce.

Before I can think of another thing to say, his hand slides down between my legs. I bite my lip to stop from making some weird sex noise that would be awkward for both of us. His fingers press against me. He's just checking to make sure I'm not storing pee somewhere. Nothing else. He draws his hand away.

"Done."

I turn back around with my arms over my breasts. He holds my t-shirt, running his hands along it before righting it. He lifts his eyes to mine and slides my shirt on over my head. The fabric falls down and I slip my arms into the sleeves before backing away as he stands.

Fuck, after that I better get the job. Even the tips of my ears feel hot.

He gestures to the bathroom. "Good to go."

I duck my head and go into the bathroom, leaving the door open a crack. Pressing my cold hands to my hot face, I feel like screaming, but that would be inappropriate. Instead I release the breath I'm holding and get ready to pee in a cup.

Suddenly it's too quiet. I can literally hear Aiden's breath in here.

"Performance anxiety?" he asks after a few long minutes.

"I swear this never happens." But sitting on a toilet holding a cup between my legs while one of the hottest actors stands outside waiting to hear me pee is just a step too far for my poor bladder. "Can you maybe sing?"

His dark chuckle makes my insides warm. "Not even if you paid me to."

"If I turned on the water—"

"Not an option." His voice goes away and then comes back. "How about a monologue?"

"Anything." To cover the silence and awkwardness of this moment.

He takes a breath and begins the lines from one of the superhero movies he starred in. The words flow from him like water and for a minute, I forget the strip search and pat down. Better yet, I relax enough to pee. Thankfully, he doesn't even pause at the sound and continues going on about the way of the world.

Setting the cup on the counter, I finish and stand without flushing. My cheeks heat as I call out, "Done."

The door opens and he nods at the toilet. I flush and move to the sink to wash my hands. He passes behind me. My breath catches at his nearness. I can still feel the ghost of his hands running over me.

He pulls out a test strip and dips it in my urine.

"Now what?" I dry my hands on the towel.

He leans against the counter. "We wait for the results."

I nod and sit on the edge of the tub. "That's from my favorite movie."

He smiles and dips his head, making his curls fall over his forehead. "It's most people's favorite movie."

"True." I kick my legs out in front of me. It was the movie that launched him into super stardom. "But do most people go as the character for Halloween?"

He raises his eyebrow like I'm foolish to ask.

"As a gender-bending version of your character?" I grin, remembering Chad being disgusted that I didn't go as the female lead character to his male superhero.

"More than you think." The corner of his lips quirks up in a sly smile. He glances at the test strip.

"How does this work?" I'm curious and we have a few minutes alone.

"The drug test or this arrangement?" He cocks his head to the side as he maintains eye contact.

"The arrangement. What do you expect from your personal assistant?" I straighten the hem of my shirt and his gaze drops to my breasts for a second. My face burns and an urge to cover my breasts flows through me.

"You're in charge of making sure I don't crash and burn again."

I bite out a sarcastic laugh. "So no pressure?"

He gives me a half grin that makes him seem approachable. "You keep me away from alcohol and drugs. The other parts are mostly what the guys need. Someone to make sure our house is taken care of while we work fourteen-hour days on set. Make sure we have food in the fridge and on the table."

"Will I need to go to set with you?" I've never been on a film set before. It feels odd even asking.

"Sometimes." He shrugs. "You're here to keep me from wanting to drown myself in substances."

That speaks to a place deep inside me. There's a reason I ended up in foster care. The person who was supposed to love me loved drugs more.

"My mom was an addict," I say softly. "I couldn't save her."

After glancing at his phone and the strip again, Aiden lowers himself to sit on the floor. "How old were you?"

"Ten." Normally, I'd let my hair fall around my face, but right now my hair is pulled back. My need to hide goes unfulfilled, ashamed of who I was. Who I am. The daughter of an addict.

"Hey." The word is soft and compelling.

When I lift my gaze to his, he gives me a world-weary smile.

"Sometimes it doesn't matter how much we love someone. Sometimes the addiction wins." He rubs his fingers together. "I've been through rehab. I did all the steps. I don't want addiction to win."

There's a light in the darkness of his eyes. He's battling this demon and he just needs me to keep him on track. He's willing to fight. That's a step in the right direction.

"I don't drink alcohol or take drugs because I don't want to become her. I don't want anyone to end up like her." A shiver races through me as the memory presses forward of her blank brown eyes staring into nothing. I push it down, hide it away like I've done for years.

"I promise I'm fighting." His words flow over me and I can see the strength in his eyes.

"If you choose me to go into the fight with you, I'll fight harder than anyone else. That I promise you." It comes from somewhere deep inside. This need to make sure no one loses their loved one. To make sure we don't lose Aiden to the darkness.

"I believe you, little warrior." Aiden's lips tip into a smile as the timer goes off on his phone.

My insides warm as I return his smile. Maybe this is what I need too. A mission. Someone to save.

Chapter 3

Heat Waves

Aiden

Greer Morrow is not who I expected to show up for this job. She's young maybe barely in her twenties while we're all almost thirty. She's small and swimming in her oversized t-shirt and baggy pants. Her chipped pink toenails peek out of a pair of bright pink flip flops.

Her voice has this husky factor that makes my balls tighten. Which is probably why Roarke insisted she come interview. She's small, compact, but refreshing. Fuck, if she'd shown up here in a dress that showed off those curves she hides, Roarke would have fucked her before we could even get a drug test.

As it is, I don't think the baggy clothes are putting him off at all.

Mason and I discussed hiring a guy to do the job just so we don't have to deal with a woman crawling into our beds. But I'm not sure I'd hate if Greer crawled into my bed. Besides we didn't have much luck with the last guy.

"Shouldn't we check the dipstick?" she says softly. Her light brown eyes flick to the strip on the counter before returning to mine.

I shift to move to my feet and catch her sweet vanilla scent. I'm glad she didn't notice my erection from patting her down earlier. That shirt is a fucking disappointment when I realized what lay beneath. Her breasts are perky and not as small as I thought. They'd fill my hand and my mouth nicely.

Fuck. Those aren't the thoughts I should have about my employee. I should probably say no to hiring her. But when I meet those wide eyes, I also don't want her to leave.

Turning, I check the test and note that everything is negative. I didn't expect anything less. The pain on her face when she discussed her mother was like a kick to the groin which helped to make my erection retreat. That I made the people around me feel like she must have felt guts me.

My friends are my family and I hurt them. Trying to stop the pain I felt was the only thing on my mind. To erase the pain caused by my failed marriage.

"Did I pass?" She stands behind me. Her flip flops slap as she draws near to look around me.

"With flying colors." I take a breath, inhaling her intoxicating scent. Fuck. I do the only thing I know will make my cock stand down, I think about preparing for a role.

"Good. What's next?" Her husky voice teases my ears. She's close enough that her warmth claws at me, making me want to turn and lift her onto the counter and bite those lips she keeps worrying with her teeth to discover how they taste. Then lick them to sooth them.

It's been too fucking long since I've had sex. That's the only reasonable explanation that this pixie of a woman tempts me.

"We should go back upstairs." I take another moment to get myself under control. My eyes close and I let my thoughts drift away until nothing remains.

She doesn't say anything as she dumps the cup into the toilet and flushes. Her hip brushes mine as she turns on the water and washes her hands.

"Do you want to wash your hands too?" That voice. Fuck me.

"Yeah." Opening my eyes, I find her watching me in the mirror.

Concern pulls at her pixie-like face. Her brown hair is pulled into a bun revealing her long neck and smooth jawline. I flash her my signature smile and wash my hands.

Her brow furrows a little but then she plasters on a fake smile too. It looks just as practiced. Ten years old and couldn't save her mother. My heart tightens for her. What ten-year-old could?

Fuck, the guys almost couldn't reach me. But once I realized what I was doing, it all came crashing down around me and I willingly went into rehab.

"Come on." I dry my hands and lead her back upstairs to the others.

The guys are on the couch. As soon as we come into view, the murmur of conversation dies. Mason's hawklike gaze scans both of us.

"Come here, poppet." Roarke holds his hand out to her. She glances at me for confirmation.

Something settles inside me at that look. Maybe she trusts me. My chest warms. Even though she shouldn't. Addiction is an evil mistress to live with. Staying clean will be a hard road with all the temptations lingering in my life. I give her an encouraging nod.

Roarke takes her hand and makes her sit next to him. Thigh to thigh. Greer couldn't get more red. Even the tips of her ears glow with color. I shut down every image my conscious tries to send me of how she'd look spread out beneath me, flushed and writhing with pleasure.

I try to focus on the conversation. Only getting small bits and pieces as I try to figure out why Greer is the first woman to make me want to fuck her since my ex.

As she answers Mason's questions, they filter into my brain. She's twenty-one, high school diploma, some college. Her pussy was warm against my fingers and the tang of her arousal filled the space between us mixed with that vanilla scent intoxicating me.

She's pretty, but I've been surrounded with the most beautiful women in the world and not responded like I do to her.

"What other obligations do you have?" Mason's firm voice brings me back as I tuck away the unwanted attraction.

Her lips part slightly before she licks them.

"None. I'm down to part time at the diner which I could quit. They're overstaffed." Her gaze flicks up to mine. "I don't have anyone who needs my attention."

"What about the fucking asshole?" Roarke says.

She winces and I perk up. Maybe she's unavailable. That would make this attraction easy to ignore. She blows out a breath.

"We moved in too soon. He's a cheating bastard, but I don't really have anywhere else to go." She shrugs and gives all of us a smile. "I'm like a cat though. I always land on my feet."

I'm sure she does, but fuck if I'm going to let her go and wind up another statistic of this town. She doesn't have anywhere else to go. What does the guy want her to do to stay? My insides knot up.

"Wyatt, why don't you show Greer around the house?" I give her my interview smile. I want to see where Mason's head is on this. Pretty sure Roarke is already signing up to be her number one fuck buddy. Which is why I didn't ask him to show her the place.

Wyatt rubs his hands on his sweats and stands. "This way, we'll start downstairs."

Greer's eyes flick to mine before she follows Wyatt. Checking in with me again. My chest swells as does my cock.

Fuck, why this woman? It's going to drive me mental. But I can't kick her out with nowhere to go.

"I like her." Roarke flashes his movie star smile.

"You like anything female." Mason shakes his head and meets my gaze. We've both seen Roarke 'in love' and then a week later, he's in love with someone new. Love is a throwaway term to him. I'm surprised he said he likes her though. That's high praise from the guy.

Roarke chuckles darkly. "Can you blame me? That voice alone will haunt my dreams tonight. Such a compact little piece of ass."

"She's not a piece of ass if she works here." Mason glares at Roarke before his eyes narrow on me. "What do you think?"

I think my cock will be hard all the time with her around, but I can get over that. That soft look she gave me in the bathroom makes me warm in a different way though. One I'm not entirely comfortable with. I clear my throat.

"She knows addicts. She's in a pinch and so are we." I lean back on the counter. We don't have much time to get someone new. The last guy tried to sell me drugs. He promised me he'd cover for me if I got him a role in the movie.

"We can take our time and find the right person for the job." Mason glances at Roarke. "Maybe a male applicant?"

"And get rid of my poppet?" Roarke acts like that would be an offense to him. My guts tighten at the thought of her walking out of here and never seeing her again. She'd become just another face in the crowd. No one special.

That would be a shame.

"Are you going to fuck her?" Mason's gaze drills into Roarke.

Roarke grins. "Why not? Besides I saw the way you looked at her. And Aiden..."

I tense as they both look at me. "What?"

Mason's eyes widen.

Roarke smirks. "This is the first time I've seen him want to fuck someone since Siobhan."

Wincing at my ex's name, I glare at Roarke. "We aren't hiring her to fuck us, Roarke."

"Why not?" He grins. "She's a woman and we're men. Seems like a good solution all around."

"Because she's not a prostitute." I straighten. "This is a job. She keeps me on the straight and narrow and helps out around the place. We aren't paying her to have sex with us."

"But that doesn't mean we *can't* have sex with her." Roarke wiggles his eyebrows. It was the right call sending Wyatt with Greer because she would have returned well fucked if Roarke had his way. And he usually does.

"Fuck." Mason leans back. His shoulders slump. "This is going to become a thing."

"Most likely." Roarke sinks back into the couch with a grin. "Pretty sure my little poppet wants all of us too. She got that look of a kid in a candy store who can't make up her mind."

"We can't lose her halfway through the filming because you couldn't keep your dick in your pants." Mason stands and clenches his fists. "If she thinks you're dumping her, which you will, she'll leave us high and dry."

Good, at least Mason is on board with having her as our assistant. That's one barrier down.

"Studios add morality clauses all the time to contracts." I should know. "What if we make it clear—"

Roarke stands, so now we're all standing. "If you cockblock me—"

"For fuck's sake, let me finish." I wet my lips and listen for a second to see if I hear Wyatt and Greer nearby. Nothing.

"Please continue." Roarke gestures with a scowl on his face like he knows what I'm going to say.

Mason watches me carefully. He's been looking for cracks since I returned from rehab. I deserve it, but it's annoying as hell. I'm fine. I did my time. Sure there are still demons lurking to drag me down, but I'll fight them off.

With her help.

"We put in a consent clause in addition to the NDA." I rub my jaw as I think it through.

"What exactly will we be putting in this consent clause?" Mason does look a little too interested. He didn't want her here because he's attracted to her? Is Wyatt interested in my little warrior as well?

"What we want." I swallow and straighten. "Her to commit to the full length of time and give us permission to explore our attraction without having to worry about her growing attached to any one of us. We can give her a bonus if she makes it to the end of the filming to make it more tempting."

"You want the woman who will be with us for four months—plus probably post-production until the premier, which could be at least another year—to consider fucking us with no strings attached?" Mason gives me a look that clearly says he thinks I'm crazy. "All of us?"

"It's not like we'd be taking away the woman's free will." I lean back against the counter as Roarke lowers to the couch with a thoughtful look. "She can choose to engage or not."

"I like it." Roarke grins.

"Of course you do." Mason shakes his head. "I'm not sure sharing a woman is a good idea. Especially if Roarke continues his manwhore ways."

Roarke laughs loud and booming. "If my poppet gives it up, I'm willing to forego extracurricular fucking. At least until I tire of her."

"How sweet. Willing to be monogamous for a whole week." I roll my eyes and shake my head. "I think we need to insist on no extracurricular fucking on all those that participate."

Not that I've been very active, but Mason has Halley. She's nothing more than a warm bed, but he uses her a lot during his creative process. He's a dark motherfucker.

"If you want in…" I leave that statement open as a muscle ticks in Mason's jaw.

"Fine," he bites out.

"It might be a non-issue if Greer says no." I'll just be taking a lot of long showers while she lives with us until I can work out this attraction. "We're hiring her either way. She's here to keep me sober and I'm confident she can."

Greer

The house is massive and every new space is more amazing than the last. Wyatt didn't pull on a shirt and with the way his gray sweats hang low on his hips, I'm heated as I follow him. I'll keep all that shit on lockdown if I get the job because this is exactly what I need. A chance to escape reality for a while. Live a fantasy life for just a short time.

We've moved to the top floor with the bedrooms. Wyatt walks in front of the closed doors.

"Roarke's, mine, Mason's." He leads me a little down the hallway. "Aiden's and our assistant's."

He opens the second door and I walk into the space. It's not massive like most of the space in the house. But it's a large room with a king sized bed in it. The walls are light gray and everything else is white. The attached bathroom is lovely with a shower/tub combination done in marble tile and a pretty white vanity.

When I come out of the bathroom, Wyatt sits on the bed watching me with those hazel eyes. My gaze drops to his cut chest and abs. I've been trying not to notice the bulge in his sweats. Seriously, trying not to look, but he seems big.

Like not hard big, but big. Like double-take big.

I squeeze my thighs together as I lift my gaze back to his smirk. Fuck, he caught me checking out his dick. My face feels so hot, I'm afraid I'll combust.

"So why this?" he asks.

I lean against the door frame. "My friend heard about the job and thought it would be a great opportunity to get out of my current living arrangement."

"Escape." He nods thoughtfully. "Is this something you want to do?"

I release a breath and look out the windows at the ocean rolling in. Peace settles deep inside me. "Yes. I can clean and cook and make sure Aiden doesn't fall off the wagon."

"You won't have much of a life living with us." He raises an eyebrow and pushes his hand through his messy hair. When he was close earlier, the smell of the ocean on a sunny day along with the earthy scent of him filled my nose.

"I don't have much of a life now." I lift my hands in surrender.

"Normally, I wouldn't do something like this, but I really don't have much to lose."

I lost everything that was important a long time ago. Though part of me wonders if I ever had anything worth keeping before.

Wyatt stands fluidly and stalks across the wood floor to stop directly in front of me. My breath catches as I take in his scent and heat. I lift my gaze from the middle of his chest up to his eyes.

"Everyone has something left to lose, kitten." His voice is low and intimate as he hovers above me. "We just don't always know what it is until it's gone."

I bite my lip as I look up at this guy. Everything inside me stands at attention, waiting for his touch. Sure, he's not a movie star, but he's still hot. "What do you do?"

He smiles this sexy smile that makes me clench my thighs tighter. I'm blaming this on Chad and his asshole ways, because I'm not usually attracted to guys like these ones. They are so far out of my league I'm surprised I don't just blink into extinction in their presence. My hormones must be on overdrive.

"I'm the screenwriter." He reaches out.

I hold my breath as he brushes a strand of hair off my cheek and behind my ear. I can't seem to look away from his eyes. Brown and greens collide within his iris, mottled with little flecks of gold. It's hypnotic. His fingers brush my neck and I suck in a breath as arousal sweeps through me.

"How much of an escape do you need, kitten?"

My panties are soaked as his head begins to dip. Is he going to kiss me? What is happening right now? My heart races. My eyes flutter shut as I brace myself for impact, knowing even his kiss could destroy me.

"Wyatt, bring me my poppet!" Roarke's voice booms through the house.

My eyes pop open and Wyatt is right there, so close I can feel his breath on my lips. My heart strains against my ribcage as I search his eyes.

"Come on, kitten. Let's see what the big bad wolf wants now." Wyatt's hand tangles with mine and I suck in a breath.

What is happening? Things like this don't happen to people like me. They just don't. But I know I want more.

When we walk down the stairs, we're met with looks that make me feel like prey. My heartbeat quickens even more and I stop. Or I would have if Wyatt wasn't holding my hand and dragging me forward into a den of wolves waiting eagerly to devour this sheep.

"We want to discuss our offer with you."

My breath catches at Aiden's words. This is really happening? Because my life has been one shit show after another. So far it sounds fantastic, but there's always a catch.

"Your offer?"

Wyatt releases my hand and I stand there dumbfounded amongst gods.

"Come on, poppet." Roarke walks up to me and puts his hand on the small of my back, gently leading me over to the table. Tingles race through my veins. "We have some things to discuss."

He pulls out a chair for me. I sit and watch as the others fill the table around me. Blowing out a breath, I drag my ass out of the clouds. This is a job, just like any job, but it's also living with four really hot men who ooze sex appeal.

I don't know how this is going to end, but I'm excited to find out.

Chapter 4

Are You Going to Be My Girl?

Greer

Okay, so maybe I'm easily intimidated or maybe these guys are just beyond what nature intended, because I'm not usually attracted to guys until I get to know them a little better. Chad and I dated for a month before we even kissed, but once that happens, I'm all in for better or worse. Or terrible in Chad's case.

Which is where my new motto comes in: Sex does not equal love.

"We need to draw up some legal documents still." Mason reclines in his chair. Even though his body is at ease, there's this power to him that's undeniable. He's not as gorgeous as the two movie stars but he's still handsome and has a dark air around him that draws me.

"Okay." I expected that much.

"An NDA, obviously, and a contract." Mason glances at Aiden. He smiles and my world turns upside down even if it isn't directed at me. Mason smiling is powerful enough to make my ovaries explode.

I must have made a noise because his gaze flicks to me, knowingly. I cross my legs but don't drop my gaze. While I may be afraid of him, I don't want him to know that. He doesn't need more power over me.

"Aiden, do you want to explain everything?" Mason steeples his fingers in front of his mouth, pressing them against his full lips. Somehow these guys make me feel like I've won a lifetime membership at an all you can eat man buffet. I need to get over that shit and quick.

This is a job not a bar. I'm going to do what they need me to do and figure out my life while I have a comfortable home. I can't screw this up by sleeping with any of them. No matter how tempting.

Aiden passes me a handwritten note with numbers that make my eyes bulge. "The first number is your monthly salary."

The number is more than I made in a year at the diner with tips. I bite my lip at the next number which is a lot more. I don't think I've ever been offered so many zeroes.

"We need someone who won't ditch us during production." Aiden runs a hand through his curls and I meet his light blue eyes. He gives me his world-weary look. "We're looking for someone now because the guy we had tried to sell me drugs."

My hand covers my mouth. "That's fucked up."

"Exactly. We're due to start filming next week and we need someone immediately. The second number is the bonus in addition to your salary if you stay until the end of filming. About four months."

I swallow knowing there's an even larger number below that, but I nod.

"The next number is if you stay through during post production and the premiere. The production company wants me sober for that year as well and finding someone new is difficult." Aiden sets his hands on the table between us. "Which is why we would be willing to give you those bonuses for staying the entire time."

I do a quick calculation of the monthly salary for a year plus the bonuses. It would be more than enough to finally reenroll in college and do something with my life. It would also afford me the time to figure out exactly what that thing could be.

This is a dream job.

Dreams don't come true for someone like me, so there has to be a catch.

I scan the guys sitting before me. These are strangers. Even though two seem familiar because I've seen their bodies of work and interviews, that's not who they truly are. Those are their public personas and I need to remember not to confuse that with who they actually are.

They're asking me to live with four men and basically make sure an addict doesn't slip when I couldn't even save my own mother. The numbers swirl before me. It would get me away from Chad and I could even pay my share of the rent through the end of our contract with no problems. It's almost a ludicrous amount.

It's not like I haven't lived with strangers before. Every new home was filled with strangers. New rules. New people to avoid.

Never in my wildest dreams would I imagine I could have this life. Even for a short period of time. And then be able to pursue a dream that was so far out of reach as to be unattainable.

"I won't lie. This seems too good to be true. What's the catch?" I cross my arms and lean back in the chair. Too many times I thought I'd found a home only to be shuffled to the next family and the family after that. Every house has secrets and dangers. So what are the dangers and secrets here?

"We want to fuck you." Roarke's words make my eyes widen.

"Excuse me?" I must have misheard him. Surely he didn't just say what I think I heard. "What?"

Mason moves and my gaze darts to him. He's the authority of this group. It's in his whole demeanor, even how he sits. His blue eyes draw me in.

"What Roarke so elegantly said. Production has a crazy schedule. While Roarke has been obvious about his attraction, the rest of us find ourselves drawn enough to be curious. If you are interested, of course."

My gaze flicks to Wyatt's hazel eyes. That intimate moment in the bedroom flashes in my mind. I mean, I've thought about all of them like that, but it's just a fantasy not something I would actually act on. Right?

It would be crazy to think that I could indulge in sex with even one of them, but all of them? That I really want to hasn't escaped my thoughts. I just figured Roarke was a flirt. Aiden. My gaze flicks to him. There's so much pain in him, but that little spark between us could be something. My leg bounces beneath the table.

"I'm not sure what to say." I swallow. My throat is suddenly dry. "I'm obviously flattered, but—"

"This isn't a condition of your job." Aiden leans forward with his elbows on the table. His blue eyes hold me captive. "You can choose when and if you want to start that kind of relationship with any or all of us or none of us. Your choice."

His eyes are so earnest and there's pain. So much pain in him.

"I'm not really the type of woman to just sleep around." I press my sweaty palms against my thighs to stop them from bouncing.

"We don't want to get a week into the arrangement and someone does something that makes you quit." Aiden releases a breath. "I want you to be my sobriety buddy. I'm not saying any of us will initiate something right away—"

"Speak for yourself." Roarke winks and gives me a huge grin. "I'd fuck you on this table right now, poppet."

My face heats, but so do my insides. Roarke is gorgeous and every time he speaks my panties get wet. When he's close, the buzz of arousal drowns out almost everything else. But still... In front of these guys? Really? Desire tugs low and heavy in my belly.

Why doesn't that scare me?

"Uh..."

"Forget Roarke for a moment." Wyatt crosses his ankle over his knee. "He's always ready and willing. All we're asking for, if I'm hearing this right, is the chance to explore our attractions. We aren't paying you to sleep with us—which someone should have said from the start, seeing as you haven't signed an NDA."

He glares at the other guys for a moment before his eyes soften when he returns those chameleon eyes to me. "It's not even a given. You say no and we back down. Anytime, anywhere. Enthusiastic consent throughout or it's a no go."

I worry my lip with my teeth as I look around at their faces. Roarke smiles and gives me his Hollywood smolder. Mason's eyes study me, sizing me up to see if I'm worthy of playing with.

Wyatt is the hardest to read. He watches me like he wants to delve into my mind and pull out everything wicked. A shiver works through me.

Then there's Aiden. So much fucking pain. They say not to get involved with someone until they're a year sober. It's too easy to trade one addiction for another and then crash and burn when it goes wrong. I don't want to be the reason he crashes.

I don't need the guilt of another addict on my conscious.

Everything inside me wants to say yes, but that piece of me that stood on a new doorstep waiting to meet yet another family to take me in can't handle rejection again. Even though these men are the ones waiting for me to say yes. To them.

Unbelievable.

"You don't have to agree to anything yet." Aiden must sense what I'm about to say. "It would be no strings attached. You decide to end it. It ends. No one shows up blasting Peter Gabriel outside your window."

I smile, because I can't help it. It's an iconic scene but why is that Aiden's go to? The movie is older than I am. It's older than he is too.

"I'll think about it." Because there's this glimmer of hope in Aiden's eyes that I don't want to snuff out. "When would I start?"

How many days would I have to put up with Chad or sleep in my car?

"Filming starts on Monday."

My smile falls. It's Wednesday. That's five days. Maybe Bristol can make room for that long. I could go back to Chad's and technically my apartment. I wince, remembering the request for a blowjob and his use for my panties.

I can't go back there. After today, I know his expectations and that's not happening.

"You live with your fucking asshole ex?" Roarke asks.

I nod, not even able to conjure a smile thinking about Chad.

"You'll stay here then. Tonight," Roarke announces like it's a done deal.

"Technically, she hasn't signed an NDA so we should keep her under watch until she signs." Mason strokes his hand over the scruff on his chin. His blue eyes follow my every move, making my insides turn to jelly.

"If you want." Aiden gives Roarke a chastising look that does absolutely nothing to quell Roarke's grin. "I'm sure we could have something drawn up quickly if needed. The room is available and it will be yours. If you want it."

My mouth opens and closes. What choice do I have? That beautiful bedroom upstairs or the floor at Bristol's or the couch at Chad's. It's an easy decision.

Roarke follows me out to my car to help me grab my things that I so elegantly blurted out I have with me. The fucking Roarke Flynn! My fangirl just won't calm the fuck down. Especially knowing exactly what he wants from me. What they all want.

It's a huge boost to my ego, but I'm afraid I'd just disappoint them. Sex is good and I enjoy it, but if it were a sport, I wouldn't even qualify for a recreational league and I'd definitely get picked last for most teams.

"This is your car?" Roarke eyes Old Betsy like she's the ugly stepsister. "How is it still running? Duct tape and prayers?"

I hold up my hands to stop him. "Shh, you'll make her mad. And no one likes Old Betsy when she gets mad."

"It looks like it's two minutes from croaking." Roarke raises a golden eyebrow as he looks her over. Her paint is faded and she's been dinged, but she's gotten me this far in life.

"*She* is sensitive and a life saver, so stop dissing her." I stroke a hand over her sun-spotted hood. "She's definitely seen better days, but she's never let me down."

And I'd need a pen and a stack of paper to list all the others in my life who have let me down. I bought her used for a grand when I was eighteen, saving every penny I earned to get her was a priority.

"Fine. Old Betsy can park in my space," he concedes. "I don't have a car here yet."

"She's used to being in the sun." I pop open the trunk and grab the bag I packed. Who knows what I grabbed and if I'll be able to even make anything match. If I can't find panties, I'm going to go medieval on Chad for distracting me.

Roarke strokes his hand down his cheek. "She doesn't really go with the aesthetic of the house…"

I laugh out loud. He grins and closes in on me. My breath catches at his nearness. His sandalwood scent wraps around me making me want to lean in closer.

"You have a sexy laugh, poppet." His hand slides around the back of my neck, sending sparks through my system. My fangirl fights with my urge to put my hands on his chest to stop him. Unfortunately fangirl doesn't win.

"Roarke." My hands press into the hard muscles of his pecs and for a second I forget why I put them there. The muscles twitch beneath my palms and I snatch my hands away like they were burned. Oof, yeah, I shouldn't touch him. That's playing with fire.

"Yes, poppet." He uses that seductive tone I've heard way too often lately and in every movie. It's almost a staple of the Roarke Flynn brand.

"Does this usually work?" I tilt my head as I meet his eyes.

He pauses and smiles slyly. "Usually."

"I bet. Look, I'm a lot starstruck right now and left my apartment in a hurry because my asshole ex thought he deserved blowjobs as payment for the rent and used my panties to get himself off."

Roarke's fingers tighten on the back of my neck before he gentles and massages the muscles. "Sounds like he deserves to be an ex."

I curl into his hand like a cat needing touch. When was the last time someone touched me like this? Chad always went straight to the typical spots and rarely spent any time on my neck. A massage wasn't on the menu.

"Mmm. He cheated on me. A lot." My eyelids grow heavy and I sway toward his heat.

"Sounds like you should fuck me to get back at him." Roarke's voice lures me. But when his words register, I laugh and draw away from him.

"I'm going to have to watch you, aren't I?" I arch my eyebrow. It's hard to take him seriously. I'm not sure why he wants in my pants, but he doesn't appear put off by my rebuffs.

He takes the bag out of my hand and gives me a cheeky grin. "Being watched is my specialty."

Aiden's words come back and the flush working up my neck goes into overdrive. *Roarke enjoys watching almost as much as he enjoys being watched.* He did say he wanted to fuck me on the table. Right then and there.

In front of the others.

Heat pours through my veins. What would that be like? Their hot gazes on my naked body while Roarke touches and fucks me. Would they all touch me?

Fuck. I'm aroused and bothered just by the thought of it. This is insane. I'm supposed to be starstruck and have all these complicated feelings, but they aren't supposed to offer to fulfill my fantasies. Or tell me I'm part of theirs.

"Still with me, poppet?" Roarke gives me a cocky grin. I must have spaced out there for a moment.

Nodding, I worry my lip. His gaze drops to my lips and darkens.

An answering pulse throbs through me. For a second, we remain almost breathless in our spots.

Roarke's eyes lift to mine and for a second, the attraction flows between us and it feels like he's going to kiss me. I don't know what face I make, but Roarke is subtle in the way he pulls away slightly, making my breath slam back into me.

"This it?" He lifts the bag.

I glance toward it and notice the bulge in his pants. My cheeks heat and I spin to close the trunk. "Yup. That's all."

Twenty-four hours. I bet if I make it twenty-four hours with them, some of this heat will wear off. They'll decide they don't really want me and things will be normal. I'll be the staff and they'll be the mega-millionaires bringing home randoms.

My fingers tighten on my keys. Okay not loving the idea of randoms. I'll get over that too. I just need time. Time to adjust, just like with a new foster family.

Learn the rules and figure out how to survive. Try not to give them reasons to send me away.

Taking a cleansing breath, I follow Roarke back into the house and up the stairs to what will be my bedroom. My room is in the corner, so I look over the pool and see the ocean beyond it. Unable to resist I walk over to the window and open it. The sound of crashing waves fill the space.

Mary had a pool. She even tried to get me to swim, but I've always been terrified of the water. So I never learned how.

"Do you have a swimsuit, poppet?" Roarke closes in behind me, but he doesn't touch me like he already knows that would be too much for me. The warmth of his body is almost overwhelming.

"I don't swim." The words slip out of me as I stare at the reflection of the beautiful blue pool.

"You aren't afraid of the water, are you?" He sounds personally offended.

I turn around and he's right there, towering over me.

"No, I'm not afraid," I lie. It's an easy lie. One I've told most of my life. Being afraid only got me attention I didn't want.

"Do you not like getting wet?" His wiggling eyebrows ruin the seriousness from his previous statement.

"I just never learned." I move past him to my bag and pull out my random selections. "When I was seven, we went to the beach. I ran in and out of the water while my mom watched. We played in the sand and water all day until I was as red as a lobster. We didn't have a pool or friends with pools. We never went back to the beach. No reason to learn to swim."

Roarke sits on the bed beside my bag and pulls out a pair of panties. I snatch them from his hand. And grab a few more things to put in the dresser.

"I'm going to teach you to swim, poppet." He pulls out a t-shirt with *Fuck Off* written on it. He holds it up with a quizzical brow.

"Chad's." I take it and set it to the side. I regard the Hollywood superstar sitting on my bed, rummaging in my hastily packed bag. "Don't you have something better to do?"

He smirks. "Not until Monday. You'll have my undivided attention until then."

My cheeks burn as I pull out the last of my clothes. It's not a lot. But it will be enough for a couple days. Then I can wait for Chad to go to work and sneak into the apartment to get the rest.

"Tell me, poppet, do you like sex?"

My mouth drops open and snaps shut. I never thought I'd have conversations like this with someone like Roarke. This job isn't going to be easy.

"If you don't want to talk about sex, we could go swimming." Roarke's blue eyes alight with mischief. "Either way we'll get you nice and wet."

I honestly don't know what to say to this man. "I don't have a swimsuit."

My door is wide open and Aiden pauses in the doorway on the

way to his room, I assume. He leans against the doorframe looking effortlessly casual, but imposing at the same time.

"Roarke, give the woman some space."

Grinning, Roarke lies back on my bed. "I'm not touching my poppet. She has plenty of room to roam."

Roarke's blue eyes are heated when they meet mine and he winks. "We were just discussing her inability to swim."

"You can't swim?" Aiden makes it sound like I have a rare deadly disease.

I shrug, suddenly aware I'm in a bedroom with two actors who have both expressed an interest in me sexually. Life is strange. I grab the handful of bras and panties on the bed and shove them in a drawer.

"We need to fix that." Aiden steps into my room. My heart slams against my ribcage. Roarke's energy already keys me up, but add Aiden to the equation and my poor heart might explode from the effort.

Roarke sits up. "Just what I was thinking."

"I don't need to learn to swim." Folding the last of my clothes, I add them to the dresser. Glancing at the now empty bag, I say under my breath, "Fuck."

Chapter 5

Irreplaceable

Greer

"What's wrong?" Aiden walks up behind me. His warmth is enticing, but I ignore the attraction I believed was one-sided. This job might be too complicated. But that didn't stop me at any of my other homes. I'll do what I can to make this work.

It's worth it to get out of a bad situation. I've learned that over the years too.

"I didn't grab my sneakers." Sighing, I look down at the hot pink flip flops. I really don't want to slap through their house all weekend while I wait for Chad to go to work on Monday, besides they start work Monday and that means so do I.

"Hmm. Pretty sure Mason doesn't want us to let you out of our sight." Roarke grabs the hem of my t-shirt and tugs on it. "We could buy you some shoes."

"No," I say firmly. Never take money or presents from anyone. There's always a catch. It gives them power over you. Always. "I have shoes. I just have to go to my apartment and get them."

I don't think I hid my wince well enough. Roarke heaves out a sigh and stands, towering over me.

"I have no choice but to escort you home then."

My gaze jumps up to his as my brain struggles to process what he's saying. "What? No. No, you can't come to my apartment. No."

I can just imagine the pandemonium that would take place.

The fans and groupies would inevitably find him. Not to mention he'd see the dump I live in. It's bad enough I look like a homeless waif in my current outfit, but for him to confirm that's who I am…

He won't want me after that. Maybe I don't intend to do anything about this attraction (with any of them), but that doesn't mean I want it to disappear in a poof of smoke.

"It won't take me long. I just need to run there and back. I'll sign whatever you need me to." The words rush out of me. I'm not ready for Roarke to not want me. I'll be the first one to admit that I need to feel wanted. Even if I'm not ready to explore it.

Roarke shakes his head as he tips my chin with his knuckle. My breath catches at his touch as hot and heavy desire floods my veins. "If you think you can tell me your ex implied you needed to blow him to stay there and believe I'll let you go there alone, you have another think coming."

His stern crystal blue eyes lock with mine. My body is hyped up being so close to him. Honestly, he could pretty much ask me to do anything and I'd probably willingly do it. His smile tells me he knows it too.

A shiver rushes through me at the feel of Aiden closing in on my back. Caught between the two of them, I'm lost to the sensations flooding my body. Fuck, they're potent. I've never been really adventurous in the bedroom, but suddenly the thought of the two of them has my brain spinning.

"You shouldn't go alone if your ex is an issue." Aiden's smooth dark voice sends sparks dancing down my spine.

One, I've been going it alone for most my life. Two, what the hell am I getting myself into here? I'm going to be alone with these guys day in and day out. I don't think I'll be able to hold out for long.

They're barely touching me and my panties are soaked. Seriously, there's a bed right there and my libido is fully aware of it.

I don't want to disappoint them though and that holds me back. Guys like them are used to a certain caliber of woman and I'm not it.

"Come on, poppet." Roarke grins. "How good would it feel to walk in with me on your arm?"

Chad would lose his shit. Seriously. Which would be epic. I'm pretty sure I'm not getting out of here alone so I need to take some control. And that means rules.

"Fine, you can come with, but—" I hold up my finger. "I drive my car and you try to look like a normal human—"

"Do I look like an alien?"

"And you stay in the car," I end before I lose my nerve.

His eyes darken and his thumb trails along my jawline, making shivers course through me. "Ashamed of me, poppet?"

A nervous chuckle bursts out of me. "No, but I don't want to deal with a hoard of groupies either."

"Give me five minutes then." He chucks me under the chin before his gaze lifts to Aiden. He grins. "Keep our girl warm for me."

Butterflies spin drunkenly in my stomach at his words. No one's ever called me their girl. Even living with Chad, I didn't feel like I belonged. We were more roommates than lovers.

Our girl. Those words tempt me. Every time Roarke claims me as his, the knot in my stomach eases.

Roarke's smiling eyes meet mine. His grin softens into a smile that makes those butterflies flutter higher.

"Five minutes, poppet." He walks around me and for a moment, I just breathe, trying to find my common sense.

It's not real. None of this is. It's like the paper dolls I had as a child. Fun to play with and imagine, but eventually they fall apart or tear. This whole thing is terribly fragile and I'm worried I'll end up the torn one at the end of it when they finally throw me away.

I might interest them because I'm new, but that's all I've got going for me. It will wear off. I need a reality check and fortunately seeing Chad will do that for me.

"What are you fighting now, little warrior?" Aiden's words are soft. He lifts his hand like he's going to touch me and my breath stalls in my chest.

"This is a mistake." The words tumble from my lips. I turn to look up at him.

His light blue eyes search mine. His lips are pulled down. He rests his hand on my shoulder. Even though he doesn't put any weight on it, it scorches through my t-shirt, igniting the flames inside.

"Which part?" His voice is soft and luring.

"I'm not used to this kind of attention." I glance toward the open door, knowing Roarke will be back soon. "I'm not anything special. I'm nothing."

"Just because you aren't famous doesn't mean you're nothing, Greer." When I lower my eyes, his hand cups my cheek. So fucking gently that tears press on my eyes. Sparks tingle beneath the heat of his hand. "I believe you can do this job or I wouldn't have insisted on hiring you."

I open my mouth to protest, but he presses a finger against my lips. My mind blanks as my arousal burns even higher.

"You may think you're nothing special." He tips his head like he's studying me and making mental notes. "But I'm not attracted to a lot of people. There's something here and I want to explore it. With you. When you're ready."

Aiden left me speechless. But Roarke of course one upped him by showing up in a baseball cap and sunglasses like that hides who he is. He even threw on a t-shirt to rival Chad's with a giant marijuana leaf on it. He doesn't look "normal" even when he tries. He towers over me and everyone else. We're approaching my car when he smirks.

"I should drive, poppet." He crowds me against the side of the car, but I hold the keys firmly in my grip. My breath catches in my chest with him this close. But I'm used to people trying to push me around. He isn't the first to try to overwhelm me with his size compared to me.

"She's a temperamental beast and hates anyone else driving her." I tip my chin and raise my eyebrow in challenge.

"If I'm forced to ride bitch seat in this hunk of—" he stops when I press my lips together, "metal, then I deserve some sort of compensation."

"Compensation?"

His gaze drops to my lips and I unconsciously lick them. I've had a little time to calm down my overactive hormones, but I'm very aware of his closeness and the fullness of his lips. How would it feel to kiss Roarke Flynn?

I've seen it so many times on screen.

He smirks with that knowing damn smirk and taps his finger against his cheek. "Put those lips right here and we'll call it even."

The butterflies stampede through me as he lowers to my level. My breath rushes out of me. I purse my lips and press a kiss to his cheek. His skin is warm and a little bristly from his stubble.

As I pull back, he turns his face to mine. All the air leaves me as we're eye to eye, so close it would only take a small movement to bring our lips together. The blue in his eyes is like crystallized water so deep and so hypnotic, making me want to dive in and drown with him.

For a second, I believe he'll close the distance, but then grinning, he straightens and goes to the other side of the car. I suck a breath into my starved lungs. The car door opens and shuts, but I stand here, waiting for my emotions to bottle back up.

Fuck. I'm not going to last a day without Roarke convincing me to do more. I've always been in control of my desire. I've always put off kissing until I was certain of the guy, especially after what I went through. But somehow Roarke ratchets my desire up to almost unbearable levels.

I'm not the kind of girl that goes for a fling, but right now, I really wish I were. Because I have a feeling the experience with Roarke would be earth shattering. What if I could be that girl? What if I could just have sex with these four guys and have it just be about sex? That is what my new motto is about, after all. They're willing for me to put it to the test.

I need to think it over. I need to figure out if I can or even want to. But fuck, do they tempt me.

Shaking off that feeling, I open my car door and get in.

Roarke grins. "Ready, poppet?"

Not even a little. I hold my breath as I turn the key to start Old Betsy, praying that just this once she doesn't act like the raging bitch she is. She must be feeling kind today as the engine fires to life.

"Are you positive this thing is safe?" Roarke's hand is on the dashboard like he's trying to hold her together.

"She rarely lets me down." I give him a smile as I put her in drive and head down the driveway.

He presses a button on his phone and the gate opens. "We'll need to install some apps on your phone so you can access the house."

Nodding, I turn toward my apartment. Out of this nicer area and back into the city.

"So tell me about this Chad. How did he win you?" Roarke adjusts his seat again, sliding it back as far as it goes until he's almost in the backseat.

I scrunch my nose. "He worked at the diner where I'm a server. Of course, he didn't stay long at that job, but he was nice to me."

"Is that all it takes, poppet? You need me to be nice to you?" Roarke reaches for the radio, but his hand pauses as he realizes it's only an AM radio. His brow furrows, but he leaves it off.

"I don't move in with everyone I think is nice." I shake my head.

"You're moving in with me." Roarke smirks and his hand falls onto my thigh. "I can be very nice."

The car swerves and Roarke swears, but doesn't remove his hand.

"Don't kill us, poppet."

"Maybe let me focus, Benji." I cock a smile his way.

He winces. "For fuck's sake, tell me you didn't watch that movie."

"Oh, I did." In his interviews, he always turns stony whenever someone mentions *Guardian of Moondust*. "The CGI was amazing and your acting was top notch."

He draws his hand away. "Now you're just being mean."

It really wasn't a good movie. Rotten Tomatoes gave it a 2% and that was generous. Though there is a subculture that adores it.

"I only did it because the money was good." He looks out the side window as we near my apartment building. "I was young and needed the credit."

"While I admit, it wasn't the best movie I've seen of yours. It was still better than two percent."

"You've seen my movies, poppet?" His gaze finds me again and heat rushes to my cheeks. This guy's ego does not need to be fed. "Have you seen *all* my movies?"

Biting my lip, I turn into the underground parking. He doesn't need to know that I have that image of him in *Lost in Vegas* seared into my brain and bring it out at night when I need relief.

"You have, haven't you?" His tone is so smug. I'm not going to give him this one. "Where the hell are we?"

The lights flicker as I make my way to mine and Chad's spots. At least, the parking didn't cost extra, but the whole vibe down here leaves a lot to be desired. It's more murder hotel than home.

"I'm not staying down here alone, poppet. You'll come back to my dead body."

I park the car and turn off the engine. Chad's jeep is in his spot so he hasn't gone anywhere. That doesn't mean he doesn't have someone over though.

"Fine." I release my breath and turn to him. "But you need to wait out in the hallway. Chad will recognize you. I don't need him going all fanboy and wanting your autograph. Or worse asking for you to put him in your next movie."

Roarke gets out of the car. When I join him, he grins. "Was he your first actor, poppet?"

"Yes." I arch an eyebrow. "But he didn't exactly make me want another one."

Roarke follows me to the elevator.

"An out of work actor isn't the same as someone like me. I'm A-list all the way."

I press the elevator button and look up at him. "I'm working for you. Not dating you. So you might as well be the same."

The elevator arrives and Roarke glances in the car with a doubtful look.

"This is a deathtrap, isn't it?" Roarke backs up a step.

"It's perfectly adequate." I step in and jump to show it's fine. "See, didn't even move."

"Your weight barely qualifies. I've been on less scary horror film sets, poppet." He still looks skeptical as he joins me. I press the button and the doors squeak as they shut. When the elevator groans, his eyes widen and then narrow on me like it's my fault.

"It's just an elevator." I watch the numbers, knowing he's still looking at me.

The gears grind to a halt at my floor. The doors open to the dimly lit hallway.

"Fuck, poppet, are you trying to kill me?" He steps forward. "At least fuck me before I die."

"I'm not trying to kill you. I'm just getting my stuff so I don't have to come back here ever again." Pretty sure living in my car would be preferable to this place. Even if I had the place to myself.

When I first turned eighteen, I tried living by myself. I'm used to other people. I didn't like being alone all the time.

A little shudder rushes down my spine as Roarke follows me down the hallway to my door.

I pause with my keys out. "You really need to stay out here."

His eyes narrow but he nods. "Leave the door cracked. So he doesn't do something stupid."

Shaking my head, I unlock my door. All Chad does is stupid stuff.

I walk in and close the door almost shut. The living room slash kitchen is empty, which means Chad must be in the bedroom. Where all my stuff is.

I blow out a breath. I can do this.

The bedroom door is closed, so I decide to be a decent human being and knock.

The door opens to a confused shirtless Chad. His hair is all rumpled. Hmm, napping or fucking?

"Hey, babe, now isn't a good time." He glances over his shoulder. Ah, fucking it is.

A thankfully fully dressed woman steps into view. "Who's this?"

"No one." Chad smirks down at me.

"I need to get my things." I cross my arms and glare.

He glances over his shoulder at the blond waiting behind him. "Give me fifteen minutes and then the bedroom's all yours."

Just what I want, to grab my stuff with the room smelling like sex.

"Are you fucking kidding me?" My voice rises. "It will take me five to clear out of here and then you can fuck her all you want."

Chad laughs. "You don't really want to leave me, babe. Where are you going to go? We both know I'm the only one who will put up with you."

Chapter 6

Like a Virgin

Greer

My blood pressure skyrockets. Fuck him and fuck this. With what I'm going to make, I'll be able to replace anything in that room.

The door opens behind me and I close my eyes. Fuck, he heard.

Hands wrap around my waist and draw me back against Roarke. Heat floods me from his touch.

"What's keeping you, Greer?" His voice is dark in my ears. His body is hot against mine. The way he purrs my name makes my panties melt.

I open my eyes to see the stunned look on Chad's face.

"You're. . . you're. . ." His stammer almost makes me smile.

"OMG, you're Roarke Flynn!" the blond practically screams. "I'm such a big fan. Can I get a selfie? Anna is never going to believe me."

Roarke's hands tighten against me, causing little shivers to race through me. Chad's mouth is still open as he stares at Roarke.

"Excuse us, but we're on a tight schedule." I hear the smile in Roarke's voice, but his tone says you're fucking bothering me. "Think we could get what we came for, mate?"

"Uh. . ." Chad glances down at me like I'm the one making him look like a fool.

The blond steps forward and opens the door. "Of course, Roarke. Anything you want. I'm Bunny, by the way."

She puts her hand in the center of Chad's back and pushes him into the living room. Roarke glides me out of the way.

"Thanks, Bunny." Roarke must smile at her because she practically beams.

He guides me into the bedroom and shuts the door. He gives me a gentle push into the room. "Hurry, poppet."

I rush forward and grab for a bag and fill it with my stuff.

"Yours?" Roarke holds up a pair of sneakers. Obviously mine since they look like children's. I nod and he grabs a bag off the floor to shove shoes in.

The knocking begins. "Hey, man."

Chad's found his voice. I roll my eyes. But when I meet Roarke's, he's pissed.

I bite my lip. Chad can't fuck this up for me. "I'll deal with him."

"Fuck that." Roarke takes the bag from me and lifts me up before backing me against the wall next to the door.

I squeal at the abrupt weightless feeling and then gasp when he presses against me. My legs and arms wrap around him, drawing him in close, holding on. His hand grabs my ass to hold me against him. Fuck, he feels good. All hard muscle.

My cheeks are on fire and I can't lift my gaze to his. I'm not sure what he's hoping to prove, but my cheeks aren't the only thing on fire.

The doorknob rattles. I turn to watch it, but Roarke grabs my chin and makes me look into his eyes. My panties dampen at the heat there.

"Want payback, poppet?" Roarke raises his eyebrow. His thumb trails over my lips and they part for him. Pretty sure I'll do whatever he wants when he looks at me like that.

The doorknob turns. I remember Chad with my panties on the

bed. Payback would be fantastic. I lift my head in a nod and Roarke slams his lips down on mine. My breath catches.

The door opens. "What the fuck?"

But then Roarke opens his mouth over mine and his tongue teases along my lips. I part them as I finally breathe. He growls his approval, making me wet and achy for him. It's not a gentle, tentative exploring kiss like a first kiss usually is. This is hungry and greedy and the best kiss I've ever had.

He tastes like mint and something darker. I want to sink into him. His cock hardens between my thighs and presses against my pussy. My thighs tighten around his hips.

The door slams shut beside us, jolting me out of the moment. I pull away, my head hitting the wall behind me. My cheeks feel like they are on fire. Oh, hell, what the fuck did I just do?

"Uh. . ." Yeah, my brain can't be expected to function right now.

Roarke grins and nuzzles my neck. "Have you ever faked an orgasm, poppet?"

My pulse throbs in my veins. "Um, what?"

He lifts his head so our eyes meet. "Fake an orgasm so asswipe out there gets the picture."

Heat flares through me. "Um, I don't—"

Have I faked it? Yes, especially with Chad. Am I good at faking it? Probably not, but it never bothered Chad either.

"Come on, poppet. If you were with that tool, you must know how to fake it." His thumb brushes over my lip and a whimper escapes me. "I doubt he knows how to make you scream like I can."

Fuck. My breath catches at the heat in his eyes.

"I'm not..." Fuck. Time to admit that I'm kind of bad at the whole sex thing. "I'm not loud during sex."

Roarke grins wickedly. "Challenge accepted."

"What?" I push my hands against his shoulders so he'll let me down, but he doesn't budge. "We should finish getting my stuff and go."

"We'll go." He smirks. "But only if you act like you're coming so hard, you're choking the life out of my cock."

My mouth drops open. He grinds his denim-covered erection against my pussy. Oh, shit, that feels amazing. A low moan slips past my lips.

"Like that, poppet. Only louder." His hips rotate against mine in a steady rhythm. My insides boil with liquid heat, chasing away all the doubts and making me forget why we're doing this.

My fingers clutch onto his shoulders. His bright blue eyes are darker as he studies my face. My insides are winding tight with every motion of his hips. His fingers trail down my neck, sending shivers through me.

"What do you like, Greer?" He licks my lip, all while rocking his hips into mine. My lips part on a gasp.

Confession time. "I don't know what I like." I bite my lip. "I don't usually...finish with guys."

His eyes light up. "Never?"

His hand runs down my side, skating past my breast. I shake my head unable to speak.

"That's a shame, poppet." His hand finds the end of my t-shirt and slips under. "We need to fix that."

Anticipation washes over me with a heavy dose of fear. What if even he can't do anything for me?

"Roarke?" It's a whole question in my mind. What is he doing to me? What am I doing? Why am I not stopping this? Why does this feel so fucking good?

His hand slides up my waist until it rests just beneath my breast. My breath shudders in and out of me as I helplessly search his eyes. I want him to touch me and I don't. His thumb rubs on the underside of my breast. "No bra?"

I shake my head, not willing to look away from his eyes.

"Nice. Are they sensitive?" He reaches up and cups my breast.

My head thuds back against the wall as I arch into his touch. My lips part as fireworks flood my veins.

"Use your words, poppet." He squeezes my breast and then pinches my nipple.

"Ahh." His touch sends a burst of desire straight to my pussy.

"Mmm. That's what I want to hear." He teases and tortures my breasts until I'm a mass of want writhing on him.

I moan loudly as he pinches my nipple again.

A loud bang comes from the other room.

My eyes startle open. Fuck, when did I close them?

"Shh, I've got you. We're going for the grand finale." His cock grinds against my pussy.

"Roarke?" My voice is deep and questioning. What the hell are we doing? Maybe we should stop before this goes too far.

"Uh-uh, poppet." His mouth claims mine and I'm lost again. His tongue thrusts into my mouth as he plucks at my nipples, alternating between them. While his hips rock into mine in a rhythm that drives me so fucking high.

"So close, poppet," he whispers against my lips. "Do you feel it?"

"Maybe—"

He kisses me as his hand slides into my pants. Oh, shit!

"Wait. Wait," I whisper trying to find my words.

He stops and rests his forehead against mine. My heart pounds so hard. His fingers are on my belly, clenching. I'm so caught up, but I don't know what's happening.

"Greer, let me help you soar." His eyes hold mine captivated.

I shouldn't. Something else crashes in the living room, drawing my attention. This isn't who I normally am, but with him, I feel so out of control.

Roarke leans in. His breath hot on my ear. "Let me make you come, so he knows what he never got. Let's show him that he never got that piece of you."

I turn my face to meet his eyes. He wants this. This small piece of me to prove to Chad what a fucking asshole he is. To get me closure.

It doesn't hurt that I'm so fucking curious. My insides are tight and ready to explode.

"Okay," I whisper.

He kisses his way to my ear. "I can't wait to have you spread out naked before me, poppet."

His fingers slide beneath my panties.

"Roarke." I'm nervous. What if I can't? What if I'm so broken no one can ever make me come?

"Shh, poppet, let me make you feel good." His fingers slide between my legs and through my folds.

I catch my breath as my hands tighten on his shoulders. He rubs circles on my clit, winding me tighter and tighter.

"Does that feel good?"

I'm beyond words as I nod. My hips follow his fingers. His words mesmerize me.

"Next time will be in my bed, poppet. I'll kiss every inch of your body. Suck this little clit into my mouth until you scream your release. Then I'll climb over you and my cock will fill you so fucking full." He thrusts two fingers inside me.

"Roarke," I cry out, unable to comprehend what he's doing to me. I've given myself orgasms but the guys I've been with haven't ever gotten me there. Even after months of learning each other's bodies, I still can't get there with them.

But I'm right on the fucking edge with Roarke and he's barely touched me.

"Fuck, Greer, I'll spend hours tasting your pussy until you come so hard you feel like you're going to break." His words. His thrusting fingers. His thumb circles my clit. "But right now, you're going to come on my fingers like a good girl. Aren't you, poppet?"

I tip over the edge on a cry. His fingers work me through it until my cry shifts to a moan. My pussy convulses around his fingers over and over again. I cling to him because my body goes liquid with my release.

"Good girl." His hand slides out of my pants as he draws back, still holding me up. "Look at me, Greer."

I open my eyes. He holds up the fingers that were inside me, dripping with my wetness. Heat floods my cheeks.

"Don't be embarrassed, poppet. I love that you came all over my fingers." He sucks each finger into his mouth and an aftershock pulses inside me. "Next time you'll come all over my face."

"I... I honestly don't know what to say to that."

He chuckles as he lowers me down to the floor. "You taste delicious, poppet."

He catches the back of my neck and draws me in for another soul-searing kiss. I can taste myself on his tongue. When he lifts his head, my knees give. He catches my hip.

"All right, enough play time. Let's get out of this horror movie set. We can continue this later." He presses a kiss to my forehead and moves around the bed collecting anything that might be mine.

Did I honestly just let Roarke Flynn finger fuck me in my apartment while my ex listened? I turn to look at the door. It's quiet out there now. Maybe he left.

Roarke tosses a large sneaker into the corner. Chad wouldn't leave while Roarke Flynn was in his apartment. He's too much of an opportunist.

"Hurry up, poppet. We've got better things to do." Roarke taps my nose as he walks by.

Okay, focus on packing. Not on the fact Roarke gave me my first non-self-administered orgasm and it was mind blowing. Pack, so we can leave this dump for his beautiful house.

I pick up my bag and empty my drawers into it. But what does this mean? Does he think I'm going to have sex with him because of this? Do I want to have sex with him? Should I have sex with him?

What if the others find out? What will they think of me?

"Uh, Roarke?" I look over my shoulder at him.

He holds up a bra way too big for me. I shake my head and he tosses it into the corner with the shoe. "Yes?"

"Can we not tell the others about...what happened?" My mouth feels suddenly dry. I just made out with Roarke Flynn in my crappy apartment.

He grins and winks. "You want to keep me a secret, poppet? Because I'm not big on secrets. I like everything out in the open, but for you, I'll make an exception."

Good, because I don't want them to think any less of me than they already do. He takes the full bag from me, carrying both of them. I glance around the room to double check I haven't left anything behind.

"If you're missing anything, I'll buy it for you. Let's go, poppet." He jerks his head toward the door.

"Wait." I hold up my hand and go to the nightstand. I pull out the top drawer. Roarke looks over my shoulder.

"Pretty sure I could replace any of those." The drawer is full of toys Chad bought.

I shake my head and drop to my knees, reaching under it. My mind is in such a haze I almost forgot. I lift the tape careful not to tear the picture. When it's free, I bring it out and look down at the last remaining picture of my mother and father. They were young. Mom's holding her pregnant belly, while Dad has his arm wrapped around her, kissing her head.

The other pictures are all lost to moves and time, but I've kept this one safe.

"You ready?"

I stand and brush my hands on my pants. "Yes."

Roarke heads to the door. I hurry in front of him to pull it open. Not sure what's waiting for us on the other side.

"Thanks, man," Roarke's voice booms out. "We got everything we needed out of there."

I move up beside Roarke. Chad's face is red like when he's had too much to drink. But he pastes on a smile. "Don't mention it, man."

"Can I get a selfie, Roarke? Please." Bunny practically bounces up and down. I roll my eyes, but Roarke gives her a smile.

"Sure, doll." Roarke moves away from me over to Bunny.

Chad's brown eyes narrow on me. He grabs my arm, but I know better than to tell him he's hurting me. He leans down next to my ear. "You still owe me rent."

"I'll send in the check." I jerk on my arm slightly, trying not to draw Roarke's attention.

"I guess you just need dollar signs to come," he spits out. "It took me over a month to get into your pants. Congratulations on being Roarke Flynn's latest whore."

"Better his whore than yours." I jerk my arm away and cross the living room to Roarke, where Bunny is showing him the picture.

When Chad makes a move to grab me again, Roarke turns all his attention on Chad. "Are we going to have a problem?"

All laughter and playfulness are gone from Roarke's tone. A shiver slides down my spine.

"Let's go, Roarke," I say softly, touching his arm. The muscle is tense under my fingers.

Chad's eyes narrow on him for a second before he grins like he doesn't have a care in the world. "Nah, man. You can have her. I was done with her anyway. She's a lousy lay."

Chad gives me a pointed look like he didn't suggest just a few hours ago that I fuck him in lieu of rent.

Roarke steps between us. His hand lands on my hip, holding me behind him.

"Just know you mess with her you mess with me." His hand tightens on my hip and pulls me flush against his back. I breathe in his cologne and let it calm the pounding of my heart. "If you fuck with her, I'll know and you won't see me coming."

Chad laughs. "I suppose you're going to have your stunt man come after me."

Roarke moves so fast. I gasp and he has Chad up against the wall. Bunny squeals.

"Greer is mine now. Get over yourself and have fun playing with your bunny." He shoves Chad one last time before he drops him and comes over to me. "Let's go."

He grabs both my bags in one hand and wraps his arm around my shoulder. At the door, he turns, "If any of this hits the tabloids, I will sue you until you are so buried in debt this place looks like a fucking castle."

I'm still in a daze as he leads me down the hall and hits the elevator button. No one has protected me. Ever.

For years, it's been me against everybody else. I had to fight and claw to stay me. Unwanted, unloved. Broken and afraid.

"What a fucking asshole," Roarke says as he draws me into the elevator.

My hand trembles as I hit the button.

That's exactly what I said last time I entered this elevator. A laugh escapes me as the doors shut and then the tears fall like someone turned them on after all these years.

"Don't cry over him, poppet. It's not worth it." He drops the bags on the floor and pulls me into his arms, wrapping them around me. A sob breaks out.

How long had it been since I was hugged? More tears cascade out as I bury my face in his shirt.

"I'm sure he was a lovely guy, but you'll get over him." His hand rubs up and down my back. The tears keep falling and I can't stop to tell him, it's not about Chad. It's about him.

"Poppet, I don't do well with tears. Do you want me to go rough him up more? How about another orgasm? Can I buy you a new car?"

A giggle breaks through as I try to rein in my emotions, but he's unlocked a floodgate I didn't know I'd been holding closed.

"Greer," he says quietly and kisses the top of my head.

The elevator stops and he lifts me up against him. I wrap around him and rest my head against his heart as he carries me to my car. His fingers dig into my pocket for my keys, but he never puts me down.

"I hope this isn't about that asshole because you can do a lot better," he mumbles as he opens the trunk and puts my bags in it.

"You have four guys willing to do whatever you want to you for the next year or so. That's got to make you a little happy, right?"

My fingers wrap into his damp shirt. His hand covers my head as I take in a shuddering breath.

"You want to tell me what this is about?" Roarke leans back against my car with me still clinging to him. "I'm definitely not as good at this stuff as Aiden or Wyatt, but I definitely excel at it compared to Mason."

I breathe in his sandalwood cologne and begin to box back up my emotions. When I relax my legs, Roarke keeps me up against him.

"Come on. We're in the creepy dungeon where no truths are allowed to escape." Roarke tips my chin up and searches my eyes. His thumb rubs through the tears. "I'm sorry if I messed up your chance of reuniting with the fucking asshole."

"That's not it." I wipe at my face with my hands and shake my head. "It's just..."

"Creepy dungeon, poppet. Spill."

I search his blue eyes and see that he's here and being nice. I can be honest about this. "No one has stood up for me in a really, really long time. So thank you."

I lean in and kiss him on the lips. When I pull back, his brow is still furrowed.

"Can you put me down, so we can head back?" I ask softly. He looks confused about something, but that's just me. People don't usually know what to do with me.

"Of course." He lowers my feet to the ground and brushes a stray tear from my cheek. His hand holds my hip, keeping me close to him. "How long?"

I tip my head to the side. "How long what?"

"How long since someone stood up for you?"

I want to reach up and fix the wrinkles in his forehead. I shrug. "Before my dad left probably."

I blow out a breath. "It's okay. I have it under control. I'm used to it. You just surprised me. It won't happen again."

It shouldn't have happened this time. He just caught me off guard. I'll be prepared next time he does something unexpectedly nice and won't dissolve into tears.

His blue eyes narrow, but he straightens and holds out the keys. "You going to drive this bucket of bolts home or what?"

I take the keys and flash him a grin, thankful he's letting this go. "She's a perfectly good car. I don't need you to buy me a new one."

We both get in and she starts up no problem.

"That offer was based on my emotional distress." He grins and puts his hand on my thigh. "But I'm definitely on board to give you another orgasm."

A little thrill goes through me. "Maybe we should wait until we know each other better."

He laughs. "That's how I get to know women, poppet. One orgasm at a time."

Chapter 7

I've Got No Roots

Greer

Roarke actually leaves me alone to unpack my bags. I'm not sure he won't tell the others what happened at the apartment. The orgasm or the crying. But their offer was no strings attached. So it shouldn't matter?

When I finish unpacking and separating out what needs to be cleaned, I don't have any other reason to stay in here. It feels odd to even have a room. I leave my flip flops and decide it's okay to wander barefoot. After all, this is where I live now.

Fuck, I live here. In this gorgeous house with gorgeous men. I can't fuck this up.

I need a purpose, so I figure I'll go check what's available in the kitchen. If I'm going to cook, I'll need to know what I'm working with. Maybe I'll even go outside and put my toes in the grass. Or walk on the pier that leads to the ocean. A little tingle of joy races through me.

Quietly, I move through the house. It's been a while, but I'm used to feeling like a stranger in a new home. Usually someone watches me, at least the first day. One of the kids or even one of the adults. So it surprised me when Roarke set my bags down and kissed the top of my head before wandering off.

I don't know where the others are. I'm not sure if anything is off limits. Anxiety winds around me just waiting for something to happen. I may be used to starting over, but it's never a comfortable feeling.

When I get to the kitchen, movement outside draws my attention. Someone is swimming laps in the sparkling pool. I step toward the open doors but stay in the shadows of the house to avoid being seen.

Aiden's long arms cut through the water like butter as he races to the end before turning like a champion swimmer and going back the other way. Is this part of his sobriety? Or maybe just his regular routine? Routine and exercise are important in a lot of ways.

I need to find out Aiden's routine so I know when he's having an off day. Maybe I'll be bold enough to walk out and read next to the pool while he works out. Maybe.

That's if I have time to read. Mason said I would be expected to do chores. I should probably find him to clarify.

I step away from the opening and turn. My shriek cuts short as I lift my gaze to Mason's blue eyes. My pulse pounds through my veins from being startled. He's so close to me and I didn't even hear him approach.

"Greer." His tone elongates my name.

"I was just going to check the kitchen for supplies." I gesture toward the island behind him.

His gaze locks over my shoulder. "Are you easily distracted, Ms. Morrow?"

I'm not sure what that's supposed to mean, but I know the way he says my name makes my insides heat.

"This is a new place. I haven't lived around so many people in a while, but I'll get used to it." I always get used to it. I glance over my shoulder. Aiden continues to glide through the water. I could watch him all day. The way he moves is elegant. His muscles stretch with every stroke.

"Did you come from a large family?" Mason's words bring my attention back to him.

"No." Never give more information until they ask specifically. I kind of already shot that rule with Aiden, but he needs someone to confide in him. To trust him.

When Mason looks at me, it feels like he's trying to dissect me. "Sir."

"What?"

"Say no, sir." He clears his throat.

Huh. Okay. "No, sir."

No one else seems that formal, but with the vibes Mason gives off I shouldn't be surprised. I walk around him to the kitchen and open the refrigerator.

"Make a list of anything you need. We have a shopper go once a week to the grocery for us." Mason moves into the space behind me and leans against the counter. If he's trying to intimidate me, it's working.

His nearness throws me off balance. Control and power radiate from him. Strong men have always made me nervous. I'm not surprised that Mason makes me feel the same as Mary's paramour. Part of me wants to cave to any of his demands while the other part is prepared to put up a fight.

"I've made a list of chores for you. As well as our current diets. They're all on the tablet in the butler's pantry." His voice is sure and precise.

"Butler's pantry?" What the hell is a butler's pantry?

"Through that opening."

I turn to see him gesture with a nod of his chin toward the corner of the kitchen. Taking a breath in, I follow his direction past the white cabinets and white marble counters. As I draw closer, I can see the opening. When I get to the doorway, I pause.

It's like the opposite of the kitchen. The cabinets are black and in a long galley style. The counters are gray with streaks of white. It's beautiful and dark. Like the man behind me.

I move into the room and go to the stand with the tablet on it.

"These cabinets hold our dishes, especially for formal occasions." Mason's voice makes me straighten and I spin to face him. His finger trails along one of the white veins in the marble. "We'll hire a cook and staff for those parties. You'll be expected to devote all of your attention to staying at Aiden's side."

That makes sense. The booze probably flows liberally at those parties. "Is there anything else I need to know?"

"Sir," he prompts. His eyes flare with a little heat.

I need to learn what these men expect of me and do as they ask. Within reason. But this is a job I intend to keep.

"Sir." My chest tightens as he closes in on me. A hint of his earthy leather scent reaches my nose. It draws me and makes me want to move closer to get a better smell. I mentally shake myself.

"I need you to look after my friends. All of them." He stops with a hair's breadth separating us. An inhale would make my breasts bump against him. "I'm not sure what you're used to, but we have a lot of demands."

Holding his gaze is difficult. I'm pretty sure he wants my submission, but I can't give it to him. Not now. My blood thunders through my veins and I can feel my pussy pulse in want.

When he lifts his hand from the counter, my breath catches in my throat and I hold perfectly still, anticipating his touch.

"I know why they want you, little mouse." His finger traces the vein throbbing in my neck and I almost whimper at the heat that courses through me. "Do you know why?"

I shake my head at his question. I don't have a clue. Pretty sure it isn't just because I'm present, but maybe convenience has something to do with it. But these guys could get any woman they wanted.

"You're like this perfect little picture of a broken girl." Mason's hand wraps around the back of my neck as he pulls me against him. All his hard lines press against my softness. His hand wraps around my hip to keep me there. "Some of us want to coddle you and fix you, but some of us prefer to see what more we can break."

I should push him away. Fear should be pounding through me as his piercing gaze searches my eyes, but instead desire and need ache within. Curiosity has me asking, "Which are you? Sir?"

My neck strains to hold the angle to search his eyes.

The corner of his lip tips up. "I like to play with broken toys, little mouse. I like to draw out the darkness within and test it. See how it fits with my darkness."

"You think you can break me?" I wet my suddenly dry lips, drawing his attention to them. His eyes darken and I'm surprised I don't burst into flames. "Sir?"

"I'll enjoy trying." His thumb brushes against my jaw, sending sparks across my skin. "But before we can play, we need to establish limits and rules. When you're ready to see what I can do to you, little mouse."

He releases me and walks out. I manage to hold myself upright until he steps out of the room and I hear his footsteps fade. When my knees give, I catch myself on the counter.

Fuck, he's intense. I'm not sure whether I'll be able to stand up to him without falling to my knees.

Pretty sure that's where he wants me.

I take a few minutes to get myself together before grabbing the tablet and heading out into the sun. I need its warmth to chase away the darkness.

Aiden still cuts through the water effortlessly, not slowing even a little. I sit on one of the lounge chairs. Outside shouldn't be a luxury, but in the city, it is. Sure there are parks, but nothing like this where you have privacy.

Over the years I've had to build up my walls. To deal with disappointment. To deal with pain. To deal with loss. Mason's not wrong when he calls me broken. But my breaks don't make me weak, they make me stronger. He can try to poke at them, but I'm not worried.

I close my eyes and tip my face to the sun. Warmth penetrates my skin and chases away the chills of the past. I could spend all day out here like this. Even the inevitable sunburn would be worth it. This is my life for now. Cool grass under foot and blue skies overhead with the ocean rolling in nearby.

My eyes pop open. I need to call Bristol. She'll want to know how it went and what's happened. I need to thank her. Maybe buy her something nice with my first paycheck. My phone is up in the room. Next time I go up, I'll remember to text her.

I open the tablet and scroll through the list of chores.

Laundry might be a big one. Four guys. I need to figure out where they keep their laundry and where the laundry room is. Do I go into their rooms? That seems odd, but if that's the way they want me to do it.

I make a note to clarify that. Dishes. Straightening. Vacuuming the main area. Apparently they want a housewife. Which for what they intend to pay me I'll buy a bunch of fifties dresses and aprons and heels and do whatever they like around the house. Minus the martinis, of course.

"What's that smile for?" Aiden's voice still makes me starstruck.

Setting the tablet on my lap, I raise my gaze to find Aiden with his muscled arms crossed on the edge of the pool. His hair is slicked back. How long was he watching me?

"The smile, little warrior?" He cocks his eyebrow.

Shit. What was I thinking about? "Oh, that I should get fifties-style dresses, an apron, and heels to do all my chores in."

His smile spreads. "You want to be our little housewife?"

"You know I'm more than my size." I pick up the tablet and scroll through the list more.

The sound of water sliding off him makes me raise my gaze to watch him lift himself out of the pool. Where Roarke and Wyatt are built thick, Aiden is all lean muscle. I swear he gets out of the pool like he's being filmed. Graceful without a hint of awkwardness.

The sunlight glints off the water caressing his skin. His defined abs and that V disappear into his square leg tight swimsuit hugging his hips. And I'm checking out his package, noting it's large size before dropping my gaze to his legs.

Sex doesn't normally preoccupy my mind, but I'm going to blame them for even putting the thoughts into my head. They're way too gorgeous to go around saying they want to have sex with someone like me. People like me are just not used to that kind of attention.

He walks to the chair next to me and grabs his towel off it. I didn't even notice that I'd sat next to it. He pats himself dry and sits on the chair facing me.

"What are you looking at?" He rubs the towel over his hair and the curls all bounce back into place.

I hold up the tablet like a proud toddler. "My list of chores."

He smirks. "Mason likes things a certain way. I wouldn't tell him about the fifties vibe or he'll make it happen."

I set the tablet on my lap. "I get that I need to help around the house. But what do *you* need from me? It would help if I know your typical schedule."

With a smile, he reclines on the lounge chair next to me. "What I need is a loaded question, little warrior."

"Why?" I turn on my side to watch him. "I'm being hired as your sobriety buddy. You must have some expectations from me."

"I'm glad you're taking this job seriously." He turns his head my way and squints in the sunlight. "I'll give you as much access as you like. You want to know my routine, just follow me for a day."

"Okay." That sounds easy enough. It's not like I have other things to do. "What do we do first?"

"Shower." He gives me a grin that makes my insides melt.

My lips curve even though I try to hold it back. "Fine, but I'm taking one in my bedroom."

"Sounds like a plan." He sits up.

"On my own," I stress.

"Someday I'm going to use the recovery card." He eyes me up and down, making my toes curl. "Do you know how much play I could be getting?"

Probably a lot. I ignore his question and the heat pooling inside me. "Do you have therapy?"

"Individual and group. Once a week and when needed." Aiden runs a hand through his hair. "One of the guys will come with. There's a nice restaurant across from the office building that you can get something to eat while you wait."

"That sounds nice." I want to ask him more, but I also don't want to pry. Certain things always made my mother backslide. Does he have anything like that? Something I need to watch for? But when he's looking at me like this, I don't want to remind him of the bad times in his life.

He seems happy and healthy, practically glowing in the sunlight. He stands and holds his hand out to me. Without a thought, I slip my hand into his. Sparks travel up my arm as I let him help me stand.

This is all so delicate. He's recovering. Roarke made me come in my apartment. Wyatt almost kissed me. And Mason wants to dissect me. Not how I saw my day going at all.

Aiden doesn't release my hand but leads me through the house to our end of the hallway. He lifts my hand up to his mouth and brushes his lips over my knuckles. Tingles skitter down my spine as his blue eyes hold mine.

"I'm glad you applied for the job, little warrior."

"Me too." My voice sounds breathy.

His smile turns mischievous. "Change into something that will blow my mind for dinner."

Chapter 8

Let's Talk About Sex

Greer

I take the most heavenly shower of my life. Warm water throughout. A door that locks. Bottles of things that smell divine and feel silky against my skin. And the towel. It's heated and so soft I want to just go to dinner wearing this.

That would definitely make a statement I'm not ready to make. When I open the door to my bedroom, I'm not really surprised to find Roarke on my bed with the tablet. He's barefoot, in just jeans. No shirt.

I've seen his body oiled down and gritted up for movies, but the real thing is so much better. He's got pecs and abs and that pronounced V thing that makes me salivate. His jeans ride low on his hips. When he turns his head to look at me, those blue eyes are heated.

"I would have joined you but the door was locked." He makes a pouty face that makes me laugh. "That wasn't very nice, poppet."

"I'm not ready for communal showers." I'm not sure I was ready for what happened in my old apartment either. I tighten the towel over my breasts and straighten the one on my head. Two! I have two towels! Both fluffy.

"That's definitely going on your to do list." He taps on the tablet. "Communal showers."

I shake my head and go to my dresser. The problem I have is what to wear. I don't really own any *blow an actor's mind* type clothes. I'm more of a what's on sale at Old Navy type of gal or *hey, look what I found at the thrift store for one dollar and look it has pockets.*

Roarke wolf whistles and I check to make sure the back of my towel still covers me. Thankfully it does.

"Those baggie clothes do not do you justice, poppet." The bed sounds like he's moving. Him touching me is a bad idea.

I turn with one hand out and the other on my towel. "Stop right there, Benji."

He cocks an eyebrow and inches forward so he sits on the edge of the bed. "I let you get away with that in the car because you were driving. But those are tickling words."

"Tickling?" We aren't children.

I don't have time to react before he's in front of me. His hands hold my hips. Burning me even through the thick towel.

"You move really quick." The words slip out. My defenses refuse to cooperate. Mostly because I like when he touches me. My body goes all soft and willing every time he's close.

He grins as he backs me against the wall. "I played sports in high school and college."

My breathing quickens as he closes in on me, surrounding me with his intoxicating cologne. The memory of his hands and lips on me makes me weak with anticipation for whatever he'll do to me.

"Now that I've got you here. I'm not sure I want to tickle you." His voice is lower as his head dips toward mine.

"You don't?" I feel like everything is hazy as I lick my suddenly dry lips.

"No, poppet, I don't." His mouth claims mine. He lifts me off my feet and presses me against the wall as he explores my mouth with his tongue and lips, devouring every inch of me.

I can't do anything but hold on, one hand on my towel and the other on him, as he thoroughly kisses me. No one's kissed me the way he does.

"For fuck's sake, Roarke, put the poor woman down." Wyatt's voice penetrates the desire fogging up my brain. "She's been here one day. She hasn't signed an NDA. Give the woman some space before she goes to the press and tells them how much of a hound dog you really are."

Laughing, Roarke presses his forehead to mine and shakes his head.

"I'm the best kind of hound dog, poppet." After sneaking another quick kiss, he lowers me to my feet and turns to face Wyatt. I lean against the wall, letting my knees figure out how to hold me again.

"And what were you doing walking into her bedroom without knocking?" Roarke wiggles his brows at me before giving Wyatt a seriously offended face. "She might have been changing."

"I did knock. I'm sure you would have heard it if you hadn't been occupied." Wyatt's gaze drinks me in. Fuck, just that look makes my knees weak.

My cheeks heat even more. These guys are overwhelming. I clear my throat. "I need to get dressed."

"Go ahead, poppet. We'll wait." Roarke walks over to my bed and sits on the edge, after adjusting his erection in his pants. I swallow and jerk my gaze away from the bulge.

Wyatt smiles and moves to join Roarke on the bed. Both of them look at me in anticipation.

"This isn't going to work," I mumble.

"You just loosen the knot there." Roarke points toward my towel. "It should drop and then you just put on whatever you decide to wear. Or nothing. We're not formal for dinner here."

His cocky grin makes me want to throw a shoe at him. Wyatt leans back on his hands. At least he has on a shirt this time, but still wears those sweats with whatever snake he's smuggling underneath them. My god, he's big all over.

My thighs clench. I know they want me and I want them, but how much of that is this starstruck feeling and how much is actual desire? I need to figure that out, but these guys aren't going to make this easy.

Rules. All new homes have rules and enforcers. The enforcer around here seems to be Mason. But it's always best to make an attempt to resolve the situation myself before involving the enforcer.

"Look, I appreciate you like to be entertained, but I'd like to get dressed without an audience. At least until I decide whether I want to take this attraction any further." I hope I sound calm and reasonable and not like a teenage girl whose brother won't get out of her room.

"See she admits it, she's attracted to me. Aren't you, poppet?" Roarke elbows Wyatt, who shoves him sideways on the bed.

"She's attracted to all of us, asshole." Wyatt grabs Roarke's arm and hauls him off the bed toward the door. "Don't worry. I'll make sure he stays out this time."

"Thank you." I let out a breath I didn't realize I was holding.

Wyatt smirks back at me as he shoves Roarke out the door. "I'll claim my thank you properly later, kitten."

The door closes behind them. I quickly walk over to it and engage the lock. It may not be very effective but it gives me a little modicum of privacy.

And I'm left to my dilemma of what to wear. I grab a nice bra and panty set and put those on quickly before rewrapping in the towel. I can use all the barriers between me and Roarke. My lips still buzz from his kiss and my fresh panties are already damp.

I pick a loose sundress and run a comb through my hair. It will have to do. In the mirror, I just look like me. Not amazing. Not wonderful. Just me. I'm not sure what these guys are seeing.

Bristol!

Grabbing my phone, I pull up my text messages.

I plug in my charger and put my phone on it before heading out the door. Aiden's door opens and he steps into the hallway at the same time as I do.

"Did you plan that?" I smile suspiciously.

He gives me this half grin that makes my heart beat skip. His gaze flows over me. "How was the shower?"

"Heavenly," I sigh. "Whatever I do after this, I need to make a lot of money so I can get a place with a nice shower."

Aiden lifts an eyebrow and I almost slap my hand over my mouth. Why do I keep telling him things? It's bad enough that Roarke saw where I've been living and gave me an orgasm while my ex listened. But with Aiden, little things keep slipping out. Some part of me trusts him with my inner thoughts and that's dangerous.

"What's next?" I need to get back on track and focus.

"We need to figure out what's for dinner." He gestures for me to lead. As I pass him, he says, "I like the sundress, little warrior."

My cheeks warm. "Thank you."

I head down the stairs and toward the kitchen. Mason has a handful of menus. Roarke and Wyatt sit on the island stools.

"What are we ordering tonight?" Aiden's hand lands on the small of my back. I almost freeze at his warm touch and the sparks rippling out from it, but he guides me forward to join the others.

Mason's gaze roams over me, heating me even more. I'm glad I chose something light and airy. Because these guys make me hot and bothered.

"We haven't decided." Mason has two stacks of menus on the island in front of him.

I haven't seen paper menus in a while. Usually I look them up on my phone, but we don't order out like these guys probably do. Is McDonald's even an option?

"Come here, poppet." Roarke pats the stool between him and Wyatt.

I glance at Aiden. Does he want me near him? I don't want to crowd him, but I want him to know I'm here for him. He's my priority in this job.

Aiden smiles and gently urges me to go with his hand on my low back. I sit on the stool and probably look like a small child compared to the guys on either side of me. Everyone is pretty much taller than me, but these guys are taller than most everyone else.

"If you want, I can cook." There was the makings for salad and some fish in the freezer.

"Not tonight, mouse." Mason spreads out three menus on the counter and glares at Rourke. "Choose from one of these three."

The restaurants are all names I've barely heard of and never could afford to eat there. I'm really curious what they serve. Somehow I don't think I'm going to get a burger and fries from any of these.

Roarke narrows his gaze at Mason. "We could order from multiple places."

"And someone always ends up with cold food." Mason shakes his head. "Choose one."

"Fine." Roarke taps on the one in the middle.

Mason looks at Wyatt and he taps a different one. Rolling his eyes, Mason looks to Aiden. When Aiden winks at me and chooses the third one, I cover my mouth to keep from chuckling.

Mason sighs and those penetrating eyes pin me in place. "Guess the mouse gets to cast the deciding vote."

"May I look at the menus?" I don't even know what cuisine any of them serve. What if I accidentally pick a sushi place. Not my favorite.

"After you vote." Mason runs his hand through his black hair, making it stand every which way.

Biting my lip, I choose the one Aiden picked. He grins at me and then grins at the others like he just won.

"Come on, poppet. I wouldn't lead you wrong." Roarke sighs. He leans in close to my ear and whispers, "Guess I'll have to settle on eating something different for dessert."

Arousal rushes through me, hot and fast, remembering his promise at my apartment. I cross my legs against the building ache. If he got me there with his fingers, what could he do to me with his tongue?

Fuck I'm curious.

Wyatt opens the menu in front of him and moves it my way. I glance over the menu. No prices are listed next to the items.

How am I supposed to pick something if I don't know how much it costs? I don't know when I'll get my first pay check and I've got less than a hundred dollars in the bank currently. I think I have a twenty in my purse.

"How much is this going to cost?" I lean in to ask Wyatt, trying to be quiet. He seems like the most down to earth of the guys. "I'm not sure I can afford it."

He turns and smiles. "Kitten, we're paying your room *and* board. Pick whatever you want. Mason's buying. He lost a bet."

"What bet did he lose?" My gaze trails down the length of the menu. Half the stuff I don't even recognize the names of. This definitely isn't a burger and fry type place.

"He thought it would take a week to replace the drug dealer." Wyatt turns the menu to the next page.

I glance up at Mason.

He shrugs. "Aiden's particular. It took almost a month to lock that guy down and we all know how that turned out."

I swallow. "Oh."

Maybe they'll tell me to leave before I even sign anything. I haven't been here twenty-four hours yet. They haven't run a background check or anything on me. Not that anything bad should come up. But maybe I shouldn't get comfortable.

With new homes, I never know how long one is going to last. Some have personal reasons to move me on. Others thought I did something I didn't. I don't like to think about my time in the foster system, but between that and my mother's drug addiction, my childhood was less than ideal.

Roarke steals the menu from Wyatt, but I don't flinch at his sudden movement. I just absorb this beautiful place, because I could lose it all again tomorrow. I can't get attached to anything here. Not the shower, not the beautiful room, not the outside, not these guys. It's all temporary and I need to make sure I remember that.

When I lift my gaze, Mason watches me like a hawk. I quickly bottle everything back up and give him a practiced smile.

"I'm not sure what I'd like," I confess.

Roarke leans toward me. "Personally I'd prefer a burger, but there's this one item that's pretty good."

When I turn to look, Aiden's eyes catch mine. He's worried about something. I give him a slightly softened smile to reassure him. Right now, I've got nowhere to go, but as soon as I start getting paid, I'm squirreling away as much as possible.

I'm going to need money to find a place when they decide I'm not a good fit after all.

Chapter 9

Sitting, Waiting, Wishing

Wyatt

Once our order is in, Roarke takes over the conversation like he always does. There's been a subtle shift in Greer's mood. She's still smiling and laughing along at Roarke's story about the time his costume got stuck on an extra's and he had to walk around with this person attached to him for hours before they could untangle them.

Something about the fashion being vintage and irreplaceable.

She laughs in all the right spots. That smile never fades from her lips, but there's something in her soft brown eyes that looks a lot like fear.

I rerun the conversation to see where it might have happened, but not knowing her backstory makes it impossible to figure out the trigger. We don't know much about our new assistant to be honest. That should probably worry me more than it does.

I like digging into new people's thoughts and dreams and histories. Frankly, Greer's mind fascinates me almost as much as the idea of fucking her.

But even though I'm as interested in her as the others, maybe we should dig a little deeper. We basically invited a stranger into our home and gave her a room before all the background checks could be run.

"Mase."

He meets my gaze and I give him a jerk of my head. He nods and we both move outside. He grabs the wooden box off the end table, which signals to Aiden and Roarke that we're going out for a cigar.

We don't smoke often. We probably won't even smoke the cigars if we light them, but it gives us a chance to talk alone. Both of us grew up with the smell of cigars, thick in the air. So it's more a nostalgia thing than a habit.

We go to the far corner of the garden and sit in the chairs overlooking the dark ocean. Mase sets the box on the table but doesn't open it.

"You talked to the lawyers?" I glance back over my shoulder. The house is lit up from within. I can see through the openings the three of them at the table. Their laughter carries on the breeze.

"They'll have the documents for her to sign in the morning." He leans back and releases a breath.

"You think we moved too quickly?" I don't know what all went down between the others while I was giving her the tour. "She's unknown. It's not like someone we know recommended her."

"I called in a favor."

Mase and his favors. Fuck, he's like the Godfather out here. His mentor gave him the hookup and Mase ran with it. He spent years being whatever people needed him to be until he got his big break. Meanwhile, the guys worked hard on their careers while I sat in our rented house and worked on my writing credits.

We were all determined to make it and now here we are. Made.

Finally able to greenlight our own project. My script, Mason's directing, Aiden and Roarke acting.

"What did you ask for?" I tap my finger on the arm of the wooden chair, wishing I had a cigar in my hand for something to do.

"Everything." He leans forward, lacing his hands between his knees. "She's going to have access to us. She's young, but she's not stupid. We need to protect the others in case she really isn't what she seems."

That spark of intelligence in her is what draws me. Too often the people I meet have no depth. Even some of the smartest people are only one note. Greer has this darkness, not in her personality, but built into her. I want to figure out everything about her.

"She told Aiden her mom was an addict." Mase rubs his hand down his face. His gaze goes out to the ocean. "He wants her. He hasn't fucked anyone since Siobhan."

"We all want her." Which is unusual for us. I don't think there's ever been a woman we've all been attracted to. There have been plenty of women in our lives. More who would want to be with us. It's not difficult for us to find someone to have sex with, but Greer is a challenge.

"This could get complicated." Mase releases a heavy sigh.

"Or interesting," I offer. When I glance at them in the dining room, Greer lifts her eyes to mine. Not that she can see anything but an outline of me in the darkness. But I feel her gaze.

"Interesting?" He leans back.

I smile, knowing I'd draw him in. "Think of all the things we haven't explored because of who we are and what might get out. It's not like we can start every sexual encounter with an NDA."

He faces me. "What exactly are you proposing?"

"Sex. The ability to follow our desires. Sharing a woman. Think about it, Mase. She's malleable. You could mold and direct her."

His brow furrows. "Like porn? That shit always gets leaked."

I chuckle. "Not porn. Just sex. Roarke loves to be watched. I walked in on him kissing her earlier and I'm pretty sure it wasn't the first time."

"Did she like it?" His tone turns interested.

"She didn't push him away or demand we both leave her room." I know Mase will like this next bit. "She didn't go off on us for being in her room. She asked nicely for us to leave."

Mase rubs his jaw. "Fuck."

Most women are willing to do what you want, but it's rare to find someone who is actually submissive. Greer may not have explored that side of herself, but I think that's what's drawing all of us.

"We make sure the NDA locks her in tight and doesn't give her wiggle room to go to the press without consequences."

"Which would be?" Mase's gaze does that thing where he tries to pick apart my brain. It would be intimidating if I hadn't known him since we were kids.

"Something she wouldn't like. Monetary maybe?" Though she doesn't seem to have much beyond the clothes on her back. I saw the bags Roarke and her brought in. If she's truly moved out of her ex's apartment, then she doesn't have much.

"Or we could just ask her." Mase narrows his eyes. "Not everything has to be done with blackmail. This isn't a movie or TV show. Sure, there should be consequences if it gets out and she's responsible, but it doesn't have to be part of what we have with her."

I blow out a breath. He's right, but in this industry things can collapse around you fast if you put your faith in the wrong people. "I just want to make sure we're protected."

"Let me see what my guys find and then we can decide whether we need to push that particular destruct button." Mase glances back at the house. "She might be fairly submissive, but she has a little bit of a stubborn streak too."

"Just the way you like them." I laugh. Mase definitely has a type. "What are you going to tell Halley?"

"Fuck." Mase opens the box and pulls out a cigar. "I'm hoping it's a non-issue. She's filming on location for the next month. She doesn't call when she's working."

Taking a cigar, I run it under my nose, inhaling the tobacco before setting it back in the box. "Greer may not like smokers."

Mase shakes his head, but puts the cigar back. "We'll find out everything."

Greer

The food arrives and we all sit at the table. While waiting, Roarke barraged me with stories with Aiden interjecting occasionally. Stories I may have heard on a talk show before and some that I'd never heard. I still laughed and hung on every word.

Both of them have this aura that draws me in.

Aiden brings me a glass of ice tea and sets his own down, while Wyatt grabs a bottle of wine.

"Does that bother you?" I ask Aiden quietly.

He smiles and tucks my hair behind my ear. Tingles follow in his wake. I left my hair down. It's long and goes halfway down my back. Most days it's just easier to pin it up.

"No, little warrior. I've never cared for wine. My drink of choice was Scotch whisky. Expensive, full flavored." He taps me on my nose and I back away. "You can have a glass if you'd like."

"I don't drink." I shrug and look at the meal Roarke suggested I get. We replated them out of the packaging the restaurant sent per Mason's instructions. He was vehement about not eating out of boxes. Besides, at the end of the night, it will be me doing the dishes.

"Not at all?" Aiden's tone is gentle.

I force a smile. "It's better not to tempt fate. I'd rather just enjoy my life than find out I inherited that gene from my mother."

"Fair enough."

My plate is mostly roasted Brussel sprouts and carrots, and a decent portion of greens with sliced green apples and a tart dressing. The steak is a small portion with a demi-glaze. It looks delicious and decadent and way too much food for me.

"Poppet, tell me about your hopes and dreams." Roarke's voice carries in the house.

My mouth opens and closes. "No one's ever asked me that."

Maybe an early foster parent, during the getting to know you phase. But after what I went through, I didn't really think I had a future. Until their offer today, I figured I'd work until something made sense.

"Great, then your answer won't be practiced." Roarke leans back in his chair and takes a bite of his steak.

"Oh." I push my fork through the vegetables. "Maybe college? I took a few courses a while back."

"Anything in particular you want to study?" Mason asks.

I set my fork down and lift my gaze to his. "I don't know, but I have a whole year to think about it while I work here."

"Best to have a plan going in." Mason takes a bite and swallows it. "If you want to talk about it, I'm more than willing to help you figure it out."

My brow furrows. What? Why? I can't think of what's in it for him to help me piece together a makeshift future. What will he want in return? "Maybe."

Aiden clears his throat. "Filming starts Monday. We need to have all the necessary paperwork filled out by then. The bank needs your information on file as the sobriety companion."

"Is it actually in your contract?" I pop a piece of Brussel sprout in my mouth, expecting something not very good. When I bite down, flavor fills my mouth. My eyes widen. Oh my God, I think I'm in love.

"Yes, I have a sobriety clause. It's explicit and there are monetary consequences if I fail to live up to them. It's one of the reasons we all decided to move in together." Aiden cracks his neck to the side. "It doesn't matter the underlying circumstances. I behaved unprofessionally on set and cost my previous film money. To back this film with me attached, they wanted assurances."

I'm listening to Aiden and trying to focus, but I'm also trying not to stuff Brussel sprouts and carrots into my mouth as fast as possible. I don't remember when I last had something to eat and whatever it was, it wasn't this good.

I'm mostly speechless anyway. I feel for him. His marriage fell apart and it makes sense that so did he. His future was taken away from him.

I know that feeling.

"Given that we all want to fuck you, poppet, I think—"

I choke on a carrot, not expecting that to come up again. At least not while eating. I cough around the perfect food.

"Fuck, Roarke, can't you think about anything else." Aiden stands and rubs his hand down my back.

I cough, but manage to swallow the food. Aiden hands me my glass and I wash the carrot down with some tea.

"Better?" Aiden sits back in the chair next to me.

I nod and dab my napkin at my watering eyes.

"Not to be an ass, but we do need to talk about this." Roarke's blue eyes sparkle when they meet mine. "After all, we've kissed."

The world slows down and there's this whooshing noise in my ears. Damn it, I knew he wouldn't keep this to himself.

"Her ex was a dick and so I helped Greer orgasm to prove to him that he's a worthless lover. I offered to let her fake it first."

Wyatt laughs. Aiden arches an eyebrow, clearly offended on my behalf. Mason leans his elbows on the table, intensely interested. While I wonder if I can disappear.

"Are we talking full penetration?" Mason asks.

"Oh, God!" I cover my burning face. What the hell did I walk into?

"I kissed her, teased her breasts, and finger fucked her tight little pussy until she came on my hand." Roarke's eyes dance merrily when I lift mine to look at him like he's completely lost his mind. "Purely for theatrical effect. Apparently, she thinks she's quiet in the bedroom."

I close my eyes and wish to wake up on the couch in my old apartment. Dealing with Chad was way easier than this level of sharing. Aiden reaches out and takes my hand. I almost pull away, but he's not pushing for more, just offering comfort. I'm not used to that.

"You certainly have a way with words, Roarke." Aiden leans back in his chair but doesn't release my hand. "I'm glad you put the asshole in his place, but I'm not sure we needed that level of detail."

"I appreciate detail." Wyatt's smile is mischievous. His hazel eyes meet mine. My pulse quickens as I can almost see the wheels turning inside his mind.

Roarke smirks.

"Fine, do you want to discuss this now?" Aiden turns to me. "Greer, do you want to discuss this?"

My mouth opens, but words don't come out. I'm not sure whether to be humiliated or turned on. I shut my mouth and nod. Might as well get this out of the way.

Aiden laces his fingers with mine and I draw from his strength. "What matters is what Greer wants to do about this attraction, not how far each of us gets with her. Is that agreed?"

"But—" Roarke blurts.

"We all know how much you love to discuss your sex life, but that's something you need to discuss with Greer if she's part of it. She needs a say in this. In all of this. She's going to be living with us for over a year. We can't just steamroll over her whenever it's more convenient for us."

Feeling exposed, I lean back in my chair and resist the urge to draw my feet up and wrap my arms around my knees. Instead, I cling to Aiden's hand like a lifeline. I don't know why he feels like the safe wolf among these predators. Maybe I just have a soft spot for him after what he went through and what he's going through.

"If you aren't going to eliminate any of us, then we need some ground rules, mouse." Mase leans his elbows on the table. His eyes hold me in place. "Is there anyone you don't want?"

If I say no, what does that mean? Am I really willing to put my new motto to the test with these men? All of them? It's not like I'll be able to ghost them if it doesn't work out. I'll still need to live here.

"I don't know what I want," I admit because they're all watching me, dissecting me. "This is a lot for me. I'm not used to being wanted. I'm curious, but I want to think it over."

Aiden's hand tightens. His blue eyes hold mine, reassuring me. "It's been a long day. Maybe we should watch something and keep our hands to ourselves for the evening. Have a sleep on it and maybe things will be clearer in the morning."

Chapter 10

Talking in Your Sleep

Greer

The movie almost puts me to sleep. I haven't felt safe sleeping at the apartment, especially with Chad, and all that lack of sleep catches up to me now. I snuggle down in the recliner between Aiden's and Rourke's recliners and yawn again.

A blanket covers me and I open my eyes to see Wyatt adjusting it. I blink at the screen, trying to figure out if I missed some of the plot.

"We can watch it again some other time, kitten." Wyatt gives me a smile before heading back to his seat.

I straighten in my chair determined to watch more of the movie.

Someone lifts me and holds me against their chest. The smell of oranges makes me feel safe and lulls me back to sleep.

Whispers wake me slightly as I snuggle deeper under the covers and sigh against the fluffy pillows.

Something chases me in the dark and I wrestle with whatever is holding me down. I bolt upright with my heart racing, flinging off the covers trying to hold me down. For a moment, I don't know where I am or what's happening. The nightmare felt real, so real, like too close to something that happened in the past. I push it away, hurrying out of the bed and stumbling into the bathroom.

The bright light makes me close my eyes, but I crack them open. I'm still in my dress. I'm at the mansion and must have fallen asleep during the movie. A shiver ripples through me. Given my memory of oranges, Aiden probably carried me to bed.

After washing my face, I wander into my room, turning on the lamp on the nightstand to find some sleep shorts and a tank to change into. When I climb back onto the bed, the nightmare clings to me, making my heartbeat erratic. The room is bigger than I'm used to. The house is eerily quiet. Maybe I can find some tea downstairs to help me back to sleep.

Grabbing a long cardigan, I pull it on over my tank top before opening the door to the rest of the house. I pause standing in the light, listening. It's quiet in the hallway, but there's enough light from the full moon coming through the windows to see my way to the stairs. I don't really want to run into anyone. As I get to the main floor, I can see a dim light is still on.

I hesitate, but what's the worse that could happen?

I run into one of the four men who want to fuck me? It's inevitable. I'm living with them. Releasing my breath, I walk into the kitchen. The light is the undercabinet lighting. The pool is also lit, giving a soft glow to the outside space.

Releasing my held breath, I check the pantry and find a small assortment of teas. With a peppermint tea bag in hand, I return to the kitchen. Seeing a silhouette of a man, I let out a small startled noise.

"Greer?" Aiden steps into the light and my heartbeat begins to slow. Of all of them, Aiden is the easiest for me to deal with. He's interested but also respects my space. Though with just sleep pants hanging low on his hips, he's even more tempting.

"I woke and couldn't go back to sleep." I move toward the kettle and set my teabag on the counter. "Figured a cup of warm tea would do the trick. Why are you up?"

Aiden runs his hand through his curls as he leans against the counter. "Insomnia."

"Do you want some tea?" I fill the kettle with water and set it back on the pad to start heating it.

"Sure."

I head back to the pantry. "Peppermint, chamomile, lemon honey, there's a few more herbal blends."

"What are you having?" His voice is deep and quiet like the night. It skates down my spine and settles low in my belly. It's weird not to hear traffic and other city noises. Just the soft crash of ocean waves fill the room.

"Peppermint."

"I'll have that."

I grab another teabag and then get down two mugs before heading back to the kettle. "Do you get insomnia often?"

Focusing on the cups, I open the packages and put the teabags in while waiting for the water to heat.

"Some nights." He sounds off, which worries me. Off isn't good for an addict. But I also don't know him well. It's hard to remember that when he seems like such a large part of my life. Movies and interviews with him don't really count as getting to know him. I have to keep that in mind.

But he's also a recovering addict.

"What do you normally do when you can't sleep?" I glance around the kitchen. The wine is all in the wine room. He said he doesn't like it, but that doesn't mean it won't do in a pinch. I haven't seen other alcohol anywhere, but I haven't looked for it either. I'm sure they have a liquor cabinet, but it should be locked.

Tomorrow, I'll get a better tour. Maybe I'll ask Mason to show me where all the hidden dangers might be.

"Drink." He sighs. "It's been a while."

I resist the urge to turn to him. He needs my trust that he can control himself. I'm here for when things get bad, which being up alone in the middle of the night could potentially spell disaster. How often has he been restless and stood in this kitchen wanting a drink?

Fighting that battle on his own has to be draining.

The kettle whistles and I pour the hot water over the teabags. I pick up both of our cups and motion to the living room. "Come on, let's go sit over here."

I sit in the corner of the couch and set the cups on the coasters on the end table before turning on the lamp. Aiden walks in and sits down heavily beside me. The light on the pool shuts off, leaving the outside dark, with the exception of the moonlight.

"We need to let it steep a little." I tuck my feet under me and study Aiden.

He looks tired and I don't smell any alcohol on him. There weren't any glasses on the counter. Not that he would need one.

He blows out a breath. "I didn't drink, little warrior. I may want a drink, but I know I can't even have a sip. There are no drugs in this house. So I'm clean."

"That's a relief. I'd hate to have failed my job on day one." I let out a little laugh.

"You don't have to pretend for me." He rests his head on the back of the couch. "You were nervous when you found me down here alone."

"You're right. But partially because I'm in my pajamas and wasn't expecting anyone else to be up." I turn to face him more fully. "I don't know everything about you yet, but I'll figure it out. I'm committed to your recovery and want to help you however I can."

"I appreciate that." He sounds so tired, so different from the man standing up for me earlier today. While I want to say fuck it and see if I can put *sex is just sex* to the test, I'm still afraid that I'll fail. Being hung up on a normal guy is bad, but being hung up on superstars that I'll see all the time on the screen would be tragic.

My life doesn't need any more tragedy.

I hand him a mug and take a sip of my tea. "From what I understand, part of your recovery is talking to peers and your therapist. Do they know about your insomnia?"

"It's only recently become a problem again." He sips at his tea while looking at me over the rim of his mug.

"Do you know what causes it?" I set the mug down.

"My wife." He chuckles. "My ex-wife. Or rather the lack of. I always slept better with her in my bed."

"Have you tried a body pillow?" I give him a smile like I know I'm being ridiculous. It's what anyone would offer as a suggestion. Sleeping alone can be hard when you're used to having someone right next to you. At least Chad was good for that.

"I could build a fort with all the pillows I have." His gaze goes to the reflection of the moon in the pool. "The doctors gave me sleeping pills for it, but I don't like the groggy feeling in the morning."

"I can understand that. I was on them for a while as a teenager. They made me feel like I was in a fog." The nightmares I had were worse than any fog though, so I took the pills until I realized I couldn't sleep without them. I needed them and that terrified me. I flushed them down the toilet.

"Did your dad raise you?" He's steering the conversation away from his problem, but I'm not sure I want to talk about mine. I meet his blue eyes and see the pain lingering in them.

Fuck. Maybe my sad life story will help put him to sleep.

"No." I pick up my cup and take a small sip. "I went into the foster care system."

He sets his mug down. "It didn't work out well for you, did it?"

I shrug. Not sure I want to talk about it, but I can keep it mostly surface.

"I never found somewhere I fit in. It was easier once I stopped trying." I stretch a leg out before tucking it back under me. "At first I was so numb I didn't try. I think those people really cared. They took me to therapy and tried to help me, but I couldn't."

It felt like I never left the apartment. That I was still there and she was still there, so still, not even her chest rose.

Aiden's hand brushes mine and I startle back to the present. His blue eyes are haunted as he searches my face. "I'm sure you did the best you could at the time."

I force a smile and set my tea down. "There were good homes with bad people and bad homes with good people. Some homes had more kids than they could handle. It was easier to hide there."

"You never found somewhere to stay?"

"I was at a couple for a year or two." A shiver runs through me. "At that point I wanted it to work. I wanted a place to call home."

"What happened?" Aiden's hand rests behind me on the couch.

Yawning, I turn and rest my head against the couch back. "The same thing that always happens. They got rid of me when I became too much."

The emptiness inside gnaws at my stomach.

Aiden's arm wraps around my shoulder and pulls me into his side. I don't resist because I need this connection. "You can be as much as you need to be here, little warrior. I promise not to get rid of you."

I smile as my eyes shut. "You can't keep that promise."

"Watch me," he whispers.

Something tickles my face. I try to brush it away not wanting to wake up yet. The dream I'm having is too good, wrapped in safe arms, snuggled up warm. I never want to wake up.

"Someone took her job of watching Aiden's every move literally." The deep voice startles me. "Didn't you, kitten?"

Who's in my room? I open my eyes and Aiden's face is right there. His curls rest against my forehead. I don't move as I try to figure out what's happening. I came downstairs and made Aiden and me tea.

We sat on the couch and talked. He pulled me into his side. And then I woke up literally tangled up with him. His arms are wrapped around me and my leg is thrown over his, while my other leg rests in between his. We're still on the couch, but I'm tucked on the inside, while Aiden is curled around me.

I'm tempted to reach up and touch his peaceful face, but I don't want to wake him.

Movement in the corner of my eye makes me glance up. Wyatt stands behind the couch with a cup of coffee.

"Make any decisions last night, kitten?" He arches his eyebrow.

Both Aiden and I have pajamas on, but the way we're holding on is pretty intimate. I'm usually a I'll-sleep-on-this-side-of-the-bed, touch me and die type sleeper. I take in a breath of his orange cologne.

"No decisions," I whisper, watching Aiden's face, but he's out.

Wyatt sets his cup down and grabs the blanket off the back of the couch to drape over us. "Take care of him."

He grabs his cup and walks outside. That didn't sound like jealousy. He honestly worries about his friend.

I settle back into the warmth of Aiden's hold, but I can't go back to sleep. What am I doing here? This is so not normal for me, but maybe it's time to mix things up in my life. This opportunity could end up giving me a future I never dreamed of having.

My only goal before this was to not end up like my mother. After my father left, she went down a dark path and dragged me along with her. She was careful enough not to get on child protective services radar, but that doesn't mean I was taken care of.

I'm just glad I only had myself to protect. In the foster system, I met a couple of kids who had younger siblings that they were fiercely protective of. I don't know that I could have stayed present, even for a sibling that needed me, with what I went through.

That doesn't matter now. I need to live in the present. I realized that long ago. But now I have something else to live for. A future. This concept that's been missing from my life for as long as I can remember. Moving from one bad situation to the next and just surviving.

My gaze lifts to Aiden's face. I don't know if there will be bad in this situation, but there's definitely good that may outweigh the bad stuff.

His eyes don't open but he draws me in tighter. "You think too loud, little warrior."

My lips curve into a smile, but I freeze at the feel of his hard cock against my hip, stirring something hot and achy inside me.

"Just the effect of having a beautiful woman wrapped around me. Nothing to worry about," he whispers.

I relax into his arms and release the breath I held back.

"I think I've found the cure to my insomnia." His blue eyes open, shining with laughter and a heat I'm growing familiar with.

"If it keeps you from wandering around at night looking for booze..." I give a little shrug. I'm not typically a cuddler, but I like the way Aiden feels against me. He makes me feel safe, desirable, and needed.

He smirks. "Hmm, booze or a beautiful woman in my bed?"

I duck my head as heat creeps into my cheeks at him calling me beautiful again.

His leg between my thighs slides against mine, making me aware of how intimate this position really is. His lips press against my forehead.

"Thank you for the wonderful night's sleep, Greer."

I lift my chin to meet his eyes. "You're welcome."

His gaze drops to my lips. Is he going to kiss me? Will it be different than Roarke's all-consuming kiss?

"Why was I not informed of couch cuddles being an option?" Roarke's booming voice fills the room.

Aiden winces and pulls me in tight. "I'm not sharing right now. She's my support human."

I giggle as he tucks me against his chest. His skin is warm against my cheek. Sparks of awareness skate along my veins.

"But she's also the maker of breakfast." Roarke's voice is closer this time.

Aiden sighs and leans into my ear to whisper. "Next time, we sleep in my bed with the door locked."

A little shiver works through me. Aiden tosses the cover from us and maneuvers himself into a sitting position with me straddling his lap. His curls are all tussled and flat from where he slept on them. My hair can't be much better.

My eyes meet his and his cock is still hard against my stomach. My insides flow into liquid heat as I search his eyes. He cups my cheek. My breath catches.

"Chop, chop, poppet." Roarke claps his hands.

Aiden lowers his hand and shakes his head. "Better get your day started, little warrior."

I back off Aiden's lap and stand. My gaze helplessly falls to the tent of his pajama pants. Dear Lord, someone blessed these men with large cocks. I doubt Mason's is small, though I haven't felt or seen his yet.

Technically I've only seen Roarke's on the movie screen.

A torrent of heat sweeps through me as I realize my gaze has lingered much longer than necessary on Aiden's cock and that I'm thinking about four men's cocks. I close my eyes and turn, stepping into Roarke's chest.

My eyes pop open and he grins down at me. "Good morning, Roarke."

He throws his head back and releases a jovial laugh. His hands grip my waist.

"What are you doing?" My hands go over his.

He lifts me, walking me over to the counter and setting me on it. He parts my thighs and wedges himself between them. His hands cup my head, threading his fingers into my hair before his mouth descends on mine.

I don't have time to protest as he claims my mouth, kissing me like I don't have morning breath, full tongue. His hard cock presses between my legs, making my already wet pussy throb.

He pulls back and rubs his thumb next to my lips. His blue eyes sparkle. "That's how we say good morning, poppet."

I open my mouth but nothing comes out. My gaze goes to Aiden, feeling bad that we didn't kiss and he had to watch Roarke kiss me. Aiden stands and adjusts his erection in his pants.

"I think you might be on to something, Roarke." Aiden grabs our tea mugs and brings them to the sink behind me. He winks, but there's no jealousy.

Roarke backs up and sets me on my feet before turning me and smacking me on the bottom. "Upstairs with you. Make yourself presentable and then make me breakfast. Be quick, woman."

My cheeks flare hot again. But I walk to the stairs and make my way up to my room. What have I signed up for?

Chapter 11

Should I Stay or Should I Go?

Greer

I don't waste time dressing but brush my teeth and hair, and wash my face. Having looked over their diets and menus, I think I know what they want for breakfast. When I return to the kitchen, Roarke sits at the island with a cup of coffee.

He smirks and gives me a wink. "Morning, poppet."

"Morning." I grab eggs and turkey bacon out of the refrigerator and set them on the counter. It takes me a few seconds to remember where the pans are, but I finally find them.

After living in apartments for the past few years, having a full-sized kitchen is a dream come true. I'm just getting everything cooking when Wyatt comes inside. His wet hair is slicked back and he's wearing a wet suit, stripped down to his waist.

"Good waves today?" Roarke leans back against the island, facing Wyatt.

Seriously, Wyatt could be a model. He's gorgeous and his body is a masterpiece of toned golden muscles. His black inked tattoo is striking against his skin. I'm lucky I'm not drooling over him.

With all these gorgeous men surrounding me, I won't last a week without breaking down and having sex with someone, which isn't normal for me.

But my hormones are out of control.

"Good waves." He walks around the island and stops beside me. I try to pay attention to the bacon cooking. The smell of sunscreen, ocean, and sun fill my nose, making my knees weak. He grabs a Gatorade out of the refrigerator and drinks the whole thing while I watch his throat work. Fuck.

"Thirsty, poppet?" Roarke's laughter breaks my stare down with Wyatt's Adam's apple.

"Need a taste, kitten?" That's just not fair to put a voice like that on a guy like Wyatt. It slips under my skin and plays to dark fantasies I never shared with anyone.

I swallow and force a smile. "I'm good."

I quickly plate the eggs and bacon and grab the piece of toast from the toaster before setting the plate in front of Roarke. "If something isn't the way you like, let me know."

"What do I get for breakfast?" Wyatt's heat covers my back and I regret not changing into actual clothes as my nipples harden in anticipation. His hands settle on the island on either side of my hips. He's so much bigger than me. I've always been on the small side, but these men make me feel dainty.

"Yogurt, fruit, and granola," I breathe out, pulling the info from my barely functioning brain.

His head dips beside mine and he draws in a breath. Bracing myself on the island, I barely keep myself upright as my knees weaken.

"I like vanilla." His lips graze my neck.

My breath catches and my eyes close at the innocent touch that feels so naughty. When my eyes open, Roarke smirks as he shovels eggs into his mouth.

"You should kiss her." Roarke points with his fork. "She's hot for it, aren't you, poppet?"

My eyes widen. "What?"

"Maybe kissing means something to our kitten." Wyatt's thumb brushes my hip bone, making heat settle between my legs. "Not all of us kiss for a living, Roarke."

"Mmm." He finishes chewing his bite. "Kissing is like breathing. It's natural. We need it." His blue eyes drop to mine to pin me in place. "My poppet just hasn't been kissed enough or good enough. That ex of hers couldn't have made her happy. I bet she faked it all the time with him. She needs to know how real men kiss."

"I've been kissed by more guys than Chad." I'm not sure why I feel the need to defend myself. Chad wasn't exactly a sparkling example of the guys I dated. He was just easy to be swept away with. Even though we hadn't been dating long, it was easier to live with him than our separate crowded shared apartments.

Wyatt steps back and I turn to get his breakfast, but he steps in and lifts me on the counter. He tips my chin up and those hazel eyes search mine.

"If you don't want me to kiss you, just tell me no, kitten."

I should say no. I should do a lot of things I don't do. He gives me plenty of time to stop him. To lightly touch his bare chest and push him away. But my whole body hums in anticipation.

Will it be different than when Roarke kisses me? Chad was a sloppy kisser. All tongue and wet. Roarke kisses with his whole body, seriously it feels like he's making love to my mouth.

Wyatt's lips brush mine, startling me back to the present. His eyes are open watching me, waiting for me to say no. Little shocks jolt my system. His lips brush mine again. His eyes darken. He slides his hands along my jaw, holding me in place as his mouth takes mine. My lips part on a gasp, longing for more.

My hands grasp the edge of the counter as his tongue brushes my lower lip, making me open beneath him. A low growl works out of his chest, rippling through me. My panties are soaked as he claims my mouth, making me forget everything, but the taste of the salty ocean, the tanginess of Gatorade, and the dark taste of him. I want to drink him in and never let him go.

My hands have minds of their own, moving to his bare skin at his waist as my legs part so he can come closer. He steps into me and the bulk of his wetsuit doesn't distract from the large bulge pressing against my pussy.

As he explores my mouth, that bulge gets harder and larger. He lifts his lips from mine and his darkened eyes open. "Sweet, like I knew you'd taste."

I release my breath. This isn't me. But maybe it is. Maybe this is okay in this house that isn't me. With these men I would never have met if I didn't apply for this job. Maybe while I live this fantasy life, I can explore some fantasies of my own. With all of them.

"We're going to get into so much trouble, kitten." Wyatt cocks a smile that makes my belly bottom out. Fuck, he's intoxicating. He lifts me off the counter and sets me on my feet. My knees barely hold me. His thumb trails along my shorts' elastic, brushing against the trembling skin of my belly. "I'll be back after my shower."

When he steps away, his gaze flicks over my shoulder at Roarke before he walks around the corner to the stairs. My heart thunders in my ears. I can think of a million reasons not to get involved with these guys.

They're wealthy, famous, elite, and I'm me. Barely any clothes on my back. Running from a shitty ex in an even shittier apartment. No future. A twisted, fucked up past.

But they want me. The same way Chad wanted me at first. Somehow in my mind someone wanting me makes me feel like I belong. But I have to remember that it's temporary. I don't really belong to anyone. No one who was supposed to want me would keep me so why would anyone else.

"Poppet." Roarke's voice drags me from my thoughts. He looks at me like I've done something wrong. Shit, what did I do? Is he going to kick me out? As fear washes over me, his look gentles. "Come here, Greer."

Uncertainty thrums through me as I walk around the island to his side. He turns on his stool and our faces are about level.

"You're not going to cry on me again, right?" He actually looks worried that I might.

"No. I don't usually cry." I draw in a breath and wait for him to tell me to get my stuff and go.

He wraps his hand around the back of my neck.

"There's nothing to fear here, poppet. If there was, I'd take care of it for you." His thumb caresses my jaw while he searches my eyes. "Whatever bad things happened in the past. I've got you now."

I blow out a breath. If only it were that easy, but he doesn't have me. This isn't some magical story where I turn into the bell of the ball. I'm the hired help and that's it. They're just lines he's saying. He's this famous actor more comfortable playing a role than maybe in his own skin.

Again, it feels like I know him, but I don't. Not really. Who he is as a person is a complete mystery to me, but I know how he makes me feel. He makes me feel alive, but he's not here to save me.

He smirks. "I see your doubt, poppet. Trust doesn't come easy, but I can put in the time because I have a feeling you'll be worth it."

When I open my mouth to tell Roarke *I'm not*, his lips crash against mine, taking my words from me and spinning me out again. He draws me between his legs and holds me against him as he explores my mouth like Wyatt just did.

I don't think I've ever kissed two guys in the same day, let alone one right after the other. Something burns a little hotter inside me. Roarke pulls away and searches my eyes again.

"Hmm, I think we should spend the day having sex," he announces.

I laugh out loud. He has to be kidding. He grins and looks really encouraged.

"She's my emotional support human today, Roarke." Aiden's voice makes me lift my gaze to watch him walk into the room. He's dressed for the day in jeans and a shirt that hugs his lean muscles.

"I found her." Roarke's hands tighten on my waist.

"You answered the phone." Aiden holds his hand out to me and I take it. Every little touch with Aiden lights me up and makes me long for more. Roarke reluctantly lets me go.

"None of you would have invited her to interview." He picks up his bacon and points it at Aiden. "You should be thanking me. You could have gotten another boring drug dealer again."

He gives me a wink as Aiden draws me back into the kitchen. "Do you need help making breakfast?"

My cheeks feel hot as I shake my head. "I've got it."

He brushes my hair behind my ear and his focus drops to my lips. My insides tighten and heat floods me like someone dropped me on the surface of the sun. How could I want a third guy to kiss me? I've never been like this, but I want Aiden to.

I want to know what Aiden Clyborne tastes like.

My tongue darts out to wet my lips and Aiden clears his throat.

"You wanted to know my schedule. Today is a perfect day to follow me." He steps back to lean against the counter.

To cover my disappointment in not getting a kiss (because I'm greedy that way apparently), I open the refrigerator again and get out the fruit and yogurt. Then I go to the pantry and find the granola.

Both Aiden and Wyatt had similar breakfasts down. So I cut up some fruit and put together two bowls of yogurt with fruit and granola.

"Normally I would wake around the same time Wyatt is up to go surfing." Aiden talks while I work. "Then I shower and get ready for the day."

He holds his hands out to his sides to draw my attention to his outfit. His gaze trails over my bare legs and the thin sleep set I have on. Self-conscious, I draw my sweater tighter around me, knowing it won't stay that way. I should have changed. I should hide my figure.

Always leave them wanting more.

It's not surprising that Mary's words keep coming back to me. This was her life, rubbing elbows with the Hollywood elite.

My foster mother Mary wanted to keep me. She wasn't really looking for a daughter though. More of a companion to keep her occupied between visits from her director lover. As a teenager, I loved her wild life style and her novel way of looking at life.

But even that ended badly. They always do.

I hand Aiden a bowl. "And then breakfast?"

Smiling, he takes the food. "Yes, breakfast. You'll join me?"

He glances at the other bowl.

"That's for Wyatt."

"What are you having?" He raises an eyebrow in that way that makes me feel unsure of myself. It's like I suddenly remember this guy is a megastar and I'm supposed to be humbled to be in his presence.

"What do you like, poppet?" Roarke brings his plate around, trapping me between him and Aiden.

I've been short my whole life, but I've never felt small like I do around these two.

Roarke grabs the edges of my sweater and holds it open, frankly assessing my body. I roll my eyes up to the sky because what else am I supposed to do? Protest? Make an issue about it after he's had his fingers inside me? It's not like he's stripping me naked.

Trust me, I know about consent. And when I can say no. I know if I say no he'll stop. He'll apologize and we'll go on like nothing happened. But part of me longs for this attention, for all their attention. I'm not saying it's healthy, but damn does it feel good.

"You could use a little meat on your bones, poppet." His laughing eyes meet mine. His hold on my sweater draws me closer to him. "Want me to fix you a hearty breakfast?"

I'm not sure I want to know what he means.

I bite my lip. "I'm just going to make myself some yogurt."

He chuckles, but releases me. "Fine. I think my breakfast would be superior but have your yogurt."

I quickly make myself a bowl with the leftovers from the fruit I cut up. When Wyatt reappears, I hand him his bowl. Grinning, he leans down and gives me a quick kiss. I freeze.

"So that's happening?" Aiden gives Wyatt a look that I can't quite read.

"You should get in there." Roarke leads me over to the table with my bowl and sits in the chair before pulling me down on his lap. He's all hard muscle beneath me.

"I can sit in my own chair." It's more of a formal statement than an actual request.

"You barely qualify to ride in the front seat, poppet. Now eat your breakfast like a good girl while I convince Aiden to stop with the slow burn thing you two have going."

My gaze lifts to Aiden's bemused shake of his head. "Slow burn?"

"This whole will they won't they thing can only last so long." Roarke frowns like it's a tragedy.

"We haven't even known each other a whole day, Roarke."

Wyatt laughs. "If I were a betting man—"

"You normally are." Aiden's delivery is dry.

Wyatt winks at me. "But I would never bet on something like how Roarke gets under someone's skin quickly. After all, he's had his finger in her pussy already."

Even my ears burn this time. "That was a special circumstance."

"It was very special, poppet." Roarke's voice is a low rumble beneath me. "And bears repeating."

When Roarke stands with me in his arms, I'm still holding my spoon from my yogurt.

"Please put me down." I keep my tone polite but firm.

"I figured we'd go somewhere private, but we could do it right here, poppet." Roarke sits in the chair with me on his lap. His fingers toy with the waistband on my sleep shorts. "I like an audience and these two would love to watch you come first thing in the morning."

My eyes widen. Fuck, is this normal for them?

After all, he suggested it yesterday too. I've never had sex in public or somewhere I could be caught. But this is even beyond that. He wants to make me come while they watch.

Maybe it's just Roarke.

"I'm good." I shovel a spoonful of yogurt into my mouth, trying not to think about how wet his words made me.

Roarke's dark chuckle races down my spine. "Tell me, poppet, you think you're quiet when you orgasm, which you clearly aren't…"

I swallow the yogurt hard and wish I had a glass of water to wash it down.

"Did you orgasm during sex with your ex?"

Wyatt leans back with a cocky smile on his face, looking wholly entertained by Roarke's question. Aiden tilts his head slightly like he's interested in my answer.

"Are we really going to do this at the breakfast table? On day two of me being here?" I twist to meet Roarke's jovial eyes.

"Poppet, typically I'm through all this uncomfortable talk and on to more pleasurable pursuits within the first hour of meeting a woman." He catches my chin to hold me there. "You seemed almost shocked when you came around my finger. That makes me think it's either been a while since someone has gotten you off or…"

Please don't say it. Fuck, it's humiliating to be so inadequate that I can't come from being fucked. That I've faked every shared "orgasm" I had with a partner.

Yesterday could be chalked up to the stress of the situation. The rush of having someone like Roarke Flynn touch me like that. It's probably just a fluke.

"Or you've never come with anyone before, kitten." Wyatt's words make me tremble in Roarke's arms.

Roarke cocks his head to the side as he studies me. For a second, I brace myself for him to set me to the side. For all of them to say, *oh, well, that sucks for you.*

Instead, Roarke smiles. "We can fix that."

All that comes from my mouth is a squeak. Seriously. I've walked into a completely foreign land where the rules I grew up with mean nothing.

"Is it so hard to believe that I could make you feel something no one else has?" Roarke leans in until his breath caresses my lips. "I could spend all day making you come, over and over and over again, poppet. Would you like that?"

Words fail me as I contemplate what he's offering me.

"Maybe no one's touched upon her darker fantasies." Mason's deep voice draws my attention into the kitchen, where he stands in a pair of pajama pants dangling low on his hips. His body is cut, but lean. His arms flex as he lifts the coffee mug to his lips. He takes a small sip. "Want to play, little mouse?"

Chapter 12

You've Got a Friend in Me

Greer

There's something so tempting about all of them. But there's a darkness in Mason that makes me want to do as he says and defy him in the same breath.

A buzzing rings through the house, breaking the spell that held me motionless.

Wyatt taps on his phone and then says, "How may I help you?"

"Let me in, WyWy." A feminine voice makes me freeze. She giggles and a rock lodges in my gut.

He presses something on his phone and glances at me with a blank face. "There's no way to prepare you."

Roarke sets me in the chair next to him as Wyatt heads to the front door. The loss of Roarke's warmth makes me want to crawl back onto his lap, but I can't do that. Someone is coming.

Is this a girlfriend? Someone important to them? Would it matter if they all had girlfriends after their proposal to me? They didn't ask me to go steady. They only want to fuck me.

I don't tolerate cheating and wouldn't help someone cheat. But what if I already did? After kissing both Roarke and Wyatt?

Er, WyWy?

Aiden continues to eat his yogurt while watching me closely. I squirm in my chair as I pull over my yogurt for something to do with my hands. Does he already regret hiring me?

"Oh, my God! You guys have no idea what kind of day I've had already." Her voice echoes through the house from the front door. "I woke up in some stranger's house with a pineapple beside me. So fucking surreal."

The woman strides into the kitchen. She's tall. Her light brown hair with golden highlights hangs down to the middle of her back in soft waves. Her outfit is airy and flowing around her, like it was made specifically for a woman like her. Her eyes settle on me and her smile freezes.

"I didn't know we had company." She slaps the back of her hand against Wyatt's chest. "Wyatt, why didn't you tell me we had company?"

She walks past me and Roarke and sits on the other side of me. Her hazel eyes are hauntingly familiar, but I've never met this woman before. She's about my age and gorgeous. She smiles like she's my new best friend, leaning in conspiratorially. "Who did you sleep with?"

My mouth opens and my gaze goes to Aiden before I can stop myself. I literally slept with him on that couch.

She follows my gaze. "Huh? Yeah, I'm not buying that. Aiden's not into randoms. So maybe you didn't sleep with anyone..."

Her eyebrow arches when she looks at Wyatt.

"She's Aiden's sobriety buddy." Wyatt sits and returns to eating. "This is my little sister, Zoe. This is Greer. She'll be here for the next year or so."

"Fascinating." Zoe searches my eyes with hers that I now recognize as similar to Wyatt's. "A girl? You know if I thought you'd hire a girl I would have applied. I could keep Aiden on the straight and sober."

"And what were you doing last night, ZoZo?" Wyatt raises an eyebrow.

"I could be sober for Aiden." She shrugs and her attention returns to me. "I was out clubbing and drinking. The people I party with generally end up at someone's house party. Sometimes I don't leave."

She winks like I should know.

Maybe I should know, but I'm not familiar with the party scene at all. I know it exists. That's the extent of my knowledge. Bristol asked me to join her on more than one occasion but I don't like large crowds.

"Greer doesn't drink." Aiden leans back in his chair. His blue eyes remain on me like he's waiting to see what I'll do. How I'll react.

"Why the hell not? You aren't one of those religious types, are you? The kind who don't drink?" Zoe rears away from me like I'll give her a disease.

"It's not because of religion."

Zoe grins. "Drinking too much is what being young is all about. Partying, sleeping around, waking up at some random's house. How old are you?"

"Twenty-one."

Zoe glares at the guys before arching an eyebrow at me. "And you're qualified for this job how?"

"Because I want her here." Aiden blows out a breath. His words light up my insides. That obsessive need of mine to be wanted is going to lead me straight into trouble like it always does. His gaze flicks to Zoe. "That's all the matters, Zoe."

"Hmph." Zoe pouts at Aiden, but then brushes it off. "Fine. If you like her, I like her."

She turns her gorgeous smile my way and tucks my hair behind my ear. It's oddly intimate since we just met. "You and I are going to be besties. If you're hanging out with this lot, you'll need a friendly face. Give me your number."

She pulls her phone out of her purse.

"You don't have to give her your number." Wyatt rolls his eyes. "Zoe, behave."

I've never been around someone like Zoe before. She just says whatever's on her mind. The guys don't intimidate her at all, while I'm still star-struck just sitting here.

"You can have my number." I don't even have my phone with me. It's still up on my bedside table charging. I rattle off my number and she puts it in her phone.

"This is going to be so much fun. These guys are barely fun, except Roarke."

Roarke chuckles making Zoe smile at him indulgently with a slightly seductive gleam in her eyes. It's gone when she turns back to me. "Just wait until one of their boring parties. Then you'll wish you drank."

She puts her finger in her mouth and pretends to gag.

"Is there a purpose for this visit, ZoZo?" Wyatt looks fed up with his sister already.

She pouts. "Can't I come and see my favorite brother?"

"I'm your only brother." Wyatt doesn't look impressed.

"Do you have any siblings, Greer?" She turns those eyes on me again and it's almost like when Wyatt looks at me, like he wants to understand everything about me.

I shake my head. Foster brothers and sisters don't count. While some of them bonded with each other, I learned to stay away from them.

"See I should have been an only child." Zoe shakes her head at Wyatt.

"I'm seven years older than you, you practically were an only child." Wyatt picks up his bowl and takes it to the kitchen.

"Did you love being an only child, Greer?" Zoe's attention latches on me again. "It must have been fabulous."

My mouth opens to tell her it's complicated.

"That's enough." Aiden stops her. "Zoe, this is only Greer's second day. Maybe leave some mystery in the relationship for later."

Zoe gives Aiden this smile that makes me wonder if she likes him, but I'm the worst at figuring out relationships. "For you, sure. I'm sorry, Greer, we can get to know each other before I dig into your every thought and feeling."

Okay that sounds slightly threatening, but probably only to me. I'm not used to people wanting to know me. After the first few homes, they stopped trying. I don't think I ever tried. Maybe once...

A shudder ripples through me.

"We should go swimming!" Zoe stands and walks to the open door, overlooking the pool.

"Greer doesn't swim." Roarke lounges back as his eyes rake over my sleepwear. "Do you even own a swimsuit, poppet?"

"No." Before I can protest more, Zoe is back at my side, pulling me up.

"You could probably fit in one of mine. I keep a few dozen here for when I show up unannounced." She towers over me and grins. "You're pocket-sized."

"You don't have to let her drag you around, Greer." Wyatt leans his hands on the island, making his arm muscles bulge.

I swallow. "It's fine as long as it's okay with Aiden."

Aiden gives me a soft smile. "We can go swimming, little warrior."

My heart flutters. I could use a break from them for a few minutes, so I don't resist when Zoe drags me downstairs to the laundry room. It's a large room with two sets of washers and dryers. There's a huge table for folding and drawers beneath.

"Okay, let's see what we want to put you in." Zoe pulls open a drawer and takes out swimsuits, placing them on the table. "Strip down. We'll try on a few and see what fits."

The door to the laundry room is propped open. The guys are probably all upstairs, but anyone could walk by.

"I can take them into the bathroom."

Zoe smiles knowingly. "C'mon, Greer. We're both women here."

She pulls off her top and tosses it on the table. Her bralet is lacy.

She shimmies out of her pants, taking her panties with them. "The guys don't come down when I'm here."

She tosses her bra on the table, standing completely naked in front of me. "They worry about accidentally catching me naked."

She shrugs and grabs a black string bikini, tying it on. It barely covers her nipples. Stepping closer, I look at the swimsuits she has out on the table. A few are just different colors of the same one she has on.

I'll be lucky not to slip a nipple in one of those. There's a floral bikini with a little better coverage that I pick up.

"That will look great on you." Zoe leans against the wall. She's this sexy ethereal being. Next to her I feel small and unnoticeable. "You're not shy, are you, Greer?"

The tone. The words. They strike at something I'd rather keep buried away. *No one has to know.*

A shiver runs through me as I lock that down. It's bad enough I cried in front of Roarke yesterday. When Zoe's face shifts to concern, I tug my pajama tank off and put on the bikini top. Smiling, she settles back to watch me. The bikini has buttons down the front but provides more coverage than what Zoe has on.

When I finish buttoning it, my breasts are pressed up and together, showing a lot of cleavage. Zoe walks toward me and grabs a pair of matching bottoms.

"Here you go."

I pull off my shorts and panties and put on the low rise bikini bottoms. Chad liked me bare and it's nice to not have to worry about stray pubes sticking out in a suit like this.

"Well, damn, girl." Zoe grins and takes hold of my hips. "Look at you. You've got a sneaky hot bod."

Heat floods my cheeks. Yeah, I'm not used to someone like Zoe. "Thanks."

Laughing, Zoe winks. "My brother is going to flip his lid. Roarke definitely will too."

She grabs my hand and leads me up the stairs and out into the sunlight. When she releases me, I wrap my arm around my waist and pause until my eyes adjust to the bright sunlight. I'm not tan like Zoe, but I'm not pale either.

Still, I feel self-conscious standing here, trying to get my vision to adjust.

"Hello, mouse." Mason's dark voice wraps around me from behind. "Glad you could come out to play."

A shiver ripples through me. The heat of his skin warms my back, but I don't turn around.

"Greer, come on!" Zoe releases a laugh before a splash sounds.

"We need to have a conversation tonight, little mouse." His fingers graze my hip just above my swimsuit, lighting little trails of fire. He looms over me from behind like a shadow.

I let out a shuddering breath at the flood of heat rushing through me.

"Fuck, Greer." The edge to his voice, as he digs his fingers into my skin, makes me inhale sharply. "I want to do wicked things to your tight little body."

Need, aching and hot, courses through my veins. A whimper escapes me.

"Greer!" Zoe lurches in the water our way.

Mason's hand slips from my skin like he was never there. I suck a breath into my aching lungs. Fuck, he's potent and dangerous. A thrilling combination.

I glance at my skin where his fingers were, surprised I don't find burn marks left behind. Zoe puts her arms on the edge of the pool and looks at me, jerking her head. "Come in, hot stuff. The water is perfect."

Stepping out onto the patio, I see Roarke and Aiden talking off to the side. Both of them turn to watch me. Roarke grins and adjusts his cock. I'm not sure why that heats my insides. Aiden's gaze roams over me slowly, sparking everywhere it touches.

Suddenly, I'm looking at a well-sculpted chest and abs. I swallow and tip my head back to look at Wyatt. He's currently focused on my cleavage.

He makes a tsking noise with his tongue that does sinful things to my insides. "I can see why you hide under oversized clothes, kitten."

Not what I thought he'd say but he has me curious. "Why?"

"You wouldn't have made it past the front door if I'd known that body was hidden beneath those clothes." His heated hazel eyes lift to mine and desire pools hot and thick within me.

"You wouldn't have let me in?" I wasn't looking to seduce anyone. I just needed out of my situation.

"I would have been too focused trying to get you out of your clothes." His large hand curls around the back of my neck.

Cold, wet drops fall on my feet. Surprised, I glance down and see red painted toenails beside ours. Zoe stands next to me. Did she hear what Wyatt said? My cheeks fill with warmth.

"You can play with Greer later, WyWy." She loops her arm through mine and draws me into her side. "I have to go to work in a few hours and I need to make sure we're besties before that."

Wyatt draws his hand away, skating along my nerves. A shiver races down my spine.

"Come on. I know we McBrides are sexy beasts, but you can resist Wyatt." Zoe draws me over to the edge of the pool. My heart trips over itself at the prospect of going into the water.

"I don't know how to swim."

Zoe's eyes light up. "We'll stick to the shallow end then."

I blow out a relieved breath before following her to the steps leading into the pool. There's no demarcation between the shallow and the deep end, but if I stay near here, I should be fine.

Zoe steps down into the pool and backs away with the water covering her hips. "You know I've never had a girl to hang out with here before. We're going to have fun."

"I agree." Roarke's voice is the only warning I have before I'm lifted into the air. His arms wrapped around my waist. His hot body presses against my mostly bare back. Alarm swamps me.

"What are you doing?" I grab his hands as he walks down the steps and sinks us into the pool.

"Wouldn't want you to drown, poppet. You can hold onto me." He turns me in his arms. My hands go to his shoulders to stabilize myself. "Think of me as your personal floaty."

"She'll be fine in the shallow end, Roarke." Zoe sounds exasperated.

The water level is at my waist, but Roarke holds me up so my feet don't touch the bottom. His blue eyes twinkle with mischief as his thumbs make circles on my bare skin.

"I'll be fine. You can put me down." My voice is breathy, but I try to look stern and not scared to death of the water. I know it's irrational, but I can't help it.

Roarke grins. "Nah, poppet. We'll do your first swim lesson."

"I don't think that's a good idea." I'm trying not to let my fear show on my face.

The water shifts behind me and I look back to see Aiden making his way over to us.

"I'll be right here if you need me." Aiden's blue eyes reassure me.

Zoe comes in closer. "We didn't come into the pool for a lesson. We came in to goof around and show off our hot bodies."

"Mission accomplished." Roarke slides his gaze over her and then over me. His heated eyes return to mine. "Swimming lessons or..."

I swallow because I've seen that look in his eyes. Heat blasts through my body.

"Lessons sound good."

He leans into my ear and whispers, "Chicken."

His lips brush my ear as he straightens. My fingers tighten into his shoulders.

"Fine, I'm going to do a few laps." Zoe kicks off the wall and heads to the opposite end of the pool, leaving me with Aiden and Roarke.

"How do you feel about going underwater?" Roarke cocks an eyebrow.

My mind feeds me suffocating darkness, being drug under and held down. I gasp in a breath and focus on Aiden's clear blue eyes.

"You okay, little warrior?" His hand holds my chin.

"Yeah, what the fuck was that, poppet?" Roarke's fingers rub my waist bringing me back to myself.

"It might be more of a fear of water." I try to shrug it off. There are things from my life I purposely forget. A little shiver ripples through me. A whole year that I don't want to remember and that only visits me in the darkness of night.

"How about floating on your back with me holding you?" Roarke smirks. "I get to admire the view and you get more comfortable with the water. Win-win."

Chapter 13

Kiss Me More

Mason

Outside Roarke and Aiden take turns helping Greer float on her back, while I sit at the table with my coffee. In a few hours, the contracts will arrive via courier. I don't want to rush our little mouse, but seeing her in a bathing suit makes it difficult to be good.

She laughs in her husky way and it makes my cock twitch. We need to come up with a plan that works for all of us. Her included, but first I need to make sure she's not going to fuck our lives up.

Leaving behind her tight little body and the shrieks as they play like children in the pool, I head down to my office. Once the door closes no sound from the outside reaches me. I had this room sound-proofed so I could work undisturbed.

Tossing my cell phone on the desk, I pull up my email to see if my contact has gotten back to me.

> Subject: Greer Morrow
> Foster records will take time.
> She moved in with Chad Adams, age 24, six months
> ago. Before that she lived in an apartment with

four others. She works at Brighton Diner in West
Hollywood. She aged out of foster care. No poten-
tial adoption records were found.
Parents: Jonathan and Crystal Morrow – Jonathan
whereabouts unknown, Crystal died of overdose at
age 28. Police report attached.
Sealed juvenile file – will take time to investigate
No police record
Credit moderate

I click on the police report from her mother's overdose and skim over the details. Until the details about ten-year-old Greer come into sharp focus. Fuck.

Someone knocks on my door. I close the email as Zoe struts in, wearing jean shorts and a t-shirt.

"You didn't come out to play." She cocks her hip and pouts at me.

I don't comment. Zoe's been hanging out with us since she was a toddler. She's like the little sister I never wanted. Attention is her drug of choice. When she isn't getting it, she seeks it out in whatever way she can.

Especially when she drinks. She sits across from me, crossing her long slender legs.

"What do we think about Greer?" She swivels in the chair as her hazel eyes meet mine.

"Aiden wanted to hire her. I think she'll do a fine job." And that's all Zoe needs to know.

"You aren't worried about her sneaking into your beds at night?" She arches an eyebrow and does a fake surprised expression. "Because that's what I'd do in her position."

"And that's why we never considered you for the job." I stand, pocket my phone, and gesture to the door. "Let's go, Zoe."

"I just want to make sure you guys are safe." She stands and slides her hand over her curvy ass. Zoe is beautiful and I haven't failed to notice the woman she's grown into. But to me she's still the little girl that followed us around like a puppy.

"We've got it handled."

She opens the door. "As long as you don't fire her, because I don't want to lose my new best friend."

I shake my head as I follow her up to the kitchen. The dishes from this morning are already done and put away. The kitchen looks exactly like it always should. A calmness settles over me. I like things a certain way.

Roarke is chaos embodied. So if Greer can keep up with his mess, she'll make me very happy.

"How are you going to keep Aiden sober when you have a bunch of wine right there?" Zoe gestures to the wine room.

"He doesn't like wine." I start a fresh pot of coffee. The others may not have shit to do until Monday, but I have work to get done. I need to prepare for the shoots we have scheduled for next week. Double check the budget is accurate and that we won't have any overages. And confirm everyone who needs to be on set is aware of that fact.

Zoe hops up to sit on the island. Giving me a sneaky smile, she crosses her long legs. "I don't know. I think it's too much of a temptation. You should give me all your wine and alcohol. Or better yet, let me throw a party and I'll make sure it's all gone by the end."

"No and fuck no." I can't afford the damage a Zoe party would create.

I open the app for the exterior cameras on my phone and check now that everyone is inside. We have a security service, but I like to be aware of what's happening. There's this white car that goes by every day.

Could be paparazzi or just someone from the neighborhood. I've been trying to make out the plates, but with the camera angles, I never get a good image of the plate.

"Fine." Zoe's gaze darts to the stairs. "Everyone went to shower. Entertain me, Mason. I'm bored."

"Go find someone to do, ZoZo. Or I'm sure you could go shopping with mommy's credit card." I pour my coffee and take a sip.

"That's rude." She pouts again which only reminds me that she's still a little girl even at twenty-one. A spoiled, rich one. "I'm waiting to have lunch with my new friend."

The difference between Zoe and Greer is night and day. Greer is a survivor. Zoe's worse day was when her nail broke before prom.

I change to the hallway camera on my phone. Maybe Greer will let me put a security camera in her room.

Greer

Swimming was fun, but exhausting. We all head upstairs to take showers, while Zoe goes downstairs to change. Aiden gives me a wink before he disappears into his room.

Having their hands on my bare skin constantly and brushing against their hard muscles has me heated as I go into my bedroom. I stop at my dresser and pull out shorts, a large t-shirt, panties and a bra. The bathroom is much bigger than the one I shared with Chad.

Even the vanity is extra long, having plenty of space on either side of the sink. I set my clothes down and start the shower.

My thoughts go back to their hands on me. What would it be like to let them touch me even more? I'm curious, but after spending a day in their presence, I'm on edge and horny as hell. I bite my lip.

I could just help myself to take the edge off. It would be easier than walking around a ticking time bomb. They definitely will make me want more. If I'm going to help myself, I want to make sure no one's waiting for me on my bed again.

I open the door to the bedroom and step out. Roarke slips into my bedroom and closes the door. He's dressed in a shirt and shorts and his wet hair has been combed back. His eyes lock on me.

I'm not shocked to find him sneaking into my bedroom. He was on my bed yesterday, which is the reason I decided to check. But he really should stop coming into my bedroom uninvited.

"You shouldn't be in here," I whisper. I'm not sure why I whisper. No one else can hear me.

His lips curve into that notorious grin as he closes the distance between us. "You looked needy, poppet. Like you have an itch to scratch. I wanted to offer my services."

Services? Fuck, he smells divine after showering. The rich scent of sandalwood heats my insides, stirring my lust. His warm hands drop to the waist above my bikini bottoms. I hiss at the contact of his skin against mine as my pussy throbs.

His head dips toward mine.

"Roarke." I need to be firm about this. Boundaries are important.

His mouth takes mine. Yeah, I suck at boundaries. He backs me into the bathroom. When his tongue traces the seam of my lips, I part them and let him in because fuck, he's a good kisser. He lifts me and my ass comes down on the counter.

His mouth trails down my neck. "Do you know how hot you look in this swimsuit, poppet? Your breasts. Your ass. This waist. I've been hard for you since you walked outside."

"Just what every girl wants to hear."

He latches onto my neck, sucking and biting. Moaning, I'm getting wetter by the second here. Maybe it wouldn't hurt to let him rile me up more before I kick him out. Give me more material to get me there.

"Tell me, poppet. Have you ever come with anyone before me?" His fingers toy with the edge of the bikini bottoms as his blue eyes lock on mine.

I could lie, but I hate lying. It's too hard to keep track of. Besides, the multiple times adults lied to me growing up soured me on the experience.

This is personal. No one else knows, so no one would catch me in the lie. This isn't really something someone would figure out, but he asked and I'd rather be honest.

"No."

His eyes light up like he's won the Oscar for best actor. "We don't have to fuck, but I want to make you come again. May I do that, poppet?"

I bite my lip. I was just going to help myself get there anyway. If I had a toy, I'd use that. This wouldn't be much different than using a toy. The orgasm he gave me yesterday was amazing, but maybe it was a fluke. Maybe with Chad standing outside the door throwing a tantrum made it hotter.

Roarke kisses the throbbing pulse in my neck and heat curls inside me. But if it wasn't a fluke...

"Say I can make you come, poppet." His hand strokes between my legs over the swimsuit, pressing against my entrance.

I groan at the flood of need inside me. "Okay."

He grins and lifts me down off the counter. Before I can move around him to go to the bed, he slides my bottoms off and lifts me back to sit on the counter beside the sink.

"Later we'll do this on a bed." He presses me back to lean against the mirror and lifts my feet to the counter, spreading me wide, putting me on display. Fuck, I'm so wet already and he's barely touched me. His gaze drops to my pussy. "Fuck, poppet. You have the prettiest pussy."

Heat floods my face. I don't think anyone's ever told me that before.

He drops to kneel between my legs and pushes my knees out to the sides even more. His mouth descends on me, licking straight up my slit. A little cry leaves my lips at how good that feels.

He smiles against my pussy before using his tongue to toy with my clit. All my protests dissolve with each swipe of his tongue. A couple of guys have gone down on me, but they were nothing like Roarke. He takes his time, exploring every inch, paying extra attention when my breath hitches or I make a noise.

"You taste so fucking good." His mouth closes over my clit, sucking, as he thrusts two fingers deep inside me.

"Ah, fuck!" Pleasure bursts through me. My eyes open and movement makes me realize the bathroom door is still open.

Wyatt leans against the doorframe, hands in his shorts pockets. His heated gaze takes in everything. Every inch of me lights on fire as if his gaze is a physical caress. "You really should remember to lock that door, kitten."

My temperature ratchets up a thousand degrees. I'm riding the edge already, but when Wyatt wets his lips , the fire is ready to consume me.

"Or don't." Roarke winks at me before he goes back to licking and sucking and making me squirm. His thick fingers thrust in and out slowly, pushing me higher and higher.

"Unbutton your top, kitten." Wyatt's hazel eyes don't leave mine.

I do as he asks, slowly opening my bikini top, while panting at what Roarke is doing between my legs. It doesn't part, but my breasts are even more on display.

"Fuck, you're a good girl, aren't you, kitten?" Wyatt licks his lips as Roarke curls his fingers inside me. I shatter into a million pieces, biting my lip on a moan.

My eyes lock with Wyatt's as I ride the wave of my orgasm. I expect Roarke to stop. Instead, Roarke keeps licking and sucking and thrusting his fingers in and out until I cry out as another release crests on top of that one, dragging me into shaking ecstasy.

My legs tremble as he eases me down. My breasts are smooshed together in the top. I drop my gaze to Roarke. He leans back, sliding his fingers slowly in and out of me as my pussy flutters around them. Wyatt's gaze follows Roarke's fingers. Aftershocks pulse with every thrust.

Uh, does this count as a threesome or just voyeurism? Some part of me thinks I should be mortified by this, but instead, my insides are combusting. I don't think I know what I'm doing anymore. But I know I want more.

"You know it could just be me," Roarke says, drawing his fingers out of me and licking my slick off his fingers. I whimper at the empty feeling. "After all, I'm famous and that alone gets some women off. The thrill of me."

"What?" My brain isn't fully functioning yet. I don't think I've ever come twice in a row like that. Not even by myself.

"She's only orgasmed with you?" Wyatt runs his fingers over his lips and I remember how soft and firm they were against mine. Sparks ignite in my blood.

"We should put it to a test. Maybe she can only come with me." Grinning, Roarke grabs a towel to wipe his mouth. "Maybe you're all mine, poppet."

A shiver of awareness rips through me. I need to be wanted. To have him claim me, fuck, it's like the sweetest drug. I want more. I want to be his.

Wyatt steps into the bathroom. His hand sweeps beneath my neck. "What do you think, kitten? Want to test the theory? Do you want me to make you come?"

I swallow and look into Roarke's eager eyes. His hand strokes over his erection straining in his pants. He wants this almost as much as I do.

"Yes." My voice is breathless as Wyatt's hazel eyes darken. He looms over me, so tall.

When he smiles and lowers his face toward mine, my breath catches. He takes my mouth, sliding his tongue against mine, heating my blood to boiling. His hand lifts my breast out of the swimsuit. His thumb sweeps over my tightened tip. Once, twice, three times. I gasp as he trails kisses down my neck, leaving a line of fire in his wake.

His kisses keep moving down over the swell of my breast until his mouth closes over my nipple and sucks on it. At the same time, his fingers thrust into my pussy, deep and stretching. I moan at the overwhelming rush.

"She's so fucking tight." Roarke sits against the wall. He unbuttons his pants and releases his cock. "Squeezing all around my fingers. Fuck, poppet, I can't wait to have you squeeze around my cock."

My pussy pulses around Wyatt's fingers. I've seen Roarke's cock on screen, but it seems even larger in real life. He strokes his hand down it and I want to touch him, feel the smooth skin under my palm, taste his salty cum on my tongue.

When I wet my lips, Roarke groans.

Wyatt's tongue flicks my nipple as he thrusts his fingers in and out of my pussy, pushing me closer and closer to the edge. That warm beach smell surrounds me as his hair tickles my chin. My gaze stays on Roarke's hand slowly working his cock.

Leaving my nipple with a kiss, Wyatt lowers to his knee. He spreads me obscenely wide, pushing my knees out, and stares at my wet, glistening pussy. Anticipation swells inside me. I bite my lip waiting, wanting, aching.

When he leans in, my breath catches, and he presses his tongue inside my entrance. Moaning, I arch against his mouth. Fuck, I've never felt like this in my life. I'm burning for more.

These men are giving me pleasure without taking it from me. It's heady.

My gaze falls on Roarke's hard cock and his hand that pumps it. Wyatt's tongue explores before he sucks on my clit. He thrusts his two fingers back inside me before stretching me to slide in a third.

"Wyatt!" I can't stop the wave that crashes over me, taking me under as he thrusts his fingers deep inside me. I scramble to get away from the sensation as it becomes too much again, but his hand on my hip keeps me under his onslaught.

"Sweet poppet, let go." Roarke's voice draws me as my heart races.

Wyatt tips me over the edge again, making me fly. My pussy gushes my release as my moan fills the air. Roarke groans as he comes. His cum falls on his hand, making me want to taste it. My pussy convulses around Wyatt's fingers as he holds them inside. He lifts his glistening mouth and smiles knowingly. His hazel eyes sparkle.

"Not just you, Roarke." Wyatt glances over, but doesn't seem disturbed by Roarke jacking off behind him.

Roarke takes the towel and wipes his cock off. He stands and offers me his hand with his cum on it. "I'm clean, poppet. Taste it."

Wyatt's fingers pump inside me as I hold Roarke's gaze and lick his cum from his finger. I give a little shiver at the salty taste. Needing more, I take hold of his wrist and clean his hand, licking and sucking on his fingers.

"Fuck me." Wyatt covers my pussy with his mouth and sucks.

I moan as I come again, a small wave hits me and I just want to curl up and sleep. He slips his fingers from me and licks my slick from them.

"So fucking sweet."

Roarke helps me stand before he takes off my swim top. I'm sure my eyes are hooded. They could ask me to do anything right now and I would. I'm not even sure I'd regret it.

Wyatt draws my back against his front, and I gladly give him my weight. My knees try to give out. My legs tremble, barely able to support me. His hand strokes over my stomach and up to cup my breast. I sigh softly. I could get used to this.

Roarke strips. Every inch of him hard and sculpted muscle. He takes my hand and brings me into the shower. For a second, I'm confused. I assumed he'd fuck me, after all he's still hard.

Instead, Roarke lathers the soap in his hands before rubbing it all over my body. Curious, I tentatively reach out to touch his pecs. When he doesn't tell me to stop, I follow the hills and valleys of his body, mesmerized by the way the muscles tense, twitch, and relax beneath my fingertips. His skin is hot to the touch, making me want to lean into his heat.

His slippery hand slides between my legs and my gaze darts up to his.

"Just being thorough, poppet." He grins and spins me to face the wall, trailing his hands over my ass, sliding one between my ass cheeks. "Tell me has anyone fucked your ass."

I lean my forehead against the tile as his soapy fingers stroke around my asshole, adding kindling to the raging fire within.

"No," I whisper.

He pulls my back flush against his front. His hard cock presses into my soft flesh. "Good."

He rinses me and then shampoos and conditions my hair. Turning off the shower, he opens the door and Wyatt holds a towel for me. My cheeks burn as I realize I'm naked with these two men. They both went down on me and made me come multiple times, while I've done nothing in return. It's always been expected.

Wyatt tips my chin up and studies my eyes. "What's wrong, kitten?"

"You didn't..." My gaze drops to his erection.

"This wasn't about me, kitten. Or even Roarke." He rubs the towel over me. "This was for you. If you don't want to take it any further, that's up to you. But right now, I'm sure you've got a lot on your mind. So let's go have lunch with my sister."

My eyes widen and my mouth forms an O. "Your sister! Zoe. Shit."

I completely forgot she was waiting for me for lunch. What a shit friend she must think I am? I grab my panties and pull them on, followed by my bra.

"She'll wait, kitten." Wyatt leans against the counter they just ate me out on.

My brain skids to a halt. Fuck, two guys just went down on me. I wanted it. Was eager for it. I want it to happen again. Maybe Mary was right about me.

I shake myself out of the past. I don't live in there anymore. I live in the here and now. She's not here. None of them are. But I'm here with these men.

Roarke stops beside me fully dressed and kisses the top of my head. "Everything's good, poppet. See you downstairs."

He smacks my ass before laughing on his way out of the bathroom.

"Zoe will bug Mason and Aiden until we come down." Wyatt's hazel eyes meet mine.

"I don't want to make her mad at me." I brush through my hair anxiously. What if she decides she doesn't want to be my friend? What if she starts treating me like some of the girls at my foster families or at school?

"Hey." Wyatt plucks the brush from my hand. He moves behind me and lifts my hair before smoothing the brush through the strands. "Zoe is cool. She's okay if you take a little longer. At some point you'll have to wait for her to get ready. See how long she expects you to wait and you won't feel so bad."

He finishes and sets the brush down. I'm still staring at him in the mirror.

"You just brushed my hair." I can't disguise the awe in my voice. I can't remember the last time someone brushed my hair.

He shrugs. "I had a much younger sister and an overworked mother who needed help. You want any kind of braid. I'm your man."

His grin makes my heart feel funny. I turn and put my arms around his waist, squeezing quickly before releasing.

"What was that for?" He rubs my jawline, tipping my face up to search my eyes. That's too much for me and I duck my head.

"Thank you." I look at the floor because it's easier. "Thank you for helping me get ready."

He plucks the t-shirt and shorts from the counter. "Not quite ready."

Smiling, I finish dressing. I don't know what any of this means, but I know I feel different. Almost lighter, even if I'm confused. How could I want more than one guy? How could I make a connection with one guy while another was making my toes curl?

How could I want to do it all over again?

Chapter 14

T-Shirt

Greer

I chop vegetables and chicken for toppings and toss a salad together for lunch.

"Mmm, see now I could get used to this." Zoe waves her fork in the air. "Someone to fix me food all day. You sure you want to work for these smelly guys. You could come live with me and we could party it up."

My cheeks flush as I glance at Aiden. He gives me an encouraging smile. Heat scorches my cheeks. He's such a nice guy, but will he really be okay with what happened in my bathroom? He said he's attracted to me, but he really hasn't made any moves.

"Give it up, ZoZo. Greer is ours. Find your own personal assistant." Wyatt winks. But his words make a funny feeling start in my chest, like a small candle is lit in the darkness.

"Maybe I will. Maybe I'll get myself a guy with a sneaky hot bod like Greer." Zoe tugs at the end of my oversized shirt.

"It's comfortable." I shrug. And it keeps most guys at bay. While I want to be wanted, I don't want attention like that either.

"So am I, darling. You and I need to go shopping. Pronto. Maybe something a little less hobo chic?" She squints her hazel eyes. "At least upgrade to—I don't know... What's a store that's slightly better that poor people go to?"

"Zoe, enough." Wyatt gives her a warning look, but I'm not sure what happens if she keeps pushing. After all, I don't mind. I am poor. I make ends meet, but I don't have extra money needing to be spent. I don't want Wyatt to punish her over me.

I've seen foster brothers and sisters fight. Most of them hid it from the foster parents. That's one of the reasons I stayed away from them.

Zoe sticks her tongue out. "I'm just saying, Greer could have a little more fashion sense, especially if she's going to hang out with you lot."

She turns and puts her hand over mine on the table. Her hazel eyes are warm with her eyebrows knitted. "Most people work on the production and don't give a fuck what you're wearing, but the second you step out with one of these hotties, your picture will be everywhere. And we don't need you to be seen as a hot mess."

That's something I hadn't considered. Maybe a shopping trip would be a good idea.

"Don't worry about that." Mason scrolls through his phone as he eats. I didn't know he was paying attention. His blue eyes meet mine. "I'll make sure she's dressed appropriately before going outside of the house, but in here, she can wear whatever she wants."

His gaze drops to his phone and I can breathe again. I cock my head to the side. What does he mean that he'll make sure I'm dressed appropriately?

Zoe drops the subject about buying me new clothes. We finish lunch. While I'm cleaning up the lunch dishes, Zoe hops up on the counter next to me.

"We should go out sometime."

"I don't think that's a good idea." I don't run in the crowds Zoe seems to. I wouldn't be able to keep up.

She tips her head. "Why not? We're around the same age. You could even wear some of my clothes. Maybe get laid since that's not likely to happen around here."

My cheeks get warm as I avoid her eyes. "My ex and I just broke up."

Not that I give two shits about him. I was over him before we were even finished.

"Man, that sucks." Zoe grins. "All the more reason to get you back under someone else."

My mouth opens.

"Are you trying to convince my poppet to find someone to fuck?" Roarke leans against the counter behind me. My insides go soft and warm at his voice.

"It's not like any of you will fuck the hired help." Zoe laughs like the idea is ludicrous. "Besides you all are almost thirty. Greer needs a young man to really pound her good."

She pushes her fist against my shoulder. Thankfully, she doesn't have a clue about what happened earlier in my bathroom.

"You don't think I could give her a good pounding." There's laughter in Roarke's voice, but a little hint of promise too.

I glance over my shoulder. He's smiling when he gives me a wink. I'm so out of my league here.

Finishing loading the dishwasher, I set it to run.

"Sure, Roarke. With your tiny dick, you could probably pound her a few centimeters." Zoe rolls her eyes. At my stunned look, she uses her hand to block her mouth from Roarke, but then says in a regular voice, "Never meet your heroes, Greer. That one scene in the movie? Body double."

She holds her fingers about an inch apart and shakes her head with a fake frown. Zoe straightens and meets Roarke's amused eyes.

"Tiny dick was Roarke's nickname all through high school." She jumps off the counter and puts her arm around me. "Friends don't let friends fuck guys with little wieners."

I laugh, because somewhere along the way she got some misinformation. Roarke's laughing eyes meet mine as Zoe navigates me to the couches and pulls me to sit beside her.

"Okay, so what kind of guys do you like?" Zoe stretches. Her body one long line. She's the kind of woman these guys are used to fucking. So why are they interested in me?

"Yeah, poppet. The ex asshole couldn't have been your type." Roarke sits in the chair opposite us.

"You know him?" She tips her head like that doesn't make sense.

"He's a special kind of douchebag." He rubs his jaw. "Probably right up your alley, ZoZo."

Her eyes narrow. "Not every guy I date is an asshole."

Roarke holds up his fist and with every name pops up a finger. "Brandon, Alexi, Marcus, Chet—"

"Chet wasn't an asshole."

"Did he ever pay when you went out?"

Zoe's lips tighten.

"I rest my case. Asshole." Roarke puts his hand down.

"We aren't talking about me. We're talking about Greer." She flashes me a smile. "Do you have a type?"

I shrug. "I don't really know."

"How many boyfriends have you had?" She leans back as she looks me over.

I shrug again. "Dating? A couple. Hanging out? A few."

"Sex?" Roarke asks leaning forward with his hands clasped between his knees. His large shoulders tug the shirt tightly, making me swallow hard as I remember his naked wet body rubbing against mine in the shower.

"Yeah, that's not personal at all." Zoe rolls her eyes. "Out with it, bestie. How many dudes have you done the deed with?"

My mouth opens and closes as I think about the bathroom. Does that count? "What counts?"

Roarke grins, but I ignore his smug smile. Zoe taps her fingers on her lips.

"Hmm. We'll go old school. Dick in pussy or ass." Zoe grins.

My face heats. "Five."

"See this is why we need to get you out of this house." She turns to Roarke. "Don't you agree? I mean, five is like sad. You can't even know what you like with only five guys."

Yeah, I'm not in Zoe's league either. I know she'll figure it out and drop me. Most girls do.

"Five is plenty." Roarke shrugs and his gaze stays fixed on Zoe. "Especially when you are used to monogamy. Maybe she's particular about who she has sex with. Nothing wrong with that."

She turns and looks me up and down. "Okay. Okay. I could see that. But that doesn't mean she shouldn't get back out there."

A buzz comes from Zoe's phone. She glances at the screen and rolls her eyes.

"Fuck, I hate work." She scoots close to me and pulls me into her arms. "All right, bestie. I'll text. If I lose this job, Mom's threatened to turn off my credit cards again."

She hugs me and waits for me to hug her back before she backs up and tucks my hair behind my ear. Her hazel eyes focus on me and it's intense.

"I still want to get you out of here some night. But get comfortable and keep these guys in line." She sticks her tongue out at Roarke as she stands. "WyWy, I'm leaving," she yells.

His footsteps are on the stairs and then he holds out his arms. She rushes across the room and flings herself into him. "Be good, ZoZo."

"You too."

He walks her out of our sight. The door opens and closes and their voices go away. Roarke clears his throat, getting my attention.

"I don't have a tiny penis." He smirks. "It was a joke in high school, but Wyatt didn't want his little sister trying to get with me either."

"Umm, I know you don't." I squirm in my chair, thinking of his hand stroking his thick cock. It's bigger than any guy I've been with in the past.

"Want to almost double your number, poppet?" Roarke winks. Four guys. Damn. Just thinking about it winds me up.

Standing, I gesture toward the kitchen. "I have chores I need to do."

"Running away?"

Yes, I am.

An hour later, I hesitate outside of Mason's office. I need some clarification and I know he'll give it to me, but I don't want to disrupt his work.

Taking a deep breath, I knock on the door.

"Come in." His low voice calls out.

"Hey, Greer." Aiden walks toward me. He went to work out after lunch in the gym down here. His hair is damp like he took a shower. "What are you up to?"

I point to the door but before I can say anything, it opens.

"What?" Mason's voice is tinged with anger and I step back. He scrubs his face before he seems to soften. "What do you need, mouse?"

My gaze darts from Aiden to Mason. I'm used to dealing with angry men, but it still makes me nervous. Another reminder that I don't know these men. I don't know what they do behind closed doors.

"I—" I draw in a breath and straighten to my full height. This is for my job that they hired me for. "I need some clarification on some of the chores."

Mason glances at Aiden before disappearing into his office. Aiden's hand settles on my low back and he guides me into the office before shutting the door. Mason sits behind a large desk. He has multiple monitors with pages of script, artwork and a few shows playing in the background with the sound off.

"I'm sorry if I was harsh. I don't like to be disturbed while I'm working." He slides a hand through his dark hair and his blue eyes pin me in place.

Aiden leads me to the chair before sitting next to me.

"Go on, little warrior," he encourages.

"Uh..." I glance at Aiden, worried that he'll think I'm going behind his back, but I'll start with something easy. "The laundry. Is there a specific place I get it from? How often should it be done? Do I need to separate the clothes? And do I put them away and where?"

"Our rooms. Aiden and I have hampers in our closets. Roarke's floor is his hamper along with his closet and bathroom floor. Wyatt brings his down to the laundry room. With Roarke, every day you should pick it up, but you can put it in his hamper. Pick a rotation for how you do it, but I wouldn't mix our clothes, which will make the sorting easier. In our closets and drawers. We can each show you our organization system. For Roarke, create your own. He'll figure it out."

I nod. Okay, one thing down. I draw in a breath.

"Can you show me where all the alcohol and drugs are stored throughout the house?"

Aiden's gaze burns into me, but I don't look at him. When his hand slides under mine and gently threads our fingers together, I release my breath.

"That's a good idea, little warrior."

When I face him, he smiles and the tension eases from squeezing my gut. He knows why I'm asking and it doesn't bother him. Mom used to get furious when I hid her stuff. She wasn't my mom when that happened. A little shudder runs through me and I squeeze Aiden's hand.

"Of course. The liquor is in a cabinet. I hold the only key, but we should check to make sure that only over the counter drugs are accessible." Mason doesn't lift his gaze from me. His attention makes me squirm in my chair. "Anything else?"

My cheeks heat, should I tell them about the other two? "Are we going to talk tonight?"

Mason's lips tip into a smile. "The documents have been couriered over. The NDA. The contract. I'll need your banking information."

"Of course." Relief pours through me. That's stuff I can handle.

Mason leans forward putting his elbows on his desk. His piercing gaze holds mine. "Will you explain something to me, mouse?"

I nod, but swallow down my fear.

"This afternoon. Roarke and Wyatt were in your room..."

It's not a question, but my heart quickens. I nod jerkily.

"While you took your shower..."

I can't break our eye contact, but Aiden doesn't snatch his hand away from me like I'm damaged goods.

"Breathe, Greer." Aiden's voice is gentle.

I suck a breath into my starving lungs. Mason cocks his eyebrow, waiting for me to reply.

"Yes," I say softly, wondering if I'll get in trouble.

"Tell me what happened." Leaning back, Mason steeples his fingers against his lips. "Don't leave out any details."

I haven't even kissed either of these men. Awareness falls over me like a summer rain storm, hot and heavy.

"I was getting ready to take a shower." I glance at Aiden and he gives me an encouraging smile. Fuck, I'm not sure if this is going to hurt them. Hurt him. His arms were so warm around me this morning. I blow out a breath.

Is it cheating? If everyone is okay with it?

"What happened next, mouse?" Mason's voice is stern and something in me responds to the authority in his tone.

"Roarke came into my room. I told him he should leave, but he kissed me and backed me into the bathroom." Even the tips of my ears feel hot. I'm sure my face is mottled with redness. The urge to let my hair hide me is right there.

"Keep going."

I bite my lip and look at my hand in Aiden's. His long fingers engulf my small hand. I meet Aiden's curious eyes. This morning there hadn't been any jealousy. Even when the others kissed me.

Maybe they play these games all the time. Maybe I'm not special at all.

Maybe I should just enjoy the ride. My heart clatters against my chest.

"Uh, Roarke asked if he could help me." I draw in a breath, needing to find some courage.

"Help with what?" Mason's voice draws me back to him.

"Help me come," I admit. Heat flares in his blue eyes.

"How?"

That spark of defiance rears its head. "Do you want just the summary or play by play?"

Mason leans forward and his smile should have warned me. Instead, it makes my toes curl and my already damp panties, soaking wet. "Show me."

My breath catches. Fuck. Do I really want to go there? I've only spent twenty-four hours with these guys and I've slept with one of them, kissed two of them, had two go down on me, and now... Does he want me to... What?

"Uh, I can't do what they did." I'm sure my face and neck are mottled with blotchy red.

"Use your hands and your words, mouse." Mason smirks. "I want to see what they did to you."

Fuck. I take a deep breath and sneak a glance at Aiden. He releases my hand and gestures for me to continue with a nod of his head.

"Roarke kissed me—"

"Touch your lips."

My gaze locks with Mason's unyielding one. My trembling hand touches my lips and I suck in a harsh breath. Mason's gaze drops for a moment to them. My nipples tighten as if he's the one kissing me.

Focusing, I try to think what happened in what order. "Then he took off my bikini bottoms and lifted me onto the counter."

Mason stands and my eyes widen as he walks around his desk. Casually, he clears the desk before me and Aiden. He holds his hand out and I automatically take it. He pulls me to standing and sets me in front of him with my back to the desk.

"Show us, mouse." Mason looms over me.

"You want me to...?" I nibble on my lip.

"Take off your shorts and panties."

Oh, fuck. I search his eyes. He seems harsh and unyielding, but if I told him no, would he back off? Consent seems important to him. I haven't signed the NDA, so he wouldn't do this if he wasn't sure I'm okay with it.

Am I okay with getting half naked in front of these two men? An ache pulses inside me as an answer. I want to. I really want to. I can't believe I'm going to do this.

Unsnapping my shorts, I let them drop to my ankles. My eyes never leave Mason's as I reach below my t-shirt and shimmy out of my panties, letting them fall to the floor. Technically, I'm not exposed with my oversized t-shirt on, but it feels decadent to be standing before these two powerhouses of man in nothing but a t-shirt.

Mason grabs my waist and for a moment I panic, but he sets me on the desk and then sits in the chair I was in. My eyes widen as the two men's eyes trail over me. I'm so conscious of my naked lower half barely covered by the t-shirt.

I press my thighs together against the ache pulsing there.

"Then what happened, mouse?"

Oh, shit. My heart races, but the curious lust I see in both their eyes feeds me. They want me. They want me to touch myself for them. This is making me even more aroused than earlier.

"He pushed me back." I lean back bracing my hands on Mason's desk. The wood is solid beneath me. I want to do this and maybe that's the most fucked up thing. Not that they're asking me to, but that I want to. I've never wanted anything like this before in my life.

But for them...

"And had me put my feet on the counter." I lift my feet and open myself up to their view. They can see my pussy and how wet I am. Some of the embarrassment fades at their soft inhale of breath.

"He went down on me. As I was about to come, I noticed Wyatt watching in the doorway." My pussy aches with the memory.

"She came twice on Roarke's fingers and face." At Wyatt's voice, my gaze jerks to the door. He leans against the doorframe. "Showing off, kitten?"

Chapter 15

Wow

Greer

"She was telling us what happened in her bathroom." Mason's gaze flicks from my eyes to my pussy. "But now that you're here, we can let her off the hook and you can just give us a demonstration."

My eyes widen. Wyatt's hazel eyes glint with mischief. He smirks and rubs his lips with two fingers.

"It'd be my pleasure."

I'm not sure if they can tell but I just got even wetter.

"I asked her to unbutton her top." Wyatt walks over to me. "Pretty sure we can get the same effect without this shirt."

I blink up at him as he steps between my legs and slides his hand on my back beneath my t-shirt.

"Arms up, kitten." He effortlessly holds me as I lift my arms. With one hand, he takes off my t-shirt, leaving me in my bra. "Put your arms back."

I do as he says. My breathing is chaotic. When he steps away, the others can see me. Almost all of me.

"Apparently, our kitten never had orgasms with someone else, so Roarke was her first." His words don't seem to phase the others. But all three men have visible erections. The temptation to lay back on this desk and let them take me one after the other floats through me like a siren's song. Just the thought of it has me aching with need.

"He wondered if it was just him. So I volunteered to test that theory."

My eyes clash with his hazel ones. The heat within nearly scorches me.

"Interesting." Mason draws my helpless gaze back to him. "Then what?"

"While I'm great with words on paper, I prefer to show not tell." Wyatt touches my knee and it's like sparks igniting under my skin.

I whimper because I know exactly what he'll do and it won't fail to get me off.

"Go right ahead." Mason smirks, gesturing to my pussy.

Aiden has been quiet, but I feel his presence more than the others. I want his mouth on me. I want all their mouths on me.

Wyatt steps between my legs again and slides his hand around the back of my neck. Our eyes lock and he waits a moment, like he wants me to acknowledge it's him that's going to do this to me.

Leaning in, he takes my mouth. I open beneath him, eager for his touch. His hand cups my breast and I moan. When he lifts his lips, his eyes are darkened. "Things are a little different. Roarke was stroking his cock while I teased her. But it would be good to know if she needs Roarke as stimuli to make her come."

"It may be the audience that gets her off." Aiden's voice arouses me. "We'll definitely need to experiment more."

My lips part as I pant in need with Wyatt hovering over me. He takes my nipple in his hot mouth. This needy noise releases in the back of my throat as I arch into him, pushing more of my breast into his mouth.

He licks and sucks, making those noises fill the room. I can't even be embarrassed. I'm too turned on. His fingers slide over my clit and he moves his body a little to the side, making me aware that both the other men can see his fingers on my pussy.

When he slips a finger into me, he sucks a little harder.

"Ah, fuck." My head falls back as desire consumes me.

"So fucking wet, kitten." He slides a second finger along his first, pressing them both deep inside me. The slick sound of his fingers thrusting in and out make me want to hide and glorify in what he's doing at the same time.

Wyatt kneels between my legs and latches onto my clit with his mouth. I cry out as wave after wave of ecstasy flows over me. My pussy convulses around his finger as I come.

"No Roarke needed." Mason's voice sends an aftershock through me, but Wyatt doesn't let up.

He adds a third finger as his tongue circles my clit. My breath catches as I fall over the edge again, coming in a rush of fluid onto his hand. Slowly, he eases me down and draws his fingers out of me, before kissing my pussy.

My breath shudders in and out of my lungs. Fuck, I could get used to that.

Standing, Wyatt kisses me. I can taste myself on his tongue, but I don't shy away from the kiss.

"You did well, kitten," he says so only I can hear.

When he steps back, he adjusts his cock. "While I went down on her, she watched Roarke stroke himself off and afterwards, licked his cum off his hand. Then Roarke showered with her and I dried her off."

He leans back against the wall, his hard cock pressing against his shorts. My pussy flutters, imagining how thick he'd be inside me.

Mason stands. "May I, mouse?"

I bite my lip, having no idea what he's asking for. But right now, I'd let him do just about anything to me. I nod, watching his every move as anticipation swells again.

His finger touches my wet pussy and I exhale sharply.

"Soft and wet. Do you desire us, mouse?"

It's not even a question. Not to me. These men are attractive, but there's something deeper that makes me want them all. Maybe it's that broken piece of me that will never truly be whole. Maybe I'm just searching for something to hold onto for a little while.

"Yes, sir." I remember the kitchen yesterday. How he wanted me to call him sir.

He circles my clit with his finger before drawing a line with the tip down to my entrance. "Are you considering what we want?"

His finger slides into me, taking my breath away. The temptation to rock against his finger is so fucking hard to resist, but I do. "I don't know what you want of me."

"Hmm." He begins to slide his finger in and out slowly, just the one finger over and over as he watches. "I have a packet of documents for you to look over. I've included a separate list. Before we can truly continue this, we need information."

"What kind of information?" My voice is breathier than normal.

He adds a second finger, making me moan at the stretch. His eyes seem uninterested in what he's doing to me. If it weren't for the outline of his hard cock in his pants and the darkening of his light eyes, I might believe he's indifferent.

"Before we can go forward with a sexual arrangement, we need to know your limits and what you're comfortable with."

My legs tremble with the need to rock into his achingly slow fingers.

"Your current health status." His gaze drops to my pussy and his other fingers part my folds and slide around my clit. "Have you been tested recently, mouse?"

I nod, because I'm so close to coming.

"When was the last time you were tested?" He curls his fingers inside me.

"Ah." I arch as he hits something inside me that makes me see stars. I'm not coming, but fuck that feels good.

"Come on, mouse. Focus." He slides his fingers over my clit. "When?"

"Last month and then last week." I pant as he rewards me with his finger pressing on my clit. The words come out in a rush. "Chad and I always used condoms, but he cheated on me. So one test when we stopped having sex and later when it had been enough time to make sure the test was accurate."

"Hmm." His fingers slide lazily in and out of my core, giving me friction, but not enough. "Are you on birth control, mouse?"

"Yes." Since I was fifteen.

"Do you like it when someone watches you being fucked?"

My body flushes with heat. "I haven't ever had anyone watch me be fucked."

He removes his finger from my clit and I whimper. His hand smacks my ass and I moan because it's a little burst of pain. But with his fingers buried inside me, it felt really fucking good.

"Semantics, mouse. Do you like being a dirty whore that everyone gets off on watching? Or would you rather be a good girl who likes her men to watch each other take her?"

Crying out, I come all over his fingers. His words were the push I needed over the edge. I'm not sure which one tipped me over. The degradation or the praise or maybe both.

He pulls his fingers out and waits for my dazed eyes to meet his. He places his fingers on my lips. "Clean them."

Keeping my eyes on his, I part my lips and he thrusts his fingers inside. I suck and lick them as little aftershocks trip in my pussy. Maybe I am a dirty little whore. He hasn't even kissed me yet, but he's finger fucked me.

He draws his fingers out of my mouth and pulls a handkerchief from his pocket, wiping them off. Pocketing the cloth, he takes my legs and lowers them over the edge of the desk before lifting me down to stand before him.

With efficient movements, he straightens the cup on my bra. Wyatt hands him my t-shirt that Mason draws on over my head. I feel like a doll as I stare at him with wide eyes. Part of me is still reconciling what I just did. Three guys have touched me and brought me to orgasm today. A fourth watched.

Wyatt hands him my panties and shorts. Mason holds them out for me to step into and finishes dressing me.

"Do you have any other questions, mouse?"

I shake my head. Even if I did, I can't remember them. I barely remember why I came in here.

"I'll show you around after work, until then..." He looks at Aiden. "Take a nap. I'm sure it's been a while since you've slept well, Aiden."

Aiden stands behind me and puts his hands on my shoulders. "Let's go, little warrior. You've earned it."

Wyatt kisses the top of my head as Aiden ushers me out into the hallway. Before I know it, I'm in Aiden's bedroom. He closes the door as I take in the light colored walls. His orange cologne is strong in here. It smells comforting.

His king bed faces the window with the ocean. He walks over and cracks a side window open. The sound of waves crashing fills the room. When he draws the curtains closed, the room darkens.

I shiver slightly at how completely the room closes in on me.

"We have night shoots and sleep during the day occasionally." His voice warms me. His hand on the small of my back guides me to the side of the bed.

"I'm going to undress down to my underwear. Feel free to get as comfortable as you want." He fades into the blackness again until a dim light comes on in the bathroom. His silhouette blocks some of it.

"To freshen up." He walks to the edge of the bed and strips off his shirt with one hand. He's not thick like Roarke or as cut as Wyatt, but Aiden's chest is defined and solid.

I finally breathe in a gasp of air. This whole day has been surreal. We both fell asleep downstairs in the middle of the night. Aiden must be exhausted, but he doesn't show it. If he needs me to sleep, who am I to tell him no?

I'm literally here to help him in any way I can. I go into the bathroom as he drags his belt out of his shorts. After taking care of clean up, I take my shorts off, fold them, and set them on the counter.

When I open the door, Aiden is in the bed, lying on his back. His eyes are open. I turn out the light and shut the door before edging around the bed to the other side. If I thought my bed was comfortable, this mattress is next level dreamy.

"I'm not sure how you don't immediately fall asleep on this." I snuggle down under the covers.

His chuckle sparks something low and hungry inside me. He hasn't kissed me. Hasn't touched me intimately. But I want him to.

But I don't want to derail his recovery.

"Stop thinking so much and come here, little warrior." He holds out his arm and I don't hesitate to take his hand. He draws me closer.

"I don't want to mess things up for you."

He settles me against him under the crook of his arm and pushes my head down onto his warm pec. "You won't. You may be in charge of keeping me clean, but it's still my responsibility, not yours."

Capturing my knee, he draws it over his. My hand rests over his solid heartbeat and I release a sigh.

"You can say no to them if you want." His hand brushes over my hair, soothing me.

"Do you want me to say no to them?"

He chuckles. "I don't know. It's pretty hot watching them make you come."

I squirm against his side.

"Did you like it?" he asks.

The darkness blankets us while the ocean drowns out all the other noises, making me feel isolated with just him.

"I did." I can admit that, especially to him. I stifle a yawn.

"Good." His word follows me into sleep.

I wake to a tickle on my forehead and a thigh pressed against my pussy. His breath brushes over my lips. When I open my eyes, I can barely make out the structure of Aiden's cheek bones and nose in the darkness. His hair against my forehead is what woke me again.

We're curled together, even on this huge bed, like we can't get close enough to each other, especially in sleep. I release the breath I'm holding and trace my hand along his chiseled jaw line.

Aiden Clyborne sleeps with me. Roarke Flynn has given me multiple orgasms. That would be amazing to me by itself, but add in Wyatt and Mason and I'm in a tailspin.

My need to be wanted is fulfilled, but the fear lingers in the back of my mind. The fear of losing their interest. Of them no longer wanting me. Am I just an oddity they want to take apart and put back together?

I know this isn't long term, but how will I feel when they all move on? I'll still have to live here with them. Can I watch Roarke with another woman?

I guess that's why they offered me all that money. The money that could really give me a fresh start. I can go anywhere in the world with that kind of money. The bonus would be spending a couple of weeks experiencing sex like I never have before. On my terms.

And then do my job.

Make sure Aiden remains sober. Clean and straighten their lives so they don't have to worry about anything else. So what if after they finish with me they want to date other women? Maybe I'll date after they're done.

Maybe I'll find a nice normal guy who isn't a douchebag like Chad. I cup Aiden's jaw and my focus falls to his lips. Sparks light up along my fingertips. What would it be like to kiss him? To be kissed by him?

Mason hasn't kissed me yet either, but I know how his finger feels buried inside me. How his words can work me into a frenzy?

"Such a noisy brain you have." Aiden's eyes open as he smiles. "Thankfully it's peaceful when we sleep."

He captures my hand before I can draw it away and touches his forehead against mine. He takes a deep breath and releases it.

"I like the way you make me feel, little warrior."

It's too dark to read his eyes. "How do I make you feel?"

"Alive. Present. Ravenous."

Sparks ignite low in my stomach, but he doesn't bring me in closer. He doesn't lean in to kiss me. He just holds me.

Knocks sound on the door. "I can hear you two talking. I'm bored, poppet. Come out and play."

I grin at Roarke's ridiculous statement. Like somehow I can tame his boredom.

"I like your smile, little warrior. I'm glad they make you smile."

"You make me smile too."

His thumb trails over my lower lip before he rolls onto his back. "Time to face the music."

Chapter 16

I Want You to Want Me

Roarke

While Greer is Aiden's assistant, that doesn't mean he has to keep her to himself. I've got a reputation to maintain. And that means making my little poppet come again. Wyatt told me about Mason's office.

I'm all for public showings, so I'm disappointed I didn't get to participate. But if it means I can fuck my little poppet anywhere, in front of anyone in the house, I'm all for it. We've all seen her hot little body and touched her tight pussy.

Well, except Aiden hasn't touched her or kissed her, but he's a hard nut to crack. If I didn't push Greer, she'd probably go at Aiden's speed. Glacial.

That'd be a fucking shame. So much time and bad sex to make up for.

She's primed for it. Her hot little body knows exactly what it wants. She just needs to trust it more.

When she finally opens the door, she blinks up owlishly. The room behind her is dark, but she doesn't smell like sex. Just like Aiden to miss a golden opportunity.

"Did Aiden finally fuck you?"

Her mouth drops open in surprise.

"Fuck off, Roarke." Aiden appears. He wraps his arm around her waist and pulls her into his solid form. Fuck, she's so little compared to us.

Her eyes close as if savoring his touch. These two are going to dance around each other forever if no one shoves them together.

He wants her. She wants him. I'm sure his ex is the problem, but he's not marrying Greer. He just needs to fuck her. Fuck, I need to fuck her tight little pussy too.

"I haven't had penis in vagina sex with anyone in this house, Roarke." Greer's husky voice makes me want to make her scream my name. Every time my name passes her lips my cock twitches and gets hard.

"We should fix that, poppet." I wiggle my eyebrows.

Her cheeks flush even redder. She's not ready yet. I know women. We still need to have our talk, but I can make her climax again.

"We need to go over laundry." Aiden nods toward my door. "Let's have a look."

I grin. Fuck, yeah, I want Greer in my bedroom, preferably splayed out on my bed, screaming my name as I fuck her.

Her eyes darken and widen when she meets mine. That's the thing with Aiden. He doesn't notice how turned on she gets. How hot she is for even the smallest amount of attention. She's starved for it. Or maybe he does know and he's still immune from being married for years.

If anyone understands a lust for attention, it's me. Fuck, I crave it.

I fall back and they follow me as I head into my room. Throwing open the curtains, I let in the light and the view of the ocean. As a kid, I could only dream of a house like this. Near the ocean, lots of things to do. It's pretty sick.

"I apologize for the mess." I turn to find Aiden standing in the doorway, while Greer picks up my discarded clothes. I might feel a little shame, but when she bends over, she flashes me her curvy ass.

Fuck, I love ass. The number of women I've convinced into a little ass play is staggering. I'm curious how Greer will react. She didn't tense in the shower and that makes me wonder how curious our little assistant is.

I open my closet door and she follows the trail of clothes into it before dropping it all in the hamper. She straightens and her gaze takes in everything in my closet. I'm not a neat freak like the others, but I try.

She glances over her shoulder. "Do you mind if I rearrange a little?"

"Go ahead, poppet." I sit on the edge of the bed and watch her. She's a little enigma. Her voice was enough to spark my interest on the phone, but when she showed up wearing a t-shirt that swallowed her whole and pants that left everything to the imagination, the urge to discover her secrets consumed me.

I fall quick for women and then lose interest in a week or two. Usually, there's just not enough spark to maintain the fire and eventually it flickers out.

Greer... fuck, I knew she had walls up. Being an actor usually gets me around some walls because people think they know me. You better believe I take advantage of that shit. But when I stood up for her and she fell apart, it made my heart ache in a way I've never felt before.

In that moment, I wanted to be her champion. I wanted to face all her demons and destroy whatever put that sad look in her eyes.

The only problem: I'm not that man.

Fuck. I know it. The guys know it. And I'm pretty sure Greer knows I can't be that man.

But when she's near me with her sweet vanilla scent and that husky voice, all I want to do is wrap her in my arms and fuck her brains out. But I'd definitely hold her after.

She slips out of my closet and into the bathroom, returning with a few pairs of boxers to add to the hamper in the closet. She glances at me before saying, "Maybe you can help me determine what's work wear and going out wear and home wear?"

"Of course, poppet. But first I want to play with you more." I move to block the closet opening, hanging my fingers on the trim above the door and leaning in. I love making her come, knowing that no one else got her there is a rush. I can't wait to make her come on my cock.

Her eyes take in every inch of my sculpted figure. I'm proud of my body. I work hard to look like this. It gets me parts and lots of pussy. Right now, I just want to see how far Greer is willing to let me push her.

Her darkened eyes practically glow, and her lips part. Yeah, she wants another fucking orgasm and I'm just the guy to give her one.

"Not sex, poppet." Pretty sure I could have fucked her yesterday up against the wall while her ex listened. Or earlier in her bathroom. Or in the shower. Fuck, to be naked with her and not thrust my cock into that sweet tight pussy was torture. But she's like a fine wine. She needs to breathe a little before I drink her.

Aiden sits on my bed. "You don't have to do anything he asks you to, little warrior."

I don't bother giving him the finger. Instead, my gaze remains fixed on her as she worries her lip. Those wide brown eyes flit from my eyes down my body to the clothes.

"I should keep working." She sighs like that's the last thing she wants to do. Or I'm just convincing myself that's what it means because I want to play with her.

"Technically, you don't work for us. Yet."

Her wide eyes lift and search mine.

I'm an open fucking book, so I'm not worried what she'll find. I want her. I want to explore her divine little body. I want to make her come so loud that everyone in this house hears it.

"Come on, poppet," I turn on the charm. "I know you want to play."

"You won't get anything done with him hounding you," Aiden concedes. "If you want, I can leave you two alone."

Disappointment and a flicker of rejection crosses her face.

I hold my hand out to stop him from getting up. She wants Aiden, but his cold attitude will destroy my little poppet. When she worries her lip, I give her my best coaxing smile.

"Aiden isn't going anywhere, poppet, because he likes seeing you naked and writhing in pleasure, even if it's at my hand." I glance over my shoulder at Aiden's purposefully blank face. "Don't you, Aiden?"

He rolls his eyes at me, knowing exactly what I'm doing, before saying, "Come here, Greer."

She slides between me and the doorframe, putting her hands on my body. Sparks ignite beneath my skin at her touch. I turn to watch her make her way out to Aiden.

She patiently stops in front of him, waiting for his next move. He cups her cheek. She leans into his hand like a stray cat seeking affection, willing to take whatever her master is willing to dole out.

I close in behind her and drag her hips back into mine, making sure she feels exactly how hard she makes me. She needs to know I want her. We want her.

"Put your hands on his knees, poppet."

She does as I ask, bending herself over. Fuck, I love this ass.

"Aiden, if you would help our girl take her shirt off." I don't miss her shiver at *our girl*. I enjoy watching my friends touch her. But when Chad grabbed her arm, I wanted to rip his off and beat him with it. He's lucky I didn't see the bruises on her until this morning.

No one is touching her like that ever again. If I see that guy, I'm decking him. Fuck the news.

The thought startles me, but Aiden dragging her shirt off distracts me. Her full breasts swell. Now beautifully held by her bra. I'm tempted to free them, but I like the thought of them swaying together for Aiden while I make her come on my fingers.

Slipping my hands around her waist, I undo her shorts, letting them fall to her ankles. A shiver ripples through her again. Fuck, I get even harder at every little quiver she makes.

"How wet are you, poppet?" I say softly as I smooth a hand over the curve of her ass. Her panties are silky under my hand. I can see the damp spot between her legs. So fucking responsive.

She makes a little needy noise as my hand strays toward her center. I chuckle darkly.

"I should warn you, Mason will expect you to answer with words or he'll punish you."

Her head comes up and Aiden searches her eyes.

"Agreed upon punishments, little warrior, with limits and safe words." Aiden strokes his fingers along her jawline. "Always consensual."

I slide my fingers under the sides of her panties and draw them down to flutter on top of her shorts. Her pussy glistens with her wetness and I can't resist easing my finger into her warm, tight cunt.

"So wet, poppet, and tight. Fuck, you're divine." I thrust my finger in and out a few times before removing it. Putting it in my mouth, I suck her sweetness off. "You should taste her, Aiden. Sweet and tangy. Fucking addictive. I could spend hours eating you, poppet."

Stepping away from her delectable body, I adjust my throbbing cock and open my nightstand drawer to pull out a fresh bottle of lube. I'm going to see what she can take.

Greer

"I know how responsive you are to having your pussy played with, but there's so much more we can do." Roarke steps back behind me. His every word is torture because my body is ready to explode for him.

My hands grip Aiden's knees and I raise my gaze to his blue eyes.

His hand falls over mine and he gently strokes my fingers. His heated gaze drops to our hands. The desire is there. I'm not just making it up, but he only holds my hand.

Roarke squirts something behind me, but I keep my gaze fixed on Aiden. He's not like the others who all have touched me intimately today. Aiden's only watched.

"No one's fucked your ass, but has anyone played with it?" Roarke spreads my ass cheeks. Fuck, is he looking at my asshole? My cheeks heat at the thought of him looking there. But desire rolls through me hot and heavy.

"No," I answer, but it comes out sounding like a question.

Roarke chuckles darkly before sliding a wet finger down the cleft between my ass cheeks. He stops and circles my asshole with his lubed fingertip. My breath catches at the unfamiliar feel of someone touching me there. Fireworks of pleasure singe me.

"What do you think, little warrior?" Aiden's voice makes me focus on his eyes again. "Do you like someone playing with your asshole?"

Suddenly, Roarke's mouth is on my ass, kissing my cheek down to where his finger circles. I startle and turn to see what he's doing.

Aiden's fingers tip my chin back until our gazes lock. "Eyes on me, Greer. I want to watch you fall apart."

A gush of arousal flows through me. Roarke's finger moves away, but then his mouth closes over my puckered hole, licking me. Heat pours over me.

My lips part and I struggle to keep my eyes focused on Aiden as overwhelming desire pulses through my veins. When Roarke's tongue thrusts into my ass, I moan loudly.

"That's it, little warrior. Take your pleasure. It's yours." Aiden's blue eyes are so dark as his pupil enlarges. "You're gorgeous, Greer."

His hand sinks into my hair and tugs slightly to make sure I stay focused on him, while Roarke does wicked things to my ass with his tongue and teeth. My pussy drips with wetness, aching to be touched, to be filled. My breasts feel heavy and tight.

I swear one brush of my clit and I'd explode.

Roarke's kisses move away from my asshole. I whimper as the edge fades a little.

His dark chuckle sends a wave of longing through me.

"Don't worry, poppet. I'll get you there. I'm not finished playing yet." His finger returns but this time he eases it inside my asshole.

My eyes widen at the feel of something pushing into my ass. My breathing stutters in and out as it feels really fucking good. Aiden gives my hair a little tug that pulls at something wanton inside me. I moan.

"Eyes open, Greer. Next time we'll do this in a mirror so you can watch as he buries his finger in your ass."

"Relax, poppet," Roarke's voice is soothing as he pushes a little deeper inside me, brushing against nerves that make tingles flood my system. "We'll work this ass until you're able to take a cock deep inside. Then three cocks will fill your sweet cunt, your mouth, and your ass at the same time. Would you like that?"

If Aiden's hand wasn't holding my hair, my head would drop. My eyelids lower as I feel Roarke's knuckles against my ass. His finger deep inside me.

"Want to feel what that would be like, poppet?"

My pussy gets even wetter as he drags his finger out of my ass slowly. Every inch sparking along my nerves and lifting me higher. He presses the walls around the opening of my puckered hole.

"Do you, little warrior?" Aiden asks. My pussy clenches in response, but I give a slight nod. Aiden's finger traces my lower lip. My tongue darts out to taste him and he gives a little groan of approval. "Suck my fingers like you would my cock."

He slides two fingers across my lower lip. My lips part at his touch. Our eyes remain steady on each other as he slides them into my mouth, while Roarke thrusts his finger deep and fucks my ass, in and out, over and over.

My hips rock with his finger as every stroke pushes me higher.

My hands clench on Aiden's knees as I suck on his fingers, sliding my tongue along them. His eyes darken further as he thrusts his fingers in deep.

I'm building to a climax and they've barely touched my pussy or any of the places other guys would touch. Roarke slides another finger in with his first. At the stretch and increased fullness, I moan around Aiden's finger.

"What a good girl you are, poppet. Do you feel that stretch?" He eases in and out slowly, dragging his fingers along the sensitive nerves of my opening, making me take every inch of his fingers. "I bet you could come just from me fucking this ass. You'll be taking cock in no time."

His words, the feel of him sliding in and out of my ass, Aiden's fingers in my mouth while his heated gaze holds mine, it's all too much and I shatter. My ass tightens around his fingers as I cry out.

Roarke holds his fingers still inside me while Aiden presses down on my tongue.

"How did that feel, poppet?"

Moaning around Aiden's finger, I suck again. Roarke's other hand slides over my clit before circling my pussy's entrance. Little shivers of pleasure ripple through me, winding me back up.

"Ready, poppet." It's not a question. It's a warning. Roarke slides two fingers into my wet pussy. "So fucking wet. You'll feel so good wrapped around my cock."

Aiden tugs on my hair. His heated eyes making me want to suck his cock, not just his fingers. "Suck my fingers, little warrior. Show me what that talented tongue can do."

When Aiden draws his fingers back, so does Roarke. As Aiden thrusts into my mouth again, Roarke's fingers go deep inside my pussy and my ass. I moan at the delicious sparks cascading throughout me.

Every inch of me is hyperaware. The slight breeze of the air conditioning tickles every inch of my naked flesh. My hands clench on the fabric of Aiden's shorts and his muscle tensing beneath them.

The guys fuck me in sync. Their fingers thrusting in and out of me, winding me back up.

"Fuck, little warrior. You're going to feel so good wrapped around our cocks." Aiden's words stir something inside me that lay dormant until I met these guys. Some hedonistic tendency that life squashed.

"I can't decide which hole I want to fuck first, poppet." Roarke slips his thumb over my clit and presses firmly. "Be our good girl and come for us again."

Like my body was waiting for his order, my whole being shatters. A scream wells in my throat as they continue to fuck me through my release. Fireworks burst in my vision as my toes curl.

"Such a good girl." Aiden's praise makes my pussy pulse harder around Roarke's fingers. When Aiden draws his fingers out of my mouth, his hand falls to his erection in his pants. He shifts it and I lick my lips.

I want to taste him. My gaze rises to his heated blue eyes, like warm pools I want to dive into. But he holds my head steady.

Roarke thrusts in deep again and his mouth closes over my clit and sucks.

This time the scream escapes as he shoves me over the edge. My eyes squeeze shut at the intensity of the orgasm tearing me apart.

"Eyes on me, little warrior."

I don't resist Aiden's order and the look on his face makes me climb higher than I thought possible. My knees begin to give out, but hands support my waist.

"Fuck, kitten. Getting ready for the big show?"

I don't turn to Wyatt, still locked in Aiden's eyes. Roarke's fingers gently withdraw. He gives a dark chuckle. "We wouldn't want our girl to walk in unprepared."

Wyatt holds me in place, while Roarke walks to the bathroom. When he returns, a warm cloth glides over my pussy and then between my ass cheeks. My cheeks heat. Aiden's hand in my hair keeps me from dropping my head.

Lifting me against him, Wyatt settles me onto Aiden's lap. I rest my head over Aiden's heart and close my eyes. I don't know what these men have planned for me, but I can feel the walls around my heart crack just a little.

Alarms sound in my brain, but I ignore them as I snuggle into Aiden and take a deep breath. I'll deal with the consequences later. Right now, I just want to enjoy this moment.

Chapter 17

I Will Wait

Aiden

When Greer's heart and breathing slows, Roarke and I help her back into her clothes. Her gaze keeps returning to my eyes and dropping to my mouth. My cock twitches at the memory of her warm, wet mouth sucking on my fingers. How her brown eyes held mine.

Her soft lips brushing against my skin made me want to lean in and taste her. But I can't. Not yet. I'm not sure if it's the ghost of my ex haunting me or something else. Something darker.

Maybe I worry about my desire for her.

It draws me in and makes me crave her, just like my addiction. I fight so hard every day to stay sober. Even though I haven't tasted her, I'm worried she'll become another addiction. One I won't be able to fight off if I have to.

After she sorts through Roarke's closet, we take a load of his clothes to the laundry room. Unable to resist, I kiss the top of her head and inhale that sweet intoxicating vanilla scent mixed with her unique scent.

"I'll be on the main floor, reviewing my script."

The heat of her body lures me, making me hesitate to pull away from her. She tips her face up.

When her light brown eyes collide with mine, for a moment, I almost forget myself and lean in to taste her. Almost. I worry a taste won't be enough. A spark of hope lights in her eyes before it goes out when I draw away.

My chest tightens as I climb the stairs. It hurts that I'm hurting her, but this is for the best. At least for now.

It's almost like a test to see if I can resist. But eventually I'll succumb to her, it's inevitable. I want the taste of her on my lips and that sweet body writhing beneath mine.

She comes up a few minutes later and heads into the kitchen, working quietly, while I read. It's blissfully domestic and I consider getting her that fifties dress, imagining her greeting me at the door when I get home from set with a smile and a martini—

And that's where the fantasy crashes and burns.

I'm an addict. My failed marriage drove me to drink. Excessively. To hide from the world that wanted to drag me through the press. Siobhan left me, but she was the injured party. I didn't spend enough time with her. I was too cold. Allegations of an affair hit the entertainment news like a ton of bricks.

I never cheated on my wife. But I loved her and needed her. She kept me grounded in an industry that can make you feel invincible when it loves you. And can brutalize you while you're already on your way down.

When she left me, I lost an important part of me. The fear of becoming reliant on a woman again, even one as sweet and submissive as Greer, plagues me and keeps me from giving in to the desire she stirs.

I focus on the script as Roarke walks through on his way to the workout room. His shorts hang low on his hips and his tank top shows off his massive arms. He lifts Greer onto the counter, making her squeak, before claiming those full lips of hers. The rise of jealous heat inside me isn't from him kissing her, but the fact he *can* kiss her without a second thought.

He can taste her sweetness without worrying if she'll just become another addiction. Something I can't seem to live without.

When he lifts his head, his gaze meets mine. Roarke knows my brain. He knows how I work. We've been friends too long. He knows I want her without me telling him and he knows that every time I don't do what I want to, it hurts her.

She's this fragile flower that wilts without praise and blooms with it. She hesitates but we don't. Well, except me.

So far Roarke's allowing me to withdraw, but only when it doesn't hurt her. Which makes me curious. Does he want more from her or is this his normal two week fling? He murmurs something to her that I can't hear.

She releases a little laugh and it curls around my insides and tugs. It would be easier if I only wanted her body, but I want those smiles and that laughter. I want to hold her in the dark and chase away her demons. But I'm barely chasing away my own.

He sets her back on her feet. As she walks away, he smacks her ass. She turns and glares at him, but he just chuckles as he heads downstairs.

Her eyes seek me out. I love that she does that. I love that she relies on me to guide her. It's a need. Almost as addicting as the feel of her warm body pressed into mine when we sleep.

When she finishes working in the kitchen, she stares outside for a second. A wistful look falls over her.

The next few lines of the script jumble together and I set it to the side.

When I stand, she straightens.

"Come on, little warrior. Let's go for a walk." I hold my hand out and she joins me. My large hand swallows hers. Siobhan was almost as tall as me with her heels. Our hands naturally fell together with her thumb over mine.

Greer's thumb slides beneath mine, and it feels different but right.

She tugs me to a stop at the door. "Oh, wait, shoes."

She holds up her bare feet. I can't help smiling at her dainty feet and toes.

"We're walking on the beach. You don't need shoes."

Shrugging, she follows me around the pool deck. When we climb past the chairs Wyatt and Mason smoke in, she pauses and checks out their setup. They didn't actually smoke last night.

I'm curious what they discussed, but I'm sure it's the same thing that has me spinning.

Greer. She's already beginning to change things around here. I don't know if it's for the better yet.

Greer

We crest the dune and a wooden pier stretches all the way to the beach and ocean. The smell is amazing. Crashing waves, sea birds, and my pounding heart fill my ears.

My hand tightens around Aiden's as the ocean spreads out before me, seemingly endless. I can't contain my grin. It's just how I remember it. Though the beach was more crowded wherever we were.

My mother was healthy then. I have vague memories, but the warm ball of love in my heart I remember clearly. The hazy picture of a man with us that I can only assume is my father, but the only proof I have of him is that one picture.

My mind can't lock on him or memories of him. Except that one day at the beach. The memory I held onto during the hard years that followed. The way I want to remember my mother and not the cold stare.

Aiden wraps his arms around me and rubs my arm. "I should have let you grab a sweater."

"I'm not cold." Automatically comes out of my mouth before I even check to see if I am. *Don't be a bother*. It's been drilled into me by foster parent after foster parent. If you're too needy, they send you away.

His hand runs up my arm. "I can feel your goosebumps."

"I don't want to go back. I'm fine." I give him a genuine smile. "Let's take a walk."

I want this time with him. Alone when we aren't fast asleep in each other's arms. Maybe I should feel embarrassed that I'm becoming comfortable being manhandled by Roarke. Or that I'm not ashamed that Wyatt and Mason both made me come too. Or even that Aiden watched me.

I've never had a chance to embrace life before and I can't wait to do more. Aiden leads me down to the sand and I pause when my feet sink into the soft, warm sand.

"How long has it been?" He smiles down at my wiggling toes.

"I don't know, honestly. Before Dad left, back when Mom wasn't addicted." It's hard to remember that there were good times. Hard to remember that at one point my mom and dad took care of me and not the other way around.

Aiden pulls on my hand to draw me away from the pier. We walk for a few minutes, hand in hand. The breeze plays with my hair. The air smells salty and fresh. The waves curl up on shore only to stretch back out to the ocean. A few other people walk on the beach, but no one bothers us.

When a dog runs up to us, I instinctively take a step behind Aiden. He laughs as he pats the dog on the head and it runs back off to its master.

"Are you afraid of dogs, little warrior?" Aiden draws me into his side and wraps his arm protectively around my shoulder.

"Every dog, no. Strange dogs, yes. Reasonably so, I might add." Dogs were tricky animals. Usually how they responded told me a lot about their master. If they were friendly, the foster parent usually was nice enough. If the dog was aggressive or downtrodden, the foster parent wouldn't be a good fit.

"Did you have a lot of experiences with dogs growing up?" His thumb strokes over my shoulder, sending little jolts of desire through me.

"Only a few homes had dogs. We never had one growing up. Mom said they were too much work." I shrug. "I wanted a pet, but I figured I'd like a cat more. They seem a lot more chill."

Aiden chuckles. "We had dogs. My older brothers usually took them for walks and helped with the care. The dogs obeyed them. Pretty sure the dogs saw me as another dog to pick on."

I glance up at his smile. He's radiant in the sunlight. I'm sure anyone seeing us together probably wonders what he's doing with me. I'm average at best. Maybe slightly pretty, but I definitely am not equal to any of the men in that house.

Maybe that should bother me, make me feel like they're using me, but it doesn't. I don't know why they're interested in me, but the attraction is intense. There shouldn't be an issue exploring that attraction as long as there are rules so no one gets hurt.

"Can I ask you something?" I push my hands in my back pockets to keep from fiddling with my shirt.

"Sure." He doesn't remove his arm and we continue walking down the beach.

"How long have you been sober?"

"I stayed in rehab for six months. I've been out for about two months now." His gaze remains on the ocean, but his thumb still skids across my skin. "I don't want to relapse and we decided that a longer term in rehab would help the producers take my recovery seriously."

Eight months sober. "That's good."

And I mean it. That means he's got a good foundation. I just need to help him hold his boundaries.

He squeezes me against him. "It is, but it also means I can't give in to this attraction yet."

My heart skips a beat. He stops walking and turns me to face him, tipping my chin up. His light blue eyes search mine and he sighs.

"I haven't been with anyone since Siobhan. If we go down this road, it has to be slow and we have to check in often. It's too easy to give up one addiction and pick up another to fill the void."

I read that somewhere, but it still sucks.

After glancing around, he slides his hand around my neck to hold the back of my head. "I want you, Greer, but I can't have you. Yet."

My pulse quickens as his thumb traces my jaw.

"The others won't wait and I don't expect you to wait either. I can wait. You can help me sleep and we'll let that be the extent of our codependence until the one year mark."

Four months? I bite my lip. I've had longer dry spells than that, but never have I felt an attraction like this one. This need to be close to him, to touch him. It's only been two days and I'm already longing for more.

If it's what he needs though, I can do that.

I smile softly. "Four months isn't that long."

He chuckles. "Tell that to my dick."

He pulls me in for a hug before I can glance down at his dick. I breathe in his citrus scent and soften against him.

"Come on, we should head back to the house." He wraps his arm around my shoulders again and we turn back.

"So we have to wait four months for everything?" I can't help but ask.

"Greedy, little warrior?" He laughs. "Maybe not everything, but definitely as you so elegantly put it no penis in vagina sex."

My face turns red. Roarke flusters me on so many levels. He gets under my skin and I can't help what comes out of my mouth when he provokes me.

"At least not with me," Aiden finishes as we walk up the steps to the pier. The house is lit from within and it looks cozy and warm, inviting. Like a home.

A shiver works through me. I can't think like that. It's like everything else in my life. This is temporary. Sure it may be for over a year, but it's not going to last.

I'm not the girl that ends up with the guy, but I will end up with a future.

That's enough for me.

He leads me down the walkway and stops at the lounge chairs, a good distance from the house, but we're no longer visible from the beach.

"I'll be honest with you." He sits in a chair and draws me down sideways on his lap. His eyes hold me captive. "I want to kiss you. I want to feel your breasts in my hands and taste your nipples in my mouth."

My breath catches as his words spark a fire in me.

"I long to trail my hand across your stomach and slip beneath your panties. Feel the heat of your pussy against my palm before sliding my fingers deep inside you until you come all over my hand."

I whimper as his hand slides along the outside of my bare thigh. Fuck, I want him.

"I love watching them with you, knowing they can bring you pleasure when I have to hold back." He slides his other hand into my hair and rests his forehead against mine. I breathe him in, aching for him. "But I'm also a possessive man and crave to make you feel what they do. I can't promise that I'll always be okay watching from the sidelines, but I won't lie to you about it either."

I open my eyes and pull back. "I don't want to hurt you."

He smiles and tugs my hair slightly back. His darkened gaze drops to my lips and they part in anticipation.

"Fuck, what I wouldn't give for a taste, but I don't trust myself to stop at just a taste." He brushes his cheek against mine as his lips touch my earlobe. "You see, little warrior, I can see you becoming my drug of choice. Burying my cock inside you to get a fix. Needing you to start and end my day. Craving you when I should be working."

A little needy noise escapes me, because fuck, I want him so badly. I want to be his addiction and I know that's wrong.

"Waiting for you will be hard, but I know you'll be worth it, little warrior." His lips skim my cheek as he pulls back. His gaze captures me again, holding me there. "You don't have to wait for me though. I don't expect you to or want you to. You should find whatever you're craving with the others."

It doesn't seem fair. "But—"

He presses his finger against my lips and then traces the outline. "You aren't battling addiction like I am. You need this awakening. Roarke is right. Don't worry I'll be along for the ride."

I cup his jaw between my hands and cock an eyebrow. "Can we ease the tension?"

He chuckles darkly. I reach for his hand against my lips and hold it while I suck on his finger. His confession helps to make me bolder. Just because we can't be intimate in a lot of ways doesn't mean he has to be in pain or need.

"Can I help you ease the tension?" I clarify, stroking my tongue along his finger. "You can use me when the pressure gets too much."

"You want me to fuck your mouth for relief?" His eyes hold mine. My heart pounds as my fear of rejection races through me.

"Yes," I whisper, suddenly unsure of myself. I'm offering an A-list actor the use of my mouth. How many other women have offered him that? My cheeks heat and I close my eyes.

"Only if you fuck your pussy with your fingers while I do it."

My eyes pop open to his smile.

"I'd hate to take pleasure and give none in return, little warrior."

Chapter 18

Promises

I'm in the kitchen cooking dinner. My insides are a jumbled up mess after Aiden brought me back and disappeared upstairs. I want to do what he said. Give him pleasure while taking my own. He came down changed and headed downstairs to the workout room.

The others haven't come around while I prepared dinner. I imagine both Mason and Wyatt worked today. I'm not sure what else Roarke got up to, but he probably had to review his script too. Or whatever actors do to prepare for a role.

I'm not sure what time they expect to eat, but I finish cooking around six thirty. I bite my lip. Should I call for them? Is there a bell to ring? Maybe text them?

I only have the one number.

"What's wrong, mouse?" Mason's dark voice sends chills coursing down my back, half because he startled me and half because his voice makes my toes curl.

I turn around and he leans on the counter, watching me with those piercing eyes. My insides melt at the heat in them. How long did he watch me before he spoke?

"I don't know how to let everyone know dinner is ready." I shrug.

Mason stalks across the kitchen, closing the distance between us. My breath catches in anticipation. He tips my chin up. "I'm sure they'll be down. It smells delicious."

His gaze drops to my lips. Is he talking about the food?

When his thumb grazes my lower lip, I suck in a breath.

"Fuck, that smells good, poppet." Roarke's boisterous voice dispels the web Mason wove around me.

Flustered, I take a step back and he lets me with a cocky grin. Each of these guys is different, maybe that's why I find them all attractive. Or maybe they all are just fucking hot and my hormones didn't stand a chance.

Grabbing pot holders, I lift the pasta bake off the stove to carry to the table. Wyatt and Aiden come from the direction of the stairs and join us.

"Did you make this, poppet?" Roarke hovers behind me as I lean over to set the pasta down. His hands curve over my ass and I only flinch a little at the intimate touch. His need to touch me is becoming familiar.

"Yes." I straighten and turn.

Roarke smiles, blocking my way.

"I need to get the focaccia." I gesture to the island.

He tips my chin and brushes his lips across mine. I suck in a breath at the tingles chasing through my blood. "We need to spend some quality time together, poppet."

His darkened blue eyes give away his intent with *quality time*. My cheeks burn, but he lets me slide past to bring the rest of dinner to the table. They all take their seats and I sit beside Aiden, next to Wyatt.

Roarke spoons a huge portion onto his plate before passing it on. I did some research on the internet to figure out what I could feed these guys as they all seem healthy. Their diet preferences all call for certain things. Feeding them might be a full time job in itself.

I take a small portion and Roarke gives me a disapproving look. I add some more and when he smiles in approval, I almost preen.

While we eat, Roarke tells another story about a time on set when he had to work with the stunt coordinator. The producer was against him doing this particular stunt, but he insisted.

"Fifteen stitches and a broken ankle." Roarke pulls his shirt aside to show the white scar right beneath his pec.

My fingers twitch to trace the line and I lift my wide eyes to Roarke. He grins with that knowing look.

"Don't worry, Mason won't allow me to do stunts this time." He winks before turning to Mason. "Pretty sure, he'd lock me in my trailer before he let that happen."

"Good." I'd hate for him to get hurt.

Everyone's plates are almost empty or empty. They ate most of the pasta and all of the bread.

When I begin to rise to pick up the dishes, Mason clears his throat, drawing my attention. I lower back in my seat.

He pushes his plate toward the center. "We need to discuss this situation."

My heart trips over itself. Me and them and what happened today and what more we want to happen. There's still this fear that they'll decide they don't want me.

"Why don't I get dessert and we can talk then?" I stand and grab plates before anyone can tell me to stop.

"I love dessert." Roarke's hand caresses my hip as I take his plate. "You can just sit on the table in front of me and I'll take all the dessert we can handle."

My cheeks burn, but I'm getting used to Roarke and him wanting an audience. I'm kind of into it, especially if that audience is the other three at this table. Quickly, I put the plates and the leftovers in the kitchen before bringing out the small chocolate cake I made.

The guys are talking low, but it's about next week.

I hurry back and grab the plates and forks. When I turn, Wyatt takes the plates.

"Go sit down, kitten. We have a lot to discuss."

As I approach the table, they all watch me and part of me wants to sink into the floor and disappear. Another quieter part wants to slide onto the table and let them do what they want with me. Instead, I sit back in my seat and cut the cake.

Wyatt hands me a plate and I put a piece on it. We do that until everyone has a piece.

"Fuck." Roarke chews his cake but looks at Mason. "Quick, make her sign the NDA so I can ask her to marry me. This cake is spectacular, poppet."

I'm resigned to being a permanent shade of red around Roarke.

"While he's not wrong about the cake, we should get you to sign the NDA before we discuss things." Mason walks to the island and grabs a stack of papers. He licks his finger and shifts through it to separate a small section. "Nothing unusual here. You'll be living with us and working for us, so just don't talk to the press and everything will be fine."

When he sets the papers next to me, I push my cake to the side, wiping my hands on a napkin. I skim the first page that seems like legal mumbo-jumbo.

"If you'd like to have your lawyer look it over..."

I laugh at Mason's words and lift my gaze. "I wouldn't know where to get a lawyer if I needed one."

He nods thoughtfully. "If you'd like, I can have our lawyer come over and explain to you the details."

"Oh." I sit back and look at him in shock. He would do that for me? He has to know I can't afford his lawyer either.

"I'd rather you be informed of your rights and duties. Rather than steamroll over you because you don't have money." Mason's eyes hold me locked in place. "We're not here to take advantage of you, little mouse."

I breathe out. "I'll just read it myself and if I have questions, I'll ask."

Mason lifts his fork. I concentrate on reading while they discuss some things to expect on set next week. The NDA seems fairly straightforward. If I break the NDA, there will be repercussions. A fine and depending on damages, charges being pressed against me.

I have no intention of selling my story to anyone, but I could see someone in my situation with dollar signs in their eyes and the need for fifteen minutes of fame taking advantage. They trusted me these past couple days.

I could have run off to the press and there would have been no repercussions. But that's not who I am.

"Do you have a pen I can use?" I ask when the conversation lulls.

Mason slides one across the table, but when I reach for it, he doesn't let go. Our eyes meet.

"You understand the risk you're taking if you sell your story, little mouse?"

I swallow and nod. "Fines and a potential lawsuit."

"They'll offer you a lot of money. Far more than what we'll pay you." He studies me, but he won't find a crack.

"Loyalty means something to me. Even if I don't sign this, I'll keep my word to you. I wouldn't want you to betray me, so I'll give you the same respect in return."

"What if one of us betrays you?" Mason raises an eyebrow in challenge.

I sigh. Lying won't do any good. "I still won't break my word, but I'll either deal with it or move on. Chad cheated on me, but we stayed in that apartment because I had nowhere else to go. If one of you betrays me, I may stay for the others. But you're giving me enough money that I can leave if I need to."

He releases the pen with a nod. My shoulders ease and I quickly sign next to all the tabs on the NDA. Could I get rich selling my story? Maybe. But I would have to betray them to do that and I can't do that.

Almost everyone I've known betrayed me. I know how deep that can cut.

I hand the pen back to Mason and slide the papers across the table to him. He adds them to the bottom of his pile and lifts off another section.

"This is our employment contract. The money we'll pay you plus the expectations and terminating offenses."

I take the stack and slowly read through it, while eating my cake. The numbers are the same. Everything we've discussed is in there. The chores I'll be expected to complete. My main priority is Aiden and making sure he stays sober. Nothing about sex as an expectation or anything like that.

When I finish, I reach for the pen. This time he lets me take it and I sign on all the flagged areas. The opportunity to have a nest egg to build a future with is just too irresistible.

I pass the papers to Mason and he adds them to the bottom.

"Before I give you the next document, we need to talk."

I straighten and push away my empty plate. The others have been quietly eating their cake. Wyatt rises and takes the plates. When I try to help him, he puts his hand on my shoulder and shakes his head.

I return my focus to Mason.

"Tell us your sexual experiences so far."

Uh. My brain blanks as my mouth drops open.

"She's had five lovers." Roarke leans back and gives me a grin. "Obviously Chad was a dumb fuck who couldn't give her what she needed."

My mouth opens and closes. I always figured it was my fault that Chad cheated.

"I'm not that skilled at sex," I admit softly, looking down at my hands. "I haven't had the best experiences with it. It usually takes me a while before I'll even kiss a guy."

I don't want to talk about the few guys I've been with. Some I'd rather forget entirely. Not all were bad though.

The guys are quiet. No one touches me. Maybe I've finally pushed them away. No one wants a defective doll. They want someone like Zoe (not specifically her) or like Bristol. Open, fun, sexually experienced, and down for anything.

"Greer," Roarke's voice is coaxing and I lift my gaze to his serious eyes.

"Yes?" I won't break down until I get back to my room. I'll keep my head up and listen to them tell me they don't want me. It's not a big deal. I keep expecting it. Finally it's over.

"Fuck, poppet. Come here." His blue eyes soften as he beckons me over.

I rise slowly and walk to stand beside him.

He pats his lap. "Climb on."

I step back, but he grabs my waist and draws me down to straddle his lap facing him. My back presses against the table.

"It's just you and me. In the creepy dungeon below your apartment. Only the truth." He holds my chin in his hand, making me meet his eyes. "I don't know how to ask this and not sound like an asshole."

"Then don't ask it." I'm afraid of what he'll ask. I don't want to lie to him, but what can I say? He could ask me anything or he could ask me the thing I've never wanted to admit.

His blue eyes search mine. Whatever he finds makes his lips tighten, but then he leans his forehead against mine. I release the breath I held in.

"Fuck, poppet," he whispers. He pulls me into his arms and holds me against his heart. "Someday you'll know you can trust us with your secrets like we'll trust you with ours."

The tension leaves my body as I realize he isn't going to push. A tear slips out, but I rub my face into his shirt.

"I'm not giving up on you, Greer, so don't give up on me." Roarke leans back and tips my chin up. "I'm going to ask you questions that are just yes or no about what you've done sexually. Only say yes if you consented to the act."

Tears choke the back of my throat, but I nod to let him know I understand. Relief floods through me.

"You've had a dick in your pussy, but not your ass. What about your mouth?"

"Yes." My insides warm.

Roarke gives me an encouraging smile. "See easy. Have you ever been tied up during sex?"

"No." I bite my lip, feeling a rush of awareness flow through me.

"Would you be willing to try it?" Roarke's hands slide around my waist.

With these guys? "Yes."

"What about being blindfolded? Have you?"

"No."

"Would you?"

I squirm a little on his lap. "Maybe."

"Outside of us, have you had sexual encounters with more than one person before?" He slides down in the chair and pulls me closer, so I can feel his erection between my legs.

"No," I breathe out. My pulse quickens.

"We'll definitely change that, poppet." His hands guide my hips over him, sending sparks of arousal burning through me as his darkened eyes hold mine.

"Are you open to me fucking your ass?"

My lips part as he rocks his hard cock against my pussy. There are too many layers between us. "Yes, Roarke."

"Good girl. Hands on my shoulders." He grins. "Mason? Have anything to add?"

Roarke's fingers find the button to my shorts. He opens them and his hand goes inside my panties and his fingers thrust up inside me. I shudder at the feel of him inside me, but my body knows what it wants as my hips rock on his hand, chasing that feeling.

"Aiden wants to wait four months before he takes your pussy, mouse, but we're impatient men." Mason's voice sends dark thrills through me as I rock closer and closer to orgasm. "We want to continue to push against your boundaries. Is that something you're comfortable with?"

"Yes, sir," I whisper. My fingers curl into Roarke's hair as his fingers continue to move within me. It's right there. I can feel the release barreling down on me.

"We want to fuck you, poppet. Only you. Without condoms. Will you let us?" Roarke's words roll over me like a freight train.

Moaning, I come on his fingers. He strokes me through it, while I pull on his hair and ride him as waves keep crashing over me.

When my hips slow, he pulls his fingers out of my pussy and sucks them into his mouth.

"I don't know which tastes better, poppet. Your cake or your pussy?"

I watch his lips move before leaning in and taking them with mine. His lips part and he takes over the kiss, cradling the back of my head.

Chapter 19

Need Me Right

Mason

Sharing with an exhibitionist might be difficult. Roarke and Greer kiss like none of us are here. Honestly, I was shocked when he was the first to comfort her. That's not like Roarke.

Roarke has sex with women. He doesn't comfort them or try to make them smile unless it's to get into their pants. Granted, he's got into Greer's pants, but that wasn't his main objective. He wanted her to tell us the truth.

Her sexual experience may not have been with her permission. It was in her voice and how she closed up before we even asked. I saw my anger reflected on Wyatt's, Aiden's and Roarke's faces.

She was twenty-one years old now. She'd been with Chad for almost the last year that means some of the four before him hadn't been her choice. How young had she been? Did she ever get therapy or even seek help?

Roarke pulls back from her lips. "Answer me, poppet. Can we forego condoms if we swear to only be yours?"

We'd discussed this briefly earlier. We've always used condoms, except Aiden, but he was married. The idea of not having to worry about finding one in the heat of the moment appeals to me and the others. It opens up a lot of opportunities.

"Greer."

Her spine straightens at my tone and her brown eyes find me.

"Answer." I hold her with my gaze.

"If I'm with you four, I'll only be with you." Her voice is soft. "I would be willing to forego condoms, but I want some time before we cross that line."

Her gaze goes to Aiden and then she turns back to Roarke. "Can I...?"

He buttons her shorts and helps her stand up. She sits down beside him with her shoulder brushing his and leans her head against his arm.

"This is all overwhelming for me. I've barely been here over a day and I appreciate this opportunity to work with you."

Roarke takes her hand between his and looks perfectly happy to have her snuggle against him. Fucking astounding.

Greer's gaze goes to Wyatt and Aiden before stopping on me. "I want all of you. I want to experience the things I've been missing and I know you can show me that. But I also need to figure out how to do my actual job."

"That's fair." I nod. And responsible which I like. "How long?"

Her gaze flicks to Aiden and her lips press together. Fuck if she says four months, I'm going to have to get real comfortable using my hand.

Aiden gives her an encouraging smile.

"A week or two?" She glances at Roarke and he smiles and kisses her hand. Her eyes soften. "Is that okay?"

"We can work up to it, poppet. I'm not in a hurry."

I almost literally had to pick my jaw up off the floor. Roarke willing to wait a week for anyone is new. He likes to press on everyone's comfort zones, pushing them out of their safe zones, but with Greer, he holds back.

Leaning back in my chair, I study the two of them because this isn't normal. Not for Roarke. Maybe once he has her, he'll go back to his old ways. I don't know if that will hurt her or not.

Her brown eyes return to mine. "Have you done this before?"

"No. We've never shared a woman before."

Her eyes widen and her mouth forms a little O of surprise.

"This is new to us, but it should work as long as we remain open and honest with each other. That includes you, little mouse."

She straightens. "I prefer to be honest."

"Good. I have some consent forms I want you to look over." I separate the last section of paper and put it in front of me. "This is a comprehensive list. Most things aren't things we might be into, but if it's something you want to try, one of us might be willing. We've already marked our answers."

Her gaze drops in alarm to the pages.

"We'll need to know your hard limits. Things that are an absolute no. Anything that might be triggering. Your soft limits. Things you might be willing to try as long as there is a discussion first and check-ins throughout. Most of the items have a scale next to them from enthusiastic yes to maybe to absolutely no. If you're unsure what something means, you can leave it blank and we can touch base on it later."

"Okay."

"I'll be more than happy to demonstrate anything you're not sure of." Roarke grins and the tension leaves her. She rubs her head against his arm.

"Come here, little mouse."

Rising, she walks around the table to stand beside me.

"Take your clothes off."

Her gaze tries to leave mine.

"Eyes on me, mouse. We've all seen your hot little body. I won't have you do anything you haven't already done until we have a chance to discuss your limits."

She nods and slips her shorts and panties down her legs. Her shirt and bra fall into the pile on the floor until she stands before us naked.

I hand the stack of papers to Aiden who sets them on the island before returning to the table.

Her fingers twitch next to her thighs as I study her form. For her height she has a curvy, slender body. Her breasts are full and her nipples harden under my scrutiny.

I run my finger down her supple stomach and she trembles beneath my touch.

"You tasted Roarke's cum. Are you adverse to giving blow jobs and swallowing?"

"No, sir." She wets her lips and shifts slightly, rubbing her thighs together.

"What about cum on your body?" I trail my finger over her hip. "Do you want to wear our cum even if we can't come inside you yet?"

She breathes out a shaky breath. "Yes, sir."

"Good girl." I pat the table in front of me. "Sit."

Her brow furrows slightly, but she climbs onto the table in front of me. Soon, I'll be able to punish her for those slight hesitations. My hard cock twitches.

"Put your feet on my knees."

She rests her feet on my knees and I open my legs to widen hers, opening her pussy up to my view. It glistens with her wetness.

"Lean down and open my pants, mouse."

She shifts forward so she can reach my pants. I turn my head so my breath is on her ear. Shivering, she opens my fly.

"Take my cock out," I order.

She bites her lip, but her small hand slides into my boxer briefs and wraps around my cock. I hiss out a breath as she pushes my underwear down. As she pulls me out, her hand remains wrapped around my cock.

"Stroke it, little mouse."

Her breath catches as she runs her hand up my length to slide her thumb over my slit, before pushing back down. I reach forward and tug on her nipple. She gasps and I turn her face toward mine.

My lips crash down on hers and she squeezes her fist around the base of me.

Fuck, this girl. She tastes like chocolate cake.

I grab her hair and tug her head back. "You need a safe word, little mouse."

Her brown eyes meet mine. "Home."

"Good girl. Let go and lie back on the table."

She does as she's told so beautifully.

"Do you want to wait to suck cock, mouse?" I stroke my hands down her inner thighs toward her pussy. Her thighs quiver beneath my touch.

"No, sir."

I slide my hands to her folds and hold her open for me.

"Good answer." I lift my gaze and lock on Aiden. "Aiden."

Her pussy clenches at his name and she turns her head to him. Their eyes meet and for a minute I think he'll say no. Instead, he stands and opens his pants.

Good, out of everyone he needs a release. Greer is more than happy to help him with that. She relaxes ever so slightly. Fuck, let's see what she can handle.

"Roarke, Wyatt on either side of her." I blow gently over her exposed clit and she twitches. "Stroke their cocks, little mouse."

She whimpers and holds out her hands to them. Aiden slides his hand under her head and guides his cock to her lips. She parts them and flicks her tongue out to lick his tip.

"If you need this to stop at any point, snap your fingers. Show me."

She snaps her fingers.

"Good girl."

Aiden pushes his cock slowly into her mouth. Wyatt guides her hand to his cock, while Roarke leads her other hand to him.

"Fuck, kitten. You look good enough to eat." Wyatt leans down and sucks her nipple into his mouth. She arches and moans around Aiden's cock.

Roarke chuckles darkly before he cups her breast with one hand while the other sinks into the back of her hair and pushes her down on Aiden's cock. "Take him all the way in, poppet. Make him feel good."

She swallows around him, but barely gags. Watching her handle three cocks has my cock dripping with precum. Aiden strokes her cheek lightly while Roarke makes her take Aiden's cock deeper before pulling her back.

When Wyatt switches breasts, she trembles. Soon, I'll be able to thrust my cock deep inside her warm wet cunt, but for now, I lean forward and suck on her clit. She moans around Aiden's cock. As I thrust my fingers inside her, she comes with a muffled groan.

"Fuck," Aiden hisses before he fucks her face and pushes in deep. Groaning, he comes.

Her throat works to take it all down. He staggers back. Her lips are swollen as her darkened eyes meet his. He sinks down into the chair and watches her.

"Come here, poppet." Roarke turns her head his way. As he moves, she brings his cock to her lips, sucking on the tip. "Good girl, take it all."

Her pussy clenches on my fingers as he thrusts deep into her throat. I flick her clit with my tongue before working her pussy with my fingers and tongue. She tastes amazing. She responds beautifully to my commands and our touch.

My other hand strokes my cock in rhythm with Roarke's thrusts. Her hand works Wyatt's cock while he devotes his attention to sucking and plucking her nipples.

When she comes, she moans again, arching up into Wyatt and pushing her hips down onto my fingers. Standing, I push her legs up onto the table. Thrusting my fingers back into her pussy, I stroke my cock, aiming it at her clit.

Wyatt groans and comes over her hand. She begins to flutter

around my fingers again, making little needy noises in the back of her throat. Fuck.

"Come again, little mouse." I rub the tip of my cock against her clit. When she hollows her cheeks around Roarke's cock, he groans as he fucks her mouth.

"That's it, poppet. Suck me down." He makes a guttural noise as he thrusts a few more times and comes. "Swallow it all."

When he backs away, her warm brown eyes focus on me. She licks her lips and my release rips through me. My cock jets my cum right onto her clit. She cries out as her cunt convulses around my thrusting fingers.

As my cum slides down her pussy, I push it into her, needing to claim her tonight, even if we have to wait to put our cocks inside her throbbing pussy.

Her breasts heave as she tries to calm down her breathing. With his cock put away, Aiden gathers her into his arms and she straddles his lap as he holds her naked body against him. She rests her head on his shoulder as he strokes his hand down her back.

Fuck. She's so fucking responsive to us. I put my cock away.

"Greer."

She turns to look at me with those sleepy brown eyes.

"All good?"

She nods. "Yes, sir."

"Good girl." Roarke leans over her and kisses her, while Aiden holds her. This situation is not our normal, but with her, it feels natural.

Greer

Aiden lifts me against him and I wrap my legs around his waist. I'm so far gone from what's appropriate. I just want to go to sleep.

Roarke follows after us with a grin on his face. I can't even feel embarrassed about any of what just happened. My body is a limp noodle. I don't even care that I'm naked while they're clothed.

Roarke opens the door to my bedroom. Aiden carries me in and sets me on the bed. I shiver as he draws away, but Roarke goes into my bathroom while Aiden sorts through my drawers.

When Roarke returns, he has a warm washcloth and carefully wipes my hand off and cleans between my legs. As I shiver, he catches the back of my head and kisses me. My chills disappear as he explores my mouth gently, teasing my lips and tongue with his.

He presses his forehead against mine. "You were spectacular tonight, poppet."

"I did okay?" I ask softly, unsure if I did well. There was a lot going on. It felt like they did all the work. Even Wyatt helped stroke my hand over his cock.

"Wonderful, wonderful, wonderful." He kisses my eyes and nose before pressing a brief kiss to my lips. My heart fills with warmth. He sits on the bed next to me as Aiden brings over panties and pajamas.

Kneeling at my feet, he pulls the panties up my legs and over my thighs. I slip down to stand on the floor in front of him, so he can pull them over my hips.

"Was that okay with you?"

Aiden has boundaries right now for a reason. I don't know if Mason forced the issue, but I'm glad Aiden was the first cock I sucked.

He lifts his gaze to mine and his blue eyes sparkle in the dim light. "Better than I could have imagined, little warrior."

He helps me into my shorts and then draws my tank down over my arms. His hands skim my breasts. I catch my breath at the fire his touch ignites.

His blue eyes darken as his knuckles graze my stomach. "Maybe we shouldn't sleep together tonight."

I bite my lip. Roarke stands beside me, drawing me against him.

"How about we both help you out?" He's talking to Aiden. "You want to hold the line and I want to hold our girl, so win-win."

My hopeful eyes turn back to Aiden. He needs the sleep and I'd worry about him waking up and giving in to the alcohol. I'd rather him give in to me, but this could work.

"This is going to get weird." Aiden shakes his head, standing. He grabs my hand and my heart skips a beat. We all go into his bedroom.

Roarke takes off his shirt as I climb onto the bed.

"Your boxers stay on." Aiden takes off his shirt and shorts.

"Fine, but she's already seen it, held it, and tasted it."

"I'd rather not accidentally grab your dick in the night."

"Prude." Roarke chuckles as he stalks me up onto the bed, crawling over me until his mouth captures mine.

I fall into the kiss feeling the heat of his skin. Aiden releases a breath. The bed shifts as Aiden lays down next to me. He punches Roarke in the arm. Roarke chuckles again, but rolls off me as the room goes dark.

"We kiss for a living, Aiden. It won't break you to kiss our girl."

"Maybe I want to respect her boundaries."

Roarke scoffs. "By shoving your cock down her throat? My poppet needs kisses and hand holding and hugs to make up for the assholes before us."

"I'm fine, Roarke." I push him away a little before rolling toward Aiden.

He wraps his arm around my shoulder and kisses the top of my head.

"Thank you, little warrior," he whispers against my hair. "You were amazing."

Chapter 20

Nightmare

Greer

Something's definitely different this morning. I'm turned on and practically panting when I wake up. When I open my eyes, the room is dark and I have no idea what's happening to me. Hands hold down my thighs and a tongue licks my clit.

I freeze, trapped in a nightmare, knowing he'll push me over the edge. He always does and all I feel is shame. I shouldn't be here, but he'll punish me if I lock my door. I can't escape him.

"No." It comes out guttural as I try to inch away from him, but I run into another body. He'll ignore my pleas to stop. He always does. My sleep-soaked brain can't make sense of what's happening. "No, don't. Please stop."

"Fuck." That's not *his* voice.

"Greer?" That's not *his* voice either. "What's wrong?"

The light comes on and I'm huddled against the headboard staring at Aiden and Roarke. The spidery tendrils of my nightmare unravel, releasing me. I suck in a breath. My lungs starved for air. I'm shaking so bad my teeth clatter together.

My arms wrap around my legs, making myself as small as possible, as I rock back and forth.

"Hey, poppet, I'm sorry." Roarke reaches out for me, but I don't want to be touched. I curl into myself. "Fuck," he mutters. "I didn't know."

"Greer." Aiden's tone is gentle. "You're safe. No one's going to do anything to you. I'm going to hand you a blanket."

I open my eyes and grab the offered blanket to wrap around myself. I'm so cold. Every inch of me trembles. *He's* not here. I count to ten and back down again. I'm not *there*.

I'm safe. Breathe.

I'm safe. Breathe.

I'm safe. Breathe.

The last bit of the terror that clung to me falls away.

My breathing calms down and I open my eyes. Aiden's blue eyes are filled with concern, while Roarke's are sad and ashamed. I want to go to them and tell them it's my fault, but I'm bare from the waist down.

My reaction will cause problems. It always does.

"Can I have my panties?" My voice shakes, but I ignore that. I'll feel more comfortable when I'm covered.

Aiden looks around the bed and finds them. He holds them out to me, careful not to invade my space. I quickly slide them on under the blanket, feeling ridiculous after yesterday.

"Thank you," I whisper, but I can't meet their eyes. My brain processes what happened. Roarke went down on me while I was asleep. Memories assaulted me until I was back there, trapped in my room with *him*.

It wasn't Roarke giving me pleasure, but *him* taking it.

"I didn't think..." Roarke shakes his head, looking so lost. "I didn't know..."

I lift my gaze to meet Roarke's. I need to reassure him. My insides feel icky right now, but that's not his fault. "It's a new place. It brings the nightmares to the surface and sometimes they bleed into reality."

"But I knew—" He stops himself and releases his breath. Not saying what I don't want to acknowledge. Straightening, he moves to the edge of the bed to sit upright. His shoulders hunch as he puts his hands on his knees. "I'm sorry, Greer."

My insides tighten and a wave of regret hits me. My trauma isn't his trauma. I can't let him leave like this after all he's done for me in the last few days. Fighting off the need to retreat, I jerk forward and wrap my arms around him from behind.

"Don't say that," I whisper against his back. My throat closes and I squeeze my eyes shut. *Don't leave me.*

His hand falls over mine and his head drops. "Poppet."

When I open my eyes, he turns his head to face me. His blue eyes search mine.

"Can I hold you?" His voice is gentle. "Please."

Tears press at the back of my eyes, but I nod. No one has needed me for comfort. He draws me around him until I'm straddling his lap. One hand presses in the center of my back while the other cradles my head against his bare chest. Tears fall unchecked down my cheeks.

Aiden moves up next to Roarke on the side of the bed. "Is it okay if I put my hand on your back?"

I open my eyes. Aiden gives me a sad smile. Nodding, I reach out a hand toward him. When he takes it, my eyes slide shut. His other hand joins Roarke's on my back. I sink into their warmth, letting them comfort me.

My heart settles as everyone just holds me. Fuck, how long has it been since someone just held me? Before I got here? Before I met these men?

"Do you want to talk about it, poppet?" Roarke murmurs against my hair. He's solid and warm beneath me. He could crush me if he wanted to, but he holds me like I'm breakable. Fragile.

My eyes squeeze shut tighter and I shake my head. Maybe being with all of them triggered it, but I loved every minute of them touching me. I enjoy being touched and crave these men.

But the darkness brings the nightmares, I can't think about that time without falling into the broken girl I was. So I don't think about it. I don't allow it into my life. I don't want to go there again.

Drawing in a breath, I prepare myself for their withdrawal and whisper, "I'm good now. You don't have to keep holding me."

"I'm not ready to let go yet, poppet," Roarke whispers and his fingers press against me gently. My heart skips a little. "I know you're not ready to talk about it, but sometimes it helps. Whatever it is, I won't judge you. It won't change how I feel about you right now. It won't change that I want you. I just want to protect you. Even if it's from the ghosts of your past."

I lift my head, worried they're just lines. Just words he feels he has to say to make me feel better. But his eyes are clear and open to me. I can see all the way into his soul. He searches my eyes as his thumbs wipe away the tears flowing down my cheeks.

"What can we do, little warrior?" Aiden's words are soft, but his nickname for me reminds me that I'm stronger now. I have some agency over my own life now. Maybe I'm still reliant on other people, but the guys will help me find a new path. They'll help me find a way to be free.

I release a breath.

"For now? Make sure I'm awake before starting anything." I cup Roarke's jaw and meet his eyes. I give him what I can. "The darkness and being held down while asleep even by covers makes me uncomfortable."

"Okay, poppet." He leans in but stops before his lips touch mine. "May I kiss you?"

Flowers bloom in my chest at his request. At his patience. I close the distance and press my lips to his. Aiden squeezes my hand and I squeeze his back. When Roarke deepens the kiss, the desire I woke with reignites inside. He draws back and presses his forehead to mine.

"I'll do my best to stay outside your lines, poppet. But I hope someday you'll trust me enough with your story." His eyes hold me captivated. I don't know what I see in his depths but it's not something I'm familiar with. At least not that I'm aware of.

I draw in a breath and relax against him, suddenly so fucking tired.

I'm vaguely aware of being shifted around until I'm laying down with warm bodies on either side of me and being held as I fall back into oblivion.

———

Even though we slept more, I've felt off all morning. I'm not hiding anything from them. I just can't share that part of me with anyone. It's shameful and I can't let it in or it will haunt me again.

Aiden swims laps in the pool. Wyatt and Mason are working in their offices, both in the basement. Roarke had to go to a fitting of some kind. I'm hoping soaking in the sun will chase away the lingering darkness.

Earlier, Mason took my phone and installed a bunch of things on it. I'm flipping through the apps to get acquainted with them. That stack of papers remains on the island, but no one's asked me to go through them yet.

Maybe I should just take a peek through them to see what they like and start answering some of the questions. I pretty much gave them my answer to will I or won't I last night, but I'm still worried they'll realize they don't want me.

I'm also worried that even if something is on that page that I don't want to do that I will because they want it. That I won't be able to hold my own boundaries with them.

That they'll reject me and toss me out like everyone else does. I should be used to it by now. It hurts less when I know it's coming and it's always coming.

"We should go in." Aiden rises out of the water like a god.

My mouth waters as I take in every inch of him, dripping wet. No one's initiated anything today. Roarke kissed me a few times, but they were almost respectful compared to the sinful kisses he gave me yesterday. My stomach twists.

I glance down at my phone. "What are we doing today?"

His hand reaches out for me and I squint up at him against the sun.

"Come on. I need a shower and want some company."

My insides tingle and I rise to join him, taking his hand.

"Talking company?" I ask hesitantly. I don't want to push at Aiden's boundaries, but this morning pushed at mine. They didn't run away or turn their backs on me. But I'm worried they'll handle me like I could break at any moment.

The thing is I'm already broken and glued back together. But I'm strong enough to take whatever they want to give me. I'm not strong enough to be turned away so soon though. I may be able to weather rejection better now, but it still hurts.

He steps in closer and his finger tips up my chin. "We won't have much time alone during the weekend. Tonight is a dinner party to celebrate the beginning of filming. The guys will all be less busy with other things during the weekend. So their focus will be on you."

Fire rises inside me at the heat in his eyes. Anticipation of that focus has me pressing my thighs together against the ache.

"While I enjoy sharing you, I'd like a moment alone if that's okay." His thumb traces my jaw line, lighting sparks in my blood.

"I'd like that." I return his smile and he tugs me into the house.

The air cools around us, out of the sunlight. No one is on the main level as we hurry to the stairs. Quietly, we make our way upstairs and into Aiden's bedroom.

As soon as the door closes, Aiden presses me back against the door. His mouth finds my neck and his hands undo my shorts. My pulse throbs as flames scorch through me.

"I want to kiss you so badly," he murmurs against my skin. "Fuck, I want to be inside you."

My heart pounds as arousal pulses within. "I want that too. But we can wait."

I don't want to wait as he slips my shorts down my legs along with my panties. He cups my pussy and we both hiss out a breath. His fingers gently pulse against me as my heart throbs in time with it.

"That first day, I could smell your arousal while I searched you." He presses his forehead against my shoulder as he just holds his hand there, cupping me, barely touching me. "I wanted you. I want you."

He turns his head and sucks on my neck as his fingers press against me, into my folds, seeking my wetness. I suck in a breath as he grips under my knee and lifts my leg to open me for him.

"So fucking hot and wet, little warrior." He strokes his long fingers over my pussy.

Explosions of heat rock through me as he rubs my clit and circles my entrance. His mouth, tongue, and teeth work on the cord of my neck, sucking, licking, biting, sending jolts of need straight to my pussy. My head thumps back on the door as need fills me.

"Aiden," I whisper. I struggle to remember why we shouldn't do this. Why it's a bad idea. When everything inside me whispers *yes, now, please*.

"So fucking soft." His finger slides back to my entrance and pushes inside. My fingers tighten on his shoulders as I hold on for dear life.

"Oh, fuck." Having him inside me pushes me even higher. My breath shudders in and out. His finger is deep inside me, filling me as I clutch around it. His body hunches over mine, holding me open to his touch.

"So fucking tight, little warrior." He groans against my shoulder. "I shouldn't. Fuck. I just want to push you over the edge once. I just need to feel you shatter around me once. It will be enough."

He lifts his head and his darkened blue eyes meet mine. The desperation, the need, the longing swirls in them as he hovers over me. I'm not sure if he's convincing me or himself, but I want him. I need him. I ache for him. My pussy tightens around his finger.

"Tell me you want me," he demands.

"I want you." I don't hesitate.

His finger draws out and he presses two fingers back inside.

I gasp at the stretch as my gaze holds his.

"Tell me you need me." He thrusts his fingers slowly in and out. A moan escapes me.

"Aiden, I need you." I hold onto his shoulders as everything burns inside me for this man.

"Tell me you're mine." His thumb circles my clit with every thrust. His blue eyes search mine for the truth. I'm an open book to this man. His fingers push me higher and higher.

"I'm yours, Aiden. Oh, fuck." I arch against him as my release tightens everything inside me. I cry out as he works me through it, pushing me higher again until I'm falling and falling and falling. But he has me.

"Beautiful," he whispers still watching me, still buried inside me as little aftershocks ripple around his fingers. I tremble against him.

Every breath feels like a chore and a gift. I search his blue eyes and see the frustrated need inside them.

I slide my hand down his chest until I reach his cock, palming it through his swim trunks. His eyes flare with heat.

"Please, Aiden." I lick my lips. "Please let me take you in my mouth."

His gaze drops to my lips. My breath hitches, longing for him to kiss me. He lowers my leg and draws his fingers out of my pussy.

"Down on your knees, little warrior." His voice is firm and commanding, sending a thrill up my spine.

I lower to my knees and gaze up at him.

He cups my chin and smiles. "Yeah, that's not going to work with the height difference."

I reach up and drag down his shorts, releasing his cock. As I stroke him, I meet his eyes. "We can make it work."

"Fuck, Greer." He lowers to his knees in front of me and grabs the hem of the t-shirt I'm wearing, drawing it off over my head. "I need to see all of you."

I reach behind me and undo my bra. He draws it off and we're both naked on the floor together. Dangerous territory, but I couldn't stop if I wanted to. We won't go too far. Just enough to relieve this aching need.

His hand ghosts over my breast, making my nipple harden painfully. I suck in a breath, but he doesn't touch me.

"Four months is going to be difficult." His gaze rises to mine.

The temptation to straddle him and take him inside me rides me. Four months, fuck. Leaning over, I take his cock into my mouth. He gathers my hair to the side, holding it loosely so he can watch me.

"Are you wet for me, little warrior?"

I moan my response, taking him deeper until my gag reflex triggers, but wanting him inside me desperately. I push him deeper into my throat. My pussy throbs in need.

"Do you want my cock in your tight little pussy?"

Ah, fuck, my clit pulses. I want that so fucking bad. Groaning, I suck on him, hollowing out my cheeks and sliding my tongue along the underside of his cock. He tastes like the saltwater of the pool and Aiden.

"Slide your fingers into your pussy for me." His words are soft.

I suck on his tip as I slip my hand between my legs and thrust three fingers inside me. I moan, but I can't go as deep as he can. It's a poor substitute for the thick, hard cock in my mouth, but it will get me there.

"Fuck," he whispers. "Cup your breast for me. Show me how you want me to touch you."

I take him down my throat as I thrust inside my pussy with my hand and use my other hand to cup my breast. Wetness drips down the side of my hand.

"That's it, little warrior. Take me deep inside you. I want to slide my cock so deep inside your pussy that the only cock you dream about is mine." He thrusts his hips, making me take his cock deeper into my throat.

Gagging a little, I swallow around him. I want that too. I don't want to think about the time before this house anymore. I want to let this time with them wash me clean and renew me to figure out what I can be instead of what I was.

He doesn't control my head, but his hips move with my mouth, feeling him inside me makes me so fucking wet. I work my pussy in time with his thrusts until I can't distinguish what I'm doing and what he's doing. Until it feels like it's all him.

He's the one pushing me over the edge. It's him that I'm tightening around as I moan my release around his cock. His hand tightens in my hair as he takes control of me. Holding my head still as he thrusts in and out until his cock swells and his salty cum fills my mouth.

An aftershock ripples through me as I swallow him down, licking him clean while my fingers remain in my convulsing pussy. I suck on his tip because I don't want the taste of him to leave me so soon.

He draws me off his cock and lifts my face to his. Our lips hover so close I can feel his breath. My eyes open to his. The heat in them stirs the embers of my lust.

"I'm not going to kiss you, little warrior, until I can fuck you. Because once I start I know I won't be able to stop." It feels like he's already inside me.

"I want you, Aiden." I draw in his citrus scent and know he's right. He could become an addiction for me. We definitely need time to come to terms with this attraction because part of me really just wants to give in and fuck the consequences.

His forehead rests against mine. "Come talk to me while I shower, little warrior. I want to see what I can't have. Yet."

Chapter 21

Dress You Up

Greer

I sit beside Aiden on the couch while a woman and a man work in the kitchen. They're early for the party, but they need prep time. Or at least that's what Aiden told me.

Roarke bursts in the door and spots me.

"Poppet!" He lifts me off the couch and onto his lap. "I've missed you."

He kisses me like we haven't seen each other in days, devouring me whole. This isn't the casual kisses of earlier. This is the I-need-inside-you kisses that have me wet and ready for whatever he wants. His hands slide down to my hips until he's rocking his hard cock against my pussy.

I whimper into his mouth and my fingers cling to his hair.

Dishes clatter in the kitchen. I pull away on a gasp and glance toward the sound. They aren't looking this way. At least not now.

"Roarke," I chastise in a whisper. My cheeks are on fire. Fuck, I forgot there were other people in the house. His kisses are potent and consuming.

"Mmm, say my name again, poppet." He leans in but I hold him back with a hand against his chest. He smirks and gives me a look that melts my panties. "Come on, Greer. Everyone enjoys a show."

He slides his hand over my ass. Yeah, touching him is bad. I scramble to sit beside him. Aiden draws me into his side to protect me.

Grinning, Roarke shakes his head. He leans in close to me. "See this is the joy of NDAs. I could fuck you in front of the chefs and they couldn't say a word about it."

My mouth falls open because the look in his blue eyes says he wants to do just that. What the hell do I say to that? And why am I not more appalled?

"Perhaps later." Mason strides across the room. He wears a dark suit with a white shirt unbuttoned at the top. My mouth waters at how well it fits him, showing off his lean muscles. His hair is perfectly styled. Handsome doesn't describe him well enough. Dark, dangerous, devastating might be closer. "I need to take care of Greer."

My eyes widen. A flash of heat pours through me. *Take care of me?* What does that mean?

Mason holds his hand out. I stare at it for a heartbeat before I take it. He tugs me against him, making me gasp. The heat of his body covers me as he leans down to my ear.

"When we have a chance to go over my expectations, I want you to remember this moment when I punish you." His voice is low and dark and stirs something wicked inside me.

Punish me? My breath catches as I look up into his piercing eyes.

With a smirk, he leads me upstairs. We don't go toward my room, but the other direction. When he opens the door to his bedroom, my heart skips a little. Where the other bedrooms were light and bright, Mason's bedroom is dark. The walls are still light, but the furniture is dark, heavy wood and even his massive bed is covered in dark red coverings.

Silver glints in the light and I swear I see metal rings attached to his headboard. But I can't quite tell before he opens a door and pulls me inside. My jaw drops as I look around the huge closet filled with women's clothes.

"Do you have a girlfriend?" I should have asked before. A stone falls in my stomach. Just another reminder that I don't know these men that well. I assumed they were all available when they made me the offer to fuck me, but that might not be the case.

He smirks. "No girlfriend, but I have a mouse."

What? I turn to him, trying to figure out what he's saying. His focus is on the racks behind me as he mentally searches the clothes.

"Take off your clothes." He steps away from me and slides the hangers, taking in a red dress and then passing by it.

I bite my lip. Should I take off my clothes or ask him to explain himself? Part of me really wants to behave and the other part wants to question. I grab the hem of my shirt and ask, "Why?"

"You can't wear *that* to the dinner, Greer. This will go quicker if you just obey me." His tone is condescending and short, but I let it go.

Maybe Mason is worried about tonight. If I obey him, maybe that will help him.

I take my shirt and shorts off and watch him as he pulls things off the rack and holds them up in my direction before shaking his head. He hasn't asked me to try anything on yet, but he's right I have nothing to wear for a dinner party casual or otherwise.

My gaze roams around the closet to all the shirts, skirts, slacks, dresses in every color. Casual to formal. Even jeans and t-shirts at one end, but not like the kind I buy from the thrift store. Everything looks brand new.

"Mouse, take it all off." Mason hangs a black dress on the peg on the wall and moves to the wooden drawers. The dress has almost a swing skirt to it, but a modest square neckline. Well, mostly modest, it will still show some cleavage.

My focus returns to his words and I automatically put my hands over the sides of my panties. "I need underwear."

He's obviously lost his mind if he thinks I'm not wearing under-wear in someone else's dress, especially at a party. What I'm wearing won't show lines through the dress that looks like it's silk. The skirt is loose enough my underwear will be fine.

Sure they aren't fancy, but they're white and sturdy.

He sighs and holds up some bits of silk and lace. "You can't wear that. Here."

I take the bits of lace and realize they're panties and a bra. Shaking my head, I hold them back out to him. "I'm not wearing someone else's underwear."

Apparently I do have limits I'm willing to hold.

Placing down a pair of heels next to the dress, he rubs at his forehead. "Why must you be so defiant?"

"I'm not being defiant. I'm being sanitary." Honestly. Washing only does so much.

He closes in on me and I back into the wall. My breath escapes my lungs at the heat pouring off him and the chaotic energy he's giving off is so different than his usual stoic self.

My heart stampedes as Mason's intense blue eyes focus on me. He takes the panties and bra from my hand and sets them on a shelf.

"First, what makes you think those are someone else's?" Mason's hands slip behind me and he unclips my bra.

Desire skitters across my skin with his fingers as he removes my bra.

I gesture to this room. "You just happen to have women's underwear and clothing in a closet that doesn't belong to another woman?" I may be young but I'm not naïve. Maybe some woman or women left behind stuff, but this isn't a mere coincidence. He happens to have clothes for me? I'm not buying that.

"No, little mouse, I happen to have a closet filled with clothes for you. That I purchased new and brought here for you." His words make me freeze. What? Mason takes hold of the sides of my panties and lowers them to the ground.

I've only been here a couple days.

"For me?" I breathe out as panic swells inside me. This must have cost a small fortune. What will this cost me? It won't be money, because I can't afford this, not even with what they intend to pay me.

When he straightens, I stand before him naked. "Now, I asked before, but I'll ask again. Do you want to be my good girl or do I need to treat you like my whore?"

I press my thighs together at the ache his words cause. I still don't know. My wide-eyed gaze returns to him.

His gaze softens at whatever he sees, and he cups my cheek. "I said I'd take care of it, mouse, and I did. You can't be yourself in Hollywood, so let me make you into someone who can fit into this world. When we're here, alone, in our own world, you can wear whatever pleases you, but when we need you to fulfill a role, let me dress you."

My mouth opens and closes. My gaze roams helplessly through the closet with more clothes than I could wear in a year. "This is too much," I whisper. "Mason, I can't—"

"You can because it helps you fulfill your role, the job we hired you for." He lifts my hand and pulls me forward off the wall. Picking up the panties off the shelf, he turns them until they are the correct direction and lowers to his knee before me, holding them out. "Think of it as your armor or your uniform."

"My uniform has panties?" I raise an eyebrow.

He chuckles darkly. "I'd prefer you to go without, but tonight, panties seem appropriate."

I step into them and he drags them up my legs. He pauses before they cover me and leans forward to kiss my pubic bone before pulling them over my hips. A little shiver races through me, reawakening my lust.

"Feel free to wear whatever you'd like." He smooths his hands over the silk bottom of the panties, lighting the flames within. His thumbs linger on the bands of lace. "I like the idea of the softest silk panties under your huge t-shirts and shorts. It's like a present I can unwrap later."

I'm definitely not used to this. Hand me downs, thrift shops and a new pack of Hanes have been my go-to clothes for so long. Mason picks up the bra and holds it out for me to slide my arms into. No man has ever bought me clothes. Let alone a whole wardrobe.

"When we play, I'll have outfits for you to wear." He takes my hand and leads me over to the dress. Before I can step forward to take it, he unzips it and removes it from the hanger. No man has ever put more clothes on me.

"Play?" I ask a little breathless. It's too much and just being near Mason and breathing in his leather scent makes my heartbeat erratic. But this, him taking care of me... fuck. Not something I would think would make me aroused.

He smiles at the dress and my panties are damp. He gives me this sideways glance that tells me he knows how he affects me. The fire he causes to rage within. He's just waiting for me to give him permission, to let him put it out.

"You haven't filled out the forms yet, little mouse. You have no idea what I want from you." He steps forward and lowers the silky dress over my head. It whispers along my skin like a lover's touch. "I need your consent."

"I think I know a little of what you want." Control, domination. Submission. My lips part.

His blue eyes find mine and he smirks as he straightens the dress on me. "You might, but we need to be on the same page. There are things I'll need from you. Unless you want me to get them somewhere else."

"No." The reaction is automatic and I'm not sure it will change no matter what deviant thing he's into. I'll be his to mold however he wants. But I don't share. His eyes flare hot.

He turns me and presses me against the wall before reaching down to slide my zipper up. I draw in a breath, waiting, needing his touch. His fingers skate along my spine, sending desire pooling at my center.

The need to explain rises inside me. It's not just that I want to be his everything.

"I can't stand a cheater," I say softly. "I won't take another woman's man. I know how that feels."

"I don't belong to anyone." He attaches the hook and eye and turns me around, closing in on me so I'm pressed between him and the wall. His hand lifts my chin and his intense gaze searches me. "I also don't break my word. If you give me what I need, I'll remain true to you and only you."

"What do you need?" I whisper. Do I have what it takes to go toe to toe with this man?

He slides his hand around the back of my neck and leans down to my ear. "The consent forms are on your nightstand, little mouse. Read through them and you'll know exactly what I need."

My stomach flips. His hand slides up my thigh to rub on the silky panties over my pussy. Heat engulfs me.

"I will say, I love the way these look on you, but I'd prefer you without. Some night, I want you in a dress with nothing on underneath for dinner."

My hips rock with the feel of his fingers rubbing my pussy through the panties. His lips caress my ear with his every word.

"You'll sit down on my lap and take my cock inside your hot, tight cunt while we eat and talk with the others. Maybe I'll let the others play with you too or maybe I'll fuck you in front of them for dessert, so they can see what belongs to me." His finger slides beneath the silky panties and thrusts into my core.

Gasping, I reach for his arm to hold on. His smile turns to determination as he misreads what I'm doing. I don't want to pull him away. My pussy clenches around his finger. I'm strung so tight it won't take much to push me over.

"No, mouse. You're going to come on my finger so I can smell you through the dinner tonight. I'll think of your warm tight pussy with every handshake." He lifts his head and his heated eyes meet mine. "Can you do that for me, mouse? Or do you need an audience to come?"

My lips part as he pushes me higher and higher. I pant with every thrust until my insides feel like they'll combust. He holds my gaze as he makes me fall apart. Moaning, I come on his fingers, shuddering as he continues to fuck me. His pleased smile makes my insides tumble over one another.

"Good girl."

An aftershock ripples through me at his words. He draws his finger out of me and moves my panties back in place. I finally release his arm.

He tips my chin up and captures my lips with his. My toes curl into the rug as he draws me into his warmth and explores every inch of my mouth. I'm pliable in his arms and willing to let him mold me into whatever he wants. Whatever he needs.

When he lifts his lips, his breath rushes out over mine. My eyes open and gaze into his.

"Stay by Aiden's side tonight. Only let him drink what you or he pours." Mason straightens and the sensual fog lifts from my head. Orders.

"Are you worried someone will give him something?" What kind of people are coming tonight?

"We can't risk it." Mason leads me to the shoes and I slide my feet into them. "He has a drug test on Monday and you'll be getting your blood test done as well."

He turns me to face the mirror. Everything fits me like it was made for me. The dress clings to my curves and flares out at the hips. How the hell did he know my sizes? Even I don't buy the correct size for me.

I don't typically wear high heels but they barely make a difference with Mason towering over me.

His hands skate down to my hips. "You look lovely, Greer."

"Thank you." I tuck my hair behind my ear. I'll need to do something for makeup and hair. I don't have much makeup to work with, but I can probably figure out something acceptable.

Chapter 22

There She Goes

Greer

Greer

A knock sounds on the door to the closet before it opens to reveal Wyatt. He whistles low as his hazel eyes sweep over every inch of me, warming me.

"Damn, kitten. I'm glad Aiden will be watching over you tonight. Otherwise, some guy would try to lure you off into a quiet corner."

"I'm watching Aiden." I cock my eyebrow. Not the other way around.

"Sure." He smirks and comes forward as Mason steps back. "And I'm some guy wanting to take you into the corner and make you uncomfortably wet during our dinner party."

His hands go to my hips like Mason's did and he tugs me back against his erection. I look tiny compared to him. My hand barely circled his cock and I didn't really get a chance to study it last night. I'm almost afraid to see it.

Wyatt smirks and lifts my chin. "We figured you probably didn't have much for makeup or hair, so we called in reinforcements."

My brow furrows as he takes my hand. Mason smiles as he smells his finger. Heat and embarrassment flow over me. Wyatt draws me out of the closet and out of Mason's room.

"There's my new bestie." Zoe's smile is perfect and huge as she comes toward me with a large case. "I brought a ton of stuff so we can experiment if we need to."

Wyatt tugs me into his side. "I'm on hair duty."

Zoe shakes her head and rolls her eyes. "He thinks he's all that." She leans in and says, "Honestly, he did a better job than Mom could. I usually went to him."

She gives Wyatt a quizzical look. "Where are we setting up?"

Wyatt jerks his head toward his room. A little rush goes through me. This is the only bedroom I haven't seen. He pulls me inside. It's white and light blue everywhere like the ocean is inside his room.

His large windows face the water and he has them open to let the air flow through. He leads me through to his bathroom, which is large enough for two people with a vanity built into the counter. Extra lights surround it and there's even a white bench.

Wyatt shrugs when I meet his eyes. "The bedrooms are all like this. Built for double occupancy. Except yours, kitten."

Zoe stops setting things out and turns to study her brother. "Kitten?"

He rolls his eyes and helps me sit down. "She's tiny and compact, but pretty sure her claws are sharp if you get on her bad side, so kitten."

"You're weird, WyWy." Zoe's hazel eyes land on me. She smiles. "Okay, so we probably want to remain fairly neutral even though it's evening. How do you feel about red lipstick?"

I bite my lip and look at all the stuff she's unloaded. "I've never really done makeup."

One time Bristol made me sit down and let her give me a makeover when she was bored. She did a much better job than I ever could. She used so many things that I was even scared to ask her what and how she did it. I couldn't afford the kind of makeup she had.

"Hmm, blank slate. I like it." Zoe leans against the counter in front of me. "Your eyes are amazing on their own. A little eyeliner, maybe some mascara, a sprinkling of brown on the lid. Maybe a little gold. Definitely a red stain that won't smear since you'll be eating. Your skin is practically flawless on its own."

Wyatt catches my gaze in the mirror and smiles. A rush of warmth flows through me.

"Let's do tiny braids around her face and drape them back into a bun. We'll leave the rest down." Zoe taps a pencil against her lip as she studies my face and then grins. "Don't worry. The McBride siblings have you."

Aiden

We've kept to ourselves since my rehab. The guys were worried about pushing my limits. But it's time to get back out there. To celebrate my recovery and the new film we're finally working on. We've had this night planned for a couple weeks now.

On a scale from *oops someone's drinking in front of me* to *holy shit this is a rave with drugs being handed out like Halloween candy*, this party ranks a solid *I'm not the only one who's done drugs here.*

I fix my cuff links and make sure my hair isn't out of control in the mirror. My fingers tremble with nerves, but I'm good.

I'm healthy and have a new outlook on life. Greer will be beside me all night. My marriage is over, but I have someone to look forward to.

Someone knocks on my bedroom door. The guys are trying to give me space now as opposed to the constant worry after I got out of rehab. The guys didn't give me privacy because they couldn't let me slip. Mason threatened to take my door off the hinges if I ever locked it.

The knock is nice and makes my chest swell a little. They're starting to trust me again.

"Come in."

Roarke opens the door and grins. He looks like a pirate from a romance novel cover. He has on leather pants and a billowy shirt that has more buttons undone than they did in the seventies.

"Fuck, Aiden, you look good enough to kiss." He puckers his lips and starts for me.

"Fuck off, Roarke." I shake my head because he's tormenting me about my decision to not kiss Greer or fuck her for four months. I duck back into the bathroom.

"It's just ridiculous when you consider you're going to kiss someone on set at least once a week while filming." Roarke sits on the edge of my bed and shakes his head. "That and you've had your dick in her mouth."

I make a noise to acknowledge I heard him, but the reality is I want her kiss too much. I want her too much. I don't know if I'll make it a week, let alone a month, but it's just another test to make sure I'm not going to cave again.

"Next time she wants you to kiss her, let me know." Roarke's chuckle fills the room. "I'll take your kisses and mine. She needs them."

"At least I know she won't be denied the pleasure then." I step out of the bathroom. "Time to go face the music."

Roarke's smile fades as he rises. "No one's going to arrive for another hour. Fuck, I hate hosting."

He's right no one shows up to the party at the time listed. But just in case some newbie doesn't know the rules yet, we need to be ready.

I clap him on the shoulder as we walk out into the hallway and head downstairs. The chefs have been joined by a few servers in black slacks and white buttoned shirts. A woman server with her blond hair in a high ponytail tugs excitedly on the arm of the guy with his hair spiked as we walk across the floor. The dark-haired woman server stays in the back doing whatever her job of the moment is.

Roarke gives the blonde a cocky, encouraging smile, but I just ignore them as we sit down.

"Claire!" The woman chef stops and glares at the server.

The blond, whose brown eyes lit up at Roarke's attention, turns and hurries into the kitchen.

"You going to turn that off?" I ask as we sit on the couch, gesturing to all of him.

Roarke grins. "Turn what off?"

"The flirting?" I lean forward and wait for him to join me. "What will your poppet think of you flirting with other women?"

He smiles. "She is mine, isn't she?" He puffs his chest up like the rooster he is. "She'll understand that I can't turn off this kind of animal magnetism, but I won't do anything about it. I'm saving all that for her."

Sitting back, I shake my head. This is a disaster waiting to happen and I'll be left to pick up the pieces of Greer when hurricane Roarke moves on.

I'm curious how many other women Roarke will have to fawn over this evening. He knows how to work a room and not commit to any woman, but make every woman feel wanted.

Mason created the guest list, but that's the way it always is. He brings the people who want to rub elbows with us and we put on our dog and pony show. Entertaining the guests with stories and anti-dotes until the wine stops flowing. It's networking in its rawest form.

And tonight Greer will be by my side. Fuck, I shouldn't have touched her earlier. I don't regret giving her an orgasm or watching her tip over the edge from my touch, but it will be that much harder to keep from pushing further. From doing it again, until all my control shatters and I'm buried deep inside her while she cries out my name.

"Can I get you a drink?" The blonde, Claire, I think, gets my attention.

"Nothing for me, Claire." My gaze falls on the stairs behind her, waiting for Greer to make an appearance.

Claire's cheeks turn pink and her attention moves to Roarke. "For you, sir?"

"Sir? Don't tell me you don't know who I am?" Roarke's tone is teasing as he flashes her his award-winning smile.

The pink of her cheeks grows deeper. She stammers a little when she says, "Of course, Mr. Flynn. Can I bring you a drink?"

"I'd love a scotch on the rocks, love." He winks and she hurries away.

Chuckling, Roarke watches her hips sway. I clear my throat.

"What?" He smirks back at me. "It's not like I'll do anything with her."

"Greer isn't like other women, Roarke." I cross my ankle over my knee.

"No, she most definitely is not." Roarke's gaze blurs over with whatever thought he's having. Maybe this morning in my bed. Her *no* jerked me out of sleep, but she was trapped in it, struggling to the surface from her nightmare.

"Come on, kitten." Wyatt's voice draws both of our attention to the stairs.

Zoe comes down first in flowing wide legged pants and a tied top, showing off her small waist. As soon as she reaches the floor, the guy with the spiked hair comes up beside her and asks if she'd like a drink.

Smiling, Zoe puts her hand on the guy's arm, squeezing it as she leans into him and murmurs something before she laughs. Claire walks over at that moment.

"Your drink, Mr. Flynn." She holds out a glass with round ice and two fingers of scotch.

"Thank you, love." Roarke takes the drink, but his focus remains on the stairs.

Claire waits a moment, probably hoping for his attention, before she heads back to the kitchen. Her shoulders slump a little, but I'm sure it's only a momentary defeat. She'll come back stronger next time.

Wyatt walks down with Greer. Her shoes appear first before her legs. I don't realize I'm standing until I'm walking toward them. The black dress showcases her figure perfectly. Her hair falls in waves around her shoulders and down her back.

When they reach the main floor, she lifts her head and my jaw almost drops open. Greer unmade up is cute and quirky and gorgeous in her own right. Greer, with red lips and eye makeup, her hair pulled back, and clothes that fit like a second skin, is spectacular.

"Fuck, never kiss her, I'll take them all." Roarke steps in front of me and draws Greer away from Wyatt before spinning her in his arms and dipping her low. When he whispers something in her ear, her cheeks darken pink. She makes a little undignified noise, but her eyes sparkle up at him like he hung the fucking moon.

He draws her back up and holds her against his side. "You need a new sobriety buddy, Aiden. This one's mine."

She laughs that delightfully husky laugh and puts her hand on his chest before she moves away from him and over to me. Every step closer makes my blood pulse harder through my veins.

"I'm taken for the night." She stops in front of me with the best smile and it's all mine. Fuck, I want to kiss her. I want to claim her. I want to fuck her.

Her light brown eyes lift to mine and I'm speechless. There's trust in her eyes and longing. Maybe we're all playing with fire with her. Maybe we'll all let her down.

But when she looks at me like that, I feel like the superhero I play in the movies and not the broken man I've become.

Greer

Aiden takes my hand and lifts it to his lips, pressing a soft kiss to my knuckles. My heart skips a beat as he raises his light blue eyes to mine. The way he looks at me takes my breath away. A shiver of desire rushes through me.

"Good evening, Ms. Morrow." His words and his smile make my insides glow. "You look stunning."

My cheeks are already warm from Roarke, but that compliment from Aiden makes a fresh surge of heat rise.

Aiden wears a black shirt with black slacks. Silver cufflinks wink in the light. He's stunningly handsome himself. But he knows that.

Aiden draws me into his side, wrapping my hand around his elbow and putting his hand over mine. I'm not doing a good job at keeping sex and love separate, at least not in my head. It would be so easy to imagine this is more than what it is. I'm here for a job, but they're offering me this sneak peek into their lives and an opportunity to explore my sexuality with four gorgeous men.

They aren't offering me love. But I don't need love. I barely remember what it feels like. I walled off my heart years ago and every year since I fortify it a little more.

Aiden leads me over to the couch and sits me next to him. I cross my legs and Roarke sits on my other side.

He ducks his head next to mine. "Poppet, when this is over, I'm going to make you come so hard the neighbors will hear my name."

"There are those sweet nothings I was hoping for." I meet his laughing eyes with a smile.

"How about I let you ride my face?" He picks up my hand and tangles our fingers together. His eyes make my blood burn hotter. "I'm willing to drown in your cum, poppet. How is that not romantic?"

He arches his eyebrow and a giggle escapes me.

"It's very hard to take you seriously right now."

"Only right now?" He smirks. "I'll have to work harder."

Wyatt and Zoe join us on the wrap around couch. Mason walks into the room and I swear my pussy tightens at the heated look he sends my way.

"You're staying for the party, Zoe?" Mason's gaze falls on her.

"Even if it's a boring talking party and no one ends up naked on the table by the end." Zoe sighs and shrugs. "I promised Wyatt to keep him company a week ago. I still can't believe you're holding me to this."

Wyatt lounges back on the couch, stretching out his dark denim clad legs. His leather shoes are shiny. He wears a green dress shirt that brings out the color in his eyes. After helping style my hair, he slipped into his bedroom and changed his shirt.

Honestly, it should be illegal for that man to cover that chest with clothes, even if they do look good on him. He looks yummy without them.

"Don't make promises you don't want to keep, ZoZo." Wyatt winks at me.

"I was puking my guts out and you were being nice. It seemed easier to give in." She pouts and her eyes focus on Mason. "You'll keep me company, won't you, Mason?"

"I have enough to worry about." Mason steps closer to me and suddenly there's less air in the room. His gaze locks on mine. "You won't get starstruck, right?"

I shake my head. Pretty sure I've done all the fangirling over the two superstars next to me. I don't know if anyone could walk in here and distract me from these two.

"Good." He tips my chin up and studies my makeup. Zoe did a flawless job. "You do clean up well, little mouse."

I'm going to take that as a huge compliment. "Thank you."

Nodding, he removes his hand. He strides off into the kitchen to talk with the chefs and the servers. I notice the blond server eyeing Roarke like he's a prized piece of meat. His fingers slide against mine.

"Maybe we can sneak away before the other guests get here." Roarke murmurs next to my ear. His breath tickles and heats my ear. "I want you splayed out on my bed with no panties on. I promise to get you off over and over again. What do you say, poppet? Want to sneak away with me?"

I turn and his face is right there. His gaze drops to my lips and I lick them. I would happily disappear with Roarke for whatever he's offering, but my duty is to Aiden tonight. I squeeze Roarke's hand.

"I have to earn my keep tonight." I rest my head on Aiden's shoulder.

"I hope that's not the only reason you stay with me, little warrior." Aiden's words are soft.

"It's not all about the money," I admit. The promise of a future and college is a huge draw, but there's more here that I want to explore. With all of them.

"I would totally do it for the money." Zoe leans forward. "What else would a girl have to look forward to?"

My eyes meet Aiden's and he gives me a smirk. So much to look forward to.

Chapter 23

In The End

Greer

"You've been to something like this before?" I ask Zoe.

"Ugh, yes. Wyatt always needs a plus one because whatever freak of the week he has going on isn't acceptable for this part of his life." Zoe grins.

My eyebrows rise. *Freak of the week?* I swallow. Is that what I'll be to him? How much of their private lives will I be privy to? I'm also so damned curious to read the consent form now. What exactly do they want from me? I squeeze my thighs tight.

"It's not all bad though. There are plenty of inappropriate silver foxes who come to these things." Zoe straightens her shirt and shows off a little more cleavage. "They'd make great sugar daddies."

"Fuck, ZoZo, no talk about sugar daddies or any type of daddies." Wyatt shudders. "We're brother and sister. Older brothers do not want to know that shit about their little sisters."

She grins. "Do you know how much money I could be rolling in if I just send some old dude pics of my boobs? Thousands, WyWy, thousands."

Wyatt stands and glares at Zoe. "I need a drink."

"Oh, bring me one." Zoe's still smiling as she turns back to us. Her gaze goes to Aiden and the joy dims in her eyes. "Sorry, Aiden. If you want, I don't have to drink tonight."

"Just because I have a problem doesn't mean you have to abide by it." Aiden lifts my hand and entwines our fingers together before setting our hands on his thigh. "I've got Greer to keep me safe tonight."

"I'm sure she'll do a great job." Zoe smiles, but it doesn't quite reach her eyes. Her gaze pauses for a second on our hands.

I'd nibble on my lip but the lipstick. Fuck. Am I already losing Zoe as a friend? I was never good at getting to know people at new schools. After a while I just stopped trying, I never stopped wanting to be accepted. Part of me really wants Zoe to like me.

"You should come out with me tomorrow night, Greer." Zoe straightens and laughs. "Drinks and hot bods for days. This new club is opening and there's a room of beds as seating."

My eyes widen. "I don't think that's really my speed."

I'm on a tricycle while Zoe is on a racing motorcycle.

Zoe grins and leans over Roarke's lap and makes a come hither motion to draw me closer.

She glances at Roarke who smirks. "See Greer, anything can be your speed with a little medicinal help."

"For fuck's sake, Zoe." Wyatt stands over us. "What the fuck are you doing? Talking about drugs right in front of Aiden?"

Zoe pouts and looks up at Wyatt with remorseful eyes. "I'm just trying to make Greer my friend. She's young like me, and she's never had a chance to have a wild and crazy life. Maybe she'd appreciate cutting loose and being free for a night."

When she glances my way, she winks before returning to her pouting face.

"You will not corrupt Greer. She's what Aiden needs the way she is." Wyatt hands Zoe her drink before he sits beside her. "She doesn't need to be fixed."

Heat rushes to my cheeks. I turn to Aiden, "Do you want some soda or water?"

"Sparkling water would be nice." He brings my hand up to his lips before releasing it. "Thank you."

I head toward the kitchen. Mason turns as one of the servers starts for me. Mason's hand lands on my hip and he guides me over to a dry bar set up in the living room. There's even a refrigerator behind it.

"You can get your drinks here, mouse." He leans down next to my ear. "Make sure it's a fresh bottle when you get more."

I nod as he backs away and his blue eyes search mine. When he's certain of whatever he sees, he returns to the kitchen.

I grab two glasses and a bottle of sparkling water. It fills both glasses.

"Hey." Zoe's voice is soft. She hovers next to the dry bar. "Wyatt told me about your mom. I'm sorry I didn't know or I wouldn't have been offering you drugs. It's just what I do with my friends for fun on weekends."

She shrugs her elegant shoulder as I lift the glasses.

"It's okay." I exhale. "I don't expect everyone to understand how my life is without knowing the full story. I think it'd be nice to hang out some time, but maybe we find something more both of our speeds?"

She grins. "That could work."

But first I have to get through tonight.

Zoe and I walk across the house back to the guys. Aiden's gaze locks with mine. Zoe is elegance personified. Her hair falls in golden brown waves. Her makeup is flawless. She just has a grace that I'll never have. She fits into this world easily. I'm okay with that.

The look of longing in Aiden's eyes as he takes me in is enough to make my blood sing. I won't compare to Zoe in the real world, but *he* likes me. This broken, screwed up version of me.

Handing him a glass, I lower into my spot between him and Roarke like I belong here. Like I didn't steal this spot from someone else, but that it was always intended for me. Roarke slides his arm along the back of the couch behind me and I don't resist the pull of his body, as I rest my head against him.

The servers and chefs are the only ones privy to this moment. They're busy getting ready. The calm before the storm. I'm not sure why Mason checked in with me about getting starstruck. I'm firmly there.

Roarke's fingertips trail down my shoulder, sending little shivers through me as I take a drink. The conversation goes on around me as I sip at the sparkling water. At some point, Aiden holds my hand again and puts it on his thigh.

Zoe studies the three of us closely a few times. I'm not sure what she'll be privy to or what Wyatt will tell her about our situation. So I just smile like this is normal for me. Overall this is nice.

But holding patterns can only last so long. Wyatt glances at his phone.

"They're coming."

Roarke kisses my cheek. "Prepare to be amazed, poppet."

Zoe stands and straightens her outfit. When everyone else stands, Aiden reaches his hands down to help me up. I didn't realize how comfortable I'd gotten between the two of them on the couch. The words spoken around me lulled me into contentment.

Cars enter the driveway. The front door is open and people begin to flow in. Not one at a time, but in droves. Aiden pulls me in tight to his side and I cling to his arm as people come forward.

They shake his hand and he introduces me. They give me a passing glance, realize I'm nobody, and continue talking to Aiden. It's like I pop into existence when he mentions me and then I'm gone the next second. I actually prefer it.

In my experience, being overlooked and ignored is always preferable to being seen.

As we greet people, they move to the servers who show them outside and take care of their drinks. I hadn't noticed the set up outside in the garden. Long tables stretch out around the pool. The pool has floating lights on it. More lights are strung above the tables. It's beautiful. One of the servers heads out through the opened doors with a tray of hors d'oeuvres.

A lot of faces of people I've seen on TV or in movies move past me. It's practically a red carpet up close and personal. Roarke makes flirtatious comments and gives looks to every female he greets and some of the men. Between rounds, he winks at me.

On interview shows, he's always a huge flirt. I'm not surprised or alarmed by the way he's behaving.

Aiden receives a lot of "how are you *really?*" or "so good to see you up and about." None of it sounds real. It all sounds like words these people rehearsed.

Everyone is glamorous and put together. Mason was right I need this dress and makeup to blend in. If I were in my normal clothes, I'd stand out, draw attention, be seen. As it is, I'm invisible and amazed. This right here was worth the price of admission into their world.

It definitely makes me feel less than to be surrounded by such industry giants.

Mary had some parties with famous people, but they were small intimate affairs. There, I was something to look upon with pity. A prize that Mary had been gracious enough to keep for a while. She loved to tell my story. Orphaned at a young age by a mother who cared more about getting high than her only daughter.

Mary ate up every compliment for how good she was to take me in out of the kindness of her heart. I was a freak show in her home. Something to gawk at and feel better about their own life situations.

"Greer." Aiden's tone is gentle as he draws me away from the crowd for a second.

"Yes?" I blink to sweep away the past. "Do you need something?"

He smiles gently and tucks a strand of hair behind my ear. "You just checked out for a moment."

I inhale and smile. "Sorry. A lot of people."

"Almost done." He tucks my hand in his elbow. "Then we can go find a quiet corner to mingle in."

"That sounds nice." The volume in the house has risen. Some soft music plays under the din of voices. Laughter bursts outside from time to time.

When we return to the receiving line, Roarke's hand rests on my back as he leans down.

"Doing okay, poppet?" His blue eyes search mine for a second.

Hoping my smile isn't stretched too thin, I nod.

"Aiden Clybourne!" That voice. I stiffen. My insides twist with knots. My breath catches. I should have known. I should have figured it out. Mason is connected to him. "Proud of you for coming through."

He shakes Aiden's hand, and his gaze skips over me to Roarke. "Roarke Flynn, always knew Mason would have good friends."

"He learned to collect us at a young age." Roarke steps forward and shakes Sawyer Brickman's hand. The woman behind Sawyer definitely isn't Mary.

"Rita, so good to see you." Aiden kisses both of her cheeks. I never met Rita but Mary talked about her constantly. This was Sawyer Brickman's wife.

"Who do we have here?" Rita turns her green eyes on me, studying me with curiosity.

Aiden touches my hand and I remember to breathe. "This is Greer Morrow, my friend."

This isn't the first time he introduced me like that, but Rita smiles and holds out her hand to me.

"What a fascinating name. Enchanted to meet you, dear." She catches her husband's hand. "I haven't run across many Greers. Have you, Sawyer?"

He turns his dark eyes on me. I brace myself. Recognition lights in his eyes before he lets it dim. He hasn't changed much in the four years since I last saw him. A touch more gray in his dark hair, but he still has that arrogant look.

"Greer?" Sawyer smiles down at his wife. "Definitely unusual."

"Well, you're lucky to have found this one, Greer. Aiden's quite the good guy." She pats Aiden's chest before her husband leads her farther into the house.

My breath returns to me and I nearly collapse as my knees go out from under me. I cling to Aiden's arm like a life line.

Someone else greets Aiden and Roarke so they don't notice. Thankfully. After this morning, I don't need them worrying more about me. Sawyer and Rita work their way into the room. When Mason stops them, his smile is so joyous it takes my breath away.

Rita must mention me because Mason's gaze finds me. He tips his head when he finds me watching him or rather them. But he gets drawn back into the conversation.

I know that man. Sawyer, Brick on set, Mary's paramour, Mason's mentor. I should have guessed he'd be here. I should have expected it. Fuck, why didn't I prepare myself for it?

Maybe because four really great guys occupy my mind now.

The door finally shuts and Aiden turns with me toward the backyard. That rush I had earlier at seeing all these people in one place is gone. I'm exhausted. I'm also grateful Aiden is by my side and I won't have to face Sawyer alone tonight.

Aiden leads me to a quiet corner as promised. We find a loveseat in a little casual seating arrangement. Roarke mingles, touching people, leaning in to kiss cheeks, laughing.

"Should you be doing that?" I turn to Aiden. Not sure what I'm supposed to do besides stick to his side like glue.

"Don't worry, little warrior. They'll come soon enough." He takes my hand and links us together on his thigh again. I relax a little, but then his fingers tense on mine. A late arrival walks out to join the party.

Greyson Marks strides across the patio, announcing his presence. The din quiets for a moment as everyone takes in every inch of the superstar. He's as tall as Roarke and as big in Hollywood as both Roarke and Aiden. His brown hair is tucked into a bun. His blue eyes are fascinating close up like diamonds on the screen. His dark suit clings to his large form perfectly.

But I realize a second later the reason Aiden squeezed my hand.

A woman walked in behind Greyson and now steps up to cuddle into his side. Siobhan Clybourne, Aiden's ex-wife.

Chapter 24

Kiss Me

Aiden

I've known Greer for two days and could read the subtle shift in her mood when Brick walked in. Sawyer Brickman took Mason under his wing years ago and trained him, worked with him, made him the director he is today.

Surprisingly, Greer knows him but not in the how have you been kind of way. *We should totally catch up.* More in the pretend we don't know each other way. *I don't know you, you don't know me.* Which they both did, but I felt her lean on me when he left like she needed my strength.

Now I'm feeling the same way as Siobhan enters my life for the first time since our divorce. We never did the divide our friends thing or talk about how to avoid each other in the future. It isn't an option.

While the industry is big, it's also very small and we would run into each other eventually. For the rest of our careers, when one of us does something big, the other will be asked about it. And we'll lie and say we're so proud and support each other.

Hell, we might even say we're friends in the future.

When in reality, she cut my world in two and shattered me into tiny pieces that I'm still working to put back together.

"What do you want me to do?" Greer's husky voice calls me back from the brink. "How do you want to handle this?"

Siobhan laughs and her green eyes find me. They sparkle with life. Her dark hair flows down her back and she looks as gorgeous as ever. She molds herself to Greyson's body the way she used to cling to me.

"Fuck," I whisper. She's happy. She's moved on. And I'm tangled in my addiction. Barely able to move forward, crawling inch by inch.

"Let me help you." Greer's words are soft and they draw me, tempt me.

When I turn, she's right there. Beautiful, young, vibrant. I'm going to hell because I'm about to do something that should happen four months from now and in private, but because my ex is here with her new boy toy, I'm going to break my own rules.

When I cup Greer's cheek, her hand goes over mine. So fucking trusting. I touch my forehead to hers and say softly so only she can hear, "I've wanted to do this since you walked through our door. Waiting would be the smartest course, but my pain is rising and I need to lose myself in you, with you. Greer—"

I don't make it through my speech as I press my lips to hers. She gasps a little and I give in fully to temptation. I only meant to sample, but I knew one touch is all it would take.

I deepen the kiss, ransacking her mouth for the cure to my pain. As she slides her tongue against mine and whimpers in need, I find that moment of peace and bliss. A moment of pure joy that I didn't think I'd be allowed to feel again. That I don't think I deserve.

The noise around us fades until it's just me and her. I soften the kiss, losing myself in the taste of her, of Greer. I was right. She's addictive. The softness of her, the little whimper in the back of her throat, her hand clutching mine.

I already crave her, need her, but now I know her taste and I want more.

If we weren't at a party, I'd draw her on my lap and slide inside her, to make myself a whole person, to feel complete. But we aren't alone and the only reason I leapt into this is because I couldn't handle the reality of my life.

A bucket of cold water wouldn't have been more effective than that thought.

Fuck. I lift my mouth and press my forehead to hers, catching my breath. What did I just do? "I shouldn't have, little warrior."

"It's okay."

I open my eyes to her soft brown eyes. They've darkened as she smiles. I want to fall into her again.

"Didn't realize you two would need a chaperone." Wyatt pulls me out of the moment. I raise my gaze to him. And the realization of what I just did sweeps through me like an ice storm. I kissed Greer at a party.

"Fuck," I whisper. How bad is it? I'm almost afraid to ask.

Wyatt smirks. "Your ex saw but Roarke drew everyone else's attention away by proposing a fight with Greyson. Even found sticks to use as swords. You okay?"

He's asking me. Greer still holds my hand. Her worried gaze remains steady on me. Her lips are slightly swollen and so tempting that I want to lean back in and take them. To escape with her and discover every tantalizing inch of her.

"I'm good." I inhale. "Really. I just needed..."

"I get you, brother." Wyatt puts his hand on my shoulder and I feel like a complete ass. He knows exactly why I did it. Siobhan looked happy, in love even. My life fell apart while hers soared. She destroyed me. I needed to show her she didn't completely break me.

"I'm here for you, Aiden." Greer's soft voice draws my attention. "Whatever you need."

I'm an asshole. I can't even hold my own line in the sand.

"Stop." Wyatt sits on the coffee table in front of us. "Whatever the fuck you're thinking. Stop. You reacted, Aiden. That's all. You're fucking human. Your ex showed up and you didn't go for a drink or drugs. You went for Greer. I'm counting that as a win. Right, kitten?"

She smiles and my heart pounds. "Yes, definitely better than alcohol."

"We should mingle." Wyatt stands and holds his hand out to Greer. "If we go together, people will wonder what the fuck is happening if they saw the kiss."

Fortunately, these are industry professionals. Typically they won't throw someone under the bus, because they know we've seen them at their lowest or we will. It's inevitable. But there's always the possibility they'll feed the tabloids this to stop their own story going live. We'll need to tread carefully.

*****

Greer

On Wyatt's arm, I apparently gain some visibility. Or maybe it was the kiss. More people ask about me, but then Aiden steps next to me and once again I slip into the background. Honestly, I don't know how to act around these people.

Most of them seem larger than life to me. They all wear plastic smiles and talk about either business or simple small talk. Neither of which I'm very adept at talking about.

"What other projects do you have coming up?" A bald man with a white beard seems very interested in Wyatt.

"I'm focused on finishing *Creator of the Dark*." Wyatt's thumb caresses my hip as we stand close together. Does he even realize he's doing it? It's turning my insides into mush, making me not focus on all these celebrities surrounding me.

"Greer." Zoe's voice makes me turn. She stands behind me with her hand on the arm of a young guy, early twenties. His blond hair falls over his brown, soulful eyes. My eyes widen in recognition. "This is—"

"Holden Jamison." Aiden holds out his hand to the man. "I've watched your work."

Holden shakes his hand with a grin. "Aiden, big fan. Huge. Still not used to meeting someone like you and them knowing my name."

I struggle to hold down fourteen-year-old me who had a major crush on then sixteen-year-old Holden Jamison. Giddiness wells within me. He played a brooding guy in love with his best friend's girl. He was my first crush.

"Get used to it. You're already a name." Aiden smiles and his hand rests on the small of my back, pulling me back to the here and now. He centers me and I release the breath I was holding.

"Anyway," Zoe says, looking between the two men and rolling her eyes, "I brought Holden over to meet Greer."

Holden's eyes lock on me and I swear my heart kicks up a notch. If I'd had a room with posters, he definitely would have been on my wall.

"Hi, I'm Holden." He holds out his hand.

I force myself not to giggle.

Aiden fucking Clybourne had his tongue in my mouth a while ago and I'm trying not to gush about my childhood crush to the guy standing in front of me. As best I can, trying to be mature, I hold out my hand and shake his, trying to keep my smile from turning maniacal because I'm touching Holden Jamison.

"I'm Greer," I get out, still shaking his hand. Blushing, I stop and bring my hand back, rubbing it with my other. My inner fourteen-year-old wants me to never wash this hand again. I almost laugh out loud, but manage to stay grounded next to Aiden.

"Ah, Holden!" Roarke's voice booms through the party. He claps Holden on the shoulder hard enough that Holden lurches forward a little. "What are you two up to?"

He looks between Zoe and Holden.

Zoe rolls her eyes. "I just thought Greer would like to meet people her own age while she's stuck in the house with you guys.

Holden and I are friends. He's not big on the party scene though, so I figured he and Greer might get along."

Oh, my god.

Roarke raises an eyebrow. "Are you trying to set Greer up?"

Oh, my god!

White hot embarrassment floods my body. I didn't have parents to be embarrassed about growing up. Apparently, Roarke intends to make up for that loss. But then it registers, *is* Zoe trying to set me up? With Holden?

Holden runs his hand through his hair and gives me a flirty smile. I'm definitely flattered and the giggling inner fourteen-year-old can die happy. I'm currently not in a relationship, but kind of.

Oh, fuck. It's not like I can say I'm taken. Zoe knows Chad and I broke up. I haven't had time to find even a fake boyfriend. Is this something friends do? Set each other up?

"No." Zoe grins. "I'm just showing her there are better guys out there than her ex. Like Holden."

Roarke stops and looks Holden over and then turns to me. "Is this what you want, poppet?"

I can't even with him right now. My face burns. He knows exactly what I want. Roarke grins and shakes Holden's shoulder.

"Just friends then." He chucks me under the chin and wanders away.

"Roarke's in a mood. Sorry about that." Aiden gives an apologetic smile to Holden. "He's protective over Greer."

Holden nods. "Like an older brother. I get that."

Aiden chuckles but doesn't refute it. Definitely *not* like an older brother. More like a horny octopus. I shiver thinking about his hands all over me.

"Are you new to town, Greer?"

Oh, hell, Holden Jamison is talking to me. I probably have stars in my eyes. Fuck, I promised Mason I wouldn't get starstruck. I draw in a breath to still some of the butterflies running race circuits inside me. He's just another guy at this party.

"No, I grew up here." See, I can speak to the hot guy in front of me without giggling like a teenager.

"Yeah? What part?"

Zoe gives me a look that I'm not quite sure how to take. Is she trying to warn me not to say something or encourage me to say more? I suck at this part of girl world.

"I moved around a lot." I don't hide my past, but I don't lead with I'm a foster kid. It puts different labels on me depending on the person.

"That's cool." Holden looks to Zoe.

"Yeah, figured this would be a me thing." Zoe leans against a chair. "Introverts. So Greer here has to work tonight to keep Aiden on the straight and sober, but maybe sometime this week, we can get together and hang out."

"Sure, that sounds good." Holden glances from me to Aiden. He rubs the back of his neck. "If that's cool. It's hard to meet people who don't want something from you in this town. Zoe says you're cool."

My chest expands and I almost preen. Zoe thinks I'm cool. I don't want to let her down. "Yeah, I'd like that."

Holden's eyes meet mine and he smiles like he's the shy one, meeting me. It can't hurt anything to hang out. He won't want to date a nobody like me. Besides, it would be nice to meet more people in town, especially when I'm going to be at things like this with Aiden. I may have had a crush on Holden until I was fifteen, but that's long gone now.

It's still weird to meet him. But I'm also very conscious of the hand resting on my back and the man attached to it. Holden might be my age, but I'm taken for as long as these guys will have me. Very happily taken, currently.

"Me and my boy usually just play games or watch movies when we hang out." Holden scans the party. "He's more into the club scene, but he's down to chill."

"Yeah, you should totally bring him too." Zoe smiles at me with a wink. "We could play pool or Roarke has all the latest video games. There's the swimming pool."

"Oh, there he is." Holden holds up his hand and a dark-haired guy starts our way.

Aiden rubs his hand on my back. When I glance at him, he smiles and leans down close to my ear.

"It's cute that you're excited to meet Holden."

My cheeks burn again. I whisper, "Teenage crush."

He lifts his head and his blue eyes crinkle with laughter. The sounds of the guys greeting each other reaches my ears. The hair raises on the back of my neck.

When I turn to face them, Holden has his arm around a guy who's as tall as Aiden with dark hair and green eyes. "Aiden, I'd like you to meet my boy, Tripp Carter."

The world stops as Aiden talks with Tripp. I freeze as everything in me says to run, to step back, to get away from him. My heart pounds in my ears, covering the voice I haven't heard since I was sixteen.

"This is Zoe," Holden says. "And this is—"

"Greer Morrow." Tripp's tone is smug and his eyes take in every inch of me until I feel like I need a shower. I've never been able to scrub him off me. "It's been, what? Five years. Look at you all grown up."

I force a smile to my lips and let all the noise in my head fade into the background. "Five years."

Not long enough.

"You know each other?" Zoe looks from me to Tripp and back again.

"My mother went through a foster phase. Wanted to help other teens in need." Tripp smiles as his gaze falls to my cleavage, what little is showing. I resist the urge to cover it. "Greer was our one and only. You were with us a year, I think."

I nod. "A year."

A year of nightmares and hell. A year I don't like to remember and even now, I'm fighting to push all that back into the box it belongs in. I'm not that girl anymore.

Tripp rubs his fingers over his lips as his eyes meet mine.

Someone taps a bell somewhere.

"Time for dinner." Aiden draws me into his side.

Tripp's green eyes go to the movement, assessing everything. Still the predator.

"We'll talk later, Holden," Aiden says. "Nice meeting you, Tripp."

"Yeah, we'll have to find time to catch up, Greer." Tripp's words shouldn't be menacing. We knew each other a full year. It should be no different than any other foster I ran into that lived in one of the homes.

But Tripp was Cindy's son. I was the invader in his territory and he made sure I knew it.

Aiden leads me away before I have to respond.

Chapter 25

Somebody That I Used to Know

Roarke

Greer holds her hand over both her and Aiden's champagne glasses as the blonde server comes around. I'm down a ways from both of them, but I check on them from time to time.

Honestly, I can't seem to keep my gaze from wandering to Greer. She's different tonight. Still cagey as fuck, but she blends in. More than one guy has looked her over, but she's mine. I need to remind her of that tonight.

I return my gaze to the couple across from me. The server pours their champagne.

"So Greyson, how long have you and Siobhan been boning?" I give them a cocky grin and swirl my scotch.

Greyson smiles and takes Siobhan's hand on the table. "We just started seeing each other a month ago."

Siobhan smiles into Greyson's pretty face before she turns those green eyes on me. "The divorce was final before I even looked at another man."

I'm not so sure about that, but whatever. Grey's a nice guy. Too nice for Siobhan. When Aiden brought Siobhan around, at first I was skeptical of her, but now I just don't like the bitch.

"Aiden seems to be doing better." Her gaze strays down the table before watching me for clues.

I grin, thinking of that kiss. Normally I like to participate, but Greer and Aiden… Fuck, those two have chemistry that I can feel the singe from across the room. I definitely want to watch those two fuck it out. Watch Greer's pretty face bathed in ecstasy as she rides Aiden's cock.

I meet Siobhan's gaze. "Yeah, eight months now. But you knew when he went in."

That's the problem. She knew this was his party, our movie. She wasn't invited, but came along as a plus one. What's her fucking goal here? Did she want to tank Aiden's recovery? Did she miss the attention she got as the wronged party?

"Of course." She takes a sip of her champagne. "I just wanted to know he was doing okay after… everything."

"Things are definitely looking up for him." I glance meaningfully at Greer as she laughs at something Aiden says. His blue eyes say it all as he smiles at her. I don't know what that kiss meant. It was spur of the moment and he might take it back, but it's going to be harder for him to resist the temptation going forward.

I'm just glad I don't have the same rules. I'm giving her the time she needs, but fuck is it hard. She turns me inside out, makes me want things that just don't make sense to how I normally operate.

Zoe's laughter draws my attention to the other end of the table where she sits next to Wyatt. Holden blushes on the other side of her. Another young guy leans across Holden to say something to Zoe. She laughs again and touches his arm.

We're going to need to talk to Zoe, or at least Wyatt is. She's trying to set up Greer with Holden, which would be fine, but Greer is mine. Holden might be perfect for her. He's a respectful young man. Doesn't do the party scene. Is professional on set.

But not for my poppet. Fuck that.

If Greer is going to be ours, then we need to be clear about everything we expect. That means no dating Holden. No dating anyone, but us.

"Would you like another drink?" The blonde server has her sweet voice on for me. Her brown eyes darken when I turn to her. Her lips part in silent invitation.

A week ago I would have followed her into the house and pulled her into the half bath. Bent her over the sink and fucked her hard until she came on my dick.

"Sure, love, I'll take another." I wink, but I don't mean it. It's all part of playing the role of Roarke Flynn. It's expected of me at this point. But I definitely won't be fucking anyone else. Including the cute server.

She blushes and heads back to the house. My gaze tracks her until it collides and settles on Greer. Aiden talks to the couple across from them. When we're not engaging with her, she becomes this shell. Her smile is perfectly fine and she appears to everyone else like she's engaged, but I know, she's not really there.

Something preoccupies my poppet's mind. I want to know what it is, which surprises me. I'm not the kind of guy women turn to for deep and meaningful conversations. I definitely don't sit around and wonder what they're thinking about. Unless it's sex, then I'm definitely interested.

But I've seen Greer when she's overwhelmed and sad and when she's afraid. Right now, I want to draw her onto my lap and make her come to life again. Whisper in her ear all the dirty things I want to do to her until her face is on fire and she tells me off for it.

"Who is the woman with Aiden?" Siobhan holds her fork in front of her lips, trying to be casual when she asks. Like she isn't asking who her ex kissed.

This woman broke my friend.

I grin at her. "Curious?"

She chews delicately before acting like she's just making conversation. "She's pretty. And young."

I hope it hurts.

Ah, is this the he left me for a younger woman schtick? Should I feel sympathy for the woman who dumped my friend? Yeah, that's not happening.

"She's new. Just found her."

Wrinkles form around her mouth and eyes like she's trying to process it internally but it's leaking out.

"Here's your drink, Mr. Flynn." The blonde sets it down next to me. Her breast brushes against my arm. Intentionally. What did Aiden call her?

"Thank you, Claire."

She perks up. Yeah, chicks like it when you remember their names. Aiden does it because he wants people to know he values them.

"Could you help me settle a bet?" I meet her brown eyes, which darken a little more.

She looks from me to Greyson and back. "Maybe?"

The guy next to Greyson pulls his attention away from us.

"See, Siobhan over there was married to Aiden, down there... What was it? Five years?"

"What are you doing, Roarke?" Siobhan leans forward and practically growls all while smiling. Siobhan doesn't like her shit aired unless she's in control of the narrative.

"Just asking for an outsider's perspective." I return my gaze to Claire. "See, they were married for five-ish years and then Siobhan wanted a divorce. Aiden didn't see it coming, thought they were happy and all that, but then she just up and leaves him. Now that's pretty crappy, but the tabloids did claim that Aiden was having an affair. So maybe she thought she was justified. Though if you know Aiden, you'd know he'd never fuck around on someone he's loyal to, especially not his wife. So clearly, that was bullshit and everyone knew it."

"What the hell is the poin—" Siobhan glares.

"Now, Siobhan." I shake my head and give Siobhan a disappointed look. "I'm discussing this with my good friend, Claire." I return to Claire's widened, slightly panicked eyes. "That's all backstory. But do you think Siobhan gets any say in who Aiden wants to kiss or even fuck? Now that they've been divorced…" I pretend to think it over in my head. "My, it's been a year and she shows up to his party with a new guy. That's probably an important detail too, don't you think so, Claire?"

"Uh."

I swear I see the moment poor Claire's brain glitches as she ping pongs between me and Siobhan. My gaze starts on Claire but ends on Siobhan. "Do you think Siobhan has any right to know anything about Aiden after she almost destroyed him?"

Siobhan's lips press into a thin line, but she doesn't say anything.

I turn to Claire. "Thank you, love, you've been great. Sorry to keep you."

Her mouth opens and closes before she hurries off.

"You don't have to be cruel. I did love him. I'll always love him." Siobhan whisper yells across the table.

"Still doesn't mean you're part of his life anymore." I take a bite of my dinner. "My job as best friend is to keep him happy. You don't do that anymore. *She* does."

I glance down the table and Greer comes to life again. Aiden engages her in some conversation. Good. My poppet only deserves the best. With us, she'll get it. I'll make sure of it.

Greer

After dinner, people mingle again. I'm on edge. There are now two people I'd rather avoid at all costs at this party. But I'm here to do a job and Aiden keeps my mind on other things.

Those people are my past. They shaped me into who I am now, but they no longer have control of me.

Aiden is part of my present as are Roarke, Wyatt, and Mason.

"How's it going?" Mason's dark voice next to my ear sends a little jolt through me.

I turn my head to look at him. Aiden is busy talking with someone, but his fingers toy with mine as we stand next to each other.

"All good." I glance around to make sure Sawyer isn't with him. I breathe a little easier when I see Sawyer across the pool with his wife. Mary always said Rita wasn't good for Sawyer, but the two look happy enough.

Sawyer's actively avoiding me, so we're on the same page. Deny, deny, deny.

"Any issues I should be made aware of?" Mason's fingers toy with my skirt hem, making me suck in a breath.

Does Aiden kissing me count as an issue? Because it was amazing. While I want to do it again, he'll likely withdraw. And I'll be okay with it, because I know that's what he needs to do.

"Not that I know of." My eyes flick up to his.

"Not starstruck, mouse?" His fingers brush my thigh and I hiss out a breath.

"No, sir."

His chuckle is dark. "Good girl."

His touch and warmth move away like he was never there. Sighing, I turn back to listen to this guy tell Aiden about the guy's last film. I don't know how Aiden appears so interested when I'm trying not to nod off.

"If you'll excuse us," Aiden says to the man. I perk up.

"Of course." He seems surprised.

Aiden draws me away and into the house. He doesn't pay attention to anyone as he climbs the stairs and heads into his bedroom.

"Make yourself comfortable, little warrior." He kisses the top of my head and goes into the bathroom.

His room has a little seating area close to the window overlooking the ocean. I slip off my shoes and curl up in the chair, watching the waves roll in and out as the sounds of the party drift up to me. It's soothing after the loudness of everyone.

After a few minutes, Aiden comes out. "You need to use it?"

I nod and pass him on my way into his bathroom. Overall, tonight has been a success. I blended in and didn't make anyone uncomfortable with a story about my mother who overdosed because my dad left us. After which I spent years in the foster system before aging out.

Of course, no one was offering that story either so that probably helped.

Checking my makeup in the mirror, I wash my hands. As I go to open the door, I hear voices on the other side.

"You shouldn't be up here," Aiden says.

"I wanted to ask how you're doing." Female voice. I can't place it.

"I'm doing great. Now leave."

"Aiden, I still care about you even if we aren't together anymore." Hmm. Siobhan, maybe.

"I'm not your concern."

I step out of the bathroom as the woman closes in on Aiden.

"All done," I say so they know I'm in the room.

Siobhan turns. Her eyes widen. I don't hesitate to move around her to Aiden's side. His hand finds mine and he draws me against him. I'm not a woman who can intimidate another woman, especially a woman almost a foot taller than me, but I can support Aiden in whatever he wants to do.

"Shall we go back down to the party?" he asks me. His blue eyes lock with mine. They're soft and his smile warms my heart.

I nod. "I just need to put my shoes back on."

Aiden lifts his gaze to Siobhan. "We'll see you downstairs."

Her lips press together as she assesses me with her eyes. I'm young. Younger than her, but only by maybe seven or eight years. She's the same age as Aiden, but it's not like they're that much older than me.

She's gorgeous and has a thriving career. Tonight, she's on the arm of one of the most eligible, sexy actors. And yet, she's up here trying to reconnect with her ex, for what? Another chance? Would he give her one? Am I just in the way or am I helping him?

Finally, she paints on a smile. "Right. I should get back to Greyson. He's probably wondering where I've run off to."

Aiden gives her the same plastic smile as she turns and leaves. Her heels click on the stairs until they disappear into the din of the party. He sighs and pulls me into his arms, wrapping me up against him.

My ear rests against his quickened heartbeat. I don't hesitate to hug him back. Part of me always wants to be here for Aiden. To be the woman he turns to for comfort. But that's not what we're working on here.

They want me. That in itself is amazing and makes me feel some sort of way. But I want them, too. Their offer is no strings.

After Chad, that's what I need. I want someone to want me for me.

"Hey." Wyatt's voice doesn't make Aiden pull away from me this time. "I saw Siobhan on the stairs. Is everything okay?"

Wyatt closes the door and the noise fades. Outside the sounds continue but they're less noticeable.

"Yeah, everything's good." Aiden presses a kiss to my hair and draws back. "She wanted to check on me."

"I'm sorry. The chefs and servers are supposed to keep people from the stairs."

"Siobhan can be persuasive when she needs to be." Aiden takes a deep breath in and I step back. "Find your shoes, little warrior. Just a little longer."

I squeeze his hand and go over to get my shoes.

"Will you give us something to keep us until later, kitten?" The heat in Wyatt's voice slides down my spine to pool hot in my stomach.

My breath catches. I turn to find both men leaning against the bed, watching me. The rush of need, want, and power is a heady cocktail.

They want me.

All those gorgeous women outside, dripping in wealth and beauty, and these men want *me*.

"What do you want?" I straighten, knowing I'll give them anything.

"Come here, kitten."

I leave my shoes and walk over to stand before Wyatt. He holds out his hands as he sits on the bed and spreads his legs. When I take his hands, he pulls me between his knees. He licks his lips as his gaze takes me in.

"What did Mason give you to wear under that stunning dress?" Wyatt cocks his head to side as Aiden lowers to sit next to him.

"He gave me—"

"Show us, kitten."

Chapter 26

Sure Thing

Greer

A shiver works through me at Wyatt's words, the way he looks at me, the heat of his body before me. His hands leave mine and he leans them back on the bed. His hooded hazel eyes never leave me. Aiden sits next to him. His heated gaze meets mine.

I still can't believe any of this is my life.

Swallowing, I reach for my skirt's hem and lift it until they can see my panties. Black silk and lace hide my pussy from their view.

"Aiden, can you check to see if she's wet for me?"

My eyes widen as the ache increases between my thighs, but I don't want to push Aiden too far. "You don't have—"

"Shh, little warrior." His hand starts at my knee and trails up the inside of my thigh, making my breath quicken. If I weren't already soaked, I would be by the time he touches me. Just the thought of him touching me again is intoxicating, dizzying. "Spread your thighs for me."

I move my feet apart and whimper as his fingers touch the edge of my panties, tracing it between my legs along my thigh, so close to touching me, but so fucking far.

"Is she wet for us?" Wyatt's hazel eyes never leave mine. The sounds of the party drift up through the open window fighting with the sound of the ocean, but both sound so far away.

Aiden's finger slips beneath my panties and strokes over my clit. I bite my lip on a moan. Fire burns inside me.

"Soaked." Aiden draws his finger out and brings it to his lips, sucking it into his mouth as I watch helpless to move. Wishing I could just stay here for the rest of the night. Alone with Wyatt and Aiden. A shiver passes over me.

But we can't stay up here long, we have to return to the party.

"Turn around, kitten." Wyatt remains still, but I do as he asks.

The bed makes a slight noise as he shifts and his fingers release the hook and eye holding my dress. Another shiver works through me. Then the zipper slides down my back and I suck in a breath. Wyatt's hands slip beneath my dress and hold my waist.

He glides them up my sides, teasing the sides of my breasts before skimming over my shoulder and pushing the dress off. It flutters to my feet in a whisper of fabric.

"Pick it up, kitten."

I step out of it and bend to pick it up. Aiden reaches for it and lays it on the bed beside him. Wyatt gestures for me to come closer again.

My nipples ache against the silk and my pussy throbs. If they leave me like this, I'll have to face those people downstairs, feeling bound up and aroused.

"Very nice choice." Wyatt slides his thumb across my nipple and I moan, wanting more. I press my thighs together against the ache. "Take off the panties."

I meet his darkened eyes as my thumbs hook into the sides of my panties and lower them until they flutter to the ground.

"Good girl." He lays back on the bed. "Undo my pants."

I glance at Aiden and his darkened eyes meet mine. He nods slightly, giving me permission. I lick my lips and lean over Wyatt to undo his jeans. His hands cup my breasts together in my bra and he slips his thumbs beneath the cup over my tightened nipples.

Taking in a shaky breath, I finish undoing his pants.

"Pull them down, kitten."

Obeying him turns me on. I slide them down over his hips.

"That's enough. Now my boxers."

The need is overwhelming. I want to come. I need to come. I can't think of anything else as I pull his boxers down and gaze at his massive cock. I want him inside me, but how would I ever fit him? My pussy clenches.

"Fuck," I whisper. Even as wet as I am, I'm not sure I can take his cock. It's long and thick and intimidating as hell.

"Come here, kitten." He holds his hands out to me. When I hesitate, he glances at Aiden.

"He's not going to fuck you, little warrior. We just want to make you feel good." He trails his knuckles down my stomach and over my hip bone, causing a riot of butterflies to dive bomb my stomach.

When I take Wyatt's hands, he pulls me until I straddle him, my knees on either side of his hips, hovering over his cock lying on his stomach. My hands rest on his green shirt.

"Sit your wet pussy on my cock." Wyatt's hazel eyes hold mine. It's a command and one that I desperately want to obey.

Bracing myself for the feel of him, I lower myself down until his cock slots against my pussy. He groans and my breath catches at the feel of his hard cock pressed against my clit. The urge to rub is strong.

Aiden stands and moves behind me. My skin tingles with anticipation. His hands glide up my back from my hips to my shoulders, pressing me forward, gently down until I'm lying on top of Wyatt.

"You look beautiful tonight, Greer." Aiden's words caress my skin as his hands trail back down over my ass, parting my cheeks.

My insides are molten lava, swirling hotter and hotter. I whimper and Wyatt shifts beneath me, rocking his hips and sliding his cock along my clit. I gasp.

"So fucking beautiful," Wyatt whispers as he releases my bra and helps me take it off. His hands slide over my bare breasts. Every touch feels like a jolt of electricity to my core.

Aiden's fingers circle my pussy opening and I gasp, clutching into Wyatt's shirt. Molten heat pours through my veins. Aiden's fingers ease deep inside me as Wyatt slides his cock along my clit.

"Oh, fuck, I... I..." My mind can't process everything they're doing to me as they begin to slowly fuck me.

"Shh, kitten. Just feel." Wyatt pinches my nipples and I moan. My hips rock with his as Aiden's fingers thrust in and out of me. "That's it. Find your pleasure and take it."

I run my hands beneath Wyatt's shirt, feeling his muscles ripple beneath my touch. I push up a little, so I can slide his shirt up his torso, revealing all his golden skin. He groans as my bare stomach presses against his.

Tingles dance along my skin where we touch.

I kiss his chest and run my tongue along the valleys of his muscles. The salty taste of him makes me crave more.

"Fuck, kitten." Wyatt's hands hold my hips.

I'm building to an orgasm. Finding my pleasure in their touch. My heart races and my breathing is chaotic.

Aiden's fingers slide out of my pussy and trail my wetness back to my asshole, before slipping inside.

I cry out softly against Wyatt's skin.

"Good, little warrior?" Aiden's other fingers slide into my pussy, filling me full of him. I can feel his fingers slide against each other deep within me, stirring the already raging inferno until I feel like I'm going to combust.

"So good," I admit and suck on Wyatt's skin.

Wyatt slides his hands up to my breasts and pinches my nipples as we writhe together. Aiden's fingers work in tandem, sliding in and out of me until I can't think anymore. My breath stops as my release overwhelms me. My pussy and ass convulse around his fingers, tightening and releasing as he finger fucks me through my orgasm.

Wyatt's cock jerks against my clit and combine with Aiden's

fingers fucking in and out of me. Moaning, I come again, gushing around his fingers and all over Wyatt's cock. Wyatt groans as he comes between our stomachs.

He slides me up until our mouths meet. His kiss is hungry and devours me whole. The head of his cock presses against my clit, making an aftershock ripple around Aiden's fingers buried in my pussy.

His fingers leave my asshole and he slides them through Wyatt's cum before pressing his fingers back into my puckered hole. I pant into Wyatt's mouth.

I gasp as Aiden adds a third finger, stretching me, and fucks my ass with Wyatt's cum, pressing his fingers all the way inside me and pulling them all the way out before sliding back in until I'm bucking back against him.

Wanting more, needing more. Pushing me closer and closer to the edge.

"Come one more time, little warrior. I want to see how your tight ass will choke my cock when I'm buried deep inside you." Aiden's words tip me over the edge again.

I cry out into Wyatt's mouth as I tighten around Aiden's fingers.

"Good girl, kitten." Wyatt runs his hand down over my ass. I rest my head on his shoulder as my breathing slows.

"Mmm, Greer, such a good girl," Wyatt says. "But..."

I lift my head and look at him.

"Aiden didn't get to come yet, kitten. You can fix that, can't you?"

My pussy tightens around Aiden's fingers. I wet my lips already anticipating the feel of his cock sinking into my mouth, filling my throat, making me gag at how deep he goes.

"You want to make me come, Greer?" Aiden slips his fingers from me.

"Yes," I whisper. Wyatt helps me sit up and then turn around. I straddle his hips facing away from him. Wyatt's cock slowly hardens between my pussy lips.

Aiden slipped away to wash his hands, but as he comes back, he undoes his belt and opens his pants, freeing his hard cock. I'm completely naked, while Aiden has on all his clothes. I wet my lips, eager to feel him inside me, to taste him again.

"I've been thinking about this all night. Those red lips of yours wrapped around my cock." He slides his thumb along my lower lip and I meet his gaze as my tongue darts out to taste his thumb.

Holding my hips, Wyatt bucks beneath me and I moan at how good that feels against my sensitive clit.

"Open, Greer."

I put my hands on Wyatt's knees to brace myself and open my mouth for Aiden. He slides two fingers into my mouth and presses on my tongue. My pussy throbs.

"Show me what you want to do to me, little warrior."

I meet his darkened eyes as I close my lips around his fingers and hollow my cheeks as I suck on them. He slides them out and rubs the head of his cock against my lips. I lick the precum from his slit before opening and taking him inside.

"Fuck, I'll never get tired of watching you take a cock, kitten." Wyatt's is hard beneath me again and he rocks our hips together, sliding my pussy along his length. "I can't wait until you're riding my cock while sucking on Aiden's."

Wetness seeps out of me onto him as I bob on Aiden's dick in my mouth, taking him so deep I begin to gag, but I want him deeper. I swallow around his tip.

Wyatt's fingers are slick as he circles my asshole. I back off of Aiden's cock, sucking on and licking it while holding his gaze. His blue eyes are dark with desire. His hand remains on my chin as his thumb strokes up and down my neck.

Wyatt's fingers slide inside my ass and I shatter, sucking around Aiden's cock until he comes. I swallow him down greedily as I ride Wyatt's cock. His thick fingers stretch my asshole, going deeper than Aiden's.

"Your ass is so tight and warm. I can't wait to get inside your pussy, kitten. I can't wait to stretch every hole to take my cock, until you ache for me, need me to fill you."

Aiden slides out of my mouth and leans down to take my lips with his. I gasp at the feel of his kiss. It's still new and consuming. His hand slips over my breast and I'm lost as I fall over the edge into another orgasm.

Aiden takes all my noises into his mouth as he devours me like he can't get enough. Wyatt keeps working my asshole and sliding his cock between my legs until the world blurs around the edges and I come again.

He slips his hand from me and drags me up until his tip rests against my clit. I keep my mouth on Aiden's as we explore each other's mouths like this is the last time we'll ever kiss.

It might be. My heart squeezes. Tomorrow he might take it all back.

"Stroke me, kitten."

I reach down and slide my hand down Wyatt's cock, rubbing his tip over my clit, until I'm working us both. My pussy aches empty.

Aiden draws his mouth away and rests his forehead against mine. "One more, little warrior. Do you want to feel him? Just the tip of him inside you to feel how wide he'll stretch you."

My lips part and my pussy throbs at the thought. I can just ease back a little and he'll slide right inside me. Not all the way, just a little, just to feel. Fuck, I want that.

I move so my feet are beside Wyatt's hips. His large hands hold my hips as I lift a little and slide his cock back to my opening. I coat his tip in my wetness, running it back and forth against my pussy from my clit to my entrance and back again as Aiden holds my gaze.

His hand cups my breast gently, tenderly, like I'm breakable. He runs his thumb around my nipple as I slide Wyatt's cock back to my entrance. I hold him there as I lower myself just a little onto him.

"Oh, fuck, oh, fuck, oh, fuck." I roll my hips, sliding on and off of his head, feeling him slip in and out of me, stretching my pussy.

"How does it feel, kitten?" Wyatt's voice is strained as his fingers dig into my hips like he's holding back.

"So fucking good," I whisper and slide a little more inside me before coming off and doing it again, over and over.

Aiden's other hand trails down my quivering stomach before he slides his finger over my clit, circling it and then slipping back to feel my entrance stretched around Wyatt's cock. "Such a good girl, Greer."

His fingers return to my clit and rub me as I work myself on the head of Wyatt's cock.

"Fuck, kitten. I'm going to cum inside you."

Panting, I take him just a little deeper before lifting off and sliding back on. "Yes, please, oh, fuck, I want to feel you inside me."

Wyatt's hands on my hips stop my descent at just the tip. "Soon, kitten. I'll be buried so deep I'll kiss your womb. This is enough for tonight."

I reach my hand down and stroke the length of his cock that isn't inside me, surprised to find a lot still exposed with how he feels inside me. My wetness trickles down over him and I use it to stroke him faster, moving my hips in time with my hand.

Aiden's eyes meet mine before he lowers his gaze to watch me take the head of Wyatt's cock. It's all so overwhelming and freeing and amazing.

When Aiden pinches my clit, I arch back as pleasure descends over my body. My lips part in a silent scream as I come, sliding a little deeper onto Wyatt's cock. My pussy convulses around him, tightening almost painfully around his thickness. My hand stops stroking him but remains wrapped around his cock.

His cock jerks in my grip. He groans as his hot cum shoots inside me, triggering another orgasm as he fills me. Aiden catches me under my arms, to help hold me up as Wyatt struggles not to buck up into me fully. His hips thrust his cock in and out in little moves.

His thighs tense between mine and I feel every spray of his cock both as it flows through his shaft in my hand and inside me. I've never felt anything quite like it.

"Fuck, kitten. You feel like heaven." Wyatt's fingers rub my hips.

I draw in a breath. My thighs tremble from overuse as Wyatt eases me off his cock.

When Aiden lifts me into his arms, I wrap my legs around him and bury my nose into his shirt. His citrus scent helps me relax.

He carries me into the bathroom. When he sets me down, I let the wall hold me up as he starts the shower. He grabs a clip out of his drawer and hands it to Wyatt as he comes in. He's stripped naked.

Fuck, he's massive even half hard and all those sculpted muscles. I want to explore every inch of him.

My body gets ideas I no longer have the energy for. Wyatt's hazel eyes meet mine as he gathers my hair in his hands. Unable to resist, I reach out and run my hands down his abs.

"A quick rinse before we go back to the party, kitten." Wyatt carefully piles my hair on my head and clips it up.

The party. Fuck, I completely forgot about the party and that I have to go down and be seen. After orgasming how many times and for how long? Oh, hell, we've been gone for a while.

"It's okay, Greer." Aiden takes my hand and kisses it. "Just a little longer and people will begin to leave. No one stays long at a dinner party on a Friday night. Not when there are other places to be seen."

Chapter 27

Closing Time

Mason

"The last few offers I had were basically for me to play the same character all over again." Greyson crosses his ankle over his knee. A few of us sit in a small seating area off to the side. Aiden and Greer disappeared into the house a few minutes ago. "I need something more substantial, that I can really sink my teeth into."

Wyatt and Zoe stand off to the side of the pool with Holden and some guy I haven't seen around before. It's not uncommon for the young actors to have an entourage or a few buddies they bring to these type of events.

I invited Holden because he's got an it factor and a work ethic. He's not letting his fame go to his head. I just hope Zoe doesn't fuck him up.

Roarke has attracted an audience as usual. He's in his element, flirting with women, impressing men, telling stories that make people laugh. He and Aiden balance each other at parties. Aiden plays Roarke's straight man well.

"I'd love to do something like what you have going." Greyson's voice draws me back in as I realize he's looking at me. "I hoped my agent would get a look at your project."

"Casting finished months ago." Everyone knows this is our pet project. The one that Wyatt, Roarke, Aiden, and I worked on for years to put together. It all came down to timing and when we were all available. "If we have any last minute cancellations…"

I let the statement hang in the air. I can't promise him anything and I won't. We're set to start Monday and I've worked hard to make sure it goes off without a hitch.

My attention wanders to Wyatt as he walks into the house. Zoe is still flirting with the boys as usual. I'm surprised she hasn't left yet. This isn't her typical Friday night scene.

"I'm sure if Mason had a part he'd offer it to you." Rita's sweet voice has always grated on my nerves. She has a tendency to try to fix things that aren't broken.

"Dear, maybe you've had enough to drink," Sawyer says softly.

"Mmm, the champagne is really divine. Don't you think so, Mase?" Rita's green eyes latch onto me. If Sawyer is like a father to me, Rita definitely plays the part of the evil stepmother. She likes to twist conversations and situations to suit her. But she plays at being nice so well that not everyone sees it.

"I like to stay clear headed, but the champagne was good." I switched to sparkling water an hour ago.

Siobhan walks out of the house over to where we are. She's stiff. "Grey, I'd like to go now."

He grins that affable grin of his. "Siobhan, come sit with me. We're talking movies and champagne."

Siobhan's eyes flit to me for a moment. "Grey."

He shakes his head. "The woman wants what the woman wants. It was a pleasure talking with you all. Mason, I hope to hear from you on future projects. We should really work together sometime."

I nod as he stands. Siobhan glances at me almost in embarrassment before she turns and heads out. Greyson hurries to catch up. A couple of clingers wander away since Greyson is gone.

"Siobhan, such an odd name. Oh, what was the petite thing's name, Sawyer? The girl at the front?" Rita almost tips her glass, but Sawyer grabs it at the last minute. "It was so unusual for someone her age."

"Greer?" I offer, only knowing one petite thing that was at the door.

"Yes." Rita grins and touches Sawyer's arm. "So unique. And just a little doll."

"How does Aiden know her?" Sawyer meets my gaze with his unreadable eyes and a voice that almost sounds like he's bored and searching for a subject to talk about.

The thing is I know Sawyer. I know he stays with Rita out of loyalty, but that she often drinks too much so he has to leave her at home. I know he has a woman he sees frequently named Mary. Even met her a time or two. Very nice woman.

I also know when he's interested and wants to seem uninterested as in now. With Greer. And that makes me curious.

"She works for us." I also know that if he's going to fish, I'm not giving him all the answers until he throws in his largest bait. The remaining couple sitting with us leaves when someone calls them over.

"What happened to that Michael guy?" Sawyer sets Rita's glass on a passing tray. The dark-haired female server keeps moving like nothing happened, leaving Rita, Sawyer, and I alone.

"Michael decided he could make more money offering Aiden drugs." I glance around the party and see Roarke. Then Zoe and the two guys. But not Aiden, Wyatt, and Greer. My gaze lifts to Greer's room. Her lights are out, but Aiden's room is on the other side of the house.

"How do you know this girl will be any better?" Sawyer asks. His wording is careful.

"What do you really want to know, Brick?" I breathe out and meet his dark eyes. "And why are you so interested in Greer?"

"Such an unusual name." Rita smiles. "You don't hear it much these days."

Sawyer winces. "I think it's time we went home, dear."

Taking the easy way out.

"But the champagne is lovely." She looks around for her glass but can't find it. She lifts her hand like she's going to call over a server, but Sawyer takes her hand instead.

He gives me an apologetic smile. "We'll talk this week."

Rising with them, I follow leisurely as he takes her into the house to leave. It's not uncommon for Rita to focus on one thing, but Sawyer usually tries to redirect the conversation, not lean into it.

His interest in Greer makes me wonder how he could know her. Greer also looked warily at Sawyer a couple of times.

"Mase!"

I turn to find Zoe walking toward me. The two guys follow after her.

"Zoe." I nod when she reaches me.

"Holden Jamison, sir." Holden holds out his hand to me. "It's such a pleasure to meet you. I love your work."

I shake Holden's hand and look to the last guy to join our group.

"Oh, this is Tripp Carter." Holden smiles. "He's my friend."

Tripp doesn't hold his hand out so I don't offer mine. His gaze takes me in. He's tall and obviously early twenties. He's got the air of a bored rich kid. His dark hair is artfully messy and his green eyes keep scanning the party. Who is he looking for?

Zoe sighs. "I can't find Wyatt."

"Okay." Not sure how this is my problem and I'm not about to tell her I saw him go into the house.

She cocks an eyebrow like the spoiled brat she is, but she slips back into easy-going party girl for the sake of the two guys.

"Holden, Tripp, and I are heading out to hit a new club." She looks at me expectantly.

I return her look.

She breathes out an impatient breath. "Could you tell Wyatt I'm going? And say goodbye to Greer. Tell her I'll call her."

At Greer's name, Tripp glances toward Zoe.

"Send her a text. I'm not your message service."

She sticks her tongue out and probably would have stomped her foot if Holden wasn't watching her. "Fine. But I fulfilled my family obligation to Wyatt. Tell him that."

I shake my head. I almost wish she was still a toddler that I could hand a toy and get her to go away.

"I hope next time we'll have more time to talk." Holden realizes this is a networking opportunity even if the cute girl wants him to go out partying.

"Maybe at one of our smaller gatherings," I suggest. Because I am interested in spending more time getting to know him. He has real potential.

Holden smiles. "I'd like that."

Zoe blows out a breath. "Okay, let's go. Let the old people do their thing."

"Thank you for the invite, sir." Holden holds his hand up as he and his friend follow Zoe into the house.

Roarke claps his hand on my shoulder. "Mason, my friend, where are the others?"

"Inside somewhere."

The crowd thins as people move on to other parties.

"You don't think they're having a party of their own?" Roarke rubs his jaw as he looks up.

"Maybe." I look at him out of the corner of my eye. "Jealous?"

Roarke shrugs and grins. "Just wish I could watch."

I blow out a breath and look around. Even after the last guest clears out, the cleanup crew will arrive. "I still have that camera set up in Aiden's room."

Roarke's eyes widen and his grin grows.

The camera was necessary with Aiden. Yes, he did six months in rehab, but it's harder out here. We needed to make sure he was okay.

I needed to make sure he was okay. He agreed to the camera, but we never discussed when to turn it off.

"During clean up?" Roarke rubs his hands together.

"There might not be anything on it. They may be sitting in the living room talking."

"Shame if that's all that happened."

Movement at the door draws my attention. Wyatt leads out Greer and Aiden from the house. Greer's cheeks are flushed. Wyatt leans down to say something into Greer's ear. Her eyes widen and she gets even redder.

Wyatt grins and takes her hand for a quick moment.

"I'd say they look a lot more relaxed now." Roarke grins and hits my arm. "I want to watch that video."

I do, too. They make their way over to where we stand.

"What do we think? An hour? Two?" Wyatt turns and looks over the remaining guests. Most are in small groups talking, settling in.

"Definitely two," Roarke says.

Greer's eyes dart around, but then she visibly relaxes. Who was she worried about? Sawyer? I'll need to get to the bottom of that, but not tonight.

"We can move to the seating area inside," I offer.

Greer's soft brown eyes finally collide with mine. She immediately ducks her head. Shy about something. They were gone for a while...

"So, poppet, let's talk about this crush you have on Holden Jamison." Roarke rubs his hands together.

"Had a crush," she says quietly.

As Aiden and her turn to go back into the house, I step forward and redo her hook and eye. She shivers at my touch and tips her face toward me with wide eyes.

I chuckle because there's no reason it should be undone. "Details, mouse."

Greer

We're spread out in the living room. People come in and talk for a while before they leave usually for another commitment, a few to home, others just leaving. This is Wyatt, Mason, Aiden, and Roarke's life, so different from mine.

I lean against Aiden's arm, feeling sleepy after upstairs. I guess tonight was about crossing lines. Aiden kissed me and I didn't technically fuck Wyatt, but there definitely was penis in vagina action. And the whole thing was so fucking hot.

I was completely naked while they were mostly clothed.

Even now I get heated thinking about it.

Roarke moves into the seat next to me and takes my hand. He moves in close to my ear. "What dirty thoughts are you having, poppet?"

Mason talks quietly with another gentleman across the room, while Wyatt talks to the man's wife. Aiden's attention is on a group of actors who are apparently also in the movie with them.

Aiden's fingers keep absent-mindedly brushing against my thigh. No one is paying me any attention, but I like it that way. I turn so my mouth is beside Roarke's ear.

"What makes you think I'm having dirty thoughts?"

His dark chuckle makes my panties dampen. "Ah, poppet, I can't give away my secrets."

The blond server moves through the area with a drink tray to collect glasses. I back away from Roarke, feeling my cheeks heat. He's trouble.

"Another, Mr. Flynn?" She bats her eyes at Roarke.

Smiling, he sets his glass on the tray. "Not for me, Claire."

She blushes at his use of her name. I get it. He's a lot. I find myself just watching him sometimes. Like none of this is real. His hand is currently holding mine, but it still doesn't feel real.

"Is there anything else I can get you, Mr. Flynn?" She looks so damned hopeful.

When I look at Roarke, a divot forms between his brow even though he's still smiling. "No, love. I'm finished."

Her blush deepens but she takes the hint and wanders away to collect other glasses.

"I'm sorry, poppet." His blue eyes meet mine as his thumb brushes over the back of my hand.

"For what?"

He cocks his head to the side as he squeezes my hand. "I didn't mean to encourage the server."

A laugh slips out. I cover my mouth, but his quizzical look makes the laughter bubble up in me until it spills over.

"Not what I was expecting." His voice is low.

I finally reign the laughter in and say quietly, "You're a flirt, Roarke."

His brow furrows.

"It's who you are. Honestly, I'd be worried if you weren't flirting with the waitress or someone's wife or the chef or even some of the men. I'd worry you were ill." My cheeks hurt from the laughter and the smile that I can't make go away.

"Doesn't it bother you?" He pulls my hand onto his lap.

I shake my head. "It's just part of who you are. Do I think you're going to have sex with all the people you flirted with tonight? No. I trust you, Roarke."

He straightens, still a little confused but getting it. I may be having difficulty remembering this is reality, but I'm not completely lost.

I lean in close and search his eyes. "Are you going to have sex with the server, Roarke?"

"No, poppet." His thumb rubs the back of my hand and I realize how close we are.

We haven't discussed how we should all behave around others, but I'm not the one who approached Roarke. He came and sat next to me and took my hand. He makes my pulse race and butterflies launch inside me.

"Honesty is all I need." I glance over my shoulder at the people talking to Aiden. They can probably overhear our conversation, but I want Roarke to know I'm okay with this. I don't want a cheater, but I'm not going to police every interaction he has. "We can talk more later if you'd like."

His slow grin spreads and I know he's not thinking of talking. His eyes grow heated, warming my insides. "Or we can go find a quiet place to discuss your dirty thoughts from earlier."

My lips part and heat rushes through me. My gaze lifts and collides with Wyatt's. Will it always be like that? Staring into one man's eyes and kissing him while the other is fucking me. Wyatt's smile is knowing.

It's not like I'm a virgin, but having even the tip of him inside me makes me wonder why am I waiting. What am I waiting for? Permission? From who? I get to make my own decisions.

Am I waiting for feelings? Fuck, no. This is about sex not feelings. So why am I pushing them away when all I really want is to feel them inside me? I want the fantasy Wyatt spelled out, him inside me while Aiden fucks my mouth. I want to be Mason's good girl and his naughty slut. I want Roarke to hold me against a wall and fuck me until I scream.

"Poppet." My gaze shifts to Roarke. His blue eyes are so stunning. I could spend hours falling into them. His eyes widen at whatever he sees in mine. But then determination locks in his with a cocky smile. "Right."

His hand squeezes mine. "Give me ten minutes, poppet."

I cock my head to the side and my brow furrows. What does that mean?

Roarke leaves my side and walks over to join the group of six people sitting across from Aiden. I turn back to Aiden and he takes my hand while he chats. His thumb skates over the back of my hand, lighting little sparks of awareness.

For a minute, Roarke joins in the current conversation. A lull gives him an opportunity.

"What's everyone doing for the rest of the night?" Roarke asks the group.

Various answers fill the space and a few people look at their phones to see the time.

Aiden leans into my ear. "Did you put him up to this?"

I shake my head. It's like a domino effect as soon as one person realizes they have somewhere else to be. One by one they all get up and leave, excited to start filming on Monday.

Roarke winks at me before infiltrating Mason's and Wyatt's small group.

Beth Stevens stays behind and reaches her hand out to Aiden.

"It's good to see you doing so well." She lowers herself to sit beside him on the couch. "I'm so glad we finally get to work together. It always seems like we should have worked together before this."

Her red hair is long right now and her blue eyes are always captivating. She's been in a lot of films. I've seen a few and she's good, but tonight she hung back even in the group chat. Was she hoping to talk to Aiden alone?

"I'm hoping it will be amazing." Aiden squeezes her hand before releasing it. He introduced me earlier to everyone but some people I already knew their names. Of course, I'm his 'friend' tonight, but everyone on set will find out I'm his sobriety companion come Monday.

"How's this going to work on Monday?" Beth settles into the seat on Aiden's other side.

The noise rises from the other side of the room and the people Wyatt and Mason were talking with are now leaving. Roarke catches my eye and smiles like the Cheshire cat.

My lips quirk into a smile and he lights up. He's chasing away the holdouts, one by one. His determined gaze falls on the last guest, Beth.

"I've got Greer, who will keep me from falling into a bottle." Aiden's words bring me back to their conversation. "Otherwise it will be filming as usual."

Beth's gaze narrows on me and for a minute, it feels like she's sizing me up to see if I'm any competition. She smiles when she turns to Aiden. "That's good. I'm glad you found someone to replace the other guy."

"You know Aiden really needs his rest to recover." Roarke holds his hand down to Beth. "How about you and I act like we're hot for each other?"

Beth shakes her head, but takes Roarke's hand. "I'm not sleeping with you again, Roarke. One time was enough."

"Was it?" He smirks and she laughs. "You wound me."

"I get it. Time to go." Beth waves to Aiden. "I'll see you on set."

"I'll see you on set too, Beth." Roarke winks. "You know there are a few nudity scenes and I always do my own stunts."

"Good night." She shakes her head as Mason escorts her to the door.

They pause at the door and whatever Mason says, she agrees with because she keeps nodding.

"Did you sleep with Beth Stevens?" I ask when Roarke sits next to me.

He smiles slyly. "A few years ago. New Year's Eve party. We were both wasted. She told me it'd never happen again and it hasn't. Jealous, poppet?"

"Of course," I give him a sly smile. "I'd totally sleep with Beth Stevens."

Roarke's eyes widen and then he smirks. "Can I watch?"

Grinning, I shake my head. Mason approaches us as the servers finish cleaning up.

"Everyone's gone." Wyatt stands looking down at his phone.

"Good." Mason holds his hand out to me. "We need to talk in my office."

My heart skips. I slip my hand in his and he helps me stand before leading all of us down to his office. Am I in trouble? Did I do something wrong? Did Sawyer tell Mason about me?

Am I going to lose another home? Fuck. I'm not ready to leave. I should have fucked them all sooner.

Chapter 28

About Damn Time

Greer

I wring my hands as Mason closes the door and circles behind his desk to pull something up on his computer. Wyatt leans against the wall, while Aiden and Roarke take the chairs.

"Come here, poppet." Roarke motions me over and when I get close, he drags me down onto his lap.

No one talks. An empty feeling forms in the pit of my stomach. I want to get out of here, but I also want to stay.

"Am I in trouble?" I need to know. I won't cry. My chest aches, but I won't cry. This is just the way my life goes.

How many times can I lose something before I find what I need?

"What?" Aiden straightens, suddenly alert. His blue eyes widen. "No, little warrior. You've done nothing wrong."

"I assumed you didn't want me screening this where anyone else could hear it." Mason's eyes meet mine. The screens behind him come to life and there Aiden and I are in Aiden's room on the screen as Wyatt closes the door.

"Oh." Relief flows through me, but then my face heats. Oh, my God! It was recorded?

Mason turns his chair to face the monitors. Every word, every touch is there in black and white and in color. From a couple of different angles even. Roarke shifts below me when I show them my panties on the screen.

"How many times did you come, poppet?" Roarke whispers in my ear as he rearranges me on his lap. My legs fall on either side of his and then he opens his legs spreading me wide. I lean back against his chest. When the cool air brushes against my damp panties, I suck in a breath.

"I don't know," I whisper, watching myself writhe on Wyatt's cock. He felt so thick and hard against my clit. My insides are on a steady simmer, being surrounded by these men and their heated gaze on my image on the screens.

"I thought you turned off the cameras?" Aiden's voice is strong and I turn to look at him.

Is he angry?

"I hadn't yet." Mason smirks. On the screen, Aiden slides his fingers into my ass. "I'm glad I didn't."

"Me too." Aiden's words are breathless. Guess he's okay with it.

Moving in front of me, Wyatt's hazel eyes meet mine.

"I took in the live show." He drops down to kneel in front of me and Roarke. His gaze shifts to Roarke over my shoulder. "How wet is she?"

Roarke slides his hands up my thighs to where my pussy aches. Anticipation flows hot and heavy through my veins. His hand slips down the front of my panties to cup my bare pussy.

"Oh, fuck," I whisper as he thrusts his finger inside me. No teasing, just right there.

"So fucking wet." Roarke kisses my ear. Sparks tumble over themselves down to settle in my pussy. His finger thrusts in and out. My hips chase it, ready for more. "Can you hear how wet she is?"

Wyatt smirks. "That's because I came inside her. Didn't I, kitten?"

"Did you like Wyatt's thick cock in your pussy, poppet?" Roarke adds another finger, stretching me.

"He only put the tip in," I moan out as I see Aiden, Wyatt, and me on the screen. Aiden's fingers are inside me, thrusting in and out. My moan fills the room from the speakers.

"Close your legs, Roarke." Wyatt says.

Roarke does and takes his fingers out of my pussy. I whimper at the sudden emptiness, but Wyatt stands me up and draws my panties down my legs while Roarke lowers my zipper and undoes my bra. Wyatt removes the rest of my clothes.

I hear and feel Roarke moving behind me.

As soon as I'm naked, Roarke draws me back down on his lap. I hiss at the heat of his skin against my back and legs. His bare cock slots against my ass.

"I'm good with whatever you want to do, poppet, but I'd love to feel your wet pussy surrounding my cock." His voice, his words, his touch push my temperature even hotter as he widens his legs, spreading me open for Wyatt. Fuck, I'd give this man anything he wants.

Wyatt's mouth closes over my pussy as Roarke fills his hands with my breasts. I moan at the overwhelming feeling of them both surrounding me, touching me, tempting me.

"Fuck, I'll never get tired of watching you take a cock, kitten." Wyatt's words from earlier fill the room.

"Me neither, poppet," Roarke whispers in my ear. "You're such a good girl for us."

Wyatt's fingers slide inside me as he sucks my clit and I watch Aiden's cock disappear into my mouth on screen. He curves his fingers to hit that spot inside me that makes my toes curl. Everything winds me tighter and tighter until I cry out as I shatter. I'm coming down, but still wound up as Roarke teases my nipples.

Wyatt sits back against the desk and withdraws his fingers. "Do you want to take Roarke's cock, kitten?"

I'm hot all over and not making the best decisions tonight. I nod because yes, I want them. I want to feel them inside me. Especially if I can lose this at anytime, lose them. Roarke lifts me before sliding the head of his cock along my slit until he presses against my opening.

I lift my gaze and Wyatt, Mason, and Aiden are all watching me, not the screens.

Roarke's cock breaches my pussy and he slowly eases me down on him. I gasp at the fullness. Fuck, he's thick and seemingly endless as he goes in deep.

My pussy flutters around his cock as he stretches me. My mouth opens as he fills me more than I've ever been filled before. I pant at the overwhelming sensation of Roarke's thick cock inside me and these men watching.

"Fuck, poppet, you feel so good. Such a fucking tight, little pussy you have."

Tonight everyone at the party ignored me. They wanted to talk to these powerful men and I don't blame them. I'm a nobody, but right now, I'm the center of all these powerful men's attention. It's heady and makes me feel dizzy with need.

When Roarke's cock is all the way inside, he draws me back against him and keeps my legs spread open so everyone can see where we're joined. "Thank you, poppet."

"Good job, little mouse." Mason undoes his belt and my pussy throbs around Roarke's cock. "We can do better. Can't we? Live the fantasy?"

I wet my lips, ready to have two cocks inside me. Roarke's hands smooth up my ribs to cup my breasts together. His thumbs circle my nipples, sending jolts of pleasure radiating down to make my pussy squeeze around his cock.

Mason mutes the sound of me giving Aiden head on the speakers, but he doesn't stop the video. He stalks around the desk. His intense gaze taking all of me in. Roarke doesn't fuck me, content to remain buried inside my pussy.

I've never had someone just be inside me, but with Roarke it feels right.

Wyatt moves to the wall so that Mason can step in front of me. I lift my gaze to his and then drop it to his crotch. Mason draws his zipper down and pulls out his cock.

I'm sprawled naked over Roarke with his cock in my pussy like a queen. I raise my eyes to Mason's and reach out to stroke his cock. Wanting more pleasure. More touches. More of them.

"Can I fuck your mouth, little mouse?" Mason's hand slides into my hair, gripping the back of my head. I clench around Roarke's cock at just the thought of this. Roarke's hands slide up and down my thighs.

I wet my lips and nod. "Yes, sir."

"Good girl." He angles my head and I bring his cock to my lips. I kiss the tip before opening my mouth for him. His impressive cock slides across my lips and tongue. I close my lips around him and hum. He slowly fucks my mouth as I suck on him. Every suck makes my pussy pulse around Roarke's cock.

"How does it feel to be filled, little mouse?" He doesn't release me to answer, just continues to fuck my mouth. "Aiden, in my top drawer, lube and a plug. She should feel how full she'll be when we all take her." He slides his cock deep into my throat. I gag a little and tears roll down my cheeks, but I push forward, wanting to take him all.

"Your tight cunt squeezes my cock like a fist every time you choke on Mason's cock, poppet." Roarke's voice is in my ear. His warm skin brushes my back. "Do you want to come all over my cock like a good girl?"

I whimper because I do. I want him to fuck me properly.

"Take him deep, kitten." Wyatt's voice is harsh. I'm not sure which him he's referring to, but they're both in me so deep already.

Aiden steps up beside me. "Bring her forward."

Mason draws me forward. I brace my hands on Roarke's knees and the angle of his cock within me feels fuller. I moan around Mason's cock. Roarke's hands skim my sides, down to pull my ass cheeks apart.

"You're going to feel some pressure, little warrior." Aiden's fingers rub lube over my asshole, making me clench. "Just relax. If you need me to stop, tap on Roarke's leg."

Mason pulls my head back until my mouth is almost all the way off his cock, just the head is in my mouth. My gaze lifts to his darkened eyes. I lick and suck on him to distract from something thick pressing against my puckered hole. Aiden eases the plug in slowly. Backing out a little before pressing in further. Over and over.

The plug is wider than his fingers stretched me earlier.

"You're doing so well, poppet." Roarke holds open my ass cheeks as Aiden eases the plug the rest of the way in. "I can't wait to watch you take a dick in your ass. You're already squeezing my cock so fucking tight. Fuck, I love your pussy."

Everything feels tighter, fuller. It's like I can feel the plug touching Roarke's cock through my thin walls.

Roarke slides his hand around to my pussy and rubs slow circles around my clit. I moan around Mason's cock. Mason eases me into bobbing on his cock again, sinking a little deeper with each thrust.

"Little mouse, you're fucking amazing. Taking my cock and Roarke's at the same time. So fucking beautiful." Mason's words fill me with pride.

I want to please them. I want to do whatever they want.

Maybe I should be ashamed to like this, but it feels so good. Aiden's fingers caress my breast, stroking over my nipple. Roarke's fingers rub my clit while his cock twitches in my pussy. Mason's cock thrusts deep into my throat over and over.

It's too much. I moan my release as my pussy gushes around Roarke's cock. Mason fucks my mouth until he holds me still. His hot cum fills the back of my throat and I swallow it down.

"Swallow it all, mouse. Every last drop." He draws back, slipping from my mouth.

I swallow again.

He grips my chin. "Open."

I open my mouth for him and he smiles.

His eyes lift to mine and even though I'm naked, I feel more exposed in this moment like he can see that need in me to please him. "Good girl."

Fuck, an aftershock rocks through me. My hands tighten on Roarke's thighs as my pussy convulses around his cock.

Roarke lifts me off him suddenly like I'm little more than a doll in his grasp, but then he turns me to face him and thrusts back inside me.

"Oh, fuck," I whisper at how good that feels. My hands go to his shoulders. His muscles ripple beneath my fingers. We're skin to skin, making tingles light up all over my body.

Aiden tugs on the plug in my ass, rubbing against the sensitive nerves. Gasping, I'm right on the edge again, ready to explode.

"Ready, poppet?" Roarke's eyes twinkle with mischief.

The answer is probably not, but I nod. Roarke stands and I wrap myself around him. He holds me effortlessly in the middle of the room. His hips thrust up into mine. Moaning, I cling to his neck as his cock thrusts in and out, pushing me closer and closer to the edge. My breasts rub against his bare chest.

Standing behind me, Aiden brushes my hair away from my neck. His lips latch onto the spot where my neck meets my shoulder. I can't seem to catch my breath as waves of pleasure roll through me.

"Imagine it, poppet. Us both filling you."

When Roarke thrusts, Aiden eases out the plug and when Roarke pulls out, Aiden pushes the plug back in. I bite down on Roarke's shoulder, unable to process all the sensations flooding me.

"Our thick cocks making your tiny body sing. We can make it happen. You can have us both. Me in your pussy. Aiden in your ass. Fucking you until you come all over our dicks."

At the thought of them both fucking me, I tighten my arms, crushing myself against him, as my orgasm rips through me, shredding me into pieces and falling like confetti to the floor.

Roarke chuckles and pistons his hips into me, chasing my orgasm for one of his own. He groans as his thrusts grow chaotic until he stills, spilling his hot cum inside me, so deep, so warm, so fucking full.

Aiden pulls out the plug and I shatter again, crying out and pulsing around Roarke's cock, milking him. Roarke holds me close as I try to catch my breath.

He sits on the chair with me attached. He doesn't move to lift me off his cock or my arms from around him. Instead he draws me against him. His hand rubs down my back.

"Fuck, I should take up smoking." Roarke chuckles, even as I feel him growing hard within me again. I take a deep breath in. "We're definitely going to keep doing this."

Aiden slides a warm, wet towel between my ass cheeks, but I keep my head resting on Roarke's chest. I'm beyond caring at this point. His heartbeat is steady in my ear. He thrusts his hips a little to settle deeper inside me, but I don't mind. I like him there.

"So this sharing Greer..." Roarke slides his hand possessively down my back. "How's that going to work? And how do we keep Zoe from setting her up with Holden Jamison? Are we going to claim her when she goes on set? Because I saw more than one guy checking out my poppet. I may be willing to share with you lot, but no one else."

I don't need anyone else. I breathe in Roarke's sandalwood sinful scent and love that his bare skin touches me everywhere.

This isn't how sex is for me. I've never had it like this before. When he's done, we're done. Go to sleep. Go home. Not stay buried deep inside me like that's where he belongs.

I've enjoyed sex with the guys I cared about, but never this enthusiastically. They've never been able to make me come. Period. But I just figured that was a me thing. I never got that comfortable with them.

"Are you going to take your dick out of her?" Mason sits behind his desk.

Roarke shifts below me again and I roll my hips against him. The slide of him within me is divine. "Nope. Not anytime soon. She's gotta get used to having good dick inside her. I might sleep like this tonight."

I should protest, but I like the way his cock feels. The closeness of his body wrapped around mine while mine is wrapped around his. I like that he wants to stay inside me. Even all night.

Normally I'd be self-conscious. We're sitting naked in Mason's office. Just the two of us. Everyone else is fully dressed. But Roarke's body heat and heartbeat sooth me. I could definitely sleep like this.

Chapter 29

Collide

Roarke

The minute she falls asleep I feel it. All that tension rushes out of her. Fuck, this woman is under my skin. I'm happy to stay inside her as much as possible.

"Someone want to let me know when the cleaning staff is gone?" I stroke my hand down Greer's back. "She's asleep and there's a bed calling our name."

How many more times can I make her come tonight? I still haven't gotten her to scream my name. It will happen.

"We need to discuss how us sharing her is going to work." Mason leans back in his chair. "Roarke can't just keep his cock in her."

"Willing to try. Besides there are plenty of options left open." I grin. My cock is hard and eager for her again, but she's so peaceful that I don't want to disturb her sleep. Also not usually an issue with women. I'm all about keeping a chick up all night.

"I want her to sleep with me." Aiden adjusts his hard cock, tenting his trousers. "She doesn't sleep well and neither do I."

He'd sleep better if he took what she offered so sweetly.

Mason nods. "Do we want to assign days? Just take her as we like?"

"Should she be awake for this?" Wyatt remains on the floor. His hand is in his hair as he studies Greer's sleeping face.

Mason turned off the video, though I could definitely use a copy of her taking Wyatt's cock. Fuck, my little poppet wanted it so bad. I can't wait to watch her take Wyatt's cock all the way inside her. My cock pulses.

We need better equipment and angles for the video next time.

"Maybe." I run my hand down her back. She probably should have a say in this. She shivers and snuggles closer to me. "But we also need to decide how this looks to the outside world. If we don't say anything, rumors will start. They always do."

Aiden blows out a breath. He runs a hand over the back of his neck and his gaze keeps wandering to Greer's naked body. "She's obviously a live-in employee, but us keeping our hands off her in public will be the issue."

"You kissed her," I point out helpfully. "If you're willing to take things further, I'm willing to watch. Because fuck, that was hot. I almost lost to Greyson trying to watch you two."

Aiden runs a hand through his hair and his eyes focus on Greer's face. "Siobhan—"

"Is and always will be a bitch." I need him to remember that because if she comes sniffing around like a bitch in heat, I'm going to go mental on her.

"As I was saying." Aiden clears his throat and brushes Greer's hair out of her face. "I wasn't expecting her. I reacted."

"It was contained." Wyatt makes a dismissive noise. "For now."

"As far as we know," Mason mutters. The party was closed, but who knows what pictures anyone could have taken.

"Where are we on the Aiden scale?" I tilt my head, studying him. "Are you sticking with the four months for p-in-v action?"

"Fuck." Aiden stands. His hands tug at his hair as he paces away. "I know I should. It's better for my recovery."

He comes back and stares at her. "But then she's here and fuck, if we'd been anywhere else when I kissed her, I would have buried my cock deep inside her and marked her as mine."

"So, fuck her." Mason gestures to her draped over me. "She wants all of us. She's not asking for a commitment. You aren't declaring undying love for the woman."

The urge to cover her ears to protect her from this surges through me, but I don't. If she hears, she hears. She knows the deal. I slide my hand up her side to play with her breast pressed into my chest. Fuck, she's got nice firm breasts.

"We should give her time to adjust to this." Wyatt leans his head back. "She wanted to wait."

I wish I had her turned around so the others could watch the flush of arousal working its way up her neck into her cheeks and down over her breasts. My cock twitches inside her and she shifts her hips. My cock hardens more, eager to come again.

Fuck, I want her on her hands and knees, sucking off Aiden while I rail her from behind. So many fucking positions and things to try with her.

The others begin to talk logistics. But I realize I have a dilemma. Greer's sleeping and aroused and I really want to fuck her, but after this morning...

"I went down on Greer this morning while she was asleep and she freaked the fuck out." I shift her on me a little and tip her sleeping face up so I can look at her. My chest softens. "She's had some trauma in the past."

When I look at the others, I have their full attention. We all guessed when we discussed sexual partners and what she'd done, willingly, in the past. I don't know who hurt her, but I want to find him and tear him apart.

"Her ex grabbed her." My fingers stroke over the bruises on her upper arm, marring her pale skin. "I don't know if it was the first time. But I stepped in to protect her. She cried when we left. Like full on meltdown. Not because that bastard put his hands on her, but because I protected her."

I can't betray her confidence. I can't tell them about the murder basement or her confession that no one has protected her since she was a kid. But there are things that we need to know going forward. To help protect her.

"She's strong, but we might be too much for her." I don't want to let her go, but I also don't want to be the reason she's more broken.

"I take it you don't mean physically?" Mason leans his elbows on his desk. His gaze goes to the fragile girl in my arms.

I shake my head. Everyone remains quiet and thoughtful.

I've never really been a violent guy. I did sports in school. Got in stupid fights. But I never wanted to hurt someone the way I want to hurt whoever hurt Greer. It doesn't make sense, but it consumes me.

This is supposed to be a no strings attached fuck fest. I liked her from the start and the more I get to know her the more attached I'm becoming.

Me! The manwhore.

Fuck, we've known her a couple days and already she's got us locked in tight without even trying. I'm not saying I want to marry her, but I'm definitely not letting her go.

Greer

Movement wakes me. I open my eyes and meet Wyatt's hazel eyes over Roarke's shoulder. Blinking, I realize my naked body is against Roarke's naked body and we're moving up the stairs. There's a blanket wrapped around me though.

Yawning, I lift my head and find Aiden and Mason, walking with us.

"Shh, poppet. We're all going to bed." Roarke's hand strokes my back and I let out a little sigh.

I rest my head on his shoulder and we pass by the now empty kitchen. "How long was I asleep?"

Roarke chuckles. "You didn't miss anything, poppet. Mase went up and made sure the cleaners were taken care of."

My stomach grumbles. I should have eaten more dinner, but my nerves were frayed.

"Hungry, kitten?" Wyatt brushes my hair out of my face. "Take her and clean her up. I'll bring up some snacks. Her room?"

"Yes, her room," Mason answers.

I meet his intense gaze. My pussy pulses remembering him inside my mouth as Roarke remained deep inside me, while the others watched. Need throbs between my legs, empty. My level of arousal alarms me. I've never been the type to go all night, but suddenly, my libido is on overdrive. I want them even now when I should be satiated.

The door to my room opens and Roarke drops the blanket from around us. He repositions me to look him in the face.

"Up for another ride, poppet?" His blue eyes sparkle with mischief as the tip of his cock brushes my pussy.

I suck in a breath.

"Have you ever had shower sex?" Roarke grins.

When I shake my head and bite my lip, his grin grows. The shower turns on and I lift my head to see Aiden stepping out of the bathroom. He sits on the edge of my bed and gives me a smile.

"Don't take all night. We have things to discuss." Mason moves to my dresser and starts pulling things out.

"In that case." Roarke carries me into the bathroom and right into the shower. I gasp at the sudden water falling over me. He presses me back against the tile and his mouth claims mine, hungry and intense. Keying me up even more. His hand slips between my thighs and slides along my clit. Sparks ignite within my blood.

My hips follow his fingers like they're a pied piper leading me to ruin. His tongue strokes mine as he devours me. His chest brushes against my hardened nipples and his cock teases my entrance. I'm so turned on I need him inside me.

He lifts his mouth from mine and rests his head on my forehead. "Tell me, poppet, are you always this wet?"

I shake my head. "Only for you guys."

"Good girl." He presses against my clit as his thick cock thrusts inside me, stretching me open again. I draw in a shaky breath and weave my fingers into his hair. He growls against my neck. "Fuck, you feel so good, Greer."

He slowly eases out before pressing back in. He's so deep inside me. His captivating blue eyes lock with mine as he slides out and back in deep, slow and easy. My breath catches as he grins.

"Tomorrow, I'm spending an hour going down on you, poppet. Licking every inch of your pretty pussy." He sinks inside me, drawing out and right back in. The pressure swells, inching me closer and closer to the edge. My hips clumsily follow his lead. "I'll make you come until you scream and then I'm going to do it all over again until you beg me to fuck you. To put my cock in your trembling pussy and fuck you until you can't stop coming."

"Roarke," I whisper as I clench his hair in my fist and my head drops back against the tile. I'm so close. Everything tingles.

"Then I'll spend another hour figuring out this tight little body of yours. I want to find all the places that make you gasp, sigh, squirm, and come." His words push me even higher. "I'll ease my cock into that tight ass and fuck you like no one else has."

Moaning, I wind closer and closer.

He puts his hands on the tiles beside my head. "Ride me, Greer. Fuck yourself on my cock until you cover me in your cum."

I rock my hips against him, slow at first, a little uncertain, but then I find a rhythm and watch his face. His gaze is intense. His lips part and he lets out a groan when I move a certain way. It's fascinating to experiment and hot as hell to have his pleasure in my control, knowing he could take over at any moment.

He shifts his hips, changing his angle. Moaning, I rub my clit on him as he hits a spot inside me that makes my insides buzz.

"Roarke. Fuck." I close my eyes against the waves preparing to crash over me.

"Open your eyes and look at me when I fuck you, poppet."

I open my eyes and topple over the edge. Wave after wave of pleasure takes me under while Roarke keeps me grounded. I cry out as his hands grab my hips. He keeps the pleasure rolling through me as he thrusts hard and fast, pistoning in and out of my pussy.

He groans and his thrusts hit me in that spot that pushes me right back over the edge.

I cry out his name unable to hold the connection anymore as he thrusts in deep one final time. His cock jerks against my walls as warm cum fills me. I wrap around him, holding on tight.

His hands smooth over my ass. His breathing is ragged as he says, "I never want to leave this pussy."

Sighing, I laugh a little as we both take deep breaths to come down. "I'm okay with that."

He chuckles and tips my chin up. His blue eyes are so easy to lose myself in.

"I'm not sure it would work long term, but I'd be willing to give it a go." Roarke lifts me against him, still buried deep inside me. My brain knows he's talking about keeping his cock inside my pussy. It's sexual, but my heart leaps a little.

Stupid heart.

"Less fucking, more cleaning." Wyatt stands in the doorway with his arms crossed. "I've brought her food. If you're going to fuck her constantly, she'll need some calories."

"Fine." Roarke kisses me but then disengages and lowers my feet to the shower floor. He grabs the soap bottle and holds it out to me indicating he wants to pour some in my hand. He fills mine, then takes some and puts the bottle back.

He rubs his hands together and runs them over me instead of himself. I gladly put my soapy hands all over Roarke's toned and built body. Squeaking, when he cleans between my legs and ass. I spend a little extra time washing his cock while he works on his shoulders that I couldn't reach.

He backs me into the wall. I look up at him as I stroke his hard cock with soap. Sliding my hand down over his balls, I bite my lip and he groans. My pussy pulses empty, longing to feel him inside me again.

"You're going to get me into so much trouble, poppet." He kisses me senseless and drags me under the water to rinse off.

The shower door opens and Wyatt holds open a towel for me.

"Go on, poppet. I can't keep you forever." Roarke smacks my ass.

I step into the towel and Wyatt's arms. I glance back at Roarke and he's washing off the soap. He winks and my pussy throbs. Forever would be okay.

Shit, yeah no, no forever. No entanglement. Wyatt's hazel eyes watch me with a smile. His hands rub the towel over me, not missing an inch.

"Sore, kitten." He pat dries my pussy with the towel.

I shake my head. Just the few inches I took of his cock, stretched me. I'd be up to try again.

His eyebrow lifts. "We all need to talk first, kitten, but if you're still in the mood after..."

His mouth claims mine as he drops the towel and grabs my ass to draw my naked body against his clothed one. I press up on my tiptoes as he leans down. After a few uncomfortable seconds, he lifts me against him. Squealing, I wrap my legs around his waist.

Kissing me, he carries me into the bedroom and lowers me onto the bed. I release him and he gives me a look that promises so much more that I ache.

"Come here, mouse." Mason holds out his hand to me and I go willingly to him. He sits on the edge of the bed next to Aiden. "This will be less distracting with you clothed."

He holds out a pair of panties for me to step into. Putting my hands on his shoulders, I step into them and he draws them up. They're not mine and they look expensive.

I lift an eyebrow at Mason and he chuckles darkly.

"I may have confiscated your old panties and bras and replaced them with some new ones." He slides his hand over the silky material covering my ass. His gaze roams over me freely before he holds up a negligee.

"I have pajamas," I protest. The nightgown is little more than a slip that will just cover my ass by a half an inch.

"Not like this." He slips it over my head and the silk falls softly over my curves, held up by thin straps and covering the panties. "Now behave and have a seat."

When I go to sit next to him, he pulls me down onto his lap. Turning me so I face Roarke and Wyatt leaning against the wall. Roarke has a towel wrapped around his waist and a smirk on his lips.

Aiden sits next to me and tucks my hair behind my ear. "Good, little warrior?"

I nod and search his haunted blue eyes. "You?"

He nods. I don't want to push on Aiden's boundaries. But giving up his kisses is tragic. I'll deal with it. We've talked about it. It's for the best and not forever.

Wyatt steps forward and grabs a plate of cut fruit and raw veggies off the nightstand and hands it to me. "Eat, kitten."

"Thank you." I give him a grateful smile and set the plate on my lap. His gaze follows my hand as I pick a strawberry up and pop it into my mouth.

Mason grabs the pages off my nightstand and holds them in front of me. "This is a list of what we would like to do to you. You can put no next to any you aren't curious about. It's a fairly comprehensive list that gets detailed."

I nod and take a bite-sized piece of broccoli next from my plate.

"Read over and fill in your answers by Monday. For now, I'm going to list some of the things we're most interested in. I want to know if you've done them with a consenting partner. Do you understand, little mouse?"

I nod and swallow. I pick up a raspberry and eat it. Consenting.

They aren't asking to know everything. They aren't digging into my past. But tonight with those two men here in this house, I feel exposed. Was some of it consenting? It's complicated and some of it doesn't seem real.

I don't dwell on the past because it only hurts me. When Roarke's and Wyatt's cocks were inside me, it was easy to forget about the nightmares from my past. But now, Mason wants me to differentiate.

Consenting only. Fuck.

Chapter 30

Late Night Talking

Greer

I chew a carrot to buy me time. I'm not sure how I'm going to answer some of this. But I'm game.

"I understand."

Mason clears his throat and begins, "We can check off anal play. Do you love it, like it, it's okay, dislike it but it's okay in small amounts, or hate."

Swallowing hard, I cough and squirm in Mason's lap, thinking about their fingers and the plug. Roarke grins wickedly at me. Heat engulfs my face. "Love."

"Anal sex?"

Roarke catches my eye with a wider grin.

"Curious." Eating more broccoli, I lean back against Mason, feeling the hard planes of his body through his shirt. Warmth spreads through me, thinking about what they want to do with me, to me.

"Spanking?"

"Yes."

"Describe."

Oh, fuck. Didn't think he was going to ask that. "One guy I was with playfully spanked me a few times."

The other time is pretty unclear about consent. So I'll just leave it at that.

Mason's cock hardens beneath me, stoking the already burning fire within.

"Rate it?" His dark voice flows over me like a caress. He wants this one. Roarke had mentioned punishment. Is this what he wants? To spank me. My panties get wet as I pop a blueberry in my mouth.

"Liked it?" I shrug.

"You don't know, mouse?" Mason's voice next to my ear sends shivers down my spine.

"It was okay. The guy was okay." Heat blankets my neck and cheeks.

"We already know you didn't get off on it, kitten." Wyatt smiles softly. "You can enjoy something and not get off on it, but we want to know if it will get you off."

His hazel eyes hold me captive. Do I think Mason spanking me will get me off? Maybe?

"You want to try it again, mouse?" Mason's tone is hard to miss. He wants this one.

I lean my head back against his shoulder, drawing in his leather scent. With him? "Yes, sir."

His cock twitches against my ass. Right answer. I eat another strawberry.

"Biting?"

My eyes widen. "No."

"Curious?"

"Ummm..." Pretty sure I bit Roarke when he was fucking me. I glance at the slightly pink skin on his shoulder. Shit, did I do that? Do I want to do it again? Do I want him to bite me?

"Relax, mouse. No one is into it but Roarke is willing to try anything once." Mason slides his hand across my stomach.

"Then no."

"You can bite me whenever you want, poppet." Roarke rubs at his shoulder with a wink.

I pop another veggie in my mouth to hide my embarrassment.

"Blindfolds?"

I flinch. Fuck. Did someone ask me this before? Was it before my freak out with Roarke and Aiden? I don't want to freak out like that on anyone else. "No, I've never done it with anyone else."

Not consenting at least.

When I don't continue, Mason's tone softens, "Hard limit or soft limit, mouse?"

"What's the difference?" I turn to look at him.

"Hard means absolutely not under any circumstances. Soft means you can discuss it before a scene but it can't be added without prior consent."

I bite my lip and glance down at the paper, seeing that Wyatt marked that he likes blindfolding his partner. I don't want to disappoint him. "Under the right circumstances maybe."

I keep my gaze on the plate of fruit and veggies.

"You can say no, kitten. I don't want you terrified. That's not the point. And if that triggers you then it's an absolute no." Wyatt kneels before me and takes my hand. His eyes are kind and soft. "It's not a deal breaker for me."

"I don't like the dark," I whisper. "It's easier with the lights on."

"We can keep the lights on, kitten." Wyatt cups my face.

"Okay" I turn and kiss his palm.

"Exhibitionism?" Mason keeps going as Wyatt steps back to the wall.

My eyes meet Roarke's and he wiggles his eyebrows.

"I haven't done it before here," I admit as I eat more.

"And now?" Roarke asks. His blue eyes excited.

I hesitate. What am I agreeing to? Because earlier, he was willing to fuck me in front of the cooks and servers. I don't know that I want to push it that far. But I've never been pushed out of my comfort zone.

"With the four of us, mouse?" Mason sets the pages down.

"Yes, love it." That's easy. I get wet just thinking about Roarke fucking me while they watched.

"Voluntary or forced?"

"Both." I blush, but I love when they all watch me. And Mason giving me orders yesterday in his office. Yes, to that.

"Good." Roarke smirks and my pussy throbs.

"Outside of our group?" Mason asks.

I squirm on him again and his hand goes to my hip to hold me still. "Curious."

"Voluntary or forced?"

"Curious," I admit, meeting Roarke's heated eyes. I don't know that I'll ever initiate it, but if anyone will, he will.

"Kneeling for submission?" Mason's voice is dark and full of longing.

"Never done." I turn to meet his heated eyes. "Curious."

He tips my chin and kisses me softly. "Good girl."

My panties dampen at the praise. I turn back to my plate, surprised to find it empty. Wyatt steps forward and takes it from me.

"Do you want more to eat?" His hazel eyes search mine.

I shake my head. "Thank you."

"Roleplay and rape fantasy. With prior discussion and consent at the time," Mason clarifies.

I meet only Mason's eyes, because if I see the longing on someone else's face, I might cave. I'm not sure this one I can cave on. Swallowing, I ask, "Rape fantasy?"

His piercing eyes search mine. "You play like you don't want to have sex and your partner or partners force you to give in. It's fully consensual, but it can be thrilling for some to play at it."

I swallow against the knot in my throat. If he's mentioning it, one of them wants to at least try it. They're giving me so much. Anxiety fills my chest like hornets buzzing angrily.

Mason shakes his head. He holds my chin and searches my eyes. "You can't say yes just to please us, mouse. Not if it's going to terrify you or harm you mentally. You can say no or say no at the time of the scene. You'll always have a safe word. If you forget your safe word, you can use red to stop or yellow if something needs to be changed, or something is too tight or uncomfortable, or if you just need to pause the scene to use the bathroom or need a break. Just because you say yes now doesn't mean you can't say no later. We won't want you any less or think any less of you for standing your ground."

"Likewise if you want to try something later when you feel more comfortable with us. We can always discuss it more then." Aiden's knuckles drift down the outside of my thigh. I meet his light blue eyes.

A tear slips out, unbidden. "Role play, curious. Rape fantasy, soft limit."

"Greer." Aiden holds his arms out for me.

I climb onto his lap, straddling him as he holds me to his chest. I draw in a breath of his citrus scent and lock down the tears, burying my face in his shirt.

"We will always check in with you. You always have a say in whatever happens with any of us, little warrior." His hand smooths over my hair and that nervous energy leaves me.

I turn my face to Mason and wait for the next question.

"Recorded scenes for just us. For safety, we'd wear masks in case it ever got out."

Aiden's hand strokes down my back.

"Curious," I say.

"We'll go over the toys and the other items on the list later. Are you okay with two or more partners at a time up to all of us?"

I nod. "Yes."

"And voyeurism, being watched? Do you want to watch other couples have sex?"

I bite my lip. So many elements of sex I haven't had an opportunity to try. I've read smut to get off before. Chad tried to get me to watch porn, but I didn't like thinking about those girls in the videos.

"Curious."

Mason puts the stack of papers on the nightstand. "You'll need to have separate discussions with each of us, but as of now there isn't anything that's off the table that we're interested in." Mason holds my chin between his thumb and forefinger. He searches my eyes intently. "Hard limits, mouse. Anything an absolute no. Or something that will trigger you?"

I bite my lip. "I can't handle being held down in the dark when I'm asleep."

Drawing in a shaky breath, I close my eyes. "I need to feel safe sleeping. That may change, but right now, I can't do it."

"What if you're on top of me and I wake you up by fucking?" Roarke asks. "Is it the lack of control?"

"I don't know." I shake my head unwilling to share my shame with them. Unwilling to open that locked room that holds my night-mares and bad memories for fear I'll never get it shut again.

"Would you be willing to let me try, poppet?" Roarke's blue eyes hold mine. "I'll start slow and *no* will stop me. Anything negative will stop me. I don't want to hurt you or open up old wounds, but I want to give you pleasure."

I bite my lip, wanting to give him anything he wants. "We can experiment with it."

Aiden turns my chin until my eyes meet his. "You don't have to. We don't have to do anything that makes you uncomfortable."

I cup his face and peer into those light blue eyes. "What are your limits, Aiden? How can I help you hold them?"

Aiden

I rub my thumbs over the silky slip Mason dressed Greer in. Her tight nipples press against the delicate fabric. I'm already determined to sleep with this girl every night. But do I need limits to safeguard my recovery.

"What if you only have sex with Greer if one of us is with you?"

Roarke steps up behind Greer and slides his hands up her ribs to cup her breasts. She releases a soft sigh, but keeps her darkened eyes on me. "She's a needy little poppet."

Can I sleep next to her every night and not need her? Not long to feel that hot tight pussy taking my cock? Roarke slides his thumbs over her nipples and her lips part.

"Only with someone else." It makes sense. I can't develop an addiction if we share her. I won't become dependent if she's not just mine. If I can't roll over in the night and make love to her. If we just fuck.

Grabbing the hem of her slip, I lift it up and off of her. Her arms come down and weave into my hair.

"Kissing?" Her gaze drops to my lips as she licks hers. Roarke's hands stroke over her nipples and her hips rock on mine, making my already hard cock throb.

"Definitely." I wrap my hands around her hips and capture her lips with mine. She whimpers into my mouth and opens beneath me. That urge to sink deep inside her assaults my senses. My fingers slide between her thighs over the satin of her panties and her hot pussy.

"Undo his pants, little mouse." Mason sits next to me with his hands back on the bed, watching.

Greer breaks off the kiss and gives me a look asking for permission.

"Do you want me inside you, little warrior?" My gaze doesn't stray from hers. She's the only voice that matters here.

"Yes, but I can wait."

I slip my hand into her panties and part her pussy lips with my fingers. She bites her lip.

"I can't." I slide my finger into her wet heat and she gasps. "Take out my cock. Be my good girl."

She works on my pants while I fuck her pussy with my finger, sliding in and out. She's so fucking wet. Her hips roll with every thrust. When my pants are open, I draw my finger out of her and meet Roarke's eyes.

He lifts her from me and sets her on her feet. Mason reaches for her and draws her panties down her legs while I strip. I don't want to feel her through my clothes anymore. I want to feel the satin slide of her skin against mine. Her eyes widen as Roarke thrusts his finger into her pussy from behind her, teasing her nipple while they watch me undress.

"You want him, poppet?"

She nods and licks her lips.

"You want us all? Aiden can take you first, then Mason can help open you up before Wyatt thrusts so deep and thick." Roarke fucks her pussy with his finger as she moans. "Does that sound good, poppet?"

"Yes, please. What about you?" She tips her head back to see him.

"I'm going to fuck that sweet mouth while you take them. I'm going to watch my friends fuck your pussy and listen to you come while you suck on my cock. Then I'm going to lay you down and push my cock into your cunt to hold all their cum deep inside you until we go to sleep."

She whimpers and leans back against him. Her darkened eyes follow me as I stalk closer to her. Her gaze flows over my naked body. It's not the first time we've been naked together, but it's the first time for a lot of things tonight.

None of us have shared a woman before. Roarke may have had threesomes, but not on this level. Roarke takes his finger out of her pussy and sucks it clean before guiding her my way. I draw her back to the bed and sit with her standing between my legs.

"Is this what you want, Greer?"

Her brown eyes meet mine then she looks at Mason, then Wyatt and finally Roarke. When her eyes return to mine, they're determined.

"Yes."

I cup her breast and suck on her nipple. She draws in a sharp breath and her fingers tangle into my hair as she arches into me. Mason slips behind her, naked.

"You want to take all our cocks, little mouse?" He slides his hand between her legs and thrusts his fingers inside her. She moans as he pumps them in and out of her.

I switch to her other breast.

"Please," she murmurs before she cries out as her release crashes over her.

"Good girl." Mason draws her hair over her shoulder before sucking on the spot where her neck and shoulder meet.

I slip my finger over her clit and she falls into another orgasm. Her breath comes out in pants as we draw away from her.

"Kneel on the bed." I lift her and she goes to her knees. Roarke lays down on the bed with his hands behind his head. His hard cock lies on his stomach.

She turns her gaze to me. I brush her hair out of her face, thankful for the braids that hold most of it back.

"You're beautiful, Greer." I kiss her softly. Our eyes lock. "Anytime you need to stop. Yellow or red. If you're unable to speak, tap on a thigh three times and we'll stop. Do you understand, little warrior?"

She swallows. "Yes, Aiden. Are you sure you want to do this?"

"Abso-fucking-lutely."

She smiles and I'm drawn in by her. I grab the back of her neck and kiss her, sliding my tongue along hers until we're both breathless.

"Turn to Roarke, little warrior." After she turns, I take hold of her hips, rubbing my thumbs over the smooth skin of her ass. "Ass up, head down."

She lowers her head and Roarke wraps his hand with her hair. Taking hold of my cock, I drag the tip from her entrance to her clit, gathering her wetness. She makes little needy noises that will drive me nuts if I don't take her.

Holding her hip with one hand and my cock with the other, I guide my tip to her entrance and ease inside her, slowly, letting her get accustomed to my size inch by inch. I'm not as big as Wyatt, few men are.

Greer is more than ready to take me. She pushes back against me on a moan, taking me in deep.

"Aiden," she whimpers.

"Fuck, Greer, your pussy feels so hot and tight around my cock. Your mouth is exquisite, but this, fuck." I draw back and sink back into her slowly, loving the way she feels wrapped around me. "I can see why Roarke didn't want to leave this pussy."

"You ready, poppet?" Roarke holds his cock up and she lowers her mouth over him. "Just suck it, while the others fuck you."

He slides his hand down to her nipples and teases them with his fingers. Her pussy clenches around me. Fuck, I'm not sure this was a good idea, but it feels like heaven.

Chapter 31

Talking Body

Greer

My knees are spread and Aiden fucks me slowly with his thick cock. Roarke's cock is hard in my mouth but he holds my head to keep me from bobbing on it, from taking him deep and choking on him. I suck and lick what's in my mouth, liking taking his cock and Aiden's at the same time.

Aiden increases the speed of his thrusts. Both his hands hold my hips as he slides in and out of me. For a second, I get a burst of fangirl. I've got Aiden Clybourne's cock in my pussy and Roarke Flynn's cock in my mouth. I'm literally between two super stars. But that thought quickly fades to the slide of them thrusting into me, keying me up.

I moan as the pressure is building inside, ready to explode. I've never come so much in my life, but I'm not complaining.

Wyatt and Mason sit on either side of me. When their hands explore my body, I'm pushed to the edge, so close to coming as Aiden fucks me.

"Do you like sucking on his cock, kitten?" Wyatt asks as his hand explores my pussy.

I moan as he finds my clit. Everything in me tightens.

"Let go, mouse. Come on Aiden's cock so he knows he has to have you." Mason pinches my nipple.

My release swallows me whole. Their hands support me as I rock back against Aiden. His thrusts grow harder, more desperate. He groans as his cock jerks and sprays my insides with his cum. An aftershock ripples through me, milking his cock.

I draw in a deep breath around Roarke's dick. Aiden bends over me and kisses me between my shoulder blades. Little ripples of pleasure chase through me.

"You're amazing," he whispers before drawing out of me.

Before I can even think about breathing and coming down, Mason's cock presses against my entrance. He slides in as my pussy convulses around him, still coming down.

"Fuck, mouse." His fingers dig into my hips as he fucks me roughly for a few minutes. Wyatt's hand is up on my breasts while Roarke pushes my head down a little on his cock.

Mason slows down and then stops fucking me. I whimper.

"Do you remember when you disobeyed me, mouse?"

It's not like I can answer him with Roarke's cock in my mouth.

"I'm going to smack this ass twice and I want you to remember how it feels. You'll tell me when I ask, otherwise I'll punish you if you can't answer." He thrusts deep inside my pussy and then smacks my ass cheek with his hand.

I try to back away from sucking on Roarke's cock, but he holds my head still.

"If you need to tap out, kitten, tap Roarke's thigh three times." Wyatt cups my breast before I feel his hair brush my arm. He takes my nipple into his mouth and sucks on me. I moan.

Mason smacks my other cheek and I startle again, but suck through the pain. When Mason rubs my smarting ass cheek, waves of pleasure rush in.

"I know Roarke has dibs on your ass, but fuck, mouse." His hands part my ass cheeks as he stares at my puckered hole. "I want to smack this ass until you're so sore it hurts for me to grab your ass cheeks. Then I'll fuck this ass until you scream my name."

I whimper around Roarke's cock and Mason fucks me hard. Wyatt continues to suck on my nipple. When fingers pinch my clit, I roll into an orgasm that keeps going as Mason fucks me.

Screaming, I shatter into a million pieces, gushing around Mason's cock and sucking hard on Roarke's. They both push in deep and come at the same time, making me climax again. Harder, longer, as they fill me full of their cum.

After I swallow his cum, I expect Roarke to be done as his cock softens a little, but Roarke just lifts me so I can breathe. His cock remains in my mouth.

"Keep sucking on me, poppet." Roarke wipes the corner of my mouth.

Mason pulls out and I feel Wyatt behind me. His tip teases my entrance.

"You ready, kitten? Or do you need a break?"

Roarke lifts me off his hardening cock. I draw in a deep breath, taking inventory. I'm so wet from coming and from the guys' cum. I'm already stretched more than I've ever been. It probably won't be easy, but I want him inside me.

"I'm ready."

He presses in like he did before, only the tip.

I gasp at the stretch. Earlier this was enough to make me shatter. Now I want it all.

"Don't worry, little warrior. We'll help distract you."

Aiden sits beside me on the bed and Mason is on the other side. Both watch Wyatt's cock in my pussy, but Aiden's fingers stroke my clit gently. Mason palms my breast in his hand while his thumb circles my nipple.

Wyatt's thumbs rub my hips.

"Do you want to keep sucking me, poppet?"

Roarke's deep blue eyes hold mine. Everything is building up again. Sucking on his cock is comforting and pleasurable and probably the distraction I need right now to keep from tensing at each push of Wyatt's hips.

Logically, I know he'll fit, but that doesn't mean it's not freaking me out a little.

"Yes, please."

Roarke smiles and holds his cock while he lowers my head to take him into my mouth. Just the head which I suck on like a lollipop.

Wyatt draws almost all the way out before pushing in a little deeper. I widen my stance and tip my ass up a little more.

"You're doing so good, mouse. Taking all that huge cock into your tiny, tight cunt." Mason's words are punctuated by his fingers tugging at my nipples.

"So slick and warm." Aiden's voice makes me whimper. His fingers keep winding me tighter and tighter.

Wyatt slides in a little more and I moan around Roarke's cock.

"Good girl, poppet. Next time, I'm going to watch Wyatt split you open on his huge cock."

Fuck, next time. This isn't a one time thing. I'm not just dreaming of fucking four men, but am actually in the middle of it. Wyatt's stretching me so much that I'm not sure I can take much more. Aiden circles my clit and my pussy pulses, clutching at Wyatt's cock.

He draws back slowly and I feel every inch of him sliding against my walls. I suck around Roarke's cock.

"You want to take all this long, thick cock, kitten?" Wyatt's words make me tremble, already on the edge.

He slides back inside going even deeper and deeper until he presses against my cervix. I gasp as he holds there, letting me get accustomed to the length and girth stretching me open.

"Such a good girl, kitten. I can feel your cunt trembling all around me, squeezing me so fucking tight. Fuck, I want to come straight into your womb, kitten. Fill you up so much that my cum drips down your legs for days."

His dirty words, his cock, their hands tip me over the edge and I free fall into my release, squeezing his huge cock almost painfully, soaking both of us in my cum.

"That's it, kitten. Come all over my cock so I can fuck you."

I moan around Roarke's hard cock. Fuck, Wyatt isn't even fucking me yet.

"Someone take a picture because I want to see." Roarke rubs the back of my head.

"You can watch next time." Wyatt's hands grip my hips as he slowly withdraws his cock.

My pussy clutches at him in aftershocks. When just the tip of him is inside me, he thrusts in deep, touching my womb and making me moan again. Aiden kisses my breast as he works my clit gently like he knows I'm too sensitive right now.

"Good, kitten?"

"Mmhmm," I get out around Roarke's cock. So fucking good.

"I'm going to fuck you now. Remember to tap on Roarke's thigh if you need me to stop, otherwise I'm not stopping until you come on my cock and milk my cum from me."

I whimper as he draws out slowly. The anticipation thrills me. When he's almost out, he thrusts in and doesn't stop, just keeps thrusting in and out while the others play with my body.

It doesn't take long for me to be right on the edge again as he brushes my cervix with every thrust. Roarke uses his hand on the back of my head to fuck my mouth in time with Wyatt's thrusts until I can't think anymore.

Roarke comes in my mouth and I swallow on instinct. Then he lifts me off his cock. I draw in a ragged breath as my body tightens ready to explode.

Aiden pinches my clit and I explode on a scream. Fireworks light behind my eyelids as I just keep coming around Wyatt's cock. My head hangs.

"That's it, kitten. Milk my cock." He thrusts in deep and his cock jerks against my walls. I feel everything. The cum working its way through his cock to spray my insides with warmth. I cry out as it pushes me higher. I rest my head on Roarke's thigh as he strokes my hair.

Wyatt rocks a few more times as he groans. Then he settles deep inside me, holding my hips as my pussy contracts around him. I release a breath against Roarke's thigh.

Every inch of me is so sleepy. I just want to drift off while my body trembles around Wyatt's cock. Wyatt's hands lift me against him, drawing my back against his hard chest. He's still so hard and deep inside me. I sigh as his hands drift over my breasts, down my stomach. He glides his finger over my clit.

"One more, kitten," he whispers against my head.

I whimper. "I can't."

He chuckles. "Yes, you can."

His still hard cock rubs something inside that lights me up. His fingers work my clit like he's typing a masterpiece.

"Wyatt." I squirm against him even though it just makes me need more. I'm so worn out, but everything he does pushes me closer.

"You can, kitten." He thrusts deep again. I release a moan.

Roarke sits up and his heated gaze falls to where Wyatt is still buried deep inside me.

Aiden leans in and takes my breast into his hot mouth. I moan as the feeling cascades down to my pussy. Mason takes my other nipple into his mouth. Roarke strokes his cock as he watches them.

It's nothing like I imagined and my body falls over the edge, wetness drenches my thighs as I cry out, "Wyatt!"

"Shh, kitten, it's okay." He thrusts in deep again rubbing that spot and my orgasm keeps going. I arch into the others' mouths, crying out. Groaning, he comes again, holding me still against him as he pumps me full of his cum.

I can barely breathe as I come down. Mason and Aiden sit back on the bed. I meet all three of their eyes. Roarke comes toward me and cups my face.

"You're so beautiful, Greer." He kisses me softly as Wyatt pulls out of me. I whimper. The fullness gone.

Roarke slides his fingers inside my pussy and I gasp into his mouth. He chuckles against my lips. "Our cum belongs inside you, poppet."

The shades of blue in his eyes hold me captive, while everyone moves around us.

The shower turns on and Wyatt draws me back against him.

"Time to clean up, kitten."

Roarke draws his fingers out of me and holds them up to my lips. "Want a taste?"

Without dropping my eyes from his, I take his fingers into my mouth, tasting their salty cum and myself, trying to memorize this taste and the feel of them for later when I'm alone. Roarke groans as his eyes flare with heat.

"I think I'm going to like keeping you, poppet."

My heart skips. No one has ever kept me. He draws his fingers out of my mouth and takes my lips with his, kissing me breathless again.

Wyatt lifts me in his arms and carries me into the bathroom. He sets me down in the shower and gently works on undoing the braids in my hair, while I lean against him, needing him to hold me up because my legs tremble.

"You okay, kitten?"

"Yes. Better than okay." I'm going to like this too much. I'm afraid when it's time for me to leave. I won't want to.

By the time, Wyatt washes me gently and dries me, I'm almost asleep on my feet. I brush my teeth while Wyatt French braids my hair. When I finish with my teeth, I just watch him.

He's a giant behind me in the mirror. Him running his hands through my hair comforts me. When he finishes, he wraps his arms around my shoulders and draws me back against his warmth.

"You're amazing, kitten."

Mason comes in with silky panties, shorts, and a camisole. Wyatt kisses my head and walks out of the bathroom. Mason dresses me and then leads me out of my bedroom and down the hall to his.

I glance over my shoulder at Aiden's door. Will he be okay without me? Will he sleep? Will he wander and get in his head over seeing Siobhan tonight? Will crossing the line with me make him cross the line with his addiction?

Mason's door is open and low voices reach me. Mason pushes the door the rest of the way open, and I see Aiden, Roarke, and Wyatt on the bed with their boxers on.

"We figured tonight everyone would want to sleep with you." Mason draws me back against his warm chest. "My bed is big enough."

Warmth fills my chest. They all want to sleep with me? I shouldn't let myself get too comfortable, but I'm already all in on this thing. Mason brushes a kiss over my hair and leads me over to the guys.

Aiden offers me his hand and I take it, crawling on the bed to be next to him.

"How are you?" We both say at the same time.

I blush and he pulls me into his arms where he rests against the pillows.

"Let's start with you," Aiden says.

"I'm good." I breathe in his citrus scent and with everything that happened at the party tonight followed by us all fucking, I'm barely keeping my eyes open. "You?"

"Better now that you're in my arms." His hand rubs my bare arm and tingles work their way through me.

My heart feels like it's going to explode. Roarke snuggles up behind me.

"I love having my cock inside you, poppet." His lips caress the back of my neck, stirring the embers a little, but I'm too tired.

"No fucking in my bed." Mason's voice is stern. "At least not tonight. Let's let the poor woman rest so we can fuck her again tomorrow."

Heat pours through me at his words and then he turns off the lights. Darkness surrounds me, but so does the warmth of these guys. I take a deep breath. I can handle this.

Someone moves on the bed and then there are footsteps on the wood floor. A light turns on in the bathroom and Wyatt closes the door, so there's a little glow around it and the room isn't as dark.

"Better, kitten?"

My pulse quickens. They really need to stop treating me this good. I don't know how I'll ever leave them. "Thank you."

I rest my head on Aiden's chest, hearing his steady heartbeat. Roarke curls up behind me. Even though Wyatt and Mason aren't touching me, I can still feel their presence. I'm safe and warm and protected.

I want to hold onto this feeling. I don't want to sleep, but I'm exhausted.

Roarke

My hand curves over Greer's hip, cradled against mine. My cock is hard, which isn't surprising with the soft flesh of her ass pressing against it. It's still dark in the room, but it's probably sunrise. The party went late last night.

And the afterparty was the best I've ever been to. Fuck, who knew fucking a woman with my friends would be so hot. I've been involved in a couple of threesomes, once with two women and the other with a woman and a man. But being with Greer was next level.

I slide my hand between her warm thighs. She's got her leg wrapped around Aiden as they both sleep. When I cup her pussy, she whimpers slightly like a wounded animal.

Fuck.

Will she ever talk about what happened to her? She's only twenty-one. I wish I couldn't imagine what happened to a kid in the foster system. The terror on her face yesterday morning told me everything.

My poor poppet.

I move my hand back to her hip and kiss her bare shoulder, tracing the delicate bone with my tongue. She sighs and relaxes again between me and Aiden. Hmm. Maybe a more tactile approach.

Wyatt sits up and looks over at us. He raises an eyebrow as I kiss her shoulder again.

"Limits," he says softly.

I rub her hip, but I'm not about to wake her up. She was exhausted when she came to bed last night. Wyatt's right. I need to respect her limits and this one isn't one I can blow past. Not without freaking her out and maybe even driving her away.

Wyatt chuckles as he moves out of the bed. He slides his hand over her bare leg. His eyes soften when he looks at her sleeping face. She's not like other women.

I've fucked twenty-one-year-olds before. It's definitely not an age thing because my poppet definitely isn't a normal twenty-one-year-old. Yes, she doesn't have a plan for her life but how could she?

Her apartment was shit. Her boyfriend was shit. And I'm guessing her job was shit.

Whoever her friend is that gave her our number deserves a fucking finder's fee. Greer needs us as much as we need her. I want to show her all the things she hasn't experienced. Take her to premiers and parties. Show her off when she's looking as gorgeous as she did last night.

Fuck, show her off when she's bare faced and in baggie clothes.

Play with her in the ocean and the pool. Take her to a deserted island and play natives for a while. Fuck her everywhere and anywhere.

As passionate as she is, I can't help but wonder why she hadn't orgasmed with anyone else before. She's responsive to our touch. So what held her back?

I'm not a fucking therapist, but I want to dig in her brain and find out how she ticks. I want to know everything about her. I want to make her smile and sigh and come so fucking hard she passes out.

She was close last night. Pretty sure we can get her there.

Fuck. Would it be a dick move to wake her up just so I can fuck her again?

"Roarke," Mason says from behind me. "Stop grinding on the poor girl's ass. Go take care of yourself if you're so fucking horny."

"I'm not grinding on her ass," I murmur, stopping the rocking of my hips. Well, not intentionally anyway. I roll onto my back and readjust my cock in my boxers.

"What happened when you went down on her yesterday morning?" Mason lays on his back with his arm tucked under his head, staring at the ceiling like it did him wrong.

"She seemed into it, but then she said no and don't. I backed away and she cowered against the headboard like I was the monster under her bed come to get her." That helps my raging hardon go down some. "She was shaking and her eyes were glazed like she wasn't here."

I glance over at her and Aiden sleeping. They wrap around each other like they're each other's life line in sleep. I lift her braid and let it slide out of my hand.

Mason grunts in acknowledgement and then sighs. "She's glued together, but she's fragile. We need to respect the limits she puts on us, but also figure out what her real limits are. She wants to please us and that can be dangerous. She'll let us push her too far."

He's right. She hesitated before answering and would look to us for confirmation before saying no on anything. I want to know who broke her. I'm sure they didn't pay for what they did or Mason would know about it.

I'll make sure they pay for what they did to her.

"I'm going for a run." I lean over Greer and press a kiss to her temple. She releases a soft breath. What I want from her will have to wait until she's more comfortable. I like exhibition, but I also like just having her on my cock anyway I can get it.

I might hold off on her ass though, make her really want it.

Fuck, my cock is rock hard again. I get off Mason's bed and leave the dark room, stepping out into the bright sunlit hallway. I squint at the light before entering my bedroom.

Stripping off my boxers, I leave them on the floor before going into my bathroom and turning on the shower. I stop at the mirror and check my jaw. My stubble is getting a little thick. It's time to shave, but I'll wait until tomorrow.

I want to see Greer's creamy thighs marked from beard burn.

Grinning, I step into the shower and let the water pour over me. Her response is so fucking innocent, but not shy innocent. No, my girl wants it. She's not shy about taking what she wants. I stroke my hand over my cock.

Nothing is artificial about Greer. Yes, she can fake a smile like the rest of us. But every inch of her is sincere. She doesn't like lying or cheating. She hides that fantastic little body under baggie clothes like she doesn't want anyone to notice her.

Fuck, but I notice her. I glide my hand up and down my cock, rubbing my thumb over my slit, feeling it pulse with need. Her voice, husky and low. My other hand slides up the tile and I rest my head against the coolness. Closing my eyes, I play back last night.

Watching her on video, sliding into her wet heat and just feeling her twitch and convulse around me. I've always used condoms because I don't trust most women, but with Greer, I want to feel every inch of her.

Fuck, it's worth it. Even if she ends up pregnant, my cock twitches in my hand. I can picture her swollen with my child, bent over the couch while I fuck her. I stroke faster, getting close.

Watching her come in the shower, fuck I could do that over and over again. She always has this little look of shock and surprise before she topples over the edge. I can't wait to spend the day inside her, tasting her, teasing her, fucking her.

Groaning, I come all over my hand. I don't know how much fucking it will take to get Greer Morrow out of my system or if I ever will, but I'm definitely up to trying.

Chapter 32

Say Something

Aiden

Kisses on my chest wake me. I stretch, feeling the slide of skin against mine. My hand caresses her bare hip.

"Good, little mouse." Mason's dark voice surprises me for a moment. "Now kiss down his abs."

She moans as she moves down to my abs. My cock is rock hard and aching. I open my eyes to see Greer leaning over me. Her mouth sucks and teases at my flesh, sending shivers through me. Her light brown eyes flash up to mine.

She kisses lower along the waistband of my boxer briefs. She's completely naked. Mason kneels behind her with his cock buried in her pussy, slowly easing it in and out.

"Good morning, Aiden." Mason gives me a smile. "Free his cock, mouse."

Fuck, I rub my face as Greer pulls down my pants and licks my cock. Mason smacks her ass. She yelps.

"I didn't say lick it."

"Sorry, sir."

He keeps fucking her before he pulls out, still hard. "Straddle him, facing his feet. And take him into your cunt."

She glances at me with wide eyes, but I hold out my hand to help her. Fuck, this is a new world. I'm going to fuck Greer when we're with someone else. Alone, I'll maintain the boundaries, but how often will we be alone?

She straddles me and guides my cock to her entrance. She slides down on me with a moan. A groan escapes me at how good she feels. So fucking tight.

Mason moves to kneel between my legs. "Suck my cock while you fuck him, mouse."

I grab her hips as she lowers her head to take his cock all the way in her mouth. No hesitation, just takes him. She grinds her hips on me. Not giving me quite enough friction.

Sitting up, I change the angle of my cock inside her. She bounces a little on me until I guide her hips, helping her fuck me. She moans around Mason's cock.

"Faster, mouse." He grabs hold of her head and pushes her down deep on his cock. When she gags, her pussy tightens around me. "That's it. Look at you taking two cocks like a good girl."

He pulls her back and she gasps around his cock. His eyes are on hers.

"Make me come, mouse. Then I'm going to make you ride Aiden until he comes." He fucks his cock in and out of her mouth, while she sucks on him, hollowing out her cheeks. Her cunt tightens around me as she comes all over my cock on a moan.

Groaning, Mase comes in her mouth. Her throat works to swallow him all.

He sits back and tips her chin up. "Open."

She opens her mouth for him.

"Good girl." He kisses her and little aftershocks ripple around my cock.

"Fuck," I whisper, holding her hips.

Mase releases her mouth and meets my eyes. "Sit back against the headboard."

I move us back and drag her up so her back is against my chest. This part I know how to do. "Grind in slow circles, little warrior."

Guiding her hips, I thrust what little I can as she figures out what she likes. When she finds her rhythm, I slide one hand down to her clit and the other up to her hardened nipple. She moans as she keeps rubbing my cock against that spot inside her.

"You're so beautiful when you come, Greer." I kiss her behind her ear.

"Aiden," she whispers as she topples over the edge. She moans as her pussy convulses around me. I lift her off me and lay her on her back before coming down on top of her, thrusting deep inside her pussy while claiming her mouth.

Her legs wrap around my hips as I thrust inside her, chasing my release, needing the rush. I slide a finger over her clit between us and she cries out, arching into me as she comes again, milking my cock.

A few last thrusts and my balls tighten, ready to explode. Thrusting in deep, I come inside her. Her soft brown eyes search mine as her hands hold my jaw. Both of us pant to catch our breath as we lie tangled together.

The bed shifts as Mason stands. Fuck, I almost forgot he was still here.

"Wyatt got coffee and bagels for breakfast this morning." He heads to his bathroom. "When you're ready, of course."

"Good morning," Greer whispers meeting my eyes almost shyly.

My cock is still deep inside her and we're alone, but I don't want to move. This is probably a gray area. We weren't alone when we started or even finished.

"Morning." I brush the flyaway hairs from her face. "How are you?"

She blushes. "I'm good. I really enjoyed last night and this morning."

I grin. "Me too."

My cock begins to harden again. She glances down our bodies.

"I'm definitely not used to guys like you." She bites her lip and shifts her hips which quickens my arousal.

"Is that a good or bad thing?"

"Good. Definitely good." She begins to unwrap her legs as I pull back, but then I thrust back inside her. "Oh."

"Yeah, it's been a while." I kiss down her neck as I leisurely thrust my cock in and out of her. "Is this okay?"

"Mmhmm." Her fingers tangle in my hair as I suck on her neck, knowing it will leave a mark and loving the fact everyone will see it. That the guys will know I marked her. "Aiden."

She arches up against me. I reach down for her knee and lift her leg higher, opening her up so I can go even deeper. Her eyes meet mine as I slowly fuck her.

Her lips part and her skin is flushed pink.

"Fuck." It's a harsh whisper from someone else.

We both look at the open door where Roarke stands.

"Voyeurs are supposed to be quiet." I return my attention to Greer's face.

"Yeah, but do you know how hot you two look together?" Roarke chuckles.

I move Greer's face back so she can focus on me. Her eyes widen as she comes. I grind my pelvis against her clit, keeping her in her release, feeling her tighten around my cock.

"Good?" I whisper.

She clutches my hair as she arches against me, dragging me down into a kiss. I keep fucking her until my balls tingle and I find my release, gathering her into my arms and holding her against me. My cock jerks as it fills her with my cum.

I keep kissing her as I pull out, reluctant to leave her, but knowing we need to get on with the day.

"Get a shower. I'll see you downstairs."

I grab my boxers and head for the door before I do something stupid like drag her into the shower with me. Her wet body rubbing against mine would start all this over again. That wouldn't be a gray area and if I have her in my room, I won't let her leave it until we're both spent.

Greer

Aiden leaves me sprawled naked on Mason's bed. I put my hand to my chest as I catch my breath. My heart pounds in my chest. Fuck. That one is going to leave a mark and not just on my neck.

"Need a shower, poppet?" Roarke leans in the doorframe, looking hot and sweaty in a pair of workout shorts. His hair is damp and he holds out his hand for me. "Come on. I'll get you nice and wet."

Sitting up, I search the bed for my pajamas that Mason peeled off me. Fuck, Mason is going to be dangerous in a different way. My need to please him had me doing whatever he asked and liking it. I didn't have that urge to misbehave this morning when I woke and he kissed me.

He undressed me slowly and then fucked me on my hands and knees. He told me to kiss Aiden's chest and kept escalating. My pussy gets achy just thinking about it.

And then Aiden did whatever that was. Something clicked in my heart and I know it would be so easy to fall for him. I'm sure it's already happening. I need to remember what this is all about.

"You don't need clothes." Roarke's voice makes me tingle. "I'll lend you a shirt."

Roarke is exactly what this is about. Sex, pure and simple. He wants to fuck me.

I walk over and take his hand. Smirking, he leads me into his bedroom, right into his bathroom. He turns on the shower and lifts me onto the counter.

His eyes take in every inch of me, heating my blood. He parts my thighs and drags his finger through the cum leaking out, before using his finger to shove it back inside my pussy.

"Roarke." I gasp and grab onto his arm.

"Can't let any escape, poppet." He rubs his jaw against mine. His stubble prickles my skin and makes me arch into his sweaty chest. "I'm going to keep you full of cum. Mine. Theirs. Ours."

He thrusts his fingers in deep over and over again, pushing me closer and closer to the edge. When he pulls his fingers out, he holds them to my lips. His eyes meet mine, almost daring me to. I open and he slides his fingers into my mouth.

I taste me and Aiden combined. Fuck. I close my eyes and moan.

"You like the taste, poppet? Me too." He drops his shorts onto the ground and steps between my legs, teasing his cock against my entrance and tipping my head back to look at him. "Aiden's right. You could be addictive. Give me another taste."

He thrusts inside me and claims my mouth with his, lifting me against him. Kissing me deeply, he takes me into the shower and presses me against the wall. I hold onto his shoulders as he looks between us. He pulls out and pushes back in, watching his cock shuttle in and out of my pussy.

"You sore yet, poppet?" His gaze lifts to mine.

I shake my head and he smirks. His eyes turn serious.

"You tell me if it's too much. I don't ever want to hurt you. Promise me, poppet?"

My heart softens. I cup his jaw in my hands, loving the buzz of his stubble against my palms. "I promise, Roarke."

"Fuck, poppet, say my name. I love your voice." He fucks me harder, every thrust touching me so fucking deep. "I'm going to need to teach you to dirty talk. I'll get Wyatt to write you some lines."

I can't focus on his words as he fucks me.

My nipples rub against his bare chest. He goes back to watching his cock sliding in and out. Fuck, I'm already getting so close again.

"So many things to do to you. We could spend the whole day fucking, poppet. I want to see you take Wyatt's cock again. Splitting you open. You should suck him. Fuck, when you choke on him, your cunt will tighten around my cock like a vise."

"Roarke?"

"Yes?" He meets my eyes and pinches my clit.

I cry out his name as I topple over the edge. He quickens his pace.

"That's right, poppet. Say my name."

He thrusts in deep and I say in his ear, "Roarke."

Shaking, he comes with a roar deep inside me. We stay like that for a few minutes to catch our breath. When he finally lets me down, my legs shake. He pulls me against him as he washes us, telling me a story about the time a set only had one shower and everyone was coated in mud.

I rest my head against his chest and let him take care of me. Enjoying it while it lasts.

When we finally go downstairs, Roarke refused to let me go to my room to at least grab panties. Instead he put his shirt on over my head. It's almost the same length as the dress I wore last night, but I'm constantly pulling at the hem to make sure everything is covered.

"It's fine, poppet." He takes my hand and leads me into the kitchen. All playfulness vanishes as I take in the serious faces around the table. My heart pounds and I want to run back upstairs. Back where everything was good.

Wyatt holds out his hand to me and I take it, letting him pull me onto his lap.

"What's happened?" Roarke takes the chair next to me and Wyatt.

Mason sets a tablet on the table. "Someone took a picture last night. Publicity is on top of it and trying to purchase the exclusive to keep it from going out."

I glance at the picture. It's Aiden and me kissing on the patio. It's a little fuzzy, but it's clear to me. I'm not sure what this means, but it can't be good.

"Fuck." Roarke rubs the back of his neck and glances at me.

"What does this mean?" I ask.

"We have to get the exclusive or someone can publish it." Mason leans back in his chair, studying me.

Aiden stands abruptly and walks out onto the patio. My gaze follows him, but I don't know what's bothering him. This kind of thing always happens to celebrities.

"Isn't this normal tabloid fodder? Would it be bad if this got out?" I mean it's not that great of picture, but it's just a kiss. It's not like we were skinny dipping or fucking. It's barely anything.

Wyatt rubs his hand down my back. "The problem is if the bank realizes you're in a sexual relationship with Aiden, they won't allow you to be his sobriety companion for the film."

"Oh." And there's the rug pulled out from under me. It was too good to be true. I thought I'd make it for a while longer.

My heart slows and my brain quiets. This is the life I'm used to. Not fantasy all day fuck fests with celebrities. I blow out a breath. I should pack my things. Figure out my next move. I can't go back to my apartment. Not with Chad there.

Maybe Bristol would take me in for a few days, just until I get my feet back under me. I need to call the diner and see about getting back on the schedule. I still owe Chad rent, so I won't be able to afford a place of my own.

But I can find a room somewhere. I can make this work. It's no different than when I left my final foster home.

"Is her name attached?" Roarke asks.

Maybe the guys will give me something for my trouble. My brow furrows. But then am I just a prostitute if I take their money? I attended one party. I wasn't even supposed to start until Monday. I probably shouldn't take their money.

I sigh. I'll find a second job. Maybe I can build my own future. It's just going to take more time. I can go to college later. I didn't really know what I wanted to be anyway.

"No. They don't have her name." Mason watches me carefully. "Greer?"

I lift my head and meet his eyes, still trying to figure out how to fix my life after having this for a few days. It wasn't nearly long enough. I'll miss them, but that's the way my life is. I know not to get attached.

For a few moments, I thought I could have the fantasy.

"Hey, kitten." Wyatt tips my chin up and searches my eyes. "This is just a bump."

I nod, because what else am I going to do? It's always the same. It always doesn't work out. Don't get comfortable. Don't get settled. Don't think you've finally found somewhere you belong, because you don't.

You never belong.

Tears choke me. No, I don't cry. It's easier if I don't cry. The tears never change anyone's mind anyway. I can leave with some dignity left.

"Excuse me." I stand and hurry to the bathroom before any of the tears can slip free. I just need a moment and then I can start living my life again. Without them.

Roarke

I'm focused on the picture when Greer says, "Excuse me."

I catch the fear on her face before she runs off. Fuck. I know that look. When the door shuts, I turn to the others.

"Not good." I walk over and knock on the door. "Poppet?"

She doesn't answer.

"What's happening?" Wyatt asks.

I storm back over to the table. "She's fucking spiraling because you just said she's out of a job."

"No one said that." Mason glances toward the door.

"If everything in your life has been shitty up until now, what would you have heard?"

Mason sits back and shakes his head. "This is fixable."

"Is it? Because if I go tell her everything is going to be okay and we send her packing that will destroy her."

I run my hands through my hair. Fuck. I need to think. To fix this. To be the hero she needs and not the guy constantly trying to get in her pants.

"We'll figure this out." Mason sounds so confident, but he hasn't seen her like I've seen her.

I walk back to the bathroom door and knock. "Greer, please. Let me in."

"I'll be out in a minute." Her voice is soft and too high pitch.

I rest my head against the door. "We'll figure this out. You're not leaving this house. You're not out of a job. Please just come out and talk to us."

Fuck, she can be my assistant. It doesn't matter if I fuck my assistant or not. This isn't over, but it feels like she's already pulling away. Normally, that wouldn't bother me, but this time it does.

I've barely had her in my life. I need more time. I need her.

Chapter 33

Calm Down

Greer

Roarke's words make my heart race. I wipe at my eyes and take a deep breath. They aren't letting me go. Yet.

Fuck, if I feel this bad after only a few days, how will I feel in months? A year?

Maybe it would be better to leave now. If I pin all my hopes and dreams to these men, what happens when they get sick of me? When they find someone new and better?

What if I'm just a convenient mystery to them? Or like Mason said I'm a broken doll they want to fix. What happens when they can't fix me?

The last few days have been some of the best of my life so far. What cost am I willing to pay for more of those days? What cost will I have to pay?

"Greer." Roarke's voice sounds like he's directly on the other side of the door. "Please, poppet. Come out or let me in."

His coaxing voice tugs at something deep inside me that needs him. I want to be wanted. It's just part of my makeup at this point in my life, but there's something more here with these men.

This has the potential to break me, but I want them. Knowing I might have to make a decision, I hesitate to reach for the doorknob. I can't stay just to have sex with them and I won't take money for that either. That's not who I am. I never want to be that desperate.

Taking a breath and making sure my emotions are tucked away deep, I open the door.

Roarke's blue eyes sweep over my face as he cocks a grin. "We wouldn't let you go that easily, poppet."

"I just needed to freshen up." I gesture hopelessly back to the bathroom. The mirror mocks me. My eyes are still a little red, but at least, I didn't have a full meltdown.

Roarke steps into the small bathroom, closing the door and before I know what's happening he's engulfed me in a hug, drawing me deep into his arms. I stay stiff, trying to resist the urge to count on him. To trust this time, they won't send me away when I become inconvenient or useless.

His large hand holds my head against his chest. "This is something that will come up. It's the nature of our business, but I swear, everything is fixable, including this. Even if it gets out, we'll spin it. That's why we have a team of publicists working for us."

I draw in his sandalwood scent and let it seep into my veins. My muscles ease and I let him take my weight against him.

"You aren't leaving," Roarke whispers.

I nod, even though I don't believe him. I want to believe him. He could mean that. But promises are easily broken.

"You ready to go back out, poppet?" Roarke doesn't let me go from his hug.

"Yeah." When I pull away a little, he releases me.

He tips my chin up and searches my eyes like he's trying to see inside me. Satisfied with whatever he sees, Roarke holds his hand out to me. I wish I could prepare myself for the sparks but every time we touch it's like a jolt to my system. I slide my hand into his and some of the tension eases from his shoulders.

"We'll figure this out, poppet." He leads me into the kitchen.

I glance at Wyatt's concerned face and Mason's thoughtful expression. My gaze then goes to Aiden standing next to the swimming pool. Is he angry at me or angry this is happening? All I know is he's all alone, like when he was up that night. The guys are giving him space, but sometimes space isn't what's needed.

I squeeze Roarke's hand and give him a reassuring smile.

He looks out to Aiden and nods slightly. He kisses my hand.

I walk around the table to step into the sunlight with Aiden.

"Hey." My voice is soft, but he turns his head toward me.

"This is all my fault. I shouldn't have done that. I know better. Shit like this always gets out." Aiden doesn't look at me as he beats himself up. He doesn't need to worry about this.

I slide my hand in his, and his fingers curl around mine.

"I'm glad you did." I can't regret anything that happened with these guys even if it means I'm not staying. But Aiden is still vulnerable and in pain.

We just stand there staring at the sunlight reflecting off the pool. Neither of us can do anything to help the others sort this. But if this is my last day in paradise, I can spend it holding Aiden's hand.

He draws me to lean against him. His hand rests on my hip, holding me close. This morning feels like forever ago, but my insides soften at his touch. The tension eases out of me as we hold each other up.

"You won't leave," he says after several minutes.

I glance up at his face but he's still looking out at the water. "If I don't have a job, I can't stay."

I can't take from them without giving. I can't just hang around and be available for sex. Even mind-blowing, life-changing sex.

"You could simply be our assistant and not my sobriety companion." His fingers stroke over my hip, bunching up my t-shirt a little. "I need you, little warrior."

I lift my gaze to his light blue eyes. My heart thumps against my chest because the deeper I go with these guys the harder it will be to untangle myself when they drop me.

"Hey." Wyatt's voice is soft and we both turn around. "We might have a solution."

Wyatt holds out his hand to me. I take Aiden's first and then Wyatt's. He leads us both inside. The inside seems dimmer after being outside in the sunlight for so long.

Aiden sits next to Wyatt. Wyatt draws me down onto his lap.

Mason rests his forearms on the table with his hands clasped. "We managed to negotiate for exclusive rights, but that doesn't mean it won't still get out."

Roarke studies me carefully. But I can't change any of what's about to happen. I have to remind myself that this could all end. I need to prepare myself for the worst. It's easier that way.

"Which means we need a new tactic. Either a distraction or a stand in."

"A stand in?" I ask.

"Someone who resembles you enough to say that's who Aiden was kissing." Mason's intense gaze focuses on me. "He would go out and be seen with her on outings that look like dates. The public will assume that's the woman he kissed at the party and even though a few guests might try to argue, we'll all claim that's the fact."

I swallow, and Aiden takes my hand.

"It's no different from when agents try to boost one of their clients by having another client act like they're in a relationship." Aiden sounds less than enthusiastic about it.

"What's the other option?" I don't know what a distraction would be either.

"Give them something bigger with more meat, so that this kiss gets shuffled to a smaller section or isn't enough to make it onto the site." Mason moves his gaze to Aiden. "The problem with that is finding something big enough. Aiden dating after rehab will be big news especially with his divorce from Siobhan."

I bite my lip. I don't like the idea of Aiden dating anyone else, but if it's the only option, it's better than being out of a job.

"If we go with the decoy date, then the bank won't have any

reason to not approve you to work with Aiden for the course of the film." Wyatt traces his finger along my thigh, sending a shiver through me. "But we also would need to make sure they don't look at you suspiciously again."

"What does that mean?" I glance around at the guys, waiting for one of them to explain.

"It would be beneficial if you were dating someone." Mason doesn't let his gaze drop from me.

"Oh." Like I understand, but I don't. "So you want me to find someone to date?"

"Fuck, no, poppet." Roarke arches an eyebrow. "You need to date one of us."

My eyes widen. "Oh."

That wasn't part of the deal.

"If you have a boyfriend, it would be less likely that they think one or all of us is fucking around with you." Wyatt draws my back to rest against his chest.

I bite my lip. Does that mean this deal is done? No more sex with all of them? I couldn't possibly choose which guy I would want to date. This wasn't supposed to be about dating at all. Just sex no strings. Nothing to bind my heart to theirs.

"As much as I would love to show you off, poppet. The obvious choice for your relationship is Wyatt." Roarke narrows his eyes on Wyatt.

My pulse quickens as Wyatt's hand tightens on my bare hip.

Mason clasps his hands together. "The rest of us have a spotlight on us. Everyone would watch to see when one of us failed you."

"I'm safe, kitten." Wyatt rests his head on mine. "As a writer, I'm known in the industry but very few news outlets care about my social life. Roarke and Aiden are too obvious. Even if Roarke dated you, everyone would wait for him to dump you and if he didn't, people would grow suspicious or curious."

Roarke's blue eyes hold mine for a second. He gives me a soft smile and a wink.

"I'm in this thing, poppet. But at some point, I'll have to date other women just to appear like I'm doing what people expect." Roarke rubs his hand through his hair. "You don't have to worry about me straying though. I won't lie to you. If I plan to be with someone else, I'll let you know."

I swallow the lump in my throat. They might not make it a year with me. I can't see me being the one to call this thing over, but I could lose each of them slowly.

"None of us are ready to give you up, mouse." Mason draws my attention. "I'm too high profile to date as well. With me being the director, the bank might question whether my girlfriend would be the best sobriety companion for Aiden."

My heart skips when he calls me his girlfriend, even if this is all pretend, so they can keep fucking me. But hell, I don't want to stop what we just started. I need this job and I want to keep having sex with these men.

"Enough people saw you with me at the party, no one will question our relationship." Wyatt slides his hand down my arm and I turn to meet his hazel eyes. "When we go out, you stay with me unless I need to be somewhere else. No one will suspect your involvement with the others."

He cups my cheek.

"Is all this necessary?" I ask, not wanting to be a burden. "Wouldn't it just be easier to get rid of me?"

Wyatt tips my chin up. "None of us want to get rid of you, kitten. You're perfect for Aiden's recovery and we all enjoyed the past few days with you. Do you want to leave?"

The weight of four sets of eyes fall on me. If I leave now, it will only sting a little. I could protect my heart from falling deeper with these guys.

The longer I stay the harder it will be to leave. My heart is already held together by duct tape. I've tried to build a wall around it, but these guys seem to slip through the cracks. If I stay, that wall will be gone and I'll be vulnerable again.

Can I watch Aiden date someone else, knowing he'll be coming home to me? Can I watch Roarke flirt and date women he has no intentions of sleeping with until one of them catches his fancy and he leaves me behind?

The real question is can I walk away from the temptation? Roarke's boisterous playfulness. Aiden's pain-filled softness. Wyatt's quiet flirting. Mason's dark control.

I clear my throat. "So Aiden will date someone who resembles me. Wyatt and I will be a couple. And Roarke will date random women."

"Yes, and you'll remain Aiden's sobriety companion." Mason locks me in with his cool blue eyes. "And our dirty little secret toy."

Arousal spills through me at those words. While I've been with other men, none of them have made me feel what these men do. I shouldn't want them as badly as I do, but I can't resist finding out what more they have in store for me.

"It won't be easy, but we'll have each other." Roarke reaches across the table and takes my hand.

"You'll be ours in this house." Mason smiles and tingles race up my spine. "We'll work this out, little mouse. You'll see."

For now, I'm secure. For now, these men want me. I'll be theirs and no one else's for now.

TO BE CONTINUED...

TO BE CONTINUED.

Meet C.S. Berry

C.S. Berry is a combination of my love for writing and my love for reading. She began as an experiment and took off into something I absolutely adore. It's not often you can do what you love and it works as a career. As for me, I love reading and romance and heroines seriously getting railed. I assume since you've read my books, you do too.

If you want to discuss books or anything with me, come join my Facebook group, C.S. Berry's Spicy Executive Suite. And you can always catch me on Instagram @csberry.

Oh and me, I have a lovely family who aren't allowed to read my books. But are so proud, they keep leaking my pen name. My dog and cats don't care about my writing as long as I sit still long enough for them to snuggle. For more of my books and to join my newsletter, visit my website csberry.com.

XOXOXO,
C.S. Berry

For more stories and updates:
csberry.com
Join my Newsletter
C.S. Berry Direct Store